RISING
DOG.

ALSO BY VINCE KOHLER

Rainy North Woods

RISING

========= BY VINCE KOHLER =========

DOG.

ST. MARTIN'S PRESS   NEW YORK

Rising Dog is a work of fiction. The novel's characters inhabit a stretch of the southern Oregon coast that is entirely a product of the author's imagination. Any resemblance to people, places, or institutions in the real world is an enormous and shocking coincidence. In particular, the Sons of Eiden Hall and its denizens are not intended to represent any actual Scandinavian group.

Design by Judith A. Stagnitto

Library of Congress Cataloging-in-Publication Data

Kohler, Vince.
    Rising dog / Vince Kohler.
        p.   cm.
    ISBN 0-312-07075-6
    I. Title.
    PS3561.0358R57   1992
    813'.54—dc20   91-39099
                                                    CIP

First Edition: March 1992

10 9 8 7 6 5 4 3 2 1

This novel is for
Rod Fox,
professor emeritus of journalism and mass communications,
Iowa State University,
and in memory of
Jeanne Moulton, English Department,
El Camino High School, Sacramento, California,
two fine teachers of writing.

ACKNOWLEDGMENTS

Numerous people helped create *Rising Dog*. My wife, Mary Joan O'Connell, patiently edited the manuscript and constantly supported my efforts. Novelist Steve Perry gave invaluable advice about plotting and craftsmanship. Others who helped include Brian McCullough and Bridget Madill, Jim Lane, David Rosenak, Jeff Wuorio, Daniel Haché, Donna McMahon, Jordan Auslander, Steve Amick, Jim Fiscus, Foster Church, Robert Schumacher, Dr. John Schilke of the Westwood Medical Clinic, Milwaukie, Oregon, and Chief Deputy Ris Bradshaw and Captain F. Sherwood Stillman of the Clackamas County, Oregon, Sheriff's Department.

Special thanks to the staff of Oregon State University's Mark O. Hatfield Marine Science Center, Newport, Oregon, for information on the habits of wolf eels; to Sharon Jarvis, my agent; and to Michael Denneny, Keith Kahla, and John Hall of St. Martin's Press, New York.

The citations from François Villon are from *The Poems of François Villon: New Edition,* translated by Galway Kinnell, 1982. The citation from Geoffrey Chaucer is from *The Canterbury Tales,* translated into modern English by Nevill Coghill, 1951. The citation from *The Kelevala: The Land of the Heroes* is from the translation by W. F. Kirby, 1951.

The rain can make all places strange,
even places where you live.

—*ERNEST HEMINGWAY,* ''*The Porter*''

RISING
DOG.

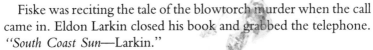

Fiske was reciting the tale of the blowtorch murder when the call came in. Eldon Larkin closed his book and grabbed the telephone. *"South Coast Sun*—Larkin."

There was only breathing on the line.

Typical, Eldon thought. They call the newspaper, then freeze up when they get a reporter. He opened his book again as the silence on the telephone dragged out. Eldon was reading the poems of François Villon in French: *I'm sure of nothing but the uncertain, Find nothing obscure but the obvious . . .*

James O. "Jimbo" Fiske leaned obliviously across the news desk, wrinkling long, curling strips of teletype paper under his elbows, adjusting his clip-on tie as he droned on into Eldon's free ear. *Doubt nothing but the things that are sure . . .* Eldon plugged the ear with a finger. "Hello? Can I help you?"

"I can help *you,"* a reedy male voice said at last. "This is the story of a lifetime."

"Um?" Eldon's gaze wandered to the big glass doors at the front of the newspaper office. It was a lovely spring day. For a short while, at least, Port Jerome and the rest of Oregon's remote, wooded South Coast were free of rain.

"It'll have to top the belly dancer who could eat broken glass," Eldon said.

There was another pause.

Eldon took his finger out of his ear. Fiske was explaining how the blowtorch flame had been played back and forth across the victim's face like a paintbrush. "—as if somebody tried to cover up that ugly wallpaper my wife put in the kitchen," Fiske said. "I didn't think of that at the time, because she put the wallpaper up years after the murder—"

Eldon jammed his finger back in his ear. *Knowledge to me is mere accident, I keep winning and remain the loser . . .* It was no good. He closed the book and sighed, stared listlessly out the glass doors at the clean blue sky. What he really wanted was to get laid. Fat chance. "Go ahead, I'm listening."

The voice on the telephone was eager. "I live out here on the road by the landfill south of town—you know, where those trucks roar up and down? Had me a little dog name of Bouncer. Know what I mean?"

"I've seen dogs, yeah." Was the voice familiar?

"Yesterday one o' those big trucks struck down my little dog. Killed him dead—just like that."

"We did a story on traffic problems a while ago—"

"Well, I reached out and laid hands on him, know what I mean? Laid hands on poor, dead little Bouncer—"

Ugh, Eldon thought.

"—and through the power of prayer, *I raised that little dog from the dead!"*

Eldon smiled. "You raised him up like Lazarus? Brought him back to life after he was crushed by one of those big rigs?"

"Yup, that's what I did. Rig had fourteen wheels."

"I don't know about doing a story. The editor's a big atheist." Eldon fought a snicker. Fiske was a Lutheran. But God-fearing or not, Jimbo showed little sign of winding up the blowtorch story, one of the most interminable in a formidably boring repertoire. It seemed to get longer with each repetition.

Just like every day that passes here, Eldon thought. I've been working here too long. Six years. It's already the spring of 1979. Christ, I'll be thirty-four in August. I've got to make a move.

The sunny outdoors was appealing, although Eldon's first love was rain.

"Where are you?" he asked the caller. "I'm coming out."

"Trail's End Mobile Home Haven."

"I'm not sure where you mean."

"Out by the county landfill. Schumacher's Landfill."

"Okay, gotcha now. You got a name?"

"You'll know me." The caller hung up.

No doubt from the flights of angels circling your head, Eldon thought. "Jimbo—there's been a miracle out by the county landfill. Guy's raised a dog from the dead."

"Dee-de-dee." Fiske rubbed his narrow mustache and grinned, showing darkening teeth backed with gold. "A religion feature would be good."

"I'm going out on it."

"I like a reporter with curiosity."

"I don't really think it's a story—"

"Get out of here, Eldon. You've got spring fever." Fiske took his pipe from the cat-food can he used as an ashtray and caressed the worn bowl. "You've sat there like a bump on a log all day. Shoot me a photo for Page One, a scenic I can run with just a caption. It's a beautiful day, just like it was for the blowtorch murder. Turned out the victim was a Chicago hood, a stoolie who'd fled here to the rainy north woods. The mob tracked him all the way to our own Nekaemas County. They identified him by his dentition—the state medical examiner did, that is, not the mob. He showed me this handful of charred teeth—"

"Right." Eldon shuddered. Teeth reminded him of dentists, and dentists gave him the creeps. He pulled his battered Nikkormat camera from his desk drawer and tugged on a floppy jungle hat studded with fly-fishing lures. His lucky fishing hat had saved his life and now he wore it faithfully. You never could tell. He put the Villon book under his arm with his notebook and went out the side door.

The salt smell of Nekaemas Bay filled Eldon's nostrils as he stepped into the parking lot. Today he was strongly aware of the contrast with the acrid odor of printer's ink that pervaded the offices of the *Sun*. Usually, he couldn't smell the ink at all.

Eldon glanced at the low-slung, orange-and-white newspaper plant, so modern and out of place among the buildings around it. As much out of place as he was himself. He walked to his van, a big beige vehicle still bearing the previous owner's California license plates. Eldon didn't like to think about Shelly—the *Sun*'s former photographer represented one of his all-too-typical failures in love. I'll have to get Oregon plates for the damn thing soon, he thought. It's been months.

He opened the driver's door, put the books and camera on the dashboard, and climbed into the cab. The van's twin bucket seats were upholstered like thrones. The van's interior looked like Scheherazade's boudoir stuffed into a delivery truck—a legacy of the gay man from whom Shelly had acquired the van.

Red velvet padding with gray trim covered the walls, the dashboard, and even the transmission hump. In the rear, a shelf bed with red satin sheets and oversize pillows lay rumpled and in disarray, left unmade after Eldon's last fishing trip. Black velvet paintings of muscle men adorned the walls. Eldon felt like a fool driving this effete vehicle around Nekaemas County, where fishermen and loggers were the social elite; but it would cost a small fortune to rip the furnishings out and replace them.

He had made one change, out of self-respect. The ivory phallus that had topped the gearshift was gone now, replaced by an eight ball. He had hoped the van somehow would improve his fortunes at seduction. No such luck.

He tilted the adjustable steering wheel comfortably above his paunch and adjusted the rearview mirror.

Eldon considered his reflection in the mirror, in something like a ritual. He saw a youthful face with fair, fleshy cheeks and sandy hair just beginning to recede. A ragged walrus mustache and blue eyes too weary for one so young. Capped front teeth. His plump cheeks and tired eyes gave Eldon an air of disappointed innocence, like an altar boy who had seen too many sins in the congregation while assisting at Holy Communion. Or so Bernice, his ex-wife, used to say back in Berkeley.

Eldon pushed Bernice from his mind and turned the van's ignition key. The engine started smoothly, nothing like his old wreck of a Citroën, gone to its rest in the junkyard the previous autumn. I miss that car, Eldon thought.

Clutching the eight ball, he shifted into first gear and edged the van from the parking lot into the traffic of downtown Port Jerome.

The sun had drawn the town's population from hiding. That was the worst thing about good weather. In the streets were women fifty to eighty pounds overweight, squeezed into blue jeans or blue or white knit polyester slacks. There were stringy, hard-faced men in grubby denims and crushed, grimy baseball caps. There were potbellied salesmen with long sideburns and lined, pouchy faces, and adolescents reveling unaware in their brief season of physical beauty before declining into the sleazy hardness of their elders. Eldon wished for rain as he turned south off Main Street onto Bayside Drive, passing the service stations, hardware stores, and shabby bars that formed Port Jerome's ugly core. He felt secure in the rain; he liked to imagine that someday a deluge might wash the town clean.

Or clean off the map, Eldon brooded as he drove down the streets he knew all too well. Covering the news was all there was to his life in Nekaemas County. That and fishing. Sometimes you hit a good story or you caught a good fish. Finding *good copy* was about all that made the place bearable.

Certainly there was very little sex.

The "resurrected" dog was no story, of course. But at least he was away from Jimbo. If he shot a decent scenic photo, he could sell it to the wire service for twenty-five dollars after it appeared in the *Sun*. God knew he could use the money. The van's air conditioner was acting up. Not that he really needed it on the breezy South Coast, but the malfunction might be a harbinger of expensive problems to come.

The southern end of town was marked by a mountain of logs at the site of the long-abandoned Wapello Head mill. The logs looked like columns for some canceled cathedral of enormous dimensions. The mill's smokestack poked nakedly into the sky, stark as a weathered bone. Log booms floated in the slough beneath the pilings of the bridge to Regret, the hamlet where Eldon lived on a hilltop.

He passed the turnoff and picked up U.S. 101.

Eldon surveyed the deep-green sea of Douglas fir and pine that covered the hills beyond town and ringed the great bay. The trees seemed to stretch to infinity. On the many days when the coastal fog rolled in, they would seem to be flying, their tops like a fleet of dark kites. But only a short distance beyond, Eldon knew, the land was clear-cut for miles. They're running out of trees, he told himself, enjoying his own sourness. And when they finally run out of trees, they'll finally run out of loggers.

The sunlight threw the reflection of the Villon book's cover onto the windshield. I'd like to meet a woman who likes medieval French poetry, he thought. Or any poetry at all.

Here was the road to the landfill. He turned onto it and drove past four signs in a row.

The first sign was of green and white metal:

SCHUMACHER'S LANDFILL
NEKAEMAS COUNTY
Landfill Closed—No Dumping

The next sign was old and hung askew:

FEARLESS FAITH LUTHERAN CHURCH
Regular Services
English & Finnish

The third was another metal sign, rusty and peppered with bullet holes by potshotting hunters:

TRAIL'S END
MOBILE HOME HAVEN
Spaces Available

And finally a big new sign, bright with paint:

FOREST VISTA ESTATES
Choice Condominiums Under Construction

The asphalt road was pitted here. Eldon slowed the van. The road skirted the closed landfill, where a few seagulls loitered. Bright young grass sprouted over the raised, gently rolling expanse. A ripe methane stench hung on the warm air. Ahead was a dilapidated little church and beyond that a huddle of rusty trailers. Farther along, indistinct among trees, was the site of Forest Vista Estates.

The road turned to gravel. Clouds of pale yellow dust billowed up as Eldon passed the landfill's locked gate. He coughed and rolled up his window, wishing again for rain. He considered the alleged miracle of the rising dog. A feeling of cool, airy wonder settled over him. The feeling had nothing to do with piety; it was professional. It protected Eldon at murder scenes, traffic accidents, and other moments of crisis—a remoteness and clarity of mind that had kept him going through six years of blood, deadlines, and rednecks. Was the strain beginning to tell? He never had bad dreams. Or not so far, he thought, passing the Fearless Faith Lutheran Church. The church had seen no services for a long time—that was obvious. The building was boarded up. Birds nested in a hole in the tilted steeple. That might make a good photo on the way home, Eldon thought.

He drove into the mobile-home park and halted. It was like so many others on the South Coast—scattered, rusted trailers, the Douglas fir and alder the only beauty in the place. Eldon spotted three invalids and a spindly little man in white who held a small black dog before a battered trailer. Eldon climbed from the van and approached them, smiling. He saw that the little man wore bright white Levi's, white T-shirt, white sneakers. He was impeccable, clean-shaven, with combed silver hair, translucent skin, and wide blue liar's eyes. The old man seemed familiar, but Eldon couldn't place him.

The dog looked like a miniature barrel covered with woolly black carpet and mounted on peg legs. The mutt yapped and wriggled happily, unrolling a long red tongue as Eldon walked up.

A scrawny, horsefaced young man sat propped askew in a wheelchair, knees knocked together, bony hands useless in his lap. A hunchbacked man leaned trembling on a cane, constantly licking bad teeth. The third fellow, a tall, skinny youth, clearly was addled. His arms and fingers seemed too short, and he wore a baseball cap backward. All were clad in ragged shirts and slack-fitting jeans. The hunchback wore a flea-market top hat. Three sets of eyes were fixed upon the old man in white.

"Eldon Larkin from the *Sun*," Eldon said. "You gave me a call?"

The old man thrust the dog at Eldon. "That was me. This is Bouncer. Not a blemish on 'im."

The dog wagged its tail and kicked stubby legs, breaking a fart. Eldon winced and rubbed the animal's shaggy head. As he did so, a huge blond man with a nose like a ruptured sausage stepped from one of the trailers.

Eldon's stomach turned over in terror. *Paavo the Finn.*

Eldon had been present months before when a titanic blow had snapped Paavo's hatchet nose across his face like a gate. Paavo would remember Eldon as an ally of the man whose fist had transformed his face forever, and the Finn's strength and ugly temper were notorious. Eldon stood rooted to the ground with fear as the Finn clumped down the trailer's flimsy steps.

Paavo's pale eyes lit with recognition. The Finn threw up gorilla arms. "Eldon Larkin! I knew you would come from the newspaper." A smile full of great spatulate teeth spread beneath the crushed nose.

"Hiya, Paavo," Eldon said with a gulp.

"I'm glad you came. This is a real miracle." Paavo turned and laid a hand fondly on the old man's shoulder.

Eldon suddenly recognized the old man. "You're Cap'n Jasper. But you're *sober*. Last time I saw you two, Paavo was trying to tear you apart—"

"That's behind us now," Jasper said with an air of serene command. "I'm a drunken ex-tugboat captain no more. I'm the Reverend Jasper O'Shay. The both of us are dry for good. Have been for months."

"I owe it all to Jasper," Paavo said. "He helped me dry out in the county jail. My wife left me—I had nothing to live for. But Jasper helped me see the light. Now I feel anger toward no man. That's as big a miracle as Bouncer here."

Jasper tossed the dog to the ground. Bouncer darted around Eldon's feet. "Made whole through the power of prayer," Jasper said. "Log truck barreled right through here and crushed 'im."

"They're clearing trees for that damn condo project down the way," Paavo said.

"There poor Bouncer lay," Jasper said, "ribs stickin' out like broken branches. But I laid hands on 'im and raised 'im up."

"Th-th-that's r-r-right," the addled boy put in.

"You saw it?" Eldon asked him.

"N-n-no . . ."

"Ah," Eldon said. "Tell me, Jasper, was it hard to do?"

"Yeah! I hadn't done it in years."

"What?"

"Well, not with animals," Jasper said. "Just people. That's why it was so hard."

"You've raised people from the dead?"

"Naw, just healed 'em. Years ago. Before I got into tugboating." Jasper cast his eyes down. "It was my downfall, too. Even a preacher sometimes needs a sideline to make ends meet. My elixir was quality stuff."

"You sold snake oil at revivals," Eldon said.

"It was good for what ailed quite a few." Jasper's voice warmed, an old enthusiasm reviving. "The alcohol ignited my prayers like fuel in a lamp. Cripples danced and sang when *I* prayed over 'em."

"Aren't you takin' all this down?" Paavo demanded.

"I'm getting it," Eldon said.

"But I was weak and fell from grace," Jasper continued. "You can figure out the rest."

"You became a drunk and couldn't preach and ran away to sea," Eldon said.

The hunchback hissed in disapproval. Eldon nodded knowingly. Many times he had seen Jasper shamble from customer to customer in Buster's tavern, begging spare change in a whine of such cutting frequency that hardened millworkers passed the hat to buy Jasper a bottle so he could stupefy himself. Now came the image of the old drunk as a fire-breathing camp-meeting healer, Bible in one hand, flask of hooch in the other.

"I went cold turkey last winter in the county jail," Jasper said. "Pink mice crawlin' all over me. When I came out of it, I knew I'd never survive another one like that. 'Jasper,' I told myself, 'you gotta face up to your nature. You're no drunk. You gotta put that behind you and be what you *are.*'"

"Then Jasper turned and helped me out, too," Paavo said. "I was at rock bottom and he lifted me up."

"I needed an assistant," Jasper said.

"I'm kind of like his Saint Peter," Paavo said.

"Bouncer proves I've still got my touch," Jasper said. "There's that old church right over there where we can set up."

"So that's it—you're trying to make a comeback as a faith healer," Eldon said. "And so here you are, with three wise men, to boot."

Jasper pointed to the hunchback. "This here's One-Square. Fella can't move is Wheelie, counta his wheelchair. They're brothers, I think. The kid, we just call 'im Beanpole. Counta how he looks. He isn't all there."

"I w-w-wanta be, though," Beanpole said.

"How'd you find 'em?" Eldon asked.

"We found 'em when we found the church," Jasper said. "They were living here in the trailer park—the last holdouts to eviction."

"We won't go, neither," One-Square said with a growl.

Jasper's expression darkened. "They're going to rip out this trailer park when they build that condo development. They'll tear down my church, too. . . . But I get Bouncer in the paper, get some publicity, I can make that church a going concern again. They won't dare tear it down."

"Could you do the miracle again?" Eldon asked.

"Why again? Dog's raised."

"How about this guy in the wheelchair, then? Can you straighten him out? I need pictures. Proof."

"I'm going to go to church a lot more from now on," Wheelie whispered.

"Amen!" said Paavo.

Eldon eyed Paavo cautiously, but the Finn's expression remained sunny as the day. "We've got to have photos," Eldon said. He clapped his hands and whistled to Bouncer, who had wandered to a man-sized hole in the landfill fence to sniff the underbrush. The dog trotted back, yapping. Eldon scooped up Bouncer in his arms. He noticed a cloud of dust boiling up the road from the direction of the highway. "There's a log truck coming."

"G-g-good sp-sp-speed on 'im," Beanpole said.

"Let's throw the dog in front of this truck," Eldon said. "Paavo's got a strong arm—he was arm-wrestling king of the town's bars. He pitches Bouncer under those wheels like a furry little bowling ball. *Sqwoonch!* Then Jasper raises him from the dead again while I photograph the whole thing!"

Beanpole bleated wordlessly. The truck rumbled closer. All eyes turned to Jasper. Jasper's nose tilted up with Olympian amusement. "I won't do it just for show. That would be presumptuous. It is written: 'Thou shalt not tempt the Lord thy God.' "

The log truck was nearly upon them, its driver sounding the horn in warning as he downshifted. It thundered through the trailer park throwing gravel, log chains bouncing and swinging on its empty trailer. The truck receded, leaving them coughing in the dust.

Eldon released Bouncer, who ran back across the road, raised a leg to a fence pole, then bounded through the hole and up the slope into the landfill.

"I th-th-th-ought ya were g-g-gonna pitch 'im," Beanpole said, a little disappointed.

"I didn't want to waste him if there wasn't going to be a miracle," Eldon said.

"G-g-guess you're right," Beanpole said. "Hey, Bouncer! Here, boy!" He scampered after the dog in a shambling, loose-jointed run.

"Bouncer's a good dog," Jasper said. "And he's here thanks to the power of prayer."

"Yeah, well, good luck, Jasper," Eldon said.

"You're not gonna do a story?" Paavo asked.

"No miracle, no photo, no story," Eldon said.

"There'll be plenty of miracles once we open the church," Paavo said.

Eldon was saved from replying by a shout from Beanpole, now atop the landfill, beckoning. Bouncer dashed barking around Beanpole's feet.

"Let's see what it is," said Paavo. He stepped behind Wheelie, released the wheelchair's brakes, and started pushing the paralytic across the road. The hunchback lurched behind. Eldon and Jasper followed.

The slope was too soft for the wheelchair. They had to leave Wheelie at the fence. One-Square jabbed his cane into the earth and struggled upward as Jasper guided him from behind.

Beanpole was hopping in a frenzy, jabbing his arms in the direction of the condo project. "It's a f-f-fight! Looks like a big fight!"

Eldon shaded his eyes with his hand. The empty truck had stopped outside the condominium site. People were milling in the road. Some kind of commotion, all right. Had the truck struck a pedestrian? "This could be your chance to do another resurrection," he told Jasper.

"Could be." Jasper started across the landfill at a dignified pace. His congregation followed. Bouncer scampered ahead, barking. Beanpole shambled after the dog, zigzagging in a kind of broken field run. Eldon heard faint shouts and quickened his pace, cocking his camera as he went.

The landfill's hummocky brown plain, speckled with spring grass like thin hair, reminded Eldon of overtanned skin crisscrossed with narrow trails like scars. Odd pieces of junk protruded from the ground like bits of an imbedded charm bracelet. The stink was pervasive. How could anyone build condos here?

Beanpole pulled up short at the far rim of the landfill berm and guffawed. "Hey, that's really c-c-cool!"

Eldon reached the edge of the landfill and looked down onto the road. Workmen in bright hard hats stood before the halted truck, squinting up into the branches of a big fir next to the road. A wordless, infantile yell of rage and frustration came from the tree. Eldon peered. Up among the branches was a man, yelling and hugging the tree's trunk. "Please don't hurt the trees!" he yelled. The rangy, black-bearded figure wore dungarees, a plaid shirt, and a headdress of branches. He had fir boughs lashed to his arms and legs.

Good copy. Eldon brought up the Nikkormat and snapped a picture. But he had to get closer. He started down the embankment.

A florid-faced man stepped to the base of the tree and cocked his hard hat back on his head. Eldon thought he resembled an angry, animated ham. The man's belly, squeezed into a grimy khaki workshirt, hung well over his jeans. The jeans were slung so low that Eldon could see the crack of the man's ass where his shirt rode up in back.

The man looked up into the tree. "Come down from there," he said sharply but not unreasonably. "You're trespassin' and you know it."

"No!" The man in the tree clutched the trunk.

Eldon climbed up on the right-side running board of the truck. "Hey, who *is* that guy?" he called through the open window to the driver.

"That's the foreman, whaddaya think?"

"No, I mean the guy in the tree."

"Who in hell're you?"

"Eldon Larkin from the *Sun.*"

"The guy's a loon. A tree-hugger."

"What's his name?"

"John Henspeter. As in chicken-dick. Now get off my truck."

"Thanks." Typical South Coast manners, Eldon thought, dropping to the ground. Six years here and it still bugged him.

"C'mon down from there," the foreman repeated to John Henspeter. "We ain't got all day to mess wif you."

Henspeter hung out from the tree and let a gob of clear saliva drop from his mouth directly into the foreman's face.

The foreman roared and yanked a red bandanna from his jeans. He wiped his eyes. "Pull that bastard down from there!"

Two workmen started warily up the tree. Their quarry screamed defiantly. Eldon heard a metallic jingle and realized that Henspeter had chained himself to the tree.

Henspeter kicked and shouted a fierce litany as the men inched closer: "Save—the—old—growth! Save—the—old—growth! Save—the—old—growth—"

One workman lost his purchase and slid back to the ground. Henspeter laughed and spat after him. The second climber grabbed one of Henspeter's legs and pulled. Henspeter threw his arms wide, letting the chain stop him. "Nail me up! Nail me up!" He kicked off the workman's hard hat as Eldon took another picture.

The man slid to the ground and plucked his helmet from the dust. "I'm not getting kicked," he told the foreman.

"Pull him down!" the foreman yelled.

"He's chained. I'm not getting kicked."

"Chained! We'll *cut* that spittin' S.O.B. outa there! Get the chain saw."

"You can't fell a tree here," someone said. "You don't know where it'll come down."

"I've been fellin' trees for thirty years," the foreman said. "I know just where it'll come down."

"Goddamn it, he's crazy," one of the climbers said. "For all we know, he's spiked the tree."

"Spiked it?" the foreman repeated in a cold voice and looked up at the man in the tree. "Look here—is this tree spiked? I'm asking straight."

The hair on the back of Eldon's neck prickled. He had read about "spiking"—driving railroad spikes deep into the trunk of a tree as a way of discouraging loggers from cutting it down. The spikes were hammered flush with the bark, making them practically undetectable; when the whirling blade of a power saw struck one, the results could be lethal. It was a tactic blamed on radical environmentalists—a tactic Eldon was certain could move a logger to murder.

Henspeter stared down at his adversary and replied with equal coldness: "No. I shoulda thought of that."

"If you had, I'd kill you and that's flat," the foreman said.

Someone lugged up a chain saw. The foreman grabbed it and pulled the cord. The saw coughed out clear bluish smoke. The motor caught; the saw roared.

Henspeter began yelling again, his voice barely audible above the chain saw. "Don't—hurt—the—old—growth! Don't—hurt—the—old—growth—"

Eldon moved closer, camera ready. The foreman lifted the vibrating saw, its cutting edge awhirl. He stepped to the tree and applied the saw.

The blade bit into the tree with an earsplitting blast and a blizzard of pale wood chips. Eldon snapped the shutter. The foreman leaned into his work. Henspeter flapped his arms and yelled as the chain saw chewed its way deeper.

Eldon moved sideways, shooting pictures. The foreman saw him and waved him away. A workman grabbed at his camera, then suddenly found himself suspended in air. Paavo the Finn had lifted the man one-handed by the collar. The man struggled vainly.

The foreman sawed on.

Another hard hat grabbed Paavo's sleeve. The Finn hurled the man he held at the attacker. Beanpole and One-Square staggered into the affray through a cloud of rising dust, the hunchback flailing with his cane. Jasper was close behind, yelling over the scream of the saw about saving his church.

The foreman shut off the saw.

Eldon flinched in the abrupt silence.

But the foreman's eyes were not upon Eldon or the tree or on Henspeter or the scuffle. Instead, he gazed into the woods beyond the condominium site, his openmouthed consternation turning into a smile: "Wouldya look at that."

The scuffle ceased. Heads turned, fists were lowered. The silence took on a worshipful quality.

Eldon looked with the others. His heart leaped. At the edge of the woods, a woman wearing cutoff blue jeans and nothing else sat astride a bay horse, watching them. Her tanned breasts were firm and medium-sized. She appeared to be in her thirties. Her light-brown hair was tied back. She had a square face and wore aviator glasses perched on her straight nose. She surveyed the men calmly, unperturbed by their stares.

Eldon gave a long sigh, conscious of the sudden drumming of his heart. It had been months—no, a year—no, more than a year since . . . Hands numb, he raised his camera and snapped a picture. She was too far away! He needed a longer lens—

Henspeter reached out like a lost waif: "Enola Gay! Oh, Enola Gay!"

The woman shook her head. After a moment, she turned her horse into the trees.

"Did you see 'em bounce?" the foreman said reverently. "That's gotta hurt!"

The tree trunk cracked. Eldon scrambled back. Henspeter howled in despair. The fir tree listed, trunk splintering. Its upper branches caught in those of adjacent trees and it toppled slowly, as if air were seeping out of it. Henspeter clutched the trunk as he was lowered unharmed to the horizontal. Eldon snapped a picture and rushed up to him. "Who is she? What's her last name?"

Henspeter only wailed. He had but one eye, luminous and blue, like a crazy jewel. His whiskered face was cobwebbed with lines radiating from the center of his collapsed right eyelid. The face was thin, yet the bony structure was powerful and seemed to contain enormous pressure, as if at any instant the face could suddenly balloon outward.

"Her name?" he said. "She's—"

Suddenly there was a bloodcurdling cry of terror behind Eldon. The reporter whirled. Beanpole was on his hands and knees in the road, eyes bugged wide, nose to nose with Bouncer. The dog stood wagging his tail, holding something in his mouth that looked like an oddly shaped lump of wood.

Beanpole tried to yell again, but the breath had gone out of him. He gasped weakly and backed up. Eldon stared. The lump of wood was almost as big as Bouncer's head. It was wedge-shaped, tapering to a row of stubby roots like gnarled toes.

Bouncer trotted proudly up to Eldon, who saw that the roots were indeed toes. The risen dog was offering him a mummified human foot.

2

Fiske was regaling two more victims with the blowtorch saga when Eldon rushed into the newsroom and stood gasping before the editor's desk.

Young Frank Juliano, who covered the county government, nodded with interest and pushed his glasses up his long nose as Fiske dragged the story toward its nauseating end. Marsha Cox sat ramrod straight behind her typewriter. Her thin features were frozen in the fierce disapproval that cowed the school boards, planning commissions, and other petty bureaucracies that were the hapless targets of her prose.

Fiske waved his pipe. "Hi, Eldon, get some good scenics? Anyway, I got home from covering the story about six in the morning, hungry as a tiger. *Good copy* always makes me that way."

"Me, too!" said Frank.

"Jimbo, there's a—" Eldon said.

"My wife cooked up a big breakfast for me," Fiske said. "Sausage and eggs. I couldn't eat the sausage because of the smell. I still think about the blowtorch murder whenever I smell sausage." Fiske closed his eyes, smiling at the memory. "But I don't have any trouble eating it now."

"Christ," said Marsha with affected drama.

Fiske opened his eyes. "Whatcha got for me, Eldon? A dog's come back from the dead, eh?"

"No. But somebody *is* dead—there was a topless woman—"

"Just the lower half, you mean?" Fiske grabbed a page dummy sheet.

"No—topless!"

"Dead naked woman?" Frank asked. "She look any good?"

"No, the woman wasn't dead—she looked great—"

"She do the killin'?" Fiske demanded.

"There was a fight, too—" Eldon said.

"Naked woman got killed in a fight," Fiske said.

"No," said Eldon. "The dog found him. Or part of him—or her. Just a foot."

"*Good copy!*" Fiske exclaimed. "You get pictures?"

Eldon rewound the roll of film he had shot and popped it from his camera. Fiske took the metal cylinder and tossed it to Frank. "Soup it."

Frank bounded for the darkroom like an awkward basketball player.

"Now," said Fiske, "what happened?"

"It's complicated," Eldon said. "I've got to write it."

He sat at his desk and rolled a sheet of newsprint into his rattletrap gray Royal 440, wishing as always that the out-of-state corporation that was the *Sun*'s indifferent owner would spring for word processors. But that was unimportant now. Eldon touched the typewriter's keys. His nerves settled down, his heart slowed, and his breathing became regular; his joints felt oiled. Cool clarity settled over him. He arranged the facts in his mind, took a deep breath, and began to write:

By Eldon Larkin
Sun *Staff Writer*

PORT JEROME—A dog found a mummified human foot Monday in Schumacher's Landfill, at the height of a brawl that climaxed in the felling of a fir tree with an environmental demonstrator chained into its top.

Nekaemas County sheriff's deputies said they did not know whether the foot had belonged to a man or a woman or how long it had lain in the landfill, which was closed in 1975.

The foot certainly was months old and possibly years old, they said.

The dried, leathery appendage was found by Bouncer, a black mongrel belonging to Jasper O'Shay, a resident of the Trail's End Mobile Home Haven near the landfill. The dog apparently dug up the foot in the landfill.

The animal's bizarre discovery halted a brawl among employees of a development company, members of O'Shay's church, and John Henspeter, an environmental activist. Henspeter had chained himself into a tree to protest the planned construction of condominiums near the landfill.

Henspeter was unhurt when the tree fell.

No corpse was found. Deputies closed the road to the landfill and prepared to search the 100-acre dump site for a body Tuesday . . .

Fiske poked Eldon's shoulder with the stem of his pipe. "Was it a right foot or a left foot?"

"I—ah—don't know."

"Well, find out. How'd they get it away from the dog?"

"Oh, he dropped it right in front of Jasper."

"You get a picture?"

"Yeah. I—I took one of the topless woman, too."

"What's she got to do with this?"

"She rode out of the woods on a horse. With no shirt on."

"We won't run that," Fiske said. "We'd get complaints about 'bad taste.' The foot is the angle for this story."

"I think she knows the environmentalist."

"What about this environmentalist, anyway?"

"He doesn't want condos built there. Something about saving old-growth timber."

Fiske wrinkled his brow. "There's no old growth over there."

"He didn't make a lot of sense."

"They arrest him?"

"The deputies cited him for trespassing and he unlocked his own chain and ran off. He was upset about being upstaged by the foot."

The darkroom door slid back with a thump. Frank emerged waving a strip of negatives. "You got some good T and A, Eldon!"

"Let's have that," Fiske said. He put a viewing lens to one eye and pulled the negatives across the plastic loupe. "Some guys standing around a tree—more guys standing around a tree—couple frames out of focus—two guys climbing a tree—fat man with a chain saw—buncha flyin' wood chips. Now, here's a good-lookin' topless gal! Gonna ask her for a date, Eldon?"

"She rode away into the woods," Eldon said sadly.

"Bet you coulda snagged her if you'd had your fly rod," said Fiske. "Dee-de-dee—here's the goods! Cute little dog with a human foot in its mouth. Reminds me of a pup I had when I was a kid, except he was a terrier." Fiske clipped the edge of the negative frame with a hole punch. "Used him to catch rats. Can't beat a terrier for rats. Print it, Frank."

"Maybe that woman will come back," Eldon said lightly, wishing it could be true.

Fiske picked up a strip of wire-service copy, looked at it regretfully. "Now we've got to spike this story."

"Another Bigfoot feature?"

"Plate tectonics," said Fiske. "Bigfoot's nothing compared to this. This is *important*. The Earth's crust is sliding around. This news desk could slip right out from under me."

Frank returned shortly with two prints of the photograph Fiske had ordered. He handed the better print to the editor and the other, still beaded with water, to Eldon for reference when he wrote the caption.

Eldon paused to admire the photo. He had snapped a good, strong horizontal. Bouncer, bright-eyed, chest out, tail high, held his desiccated discovery crosswise in his jaws. Each buckled toenail on the withered foot was in focus, the bristly hair on Bouncer's muzzle sharp and clear. A large ant crawled on the foot.

It was a left foot. Eldon resumed typing. He had a good time with the story, spicing it with the Henspeter confrontation and describing Jasper as a faith healer with a "born-again dog."

Eldon paused. Who owned the condominium project? Maybe that had been the subject of a business story—Marsha's beat. He looked around but Marsha had flounced off. No wonder I can't remember anything about it, Eldon thought. I never read her boring stories.

"Hey, Frank—can you check the clip files for me? Who owns the condo project out by Schumacher's? I think Marsha might've written about it."

Eldon continued writing while Frank rooted through the tall file cabinets full of past *Sun* stories. The cabinets were packed with yellowing clippings mounted on sheets of paper in manila folders, dated and cross-referenced—often eccentrically—by author, topic, and names of persons, companies, or government agencies involved. Such a collection once had been known as a "morgue." To Eldon's disappointment, the term had passed from use in recent years. Now the files were dignified as "the library." That was just as misleading and much less fun—except perhaps for Marsha, who corrected Eldon whenever he used the old term.

At last Frank said, "The company is Forest Vista Incorporated. The owner is Keith Howell of Port Jerome." He spelled the last name.

"Howell," Eldon said. "Where do I know that name?"

"The story says he got an award a while back. One of the big environmental lobbies recognized him as an 'ecologically conscious' developer."

"There is such a thing?"

"Story says so. The award was for a project in Coos Bay."

"What else?"

"Nothing else. Looks like Marsha just rewrote a press release."

"The names are all I need." Eldon used a pencil to amend his story. He typed "30" at the end and rolled the final page from his typewriter. The drag of his arms and body seemed to return. He was back in the lackluster real world.

Yet there was cause for satisfaction. Again Eldon admired the photograph he had taken. "Bouncer the Page One pup will stop 'em dead."

Frank dropped another photograph across the first. "Here's your new girlfriend."

Eldon turned the picture to its proper vertical angle to feast his eyes upon the woman rider. "Don't I wish. You're getting pretty good at darkroom work."

"I wish Fiske would hire a new photog."

"It's not as if they stampede to Port Jerome to apply." Eldon stared at the horsewoman's breasts.

"Thirty-four B's at the most," Frank said casually. "But she's not bad-looking."

Eldon was irritated. Frank had a new girlfriend. Pleasant, boyish Frank always had a girlfriend. But couldn't he at least be respectful? For Eldon, love was as scarce a commodity as money. How many had it been—four women in six years? *Four?* "The wire service'll pay me for the picture of the foot," he said.

"They might buy the cheesecake, too," Frank said. " 'Editors, Note Subject Matter.' I don't know who runs photos like that, I think they just post 'em on newsroom bulletin boards. I want some chili."

Eldon dropped the horsewoman's picture into a manila folder. It would get an honored place at home, among his well-thumbed collection of porno magazines. "I'll write this caption and come with you."

After Fiske had okayed Eldon's story, Eldon stashed the precious photo in his van. Then he and Frank made their way down the street to Pop's restaurant, source of the sticky sweet rolls that were often Eldon's breakfast. Eldon pondered his waistline as they sat in a booth, waiting for their chili. I have to take off some weight, he thought, unwrapping a plastic packet of crackers and munching them.

Frank was full of enthusiasm. "A mummified foot! Murder in the landfill! You always find the best stories, Eldon. I don't know how you do it."

"I just wonder who the woman on the horse is," Eldon said. "She must live around here. Maybe up Jackknife Slough. The environmentalist knew her."

"Did you ask him?"

"I couldn't get anything out of him. It would be a conflict of interest, anyway. I won't ask personal favors from someone I've written about."

"You worry too much," Frank said as the chili arrived in heavy white bowls. "You've got to keep your wits about you, is all."

Eldon opened two more packets of crackers, crushed them, and dropped them into his chili.

"Forget the cowgirl," said Frank, hefting a big spoonful of chili. "This business with the foot is the best story since the elephant case. We're talking murder most foul."

"Probably just a bum who wandered into the landfill and died."

"And became a mummy in this climate? Right."

"He was pickled in alcohol. Full of cheap wine."

"Lying out on the ground?" Frank said. "No way. He'd have moldered away in the rain. The birds and bears would've scattered his bones long ago." Frank swallowed the chili and shook his spoon. "He had to've been buried *in* the landfill, Eldon. He was *hidden*. Therefore—murder."

"If the dog was able to find him, he couldn't've been buried very deep."

"Maybe rain washed some of the earth away. We do get sixty-five inches a year."

"Well, we'll know for sure when they find the rest of him."

"That was a great photo of the foot. Two-fisted news, like in newspapers in the thirties." Frank ate and frowned. "This chili's okay, I guess."

Eldon stared at his chili and at last took a mouthful. It was tepid; the ground beef had the consistency of gravel. "It's sure not California chili. There was this great chili place Bernice and I used to go to in Berkeley—" Eldon felt cold. She had taken off six years ago and he had fled to Port Jerome. The divorce had been final for three years. If he couldn't stay fired up about his work in this dump, the best thing to do was to jump off a bridge and be done with it.

But there's always the fishing, he reminded himself and felt a little better.

And there's always murder, his mind continued. Was the foot a relic of some old robbery? Of an ancient revenge slaying? Of a cult that hacked up its victims? "Fat chance," Eldon muttered under his breath.

"Pardon?" Frank asked.

"If it's murder, maybe it was done somewhere else and the body was just dumped here. This doesn't have the South Coast's usual impulsive style."

"You may be right," Frank said. "Premeditation's too intellectual for 'em around here."

No, Eldon reflected as they ate, premeditation wasn't the style in the South Coast's rainy forests. Here murder struck like lightning, when people who had lived too long in the rain and poverty and isolation finally snapped. A millworker split another's loud-mouthed head with a crowbar. A bruised housewife plunged a carving knife into her drunken husband's guts. A pudgy teenager, goaded beyond endurance by his hardscrabble family, buttoned all their lips forever with his Christmas pump shotgun. Murder on the South Coast was a grand gesture, cathartic, almost joyful, easy for a reporter to cover.

This one won't be easy to cover, Eldon thought. That's what's bothering me. "I'll probably have to spend all day at the landfill tomorrow while they hunt for the body. I hope it doesn't get hot."

"Around here? Take a lunch. Hope it doesn't rain."

"I'd like it to rain." Eldon ate a big spoonful of chili, chewing slowly, thinking about the topless horsewoman, imagining being cozy with her in the rain. He saw himself preparing a gourmet seduction dinner in his hilltop abode. Cornish game hens stuffed with wild rice and mushrooms, a cheery fire in the stove, classical music on the stereo. And then . . .

Eldon swallowed. "I wonder if she likes classical music."

"Who? You still thinking about that woman?"

"Yeah." Eldon sighed. "I have a snowball's chance in hell of meeting her."

"Oh, crap."

"It's not possible. We haven't been properly introduced. It's like when I was a student visiting Paris. You never met anyone on the Métro—it just wasn't done."

Frank shrugged. "So how'd you meet Bernice?"

"I don't remember," Eldon said, taken aback. "At a party."

"Go to more parties."

"No one invites me," Eldon said. "And I can't party with people I might wind up writing about. And it would have to be the right party, obviously. I don't know anyone who knows her, except—"

"—this environmentalist. Like I said, you worry too much. In fact, you seem to be worrying a lot more lately."

"My elephant story last fall went national, Frank. The wire service put it in papers all over the country. But I'm still here. I didn't get a better job. There were no openings in Seattle or San Francisco. The *Oregonian* wouldn't give me the time of day. When I called the city desk about sending a résumé up to Portland, you know what the guy said? 'I don't really think—' "

" '—you'd like it here,' " Frank recited without sympathy.

Eldon fell silent. A little at a time, his old life in Berkeley was slipping away. He was stuck in Nekaemas County, doomed to go native.

"So you want a piece of the action?" Sheriff's Detective Art Nola straightened and stepped to the strip of yellow crime-scene tape. He held a chipped china saucer carefully in one hand. He wore white latex surgical gloves flecked with mud. "No way."

"Art, you know I play straight," Eldon said from the other side of the tape.

"I know you get me in Dutch," Nola said. "I'm better off when I don't talk to you."

Nola was long-jawed and long-nosed, his lined face topped with prematurely graying russet hair. Much of the landfill behind him was marked off by connecting boxes of tape, forming a giant, flimsy yellow grid that gleamed a little in the morning sun as it flexed with the breeze. Deputies dug carefully with spades or probed with long metal rods. Others sifted earth through prospector's screens.

Eldon edged closer to the tape. "Find anything?"

Art thrust out the saucer. It was a rich, deep purple-red, with gold scrolling and tiny figures in seventeenth-century pastoral settings. "I can't believe anyone would throw this away."

Eldon saw that he wasn't joking. "It's chipped."

"Only a little! It's a Beehive. Top of the line." The detective turned the saucer over. Stamped on the underside in purple was what looked like a line drawing of a pistol slug. "That's Royal Vienna, 1850 to 1864," Nola said. "The mark is embossed under the glaze. A company's logo is called a 'mark.' There are all kinds of them. Crossed swords. Flying birds. But nothing beats a Beehive."

"When the hell did you get interested in fine china?"

"Shelly got me interested, before she decamped for Seattle." Nola carefully stowed the saucer in a clear plastic evidence bag. "I never did have good judgment where a woman was concerned. My dad always said."

"Well, she was too good a photographer to hang around here." Art gave a wry smile. "At least you got a van out of it."

"So what about this foot? Any sign of who it belongs to?"

"We're digging."

"How many men?"

"Six."

Eldon jotted in his notebook. "To cover a hundred acres? We'll be out here all day."

"All week's more likely."

"So he's buried deep?"

"You said that. I didn't say that."

"Okay, okay. How deep will they dig?"

"The landfill's forty-seven feet deep at its deepest point. It's mounded in the center. We'll dig until we find something."

"So you do think he's in there."

Nola gave an exasperated shrug. "No, we're digging for more china. Wait—don't put that in the paper."

"Stop fencing with me."

They scowled at one another. At last Nola said, "I'm not fencing, Eldon. You know about as much as I do."

"What does your Missing Persons Unit say?"

Art chuckled. "How long have you been covering our department? We're too short-staffed to have one. Most law-enforcement agencies are. This week, *I'm* the Missing Persons Unit. I can tell you this case doesn't fit any recent reports in our files."

"So this case is older than that."

"We'll have to wait for the medical examiner on that one. But clearly that foot's been here awhile."

"You said it didn't fit any recent cases. How far back is that?"

"I've checked four years back. And the longer someone's missing, the colder the trail gets."

"And further back than '75?"

Nola shrugged. "After someone's been missing that long, the odds of finding anything drop off dramatically. It takes a lucky break. That's a rule of thumb."

"Let me look through your old records," Eldon said. "You'll be the first to know what I find."

"Save yourself the trouble," Nola said. "The file probably doesn't exist anymore—especially if they didn't think foul play was involved. It has to be something special or we chuck it. It's a cost thing."

"Somebody disappears and you chuck the file out?"

"Being gone isn't a crime," Nola said. "Disappearing doesn't mean you've been the victim of a crime. Being gone doesn't mean you even got reported as missing."

"That state police computer hookup—National Crime Information Center. Any hits there?"

"No. Maybe there never will be. They've only been putting missing persons into NCIC since 1975."

25

"What about dental records?"

"A lot of missing persons turn out not to have dental records."

"Why?"

"Maybe they don't have heads."

Eldon had a vision of Fiske crying *Good copy!* and asked, "The foot, Art—was it *hacked off*? Can you tell?"

"We're off the record here?"

Eldon sighed and closed his notebook. "We're off the record."

"I'm not the medical examiner, so I don't want to speak out of turn," Art said. "But a cop gets to know what to look for. That's a whole foot but no leg bones. If the foot had been chopped off, there'd be stubs of the tibia and fibula sticking out of the foot, right? Because you'd tend to chop above the ankle, which is the narrowest point."

"So the body just fell apart. It could've been a natural death."

"Absolutely. We've never ruled that out." Art gave Eldon a puzzled look. "Where'd you get the idea that he was *chopped up*? You reporters have morbid imaginations."

"Too much sun. I wish it would rain."

"It's warming up, isn't it?" Nola said. "It can get hot and I can work in the stink, or it can rain and I can work in the muck."

"Did you have the dog sniff around some more?"

"We tried that. He just stands on his hind legs and wags his tail, begging for a goody."

"I guess Bouncer has retired from forensic work," Eldon said. "When should I check back? I can't sit out here."

"Anyone's guess," Nola said. "It's a big landfill."

"I'll take some pictures and go."

Nola sighed. "Just don't cross the tape."

Eldon moved down the boundary of the grid and shot a few pictures of deputies at work. The sun burned bright in the blue sky and the landfill was beginning to stink. Beads of sweat glistened on the deputies' foreheads. They worked doggedly as the smell grew stronger. Plainly the landfill had been improperly sealed—no wonder the dog had found the foot, Eldon thought.

But *where?*

He surveyed the scene with growing frustration. Photos and copy about the search would hold Fiske at bay, but that would not satisfy Eldon. There was a corpse to be found, the more desiccated, the better. He wanted the story. And a photo. Not even Fiske would publish a shot of a mummy; but Eldon's getting the scoop would be a validation.

Eldon trudged along the line of tape, his frustration increasing with the intensity of the sun. This was a warm spring for Port Jerome, where heavy rain and ocean winds provided Frank's "natural air-conditioning." Winter temperatures much below forty degrees Fahrenheit constituted a cold snap, summer temperatures higher than eighty a heat wave. It's going to be a hot summer, Eldon thought. No rain in sight.

He noted that the searchers were working outer portions of the big grid—sensible, when you considered that Bouncer couldn't have gone very far to uncover his gruesome prize. The body ought to be in the outer reaches of the landfill, lying virtually in the open. Or perhaps not. The little dog might merely have discovered the foot protruding and merrily tugged. . . .

"Eldon!" called a distant voice.

Eldon halted. The voice was Paavo's. The sound sent chills along Eldon's spine despite the knowledge that the big Finn now walked the path of Christian love and peace.

"Eldon!"

Paavo stood on the far side of the landfill near the trailer park, beckoning vigorously. Eldon sighed and started in Paavo's direction. It was a chance to get out of the sun.

Paavo beamed as Eldon trudged up. The grin beneath the Finn's crushed nose made him look fearsomely idiotic. "This is great, huh?" Paavo said and gave a loud, coarse laugh.

"A dead body in a landfill is great?"

"It's too bad," said Paavo, leading Eldon down the slope to the road. "But it's great publicity for the church. You really wrote a fine story for us in the *Sun,* Eldon."

"I didn't write it for you. I wrote it because it was news."

"It was all absolutely true and accurate."

"That's our daily goal at the *South Coast Sun.*"

"That was a great picture of Bouncer. 'The born-again dog.' Jasper liked that. I did, too. We all did."

"Thanks, Paavo."

"We've got another story for you."

"I'm pretty busy with this body story—"

27

"If it hadn't been for Bouncer, you wouldn't *have* a story."
Paavo's expression was shrewd.

The phrase *Go to hell* formed in Eldon's mind and very nearly on
his lips. Then Eldon looked at Paavo's knuckles, thickened from
years of pounding in skulls. Eldon sighed. "Okay, Paavo, lead on."
They walked to the trailer park. There the hunchback stood
guard, squinting, cane lifted like a sword.

"It's okay, One-Square," Paavo said. "Nobody's going to run us
off just now."

Awful, random squawks came from behind a trailer. It sounded
as if someone had neglected to oil a strange machine of torture.
Eldon and Paavo rounded the trailer's side to find Beanpole labor-
ing with an old wooden concertina as Jasper and Bouncer danced.
Wheelie cheered weakly from the sidelines.

"That little dog's dancin' for the Lord," said Paavo. Jasper held
Bouncer upright by the forepaws as he shuffled in a circle. The dog
turned on its hind legs to follow its master, tail wagging.

"Gimme that," Paavo said, and grabbed the squeeze-box from
the youth. *"Saanko luvan!* Let's dance!" The Finn pumped the
concertina with a will.

The tune was "Rock of Ages" with a polka beat. Paavo played,
punching out the notes as he had punched out teeth in bars all over
Port Jerome. Jasper lifted his knees high, picking up the rhythm.
Bouncer yapped and farted. Jasper released Bouncer's paws. The
dog toddled on his hind legs in an awkward circle before dropping
to all fours.

"Tanssit oiken hyvin," Paavo told the dog. "That means, 'You
dance very well.' "

"That's Finnish?" Eldon asked.

"I just know a little so I can be nice to the old folks."

"Bouncer does better each time," Jasper said. "This smart little
dog's gonna dance for the Lord and troll the sinners in to my
church. Gonna rename the church. The Church of the Rising
Dog. Like it?"

"What about this concertina?" Eldon asked. "Nice-looking old
box."

Paavo's features took on a boyish glow. "Grandpa Wikkula
brought it over from Vaasa. He taught me how to play when I was

a kid. I still play it in his memory." He held out the concertina for Eldon to examine.

Eldon accepted the instrument carefully. Dark hexagonal wooden plates capping the bellows were carved with floral designs. The wood glowed beneath old varnish. On one plate were ten white button keys. The concertina's grips were of old black leather, although the bellows was creamy and bright.

"The bellows isn't original. Grandpa wore it out," Paavo said in answer to Eldon's questioning look. "He used to play it on the picket line during the mill strikes, years ago."

Eldon nodded. The Finns, like other Scandinavian immigrant groups, had an honorable if two-fisted place in the labor history of the Pacific Northwest. In the heyday of the Industrial Workers of the World early in the century, Finnish loggers, fishermen, and millworkers had helped slug it out with strikebreakers and company goons for the sacred right to organize. After their foes were vanquished, hard-drinking Finns joyously continued slugging it out—with Norwegians, Swedes, and Scots, among themselves, and with whomever else wandered into the rainy north woods of Oregon and Washington. If there was a fight on the Northwest coast, the tradition went, there usually was a Finn in it or running to join it or lying unconscious nearby.

Eldon clicked one of the concertina's buttons, then took the leather grips and pushed. The concertina wheezed vaguely. "There must be an art to it," he said, and felt a sudden liking for Paavo. He suppressed the feeling—business was business—and handed the concertina back.

"I still think he's with 'em," One-Square said. "He's with the cops."

"I'm a reporter," Eldon said huffily.

"We know you got to sell papers," said One-Square. "We know you got to stay on good terms with the powers that be."

Eldon bit back the impulse to tell One-Square to see a dentist and for good measure a chiropractor; instead he lifted his camera. "Let me get a picture of you with the concertina, Paavo."

"Let's get Bouncer dancin' for 'im," Jasper said.

"We've already done the dog," Eldon said.

"Bouncer found the foot," Paavo said.

"Not unless he finds the rest," Eldon said.

Jasper and his followers exchanged glances, and the prophet nodded solemnly. "We'll get right on that."

"W-w-we gotta r-r-right to s-stay here," Beanpole said. "B-b-bouncer's performed a service to s-s-society."

"They could come anytime, try to run us outa here," said One-Square. "But we won't go! We'll fight!"

"Don't start another riot on my account," Eldon said.

"Might have to," Jasper said, "to save the church."

"I'll help," Wheelie muttered from his wheelchair. "I'll ram 'em, if you gimme a push."

"You've got the landfill between you and the condos," Eldon said.

"The developer's taking over the whole area," Jasper said. "The trailer park, the church, and the landfill, too."

"What would he want with the landfill?" asked Eldon.

Jasper shrugged. "That's the way I heard it."

"Well, I'll look into it," Eldon said. "Paavo, put that squeeze-box on your knee and look as if you're playing."

Paavo knocked out a few chords while Eldon snapped pictures. The Finn had a stiff, rather formal smile that spoke to Eldon of years of emotions locked away, hoarded, and cautiously expressed. At last Paavo said, "That's enough." He set the concertina down and turned in the direction of Forest Vista Estates. "That guy in the tree had the right idea."

"What do you know about him?" Eldon asked. "I want to talk to him."

"Me, too," Paavo said. "He's got some good ideas—and a good style in a scrap. He's been around here a lot."

"Around here?"

"I think he lives up the slough. Beyond the condo site." Paavo pointed toward the woods. "He comes from over there."

Eldon felt a thrill. It was the direction from which the glorious horsewoman had come. I'm going your way, Eldon thought.

An interview with the crazy environmentalist would keep the foot story alive until the sheriff's office found the rest of the body in the landfill. And a casual question during the interview would give him the identity of the horsewoman. Eldon's heart raced.

3

Eldon entered the *Sun* office and felt the thud of the press through the soles of his feet, like a gigantic heart beating in the back shop. Most of the staff were out to lunch. Fiske was present but out to lunch in his own way, Eldon thought.

The editor gripped the edges of the news desk, a big surveyor's map spread out before him. Fiske pulled his pipe from between clenched teeth and regarded Eldon. "She runs right through here. This desk could slide out from under me anytime."

"What're you talking about?"

"Plate tectonics. Continents slipping around like hogs on ice."

"That's ridiculous."

"Scientific truth. Pull your nose out of those effete French books."

"I know about plate tectonics."

"Bet you don't know that a seam runs right through Port Jerome," Fiske said. "That's the wire story I had to spike yesterday on account of the foot. Two huge plates come together right here. A regular San Andreas Fault."

"We don't have earthquakes in Oregon."

"Not lately," Fiske said. "But all hell is waiting to bust loose— mark my words. Like San Francisco, '06. Not just shake and quake but shake and bake, too. There's fire down below, as they say in church. Just think about those volcanoes up around Portland."

"Mount Hood? Mount Saint Helens? They're dormant. Always have been. C'mon, Jimbo, you think this is the prehistoric ages? Dinosaurs and volcanoes and caveman reporters?"

Fiske grinned. "Plenty of cavemen in Nekaemas County, as I know you agree." He thrust out a copy of the day's edition. "Good thing you're not shy about burning up film."

Eldon grabbed the paper. Fresh ink smeared his fingers. On the front page was a big picture of John Henspeter, yelling and goggle-eyed in the fallen tree at the landfill. The blurred hand of a construction worker plucked at Henspeter's arm. "Hey, that's okay. I've saved you two days running, Jimbo, French poetry and all."

"You're my hottest reporter, Eldon, I've always said that. I looked over your negatives and found that picture, just ahead of the shots of the topless gal—"

"I want those negs," Eldon said.

"I had Marsha knock out a little copy saying the search for the body was continuing and asked her to call the owner of the condo project for some comment. Just to keep reader interest alive. That landfill's a sensitive area—"

"Marsha!" Eldon said in disgust. He scanned the brief story that accompanied the picture. "This copy is terrible. Why didn't you have Frank do it?"

"Frank's busy."

"Oh, that's right, the county commissioners meet this morning."

"Not that," Fiske said. "I want *you* to cover that. Frank's out at the community college, interviewing a professor about plate tectonics."

"What? There's a corpse in Schumacher's Landfill, an environmentalist starts a riot, and you're fixated on plate tectonics? Bigfoot was bad enough—"

"This is a hot story," Fiske said. "Look at the map."

Eldon glanced down in irritation—and stopped. "That's the landfill. And the area around it."

"Dee-de-dee! Old Jimbo gets your attention after all, eh? A tectonic fault is right beneath this week's focus of news in Nekaemas County."

"Right beneath?"

"Five miles off the coast. Close enough."

"It's not on the map."

"Of course not. This is just a county surveyor's map. The tectonic plates have been mapped by the University of Oregon with some kind of sonar. That's what the wire story was about. One plate under the Pacific Ocean is pushing under the other plate, which forms the shoulder of the continent."

"Right under Port Jerome?"

"Near enough for headlines," said Fiske happily. "That plate's gigantic. It extends all the way up into British Columbia and out into the Pacific for three hundred miles. South to Monterey, California, too. In our neck of the woods, it runs north–south along the highway south of town, turns inland, and goes off into the Willamette Valley, beneath Cottage Grove and so forth, out into central Oregon. But who gives a damn about those valley towns?"

"Right." Eldon studied the map. It showed the area around the landfill, with survey markers and terrain contours. There was the condo site. And there was the forest, with Jackknife Slough cutting through the trees, a narrow arm of Nekaemas Bay fed by freshwater streams. Intruding into the forest behind the landfill was a "wetland"—Oregon planning terminology for a marsh.

Eldon wrinkled his brow. "We can't do a story that there might be an earthquake at Schumacher's Landfill in five million years. That's no angle."

"It is if someone's going to build luxury condominiums near the fault."

"Ahh. What did the developer have to say to Marsha?"

"She didn't reach him. That's why her story is only about the continuing search for the body. Which is where you come in."

"Well, what about the body?"

"Wait until they find it," Fiske said. "We're not even sure it was foul play." Fiske rooted under the map until he found a typewritten sheet of paper. "The Board of Commissioners' agenda."

"They met this morning. The meeting's over."

"Today's meeting lasts through the afternoon. Land-use matters. You'll have to get moving or you'll miss the afternoon session."

"If I'm covering for Frank, when am I supposed to call the developer?"

"Read the agenda. Dee-de-dee."

Eldon looked at the agenda. The answer to his question was there in black and white: 2:30 P.M.: CONDITIONAL USE PERMIT APPLICATION—FOREST VISTA ESTATES. CU-79-28.

"That must be what the ruckus was about at the condo site," Eldon said, "with the guy chained in the tree."

"I told you it was good copy," Fiske said. "Get me a story before our whole circulation area falls into the sea."

★ ★ ★

Eldon scowled and flicked the van's air conditioner on and off without result as he steered south down the winding highway toward Preacher's Hole, the Nekaemas County seat. I've got to get this fixed, he thought.

But he couldn't save money if he spent what little he earned on the van. Yet he needed the van for his job, which paid too little. The worrisome thought went round and round in Eldon's head, a little worm turning somersaults in his brain. Even if I get the money together, there's not a mechanic in the county I'd let touch it, he thought. Certainly not in Preacher's Hole.

He was perspiring. As usual, it was ten degrees warmer around the county seat. Preacher's Hole lay twenty miles south of Port Jerome and inland, sheltered from the Pacific's cooling winds in a small valley formed by low coastal mountains. The valley floor was green with farmland, its slopes lush with trees.

Only twenty miles, Eldon thought as he drove past the modest, pleasant dairy farms. But it might as well be another world. Not a clue here that we're close to the sea.

The impression of pastoral serenity faded as he reached the outskirts of Preacher's Hole. The town's fringes consisted of sagging, rain-rotted buildings, rusty trailers and pickups. An abandoned sawmill. Farther along, things were a little better. Frame houses had long-haul trucks parked in front. Some windows held hand-lettered signs advertising homemade quilts, hairdressing, dog grooming, and fortune-telling.

At the hamlet's center lay the Nekaemas County Courthouse, the town's reason for being. The courthouse stood at the end of Main Street, set off from bars and old stores by a rich green lawn.

The lawn was the nicest thing about the hub of government. The courthouse was painted a ghastly mustard hue; the rest of Preacher's Hole glowed with muted beauty by comparison. Thrown up in the 1930s by the Works Progress Administration, the courthouse had the shabby look of Great Depression modernism left untended. Abstract designs in corroded tooled copper framed the doorway.

It looks like an abandoned exhibit from the 1939 New York World's Fair, Eldon thought as he parked the van. Frank Juliano maintained that the courthouse looked as if Jor-El lived there, and it was with wry thoughts of Superman's luckless father that

Eldon paused to read the copper plaque, green with age, memorializing William Simon U'ren, the populist reformer who had made the voters' right of recall part of the Oregon Constitution. Eldon mentally licked his chops. He had never covered a recall campaign, although the practice of citizens recalling elected officials who had displeased them had been a vigorous Oregon political institution since 1908.

He threw U'ren's plaque a quick salute and entered the courthouse to read the warning to hobnail-shod loggers in the gloomy lobby: "No calks on steps."

The Board of Commissioners' meeting room was down the hall.

". . . and just what was the earning power of these vegetables?" a harsh voice was asking as Eldon approached the hearing room.

Eldon recognized the voice. It was "Pumpkin Joe" Nedlee, chairman of the Board of Commissioners. It'd be fun if somebody decided to recall him, Eldon reflected as he slipped into the room and sat on the rear bench. Nedlee was a pompous, abrasive little boor who had fattened too long at the public trough. And here in the heart of his fiefdom, Pumpkin Joe presided like a rustic prince.

Two of the county's three commissioners were nonentities who reminded Eldon of lumps of crudely animated pastry.

Nedlee was a contrast to his colleagues.

The chairman looked like a fierce, balding monkey with chin whiskers and a flat, wide nose. He wore a string tie and a suit a decade out of date. He wielded a gavel like a scepter at a little group of county planners and other functionaries who sat to one side at a table. Nedlee stood out between his fellow commissioners if not because of his arrogance, then because of his huge, shiny forehead. Nedlee's skull seemed almost too large for his body. But his big gray eyes behind wire-frame spectacles gleamed with ornery intelligence as they fixed upon Eldon.

"We are in executive session," Nedlee said. "Closed to the public."

"The door was open. Anyway, I'm press. Eldon Larkin of the *Sun*."

Nedlee squinted. "Where's Frank?"

"Busy. Why the executive session?"

" 'Pending litigation.' Read your agenda." Nedlee scowled. "I suppose we have to let you stay. Close the door."

Eldon obeyed with annoyance. Oregon law allowed reporters to attend closed sessions of governing bodies as the public's watchdogs, although they could not report what transpired. He was within his prerogatives and expected Nedlee to be gracious about it.

The discussion resumed and Eldon swiftly decided that the matter under discussion was not newsworthy; but since it involved the threat of a lawsuit against the county, the proceedings had been closed as a matter of course. A farmer had gone to court, claiming that his vegetable truck had struck a pothole in a county road and damaged an axle. The county's attorney had proposed a token payment to settle the matter.

Nedlee reddened at the suggestion. "His squash crop isn't worth a damn anyway, and this is how he's trying to recoup. I know squash—they don't call me 'Pumpkin Joe' for nothing. His father pulled the same trick back in my first term, probably with the same truck and the same pothole. I'd like to build big potholes in front of his house!" Nedlee laughed spitefully at his own joke and began twisting a pencil with maniacal intensity, growing more agitated as the debate maundered on.

It was clear the other two commissioners wanted to settle on grounds of economy and expediency. At last the chairman surrendered with a violent snap of his gavel. "We are back in open session for the purpose of voting!" Nedlee announced the substance of the matter as the law required, recited the settlement proposal and added: "I'd like to gavel that crook's head! Clerk, call the roll!" He thrust the gavel toward Eldon. "And that last remark's off the record!"

Eldon smirked. "You should've said it in closed session, Commissioner. But I'll let you live."

"Damned right you will!"

The clerk called off the three commissioners' names. Nedlee surprised Eldon by joining the others in voting "yea." Then he gave Eldon another glare. "Open that door and let in some air."

Eldon slid down the bench to the door, twisted the knob, and pushed the door open. A big man of about thirty-five strolled into the room carrying a long, rolled-up map. He had regular, almost chiseled features and seal-brown hair counterpointed by an expensive yellow leisure suit. The jacket's cuffs were turned back to expose hairy wrists and a big gold wristwatch. The picture of South Coast affluence, the man looked as if he worked out with weights and carried himself as if he owned the place. Could this be the vegetable farmer? Eldon looked for Nedlee's reaction. But the chairman only gave a tight smile and said, "Welcome, Mr. Howell."

It was time to deal with Forest Vista Estates. Perfect timing, Eldon thought, taking out his pen and notebook.

"Good afternoon, Commissioners," said Keith Howell as he carried the map to the cork-backed easel that stood at one side of the room. Eldon was struck by the rich timbre of Howell's voice; it was part and parcel of the man's self-possession. He leaned forward, studying Howell as he unfurled the map and grandly tacked it to the easel.

The map was similar to the surveyor's map that Eldon had studied in the newsroom. Proposed condominium units were neatly indicated in colored pencil.

Nedlee announced that this was the time set for a public hearing on the application for a conditional-use permit by Forest Vista Estates. Nedlee spoke with gravity, regarding Howell steadily as he spoke. Eldon sensed tension between the two men.

Howell returned a sunny smile. "Thanks, Mr. Chairman. Or may I say 'Pumpkin Joe'?"

"Pumpkin Joe will do, as every voter knows. Describe your proposal. Then we will hear public testimony—if anyone shows up to talk."

Howell looked around the room. "I expected at least a few people in opposition. There usually are when there's a stand of trees involved."

"Looks like you're in luck," Nedlee said.

Reaves indicated the map. "Forest Vista Incorporated has a policy of environmentally responsible development. The zoning of our property allows us to build condominiums on the site. We could simply cut down the trees there and get on with it." Howell gave a self-deprecating smile. "But the result would be too few units to allow us to recoup our investment costs within a reasonable time. Like anyone else, we have to satisfy our creditors.

"But environmentally responsible development can enhance the livability of our state as well as attract desperately needed new business to Oregon." Again, Howell indicated the map. "We propose doubling the number of units in the project—and to deal with that awful landfill."

Nedlee perked up. "After all these years? How?"

"By reclaiming the landfill as a park. The park will serve as a buffer for Jackknife Slough and the wetlands to the west, which by law must be preserved as a natural area." Howell paused. "Of course, the trees will still have to come down on the condo site. But compensating plantings would be part of the park's landscaping."

Not a bad idea, Eldon thought, scribbling notes. First developer I've met who wanted to clean up his mess.

Nedlee nodded vigorously. "That can be worked out with the county Design Review Committee."

Howell gave a quick nod of agreement and continued speaking—details about applicable zoning formulas, construction costs, state land-use requirements, and other myriad technical aspects of developing real estate in Oregon. Nedlee tossed out a question about soil-quality classifications. Howell responded with scarcely a pause, neatly recapping the question, answering it, and weaving the answer into his presentation. It was a notable performance for the South Coast, where an almost willful inarticulateness was the preferred public style.

This guy's pretty sharp, even if he is bandwagon charming, Eldon thought. I wonder what he'll say about the tectonic fault— or the nut in the tree?

A dog barked. The sound was muffled, as if through glass. There was a scratching sound. Eldon looked up and saw faces outside the window: Paavo the Finn glaring, Jasper with a calculating grin, Bouncer the Born-Again Dog squirming in Jasper's grip and pressing his wet nose to the glass. And John Henspeter, single eye glittering.

Nedlee examined the lineup with a frown. "Please continue."

Henspeter shook his fist and disappeared.

Howell was unruffled. "The closed-out landfill makes the adjacent residentially zoned land better for development. But a park will make it easier to protect the nature preserve—"

Footsteps thudded in the hall. Henspeter appeared in the doorway, waving his arms. Paavo and Jasper came behind.

"Down with the land-raper!" Henspeter yelled.

Nedlee slammed his gavel. "Button your lip!"

"He doesn't want to preserve nature. He wants to cut down trees!" Henspeter cried angrily. "Down with Commissioner Nedlee! Down with the landfill! Down with Forest Vista Estates!"

Nedlee's neck seemed to stretch several inches, as if he were a scrawny old rooster about to attack a rival. Howell looked from Nedlee to Henspeter. He had a rueful yet delighted expression, like a man who has walked into a surprise party in his honor or found himself the butt of a wonderful, good-natured practical joke.

One of the other commissioners said, "If you'll take a seat, sir, we'll hear your testimony after Mr. Howell has finished."

"Mr. Howell will finish us all," Henspeter said with a snarl, crooking his fingers like claws. His eye had a lunatic glint. Paavo grinned at Eldon and gave a thumbs-up sign. Eldon checked his camera.

It was a cue for Henspeter. "Don't-hurt-the-old-growth," he chanted. "Don't-hurt-the-old-growth—"

"I'll call a deputy and have you removed!" Nedlee said.

"Not before you listen to my statement!"

"You'll *get* your turn!"

Howell waved a hand. "Mr. Chairman—if he wants to talk, I'll wait. I want to be a good neighbor."

Bouncer yapped and jumped down from Jasper's arms. He trotted over to Howell, wagged his tail, and put his forepaws in the developer's lap. Howell crooned and stroked the dog.

Henspeter roared at the betrayal. His hand snaked under his ragged denim coat. Eldon's heart jumped into his throat—and Henspeter pulled out a rope tied in a hangman's noose. "Hang all developers! Hang all commissioners!"

Eldon snapped a picture.

"I don't think I want to listen to this," Nedlee said.

"You will!" Henspeter said.

Nedlee rose. The other commissioners stood up, too. The trio faced left and filed from behind the desk and out a rear door. The planners and other functionaries rose and followed them. Eldon focused for another picture with Henspeter in the foreground and the departing commissioners in the background. He was too late. But as he swung the camera up, Howell rose and gave a good-natured shrug. Eldon snapped the picture: the developer, the environmentalist, the dog, the noose.

Howell gathered up Bouncer as if the dog were something precious. "You and I ought to talk," he said to Jasper.

"Maybe," Jasper said.

Howell, Jasper, and Paavo strolled out the door. Howell gave Eldon a wink: "See you in church."

Eldon was about to follow them when Henspeter pulled a soiled wad of paper from his pocket, unfolded it, and began to read: " 'When in the Course of human events, it becomes necessary for one People to dissolve the Political Bands that have connected them with another—' "

Oh, crap, Eldon thought, Fiske will want me to sit through this so I can report whether he read the entire Declaration of Independence. There was more movement at the window. Eldon saw the county commissioners lined up outside, staring in at Henspeter. Nedlee's boulder of a head bounced up and down as the little man hopped to peep over the window ledge. Henspeter continued obliviously reading.

Eldon scribbled in his notebook:

> PREACHER'S HOLE—The Nekaemas County Board of Commissioners today swapped places with an environmental protester who waved a hangman's noose. The comic turnaround pointed up a controversy over a proposed condominium development south of Port Jerome. . . .

Bingo, Eldon thought, reading the words back. He was proud of his ability to compose on the fly. It gave a pleasure similar to that of fly fishing—you knew you were still alive when you could hit a moving target.

Henspeter was still reading: " 'He has erected a Multitude of New Offices, and sent hither Swarms of Officers to harass our People, and eat out their substance. . . .' " He pronounced the words as if struggling with an incantation. Eldon slid down the bench and looked out the door into the hall. Jasper and Paavo were not to be seen. Nor was Keith Howell. The bigger fish, Eldon realized with frustration, had gotten clean away.

The county commissioners' faces dropped away from the window, one by one.

"There goes your audience," Eldon told Henspeter.

"You're here. You're the press. Paavo told me."

"You might as well quit reading. I don't have space to get it in." Henspeter sneered, exposing coffee-stained teeth. "I guess the Declaration of Independence doesn't sell newspapers."

"It's old news. It doesn't win land-use cases, that's for sure." Henspeter lowered the sheet of paper. His hands were trembling. "Listen, I know where the body's buried on all this."

"So what have you got for me?" Eldon asked. "If you know where the body's buried in Schumacher's Landfill, I'll have two stories."

"It's *you!*" Henspeter said suddenly, his eye bugging. "You're the one from the fight the other day! You took that picture of me in the paper." A grin spread across his face. "That was a great picture! If you were in with *them,* you wouldn't have put it in the paper. That really socked it to 'em. Now I see what Paavo was driving at."

"What *was* Paavo driving at? Never mind—I just cover the news. What've you got for me?"

Henspeter glanced cautiously at the empty window. His grin became mischievous. "You can bet that Mr. Pumpkin Joe Nedlee is going to let them build those condos. He has an interest in that landfill."

"How can that be? It was a county-owned landfill."

"Start sniffing. Call up your Deep Throat."

Eldon made a rude noise. Ever since the movie *All the President's Men,* people seemed to think that he spent all his time in parking garages, talking to a mysterious stool pigeon who had a blue light around his head. Eldon had enjoyed the romantic film but sometimes wished it had never been made. "You'll have to be more specific."

"That would be dangerous," Henspeter said proudly.

"It always is. You don't seem to be a man who scares easily."

"Damn right I don't. I've got an army behind me."

Eldon suspected that the "army" marched, limped, shuffled, and rolled via wheelchair to the pulse of Finnish concertina music and the farting of a little black dog. But then a more pleasing image returned to his mind. "Who was the woman on the horse?"

"Eh? Why?"

"You seemed to know one another."

A profound sigh escaped from Henspeter, as if his soul were leaking out through a valve. His eye rolled toward the ceiling and the tremor returned to his hands. "That was . . . Enola Gay."

"Enola Gay?"

"Enola Gay Hansen. The Blonde Bomber. Good woman. A tough woman. Really knows how to fix a car. Works at it professionally." The eye swiveled down upon Eldon with unnerving fluidity. "She's my ex. . . . Why?"

"Uh—the air conditioner's broken in my van. Got to get it fixed. I heard about her, ah, abilities." Eldon decided to take the plunge. "Where's her shop?"

"Where I used to live. Where she still lives. Up from Jackknife Slough, on Harlan Road. The mailbox has an airplane on it." Resignation was in Henspeter's voice. "It was good between us for a while. Enola Gay loves animals and nature. But she said I couldn't see the forest for the trees." He gave a short, bitter laugh and his eye began to glisten. "Just remember—Pumpkin Joe stands to profit by murdering all those trees."

At least she's not Henspeter's sister, Eldon thought as he climbed the stairs to the second floor of the courthouse on the way to Nedlee's office. A sense of triumph welled in his chest—the address of the topless horsewoman had been his for the asking! It was amazing what people would tell a reporter.

Probably Enola Gay Hansen couldn't tell him anything about the debate over Forest Vista Estates, but no doubt she could tell him something about John Henspeter. Such as whether he'd passed on any social diseases, Eldon thought with a smirk. I sure hope not.

Even if Eldon's years in Port Jerome had been ones of grinding sexual famine, he clung to his standards. He refused to prowl the bars to consort with pork-butt barfly women or their rangy sisters, all with bouffant hairdos and tight cowgirl jeans. And with hard eyes that looked through the haze of cigarette smoke as they danced absently to country-western music.

The horsewoman was not in the same class. She was too vital. Eldon considered briefly whether scoring with her would come under the heading of sleeping with a news source. He dismissed the question by assuring himself that she obviously knew nothing relevant. And she wasn't involved with Henspeter anymore.

He reached the top of the stairs, puffing. I've got to take off some weight, he thought as he approached Commissioner Nedlee's office. I've got to improve my appearance.

Eldon had never visited Pumpkin Joe's sanctum. The offices of the other county commissioners were in a less isolated part of the building, safely ensconced behind a counter and secretaries who filtered out marauding citizens. But Pumpkin Joe's office door opened directly—defiantly—onto a public corridor. Nothing barred the way as Eldon stepped up to the door and read the sign thereon:

COMMISSIONER PUMPKIN JOE NEDLEE
Knock and Enter
"Better Roads for Nekaemas County"

Eldon raised his fist but a pounding from within the office anticipated his knock. Eldon started again to knock but the pounding continued. It sounded as if a furious carpenter were punishing some resistant piece of handiwork. The hammering persisted. Eldon turned the doorknob and pushed the door open.

Nedlee's office was dark except for the soft light of a shaded desk lamp and the sun's yellow glow through window blinds. *"Well?"* Pumpkin Joe looked up from across his desk, his face an alarming shade of red.

"Got a minute?" Eldon asked in a professionally casual tone. Then his eyes adjusted to the gloom and he stared in amazement. Nedlee was hunched over his desk with a hammer, interrupted in the act of driving a large nail into its surface.

43

"I like to get things *nailed down,*" Nedlee said with a sinister chuckle. He beckoned with the hammer. "Pull up a chair. Close the door."

Eldon sat in a vinyl-covered bucket chair before the desk. The desk top seemed to glitter in the lamplight. He looked more closely. The light shone on dozens of nailheads pounded flat into the dark wood, where the shallow craters from a multitude of hammer dents cast little crescent shadows.

"I'd *chew* nails if I could," Nedlee said with satisfaction. "Calms me down. I made this desk myself, many years ago. I once was a carpenter." Another sharp chuckle. "Same as Jesus."

"I know how you mean." Eldon glanced around the office with rising interest. The place looked like a Victorian museum. The wall immediately beside Nedlee's desk was covered with plaques, certificates, and autographed photos in frames; Eldon noticed one of Nedlee, beardless and years younger, shaking hands with Lyndon Johnson. On the opposite side of the office, potted plants crowded the sill of the single large window. Their big, handlike leaves seemed to grope for the sun that glowed beyond the blinds. Tall shelves were crammed with books, folders, spiral-bound reports, and souvenirs. There were bowling trophies, a small and rather striking African mask, a statuette of a drunken leprechaun wearing a McGovern button, and a phrenology bust covered with numbers and topped with a half-melted candle. And there, serving as a bookend for a set of the Oregon Revised Statutes—was that a human brain in a jar?

Nedlee was watching Eldon. "Relics of a proud career. Now, what can I do you for?"

"When will the hearing resume on Forest Vista Estates?"

"When I'm not being heckled by crackpots!"

"Do you have a time certain?"

"Not yet. What's it to ya?"

"It's a public hearing, Commissioner," said Eldon, aware that Nedlee was goading him. "And there's some controversy about this case."

"Henspeter? I don't think he even noticed we'd left."

Eldon smiled. "Well, he noticed after I mentioned it."

Nedlee dropped the hammer on the desk with a clunk and rocked back in his high-backed leather chair. The redness in his face faded and he smiled a little. "We won't continue today. We can't work these things out under these conditions."

"You mean you won't let Henspeter have his say?"

"I mean that he doesn't want anyone else to have *their* say. Come look." Nedlee went to the window, pulled up the blinds, and pointed. Eldon followed, blinking at the sudden rush of sunlight. In the street below, Henspeter paraded with an insulting sign, followed by Jasper, Paavo, and their crippled congregation.

"I should take a picture of that," Eldon said.

"You do that." Nedlee returned to his chair. "Just remember—Henspeter doesn't want the question of whether to develop that area asked *at all*. And that's not the way our political system works."

Nedlee's earnestness made Eldon decide to take the bit in his teeth. "Why should it be developed? Talk is that you have something to gain if it is. That true?"

Nedlee sat up abruptly. The springs in his chair squealed. His face reddened again and his eyes seemed to grow larger. Eldon fantasized that Nedlee would brain him with the hammer. At last, the chairman took a deep breath, exhaled, and rocked back in his chair. "Who put that notion in your head, young man? John Henspeter? If you want to know the truth—no, that area shouldn't be developed. But it will be."

"It shouldn't?" Eldon said in surprise and reached for his notebook.

"Hold on a minute. I'll tell you why—on background. Not for attribution, including what I just said."

"This is a public matter—"

"I don't want to be quoted on an issue I'm going to vote on. Not this issue, anyway. It would only stir the pot, and in favor of that asshole Henspeter."

"All right. Fair enough. But why are you going to tell me this?"

"To show that I don't have anything to gain. And because it's a public matter, as you say. And because I'd just as soon you got the straight skinny from old Pumpkin Joe."

Said the spider to the fly, Eldon thought. "Fire away. Why shouldn't that area be developed?"

"Because it's next to a *dump*, for Christ's sake."

"So why will it be? I thought that was against the spirit of Oregon's land-use planning laws."

"It would be, except that the condo site is zoned for residential development. Has been since 1968, before all this hell-on-wheels planning got started. Grandfathered, in effect. That's the error and I was part of it. I voted with the rest of the county commission to rezone that property from forest land to residential. It was nice property. Had trees on it. A nice place to build houses, we thought."

"Next to a landfill?"

"We didn't think anything about the landfill. It'd been there since the thirties. That rezoning should never have been done— wouldn't be permitted today. Neither would the landfill, threatening a wetland like that. But that's the way we thought back then. Or didn't think, if you like. Ever look back on something you did years ago that seemed perfectly sensible at the time and wonder what the hell you were thinking about?"

Eldon thought of the failure of his marriage, which had brought him from Berkeley to Nekaemas County's rainy wilds. "So who owned it? Did you ever have any interest in that land?"

"Nah. It was owned by a cousin of Ellis Weems, my late, lamented predecessor on the county commission. He had inherited it from Ellis. The cousin wanted it rezoned so he could sell the land for development, so we granted it. That's probably what Henspeter's talking about. You didn't have all the hearings and public comment and other safeguards we have today. There wasn't the same level of public interest, either. But it was completely open and aboveboard. It was just how we did business then. The rules have changed." Nedlee chuckled. "Once the cousin got his zone change, he couldn't sell the land. It was next to that stinking dump."

"Why doesn't the landfill make a difference now?"

"Because the landfill's closed now. That makes all the difference. Not to the cousin, though—he died in 1971. Howell bought the property from the estate."

"Howell got it cheap while the landfill was still operating."

"It was a good turn of business," Nedlee said. "He acted quick. Got himself property with zoning that now allows him to develop it. He can create a public park over the landfill and swap that for density credits—build extra condos."

"Slick work."

"Keith's a slick boy." Nedlee shrugged. "It's the law. No reason he can't make the law work for him. It's too bad about those trees—but the board has to make a decision about what's best for the people of this county."

"What about utilities—sewers, water, and so forth?"

"The site is within Port Jerome's urban growth boundary. Sewer and water could go out there tomorrow, if Howell agrees to be annexed by the city."

"That would multiply the value of the property."

"Yep."

"Suppose you just tell him that he can't develop it? Refuse to approve the project?"

"If it was up to me now, I'd leave the damn trees there," Nedlee said. "But that's done. We can't waste county money on a lawsuit that Howell probably would win. We've got to make the best of the situation. That's the art of politics."

"Cutting down the trees is best?"

"Nothing sacred about trees—the whole history of Oregon teaches you that. It'll be good to get a little development into Nekaemas County. Aren't you tired of living in a rural slum? I am. I'm chairman of a shitheap. I can see it in their faces at the legislature in Salem, in the governor's office, at the Association of Oregon Counties. Condos and a nice park will be a hell of a sight better than a bunch of rusty trailers and a dump."

Eldon thought about it. "You could clear the trailers out and leave the trees alone. That must be the way Henspeter would want it."

"The way Henspeter wants it?" Nedlee's lips pulled back in a snarl of contempt. The transition was so sudden that Eldon involuntarily jerked back. "He's capable of spiking trees!" Nedlee said. "You know what happens when a chain saw blade hits a railroad spike driven into a tree?"

"Well, I can imagine—"

"Shrapnel, that's what happens! You *can't* imagine. What would you think of Henspeter if he talked about holding a loaded gun to your head just because he didn't like a story you wrote? Or just plain said he'd shoot people working in the woods or throw hand grenades at them? He's practically a terrorist."

"It's a long way from loose talk to terrorism."

47

"How can you tell? You can't, and that's his game. That's why we walked out of the hearing—because we can't let county government be intimidated. Spiking trees—that's an affront to the people of this county. Henspeter deserves the same himself. I'd like to *nail* Mr. Henspeter—" Sputtering, Nedlee snatched up the hammer and ferociously pounded another nail into the desk top. "I'd like to *nail him,* understand?"

"Yeah. . . . Thanks for the background, Commissioner."

"Drop those blinds on your way out. I can't stand to have him think I'm watching."

Henspeter and his fellow pickets had vanished by the time Eldon emerged from the courthouse. Just as well, Eldon thought. He didn't like the idea of putting them on the front page three days in a row. That would only invite constant pestering for more ink.

Eldon reflected on his ambivalence toward the controversy as he climbed into the van and started the engine. Sure, the debate was good copy, journalism at its most responsible: human passions focused on a substantive public issue, one that would influence the future shape and flavor of Oregon's life-style. It was news that informed citizens so they could better play their role as fundamental movers of democracy. Blah, blah, blah . . . as if the *Sun's* readers gave a damn. The issue wasn't *sexy.* What did they care if a real-estate speculator and a man who dressed like a tree bit one another on the ass?

The real story is that corpse somewhere in the landfill, Eldon thought, steering the van down the street. I wish Bouncer hadn't found just one foot.

He thought of the well-stacked horsewoman. Enola Gay Hansen, eh? On Harlan Road up from Jackknife Slough. Eldon fiddled with the air conditioner's controls. Happily, there was no response. A talented mechanic was just what he needed. And maybe she could give him some story leads, at that. It was a crazy impulse but desperation was driving him to those, lately. Why else would he have interviewed a man who pounded nails into his own office desk?

Nedlee's a violent little sucker, Eldon thought. He's had his own way for so long that he's sudden death to cross. Eldon imagined an enraged Nedlee flinging himself across the commissioners' desk in the middle of a hearing so he could strangle Henspeter. If Nedlee doesn't die of apoplexy, Eldon thought. That would be good copy. We should cover every hearing on this case until it's settled, just to make sure we don't miss anything like that. Or Frank should, while I'm chasing the mummified foot.

The vision of Nedlee dropping spectacularly dead, his hands locked on John Henspeter's throat and his brains cooking in his own boiling blood, made Eldon giggle. He thought gleefully that Bernice would be appalled to see him now, brought to this predatory pass by a steady six-year diet of traffic accidents, murders, dope busts, and minor human perfidy.

Or would she? Bernice was a pretty tough customer, full of artistic sensitivity but hard as nails when it had come to ditching Eldon and heading for Australia, the sunset glinting on those steel-rimmed glasses of hers. Actually, she left first and wrote later to break it off, Eldon thought. How did I let her con me into that?

That question still nagged him. It was the signal defeat of his life, the blow he had never seen coming.

Life was full of such blows. Eldon made an exciting if meager living writing about them. Misfortune was even fun—when it happened to other people.

Eldon reached the slough country south of Port Jerome and turned up Harlan Road. The two-lane road paralleled the slough's course for a time, then gradually ascended into the forested hills behind the bay's eastern shore. The foliage was dense and deep green, perpetually wet, even in this sunny season—bracken fern, alder, Oregon grape, maple, and the ubiquitous Douglas fir. The trees were touched with gold on top by the afternoon sun; beneath were deep shadows where mushrooms grew. The light had a greenish cast that Eldon loved, especially when it rained and the forest took on a comforting density. Then he slept well.

Mailboxes along the road were the only sign of habitation. The houses were hidden by the trees or tucked into wooded dells. Eldon searched for a mailbox with an airplane on it, expecting something small and crude. Decorative mailboxes were one of the South Coast's kitschy art forms, right up there with statues carved with chain saws and 3-D pictures of animals stamped in plastic. He passed mailboxes that displayed patriotic symbols, driftwood, silhouettes of animals, laminated pinups. He came around a curve and braked sharply.

Eureka! A mailbox at the foot of a rutted driveway was surmounted by an eighteen-inch-long metal reproduction of a Boeing B-29 Stratofortress of World War II, rising up from behind the box as if taking off. On the bomber's nose was the name *Enola Gay*. Beneath were the words AUTO REPAIR. Enola Gay—the blonde bomber. Ho ho, it all made sense now. Eldon's heart speeded up.

He followed the driveway over the hill and down into a sunny hollow to a low, weatherbeaten frame house. The yard was sparse but tidy. A rusty delivery truck stood next to the house. Rock 'n' roll blasted from a radio resting on the truck's fender—"Great Balls of Fire," roared out by Jerry Lee Lewis. Mechanic's tools and a toolbox lay on the ground next to the truck. Someone lay beneath the truck, working. He could see the mechanic's feet.

Eldon drove up and parked. As he climbed from the van, the topless horsewoman slid from beneath the truck, grasping a big wrench.

"Hi," she said, smiling. "What can I do for you?"

She was not topless now. She wore a grimy green mechanic's coverall. No—it was an old military flight suit, with zippered pockets and swatches of darker cloth on the chest and shoulders where badges once had been. She looked anything but glamorous, but that only accentuated her femininity. Thirty-four B's, he thought, remembering the photo and Frank's estimate. Eldon tore his gaze away from the woman's chest, dragging his eyes up the flight suit's zipper to her tanned throat and at last to her face. She wore her aviator glasses. One cheek was smudged with grease.

Eldon opened his mouth to speak. To his horror, no sound came out. He could only stare while Jerry Lee Lewis screamed about great balls of fire.

"Hi, what d'ya need?" the woman asked cheerfully, hefting the wrench. Her smile was earthy, and her blue eyes shone behind her photosensitive lenses. Eldon got the feeling she could brain him with the wrench, if necessary, with no loss of good humor.

"Ah—ah—" Eldon began. He felt as if he were again in junior high school, about to ask a girl if he could walk her to the bus.

The woman reached down and snapped off Jerry Lee Lewis. "Sorry."

"Enola Gay—Hansen?"

The woman beamed. *"C'est moi."*

God, did she speak French too? "I—I—need my van's air conditioner fixed."

Enola Gay's face lit up as if she were a bright child confronted with a delightful new jigsaw puzzle. "Okay! I haven't had much work lately. What's wrong with it?"

"It doesn't work."

Enola Gay trotted to the van, put a hand on the handle of the driver's door, cocked the monkey wrench onto her shoulder like a baseball bat. "Like how doesn't it work?"

"It—when I turn the switch. Nothing." I sound like an imbecile, Eldon thought miserably as Enola Gay put the wrench on the ground and opened the van door.

Too late, Eldon thought about the van's embarrassing interior. But before he could do more than open his mouth, Enola Gay had stepped up into the van. She stopped halfway into the cab, giving Eldon a breathtaking view of her firm ass. She looked fore and aft and gave a low whistle.

"I'm impressed," Enola Gay said. "This is fancy. I should've washed my hands before I climbed in here."

"That's—all right."

Enola Gay got into the driver's bucket seat, expertly triggered the swivel latch, and spun to the rear. "That's some artwork back there! I like that kind of thing—fancy muscle men who are real crushers, y'know? What'd you say your name was?"

"Eldon. Larkin." Eldon filled his lungs with air. "I—inherited—the van."

"From your maiden aunt?" Enola Gay spun the seat to the front. She clicked the ignition key to the first position, then tested the air conditioner controls. "Sure 'nough. It doesn't work. What'd you do to it?"

"Nothing!"

Enola Gay abruptly turned upside down in the bucket seat, pivoting on her buttocks to throw her legs up over the seat back and swing her head under the dashboard. She was limber as a gymnast. Eldon caught his breath at the way her hair tumbled. Enola Gay flipped open a plastic inspection plate. "Hm. Hm!" She pulled a pen flashlight from a pocket, snapped it on and peered in. "Thought so. This'll cost you, bud."

"I'll pay," Eldon said in a wretched whisper. Anything so that she did not slip through his fingers. "How much?"

There was a snap as Enola Gay pulled something free under the dashboard. She thrust out a grimy fist and opened it to reveal a tiny glass cylinder, capped at both ends with metal. "Oh, about as much as one new fuse. Ha, ha!"

"What?"

"You blew a fuse, that's all. The fuse box is right here under the dash."

"Thanks. I don't know much about cars."

"Bring me that toolbox," she said, still upside down.

Eldon scrambled across the gravel and seized the toolbox. He brought it back, went down on one knee on the ground, and opened it. Enola Gay, still reversed in the seat, rummaged in the top tray with her fingertips. Her fingers were surprisingly long, although the nails were clipped short and caked with grease. Eldon visualized them with long red false fingernails as Enola Gay found a fresh fuse amid the clutter in the tray and installed it.

She reached up and flicked the air conditioner switch; the fan started at once. "Here's the rule for car maintenance: Always check the obvious. Save you a wad of dough."

"What do I owe you?"

"Oh, hell, I'm not going to charge you for that."

"You're very kind."

"Quite a vehicle you've got here. I noticed it's got California plates." Enola Gay looked a little disappointed. "You're not from *California,* are you?"

"I defected years ago. I'm an Oregonian now."

"I'm native-born. Can't you tell from the rust?" Enola Gay chuckled at the ancient Oregon joke and crossed her ankles behind the seat back, apparently content to remain upside down. She glanced to her left and downward. "Hey, you've lost something under the seat—" She pulled up the manila folder and the picture Eldon had taken of her slipped halfway out.

Eldon pawed the air helplessly as Enola Gay studied the photograph through the spokes of the steering wheel. Now, Eldon knew, she would climb from the van and crush his brow with her monkey wrench—and probably charge him for replacing the fuse, too.

Enola Gay laughed. "Well, all *right!* Don't I make a pretty picture? Did you take this? You did? I want to buy it!"

"That's okay—you can have it—I—"

"You must've been at that fracas down by the landfill the other day. I *thought* I saw someone with a camera."

"That was me."

"How'd you find me?"

"I'm a reporter for the *Sun*—"

"A reporter!" said Enola Gay, delighted. "Now that must be interesting. Were you out there because of that foot they found in the landfill? You didn't take that picture that was in the paper today, did you?"

"Yeah, I did."

"Wow! You're quite a photographer." Enola Gay gazed upon her picture again. "Cheesecake and a mummy's foot, both in one day. You have an interesting job."

Eldon smiled. "Both on the same roll of film, in fact."

"If you're a reporter, no wonder you were able to find me." Enola Gay looked up from the picture, her benign expression unchanged. "How'd you do it? And why?"

It's got to come out sometime, Eldon thought, and said: "John Henspeter."

"John told you how to get here."

"Yeah. It's John I came about."

"Well." Enola Gay swung upright. "Come in and have some coffee. But I get to keep this great picture."

"You bet."

Enola Gay climbed from the van and led Eldon toward the house. At the door, Eldon was puzzled to hear the gurgle of water inside, as if there were a brook in the living room. Enola Gay led him inside and Eldon saw the source of the sound.

The living room, simply furnished, was full of afternoon sun that glinted on a big fish tank on a stand in the center. The gurgle was the rich rush of water through the tank's aerator.

"It was John's," Enola said, leading him over. "He loves nature."

53

Eldon looked in vain for fish. Much of the rectangular tank's volume was filled by a cairn of rocks and broad, brown, obscuring ferns. "I gathered that you and he are no longer an item."

"Not for a while now." The matter-of-fact tone piqued Eldon's optimism.

Politely, he peered into the tank. "This is pretty big for tropicals. Where are the fish?"

"Rap on the glass."

Eldon banged on the thick plate. A big, brown, gape-mawed snake shape lunged at him from among the submarine rocks. Eldon yelped and backed up. The thing had triangular jaws lined with rows of pyramidal teeth, like an animated bear trap with wicked, mobile little eyes.

"That's a wolf eel," Enola Gay said as the jaws worked.

"Jesus Christ," Eldon said in irritation, his skin prickling as he imagined the thing on the end of his fishing line. Then he saw that Enola Gay was not laughing but merely regarding him with that ready-for-anything air.

"John would've yelled and thrown something," she said. "They're his eels."

"He's an excitable kind of guy."

"Yeah. Let me make that coffee." With a quick motion that stopped Eldon's breath, Enola Gay unzipped the flight suit and shrugged out of it. Beneath she wore a pink tank top and cutoff blue jeans. Eldon relaxed, but only a little, thinking, No bra.

Enola Gay winked. She hung the flight suit on the coat hook by the door and went into the kitchen.

Eldon studied the aquarium. Another eel lurked among the rocks. Pumpkin Joe ought to have this tank in his office, he thought.

An electric coffee grinder started in the kitchen. Eldon felt pleasure—he would get fresh-ground coffee, not instant. This woman definitely had class.

He looked around the room while his mind toyed with the possibilities. There was a bookshelf against one wall, and above the shelf a curious metal-framed photograph. The picture was a couple of feet square. Eldon knew he had seen it reproduced before—a thick, white column of water supporting a great, furry cloud that spread to the edges of the picture. It was a nuclear explosion at sea.

In the foreground was a Pacific atoll. Palm trees bent like crazy paintbrushes in a lethal wind.

Eldon turned his attention to the books on the shelf below. He saw with pleasure that they were literary fiction and books about philosophy and art, some of them college paperback editions that he knew from Berkeley. Erasmus. A translation of *Njal's Saga* from Iceland. He opened a well-thumbed copy of Kenneth Clark's *Civilisation*. She reads about art, Eldon thought, scarcely daring to believe it.

Enola Gay came out of the kitchen, carrying coffee and oatmeal cookies on a tray. She set the tray on a table in front of the sofa and sat next to Eldon. "That's Test Bravo," she said, nodding toward the photograph. "Bikini Atoll, '52. That's a print from the original negative."

"How do you happen to have it?"

"My father knew one of the men who took the picture. He has lots of connections."

"Really? And he named you Enola Gay? After the Hiroshima bomber?"

"My mother named me. But that's right. Your history's pretty good."

"Well, I read."

"I like a man who reads," Enola Gay said. "My father read a lot of history, too. Maybe too much history. He said the atom bomb was the biggest thing in history. 'You've got a proud name, Enola Gay,' he'd tell me. 'One of the biggest names in history.' Most people don't know the significance." She nibbled a cookie. "So what do you want to know about John?"

"Why was he up in that tree?"

"Are you going to put my name in the paper?"

"Maybe. I'm doing a story about the beef over the condo development. I need to know what I'm dealing with. John made quite a scene today at the county commissioners' meeting."

Eldon recounted the confrontation. Enola Gay shook her head. "Don Quixote."

"He and Commissioner Nedlee don't get along," Eldon said.

"If you're in authority, John doesn't like you."

"The enmity seemed to go back a long way."

"John's been around a long time. So has the commissioner."

"Longer than you?"

"Well, I'm a native. But I only moved back down here about five years ago. From Astoria—it was getting too busy and crowded."

"Anyone who thinks Astoria is 'too busy and crowded' really likes the rainy north woods," Eldon said.

"John likes them—the woods," Enola Gay said. "That's how we got together."

Eldon couldn't resist. "You were out riding and—"

"Actually, yeah."

"You do that a lot?"

"When the weather's nice." Enola Gay nibbled a cookie. "I rent the horse. My big indulgence. I was riding along, getting some sun, you know, and there he was. Sitting like a monkey in a tree. No—like a satyr." She gave a satisfied smile at the recollection. "He came to dinner and stayed two years."

Eldon imagined Henspeter swinging down from the tree like Tarzan onto the topless rider. "And left just like that?"

"Look, I like nature as well as anybody. But John was getting kind of far gone about it. Off he went. Hasn't been back."

"You seem pretty matter-of-fact about it."

"I take things as they come. It was a relief, really. He needs to come and get his stuff."

"And his eels?"

"I'll feed 'em until he thinks of something. He'd been getting more and more wound up. I worried about that. He was talking pretty ugly."

"About spiking trees?"

Enola Gay nodded. "He was losing his sense of humor. Something about that developer down there who was building the condos. He never liked him."

"How do they know each other?"

"He never did say. But something about building those condos down there grabbed John's guts and wouldn't turn loose."

Eldon waited but Enola Gay did not continue. Eldon thought about how he was using his powers as a reporter for direct personal gain. I've got to invite her up to my place for dinner, he thought.

But of course it wasn't as easy as that. The old feeling crept over him. He felt as if he were twelve years old and didn't know what to say. He always regressed this way, in his mind. He had never been able to grow out of it. But oatmeal cookies were his favorite. Finally he said, "You like to read about art."

"I love the Book of Kells," Enola Gay said softly. "And the Scandinavian sagas."

Eldon nearly fell off the couch. His hand trembled. Here was a woman he could talk to! In Port Jerome! Here was—here was—

Enola Gay was watching him closely. Her eyes were large, her lips slightly parted. She leaned over and kissed him, gently but firmly, with moist, soft lips.

Eldon sighed and returned the kiss. She tasted faintly of oatmeal cookie. He felt himself melting. Enola Gay set her coffee cup down, took Eldon's cup and set it down, too. "I want you," she said.

"Yes," Eldon whispered.

He let Enola Gay pull him to his feet and lead him toward the bedroom as water rushed through the eel tank's aerator.

It was the first bedroom other than his own that Eldon had entered in years. He looked at the king-size bed with the bright quilt and the big cedar chest at the foot. The quilt was deep blue with a pattern like a gold-and-red compass rose, one major point aimed at the pillows.

Enola Gay turned and pulled the tank top over her head. Eldon grabbed her, laughing happily at the stretch of her breasts and muscles. They kissed deeply and toppled onto the bed, crumpling the symmetry of the compass-rose quilt.

Eldon got his hands on the waistband of Enola Gay's cutoffs. She squirmed free, breasts bouncing, and sprang for the foot of the bed. She yanked Eldon's shirt over his head as she passed. Eldon struggled to free himself. Enola Gay whirled around the mattress and dragged Eldon's pants down around his ankles, then slithered up his trapped legs and mouthed his engorged cock. She sucked like a vacuum cleaner. Eldon cried out with pleasure.

Enola Gay rolled away. Eldon kicked free of his trousers and scrambled after her, puffing but determined. She was at the foot of the bed now, wriggling out of her cutoffs and panties. Eldon saw with delight that her pubic hair was tawny blond. He fell atop her.

Enola Gay grabbed his shoulders and they rolled over together. Eldon's head thumped on the cedar chest. She's very strong, he thought, agreeably startled, as she mounted him.

It was a fantastic afternoon, full of sweaty wrestling as the sun settled. All methods and directions. She literally led him around the mattress. Several times. Eldon struggled to keep up. It was like spinning out of control in a jet.

"—because I wondered if you were gay," Enola Gay explained much later.

"*What?*" demanded Eldon, sitting up in bed.

"With that van and all."

Eldon twisted away from the wet spot on the sheet. "It belonged to a California fag. I inherited it."

"From the fag?"

"No, from a woman."

"Your wife? Your girlfriend?"

"Neither one." Too bad, too, Eldon thought. Then he reveled in the delicious ache in his muscles and decided it was just as well that Shelly wasn't around. Or Bernice.

"I seduced you because you were so cute and helpless with that fuse," said Enola Gay. "And you had that van. I just had to know." She nestled in Eldon's arm, slid her hand over his chest. "I think it's interesting to know people sexually."

"Just 'interesting'?"

"Nice interesting." Enola Gay's eyes closed. She dozed.

It was dark now, and Eldon could hear the wind making its hollow sound through the trees. It looked as if he was staying the night. Wait'll Frank hears about *this,* he thought with drowsy satisfaction.

It seemed that only a moment later a thought jarred him awake: My story. I never called the paper to check in with Fiske.

A clock radio by the bed read 5:32 A.M. He had slept all night! But there was still plenty of time. The *Sun* hit the streets at noon; he could easily write his story this morning in time for the day's edition.

I'll call Frank at home, ask him to do the morning cop checks for me, Eldon thought. He'll understand. He's getting up about now, anyway. And I'll call Fiske when he gets to the office about eight and promise him something colorful.

Eldon eased out of bed and padded naked through the still-dark house, searching for the telephone. His knees felt springy after the night's long exercise. He found the phone on a table near the eel tank, illuminated by the fluorescent tube in the tank's lid. Silvery hints of dawn were in the room, making odd, subtle highlights in the corners and on the furniture.

Eldon stood with the receiver in hand; Frank's phone number was in his wallet, and the wallet was in the bedroom with his clothes. Eldon tried to remember the number as he stared across the room at Test Bravo. Dawn light touched the picture's metal frame. Eldon felt rested and pleasantly light-headed, as if he were under water or still dreaming. There was a big shape in the shadows in one corner of the room, near the framed picture.

The shape was man-sized.

Then it moved and Eldon's heart thundered. A man stepped from the shadows—John Henspeter, his single eye glittering. He held a double-bladed ax.

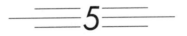

REPORTER SLAIN IN AX MURDER: The headline glared in Eldon's mind. The kicker specified that his corpse was NUDE, HEADLESS. Fiske wouldn't miss a bet. The story was written in Eldon's imagination and the *Sun*'s presses rolling before he realized Henspeter did not intend to kill him. The man merely stood there, the ax in one hand and a shopping bag stuffed with clothing in the other.

"I came for m' things," Henspeter said, mumbling like an abashed boy.

"Oh." Eldon unclasped his fingers from his genitals. His scrotum tingled as the blood rushed back in.

Henspeter set the bag on the couch and leaned the ax against the eel tank. "I have some other stuff in the bedroom."

"Enola Gay's sleeping."

"I'm kinda early, yeah. I didn't want to bother anyone."

"It's okay." Eldon suddenly felt sympathy for Henspeter, usurped in his own house. The feeling was a surprisingly palpable pang. But it was great to be the one doing the usurping. "Why don't you hang out awhile, wait 'til she gets up?"

"Thanks." Henspeter sat on the couch. "Did you get your air conditioner fixed?"

"Yeah. Fuse."

"That's what I get for giving advice." Henspeter gazed into the eel tank and brightened a little. "Like it? I'm proud of those eels. The big one's Saul Alinsky and the female's Emma Goldman."

"What d'you feed 'em?"

"Chopped meat."

"With those jaws, I guess so."

"They're pretty timid, actually. But territorial. Especially the male. Saul'd give you a pretty good bite if you messed with his territory."

"Like people."

"Like people. I caught him out in the slough. Then I decided he needed a lady, so I caught Emma. They're native Northwest critters. They come in from the ocean with the tide, and they'll come a long way up the sloughs if the salinity in the water is right. That's the real problem—keeping the right salinity level in the tank."

"What's that tank weigh? You'll have a lot of trouble moving it."

"I've gotta get a place first. I'm living up in the woods now. In a tent. I love the forest."

"Yeah." Eldon racked his mind for a topic of conversation. "Want to tell me some more about this problem with the condos?"

"I don't suppose you've conducted many interviews naked before."

"Only spiritually."

"Spirit's what all this is about," Henspeter said, seizing upon the word. "I gave up my eye for this. It's that important."

"Your eye? How?"

"Lost it in a fight like the one at the landfill the other day. Naw, scratch that. Yesterday was nothin'. You haven't *seen* a fight over that place yet."

Eldon waited. He wanted to see where this would lead. When Henspeter only smiled again, Eldon asked, "Were you ever a logger?"

"Sure I was. A two-fisted logger. How else d'you survive down here?"

"And you lost your eye in an environmental demonstration? Or just fighting?"

"That's right," said Henspeter. "And do you know something? I can see better with *just the one eye.*" His voice was taut. "I don't want to waste time tellin' ya. Gonna show ya. I'll show you my camp. C'mon."

He pulled a rumpled pair of khaki pants from the paper bag. "Put these on. There's a pair of rubber boots on the back porch."

Eldon started to say that his own clothes were in the bedroom, but he did not want to argue with a man with an ax. "Do you have any socks?"

"Here's socks."

The pants were too tight for Eldon's ample waist. He had to sling them low to button them closed. The pant legs were too long; he turned them up into fat, ridiculous cuffs. And the socks were too long in the toes; they flopped like the shoes worn by the Seven Dwarfs.

"Shirt." Henspeter threw a ragged black sweatshirt at Eldon. It said OREGON on the chest. The sleeves were hacked off. The sweatshirt was too tight in the shoulders. Eldon's belly bulged out between the sweatshirt's hem and the low-cinched trousers. Feeling like the loser at a rummage sale, he shuffled out onto the porch and stuffed his feet into the clammy rubber boots.

He looked around with a shiver as the morning air nipped his skin. Sunlight was leaking quickly into the gray sky. Mist drifted off the wet grass, and foliage glittered with dew in the new light. The forest stretched into the hills behind the house, sunrise swiftly defining its details and its many shades of green. Atop the ridge, low-hanging fog blurred the trees as if blotting them with gauze.

Henspeter strode toward the forest, leaving dark tracks in the wet grass. Eldon followed, gooseflesh on his bare arms. There was only a scanty trail. On all sides were ferns, deciduous trees, logs crusted with moss and mushrooms. "Tasty eatin'," said Henspeter, pointing at the fungi. The forest was clouded with drifting mist that

61

swallowed the trail as it wound uphill. Eldon slipped on the wet slope in his clumsy boots. Henspeter strode purposefully onward.

The slope grew steeper, the growth thicker. Then the trail was gone. Here were trees like massive temple columns, tall and straight, trunks softened by delicate coats of pale green moss. Fallen trees lay on the forest floor, surrounded by undergrowth, reminding Eldon of wrecked tanks after a colossal, mysterious battle. The trees had been toppled by age, not man. Their massive root structures had pulled up intact out of the earth. Pitched against one bole was a sagging tarpaulin that sheltered a sleeping bag on a mattress of fir boughs. The remains of a campfire smoked in a circle of stones. Beams of morning sun cut through the trees in golden swaths, but the light retained a greenish cast that made the forest seem infinite.

"Old growth," Henspeter intoned.

"Port Orford cedar," Eldon said.

Henspeter was surprised. "You recognize it?"

"A reporter learns about all sorts of stuff. I've written forestry stories, so I know about Port Orford cedar. There's not a lot of it left—it was logged out because it makes ideal ship timbers. I didn't know there was a stand this close to town."

"Some of these trees must be a couple of centuries old. Most people don't know they're here." Henspeter's voice was hushed. He was no longer the buffoon. "It's the way the forest was when the pioneers came. Imagine trying to get through this in covered wagons."

"They'd have had to hack their way through."

"And they haven't stopped hacking yet."

"Nobody's going to cut these down and build condos up here."

"Not yet, you mean." Henspeter scrambled up onto a fallen tree and walked along the trunk. "The condos down at Schumacher's are just the start of it. Howell wants to develop this whole hillside."

"He never said that."

"It's how he thinks. 'More is better.' "

"He got an award for being ecologically conscious—"

"You know how he made that project in Coos Bay pay off? He fired all the workers and hired other ones, at lower salaries."

"Hm."

"If Howell doesn't cut down these trees, then someone else

will," said Henspeter, gazing down on Eldon. "Howell would call it 'thinking big.' Once he's blazed the trail, people just like him will pour in here and cut down—all—these—trees. They'll put condos up here. With big, ugly cars and people who dress and think like Howell, people who won't give a damn about the missing trees. And that son of a bitch Nedlee will let them."

Now there was real hatred in Henspeter's voice—as pure as Nedlee's hatred for Henspeter. Nedlee is what this is really all about, Eldon thought. "The South Coast is changing," he said, deliberately echoing the commissioner.

"I don't want it to change," Henspeter said. "This is not for the better." He sat atop the great bole and gazed into the forest. "These are immortal trees. They've survived so many things. They've got to survive him. So many other people haven't."

"What do you mean by that?"

"This ought to be a nature area, that's what I mean. I'll stop 'em any way I can. I tried down there at the landfill. I'll get other people to help me. You get enough people—"

"Chained in trees? There's a land-use planning process."

"Stacked. Fouled with lawyers. Fouled with the kind of people who bury bodies in landfills. You were at that meeting. You saw Nedlee and his sheep. Nedlee's got the board in his pocket, and Howell has got this county in his pocket." Henspeter held out a hand. "Climb up. I'll show you something."

Eldon grasped Henspeter's hand and scrambled up the slippery trunk. The bones in Henspeter's hand seemed oddly fragile, as if Eldon could crush them with too tight a grip. But Henspeter pulled him up with sinewy strength, and after a moment Eldon got his footing on the fallen tree.

Henspeter pointed across Eldon's shoulder. "Look through the trees—out there, toward the bay."

"Mill stacks."

Henspeter bared his teeth. "Like having a zoo with a slaughterhouse on the premises. These beautiful trees, and that's what we do with them."

"So would you spike these trees to stop them?"

Henspeter was silent. Wind boomed through the trees. "No," he said at last. "No. I can't see killing anybody."

"You sounded like you would spike them, down at the landfill. People *say* you'd spike them."

"That was to keep 'em riled. So they can't think. Slow 'em up, anyway."

"You rile them enough that way, you're liable to get shot."

"Aw, let 'em worry. But I'll tell you something—we're not wasting any more time in Nedlee's kangaroo land-use hearings. And you can put that in the paper."

"Oh, I'll put it all in the paper."

"Good. Time you told our side of it for a change. Now—I want you to listen."

"Listen—?"

"Shh. Hear that?"

Eldon heard only the movement of the wind through the trees. Then the distant gush of water came to his ears.

"That's Jackknife Creek," Henspeter said and waited.

Slowly it dawned upon Eldon. "I fish in that creek. It's a good run for rainbow trout."

"The creek runs pretty close to this old growth. And then cuts down near the condo development on its way to feed into Jack-knife Slough. If those trees get cut, if this whole area gets developed, how good do you think the fishing's going to be?"

Henspeter had a point, Eldon thought.

Henspeter didn't wait for an answer. "I just wanted you to see that our side is your side, too. Now let's go see if we can't talk Enola Gay into frying some eggs."

His tone held no malice. Nevertheless, Eldon wanted to steer away from the subject of Enola Gay. As they slid down the tree trunk to the ground, Eldon said, "You really hate Nedlee, don't you? And he hates you."

"Does he?" Henspeter was innocent.

"I've talked to him," Eldon said. "And now I've talked to you. I saw you together in that meeting. You hate each other, and you don't get that way with one short disagreement over some trees, even if they are Port Orford cedar."

"No, you don't."

"What is it, then? You want me to be fair to you in the newspaper, you have to tell me the whole story."

"That's easy. Pumpkin Joe is Enola Gay's father."

Eldon felt a sick stab in his gut.

A baroque network of interpersonal connections among the populace was a feature of Nekaemas County's rainy isolation. It was a major reason that Eldon kept his distance, socially, from most people. As Fiske said, "People around here don't have anything better to do but fight and screw each other; so when they get worn down, they fight and screw in different combinations." The raddled chowder-house waitress might easily be the cousin of a crooked used-car salesman indiscreetly scorned during a conversation over coffee. The high school prom queen Eldon secretly lusted after might be the car salesman's daughter. And the girl might be the part-time secretary (or worse) of the salesman's silent partner, who was a major contributor to the sheriff's reelection campaign, just when you needed police cooperation in covering the story of a human foot found in a landfill. . . .

Enola Gay was sitting at the kitchen table when they returned. Dressed in jeans and a denim shirt, hair combed and tied back, she looked fresh and rested. In control. The kitchen was full of rich cooking smells. Bacon sizzled in a skillet on the stove. The table was set for three.

Enola Gay polished her glasses, a half-empty mug of coffee at her elbow. "So there you are. I found your stuff in the living room, John. Wondered if you two went up into the woods to duke it out."

"John showed me the old growth," Eldon said.

"Glad to hear that's all it was," said Enola Gay. "You never can tell with men."

"You cooking enough for three?" Henspeter asked, again wistful.

Enola Gay nodded. "I figured you'd both survive."

Eldon and Henspeter sat at the table. Enola Gay fried a skillet of eggs, then put out big platters of food and let them dig in. Eldon took three fried eggs, four strips of bacon, mounds of hash brown potatoes and toast. Sex added octane to his ample appetite. He ate heartily while Enola Gay and Henspeter matter-of-factly discussed the disposition of Henspeter's belongings.

Henspeter scorned knife and fork. He scooped up the fried eggs one by one with his fingers as if they were oysters, tipped back his head and dropped them into his open mouth. Yolk ran down the corners of his mouth and into his beard.

Enola Gay, who ate with utensils, chewed unconcernedly. "Knew you'd like it, John."

"I miss your cookin'." Henspeter threw a handful of hashbrowns onto a slice of toast and used a knife to add a glob of grape jelly. He folded the toast up like a tortilla and inhaled it.

"More coffee, Eldon?" Enola Gay asked.

"Please." Eldon glanced at the kitchen clock. It was 6:45 A.M. Still time to call Frank. Plenty of time for him to get back to town and file a story. Eldon felt relief—indeed, a growing sense of victory—as the food warmed his belly. He had gotten laid, though he'd better be discreet about that. Even if he had failed to get comment from Howell about the earthquake nonsense, he could beguile Jimbo with something better—the colorful confrontation between Henspeter and Nedlee, with a sidebar interview with Henspeter—"half two-fisted logger, half radical environmentalist," something like that.

When they finished eating there was a silence. Then Enola Gay said, "I'm going to have to toss you out, John."

"I've got to get my things."

"Take the clothes and tools you've got together and come back later. I've got company."

"I've got to be getting to work—" Eldon began.

"You can go when you feel like it," Enola Gay said. "But John's cast his dice, and now he's going to have to live with the roll." Her tone was perfectly reasonable.

Henspeter looked sadly at his plate, then gave a wan smile. "It's true, I guess. My stuff—"

"Come back for it *later,* John." Enola Gay showed the same equanimity as when Eldon had feared she would brain him.

Henspeter reddened, raised a fist to slam the table in frustration, then braked the fist and merely gave the table a light tap. "Okay," he said softly. "Okay."

"Thanks for showing me the trees," Eldon said.

"Just make sure you get it straight in the paper."

"Point of honor with me."

"I think it is," Henspeter agreed. "I'll be up there in the old growth." He left the table, went into the living room, and returned with the sack, the ax over his shoulder. "I'll be on guard. Like the wind in the trees." He went out the kitchen door, whistling.

"He likes you," Enola Gay said.

"I can't afford to like him," Eldon said, "or to dislike him. He's a source. . . . You didn't tell me you were Joe Nedlee's daughter."

"You *are* a reporter. Is that a problem? You didn't ask me."

"Your name's Hansen, not Nedlee."

"It's my mother's maiden name." Enola Gay sighed. "I was pretty small when Mom and Pumpkin Joe broke up. She broke up with a couple of husbands after that, too. Like I said, you never can tell with men. Mom's dead now. I don't see Joe much. Boy, he never liked John." She frowned. "I asked Joe where he got off, acting like my father."

"What'd he say?"

"It made him wild. Said he *was* my father, regardless."

"Well, he is your father." Immediately Eldon felt guilty—but not very. She isn't *much* of a source, he told himself. The fact that she's Commissioner Nedlee's daughter is strictly coincidental. But he felt uneasy again. This smacked of illicit gain.

Enola Gay watched him, eyes glittering merrily behind her glasses. She looked like a cat about to devour a bird. Eldon's groin stirred as she smiled. He looked at the clock. Police checks. Deadlines. Journalism, his reason for being—or for being in Nekaemas County, anyway. "I should go—"

"But you can't." Enola Gay's smile was pleasantly feral.

"Oh? And why is that?"

"Because I *insist.*"

Eldon creaked into the office three hours later, realizing that at thirty-three he was not as limber as he once had been. He felt like a racquetball smacked too many times against the wall of the playing court. Fiske seemed miles away as Eldon crept across the rough orange industrial carpet that covered the newsroom floor. The editor was a tiny figure beckoning with a pipe. The smell of tobacco and the sound of Fiske's voice floated to Eldon's senses, abruptly restoring proper perspective.

"Well, dee-de-dee," Fiske said as he came into focus not five feet away. "Where ya been, Eldon, shacked up in a whorehouse? You look like the whites of your eyes've been drained."

"I—had car trouble."

"Called your house. You musta been at the mechanic's, huh?"

"Yeah."

"I called yesterday and this morning. You were at the mechanic's all night, huh?" Fiske grinned, a great spread of gold-backed teeth.

Marsha sniffed at Eldon over her typewriter. "*I* had to make police checks this morning."

"Did you good, too," said Eldon. His head still felt as if it were floating off his shoulders.

"Fortunately, things were quiet," said Fiske. "You should have checked in. Usually you're the first one in here every morning and the last one out at night."

"Sad but true, Jimbo."

"So are you going to write a story today?"

The clock still showed more than an hour until deadline. "I've got a great story," Eldon said.

"What'd the developer have to say about the earthquakes?"

"I didn't get to ask him. I got something better—that nut Henspeter and Pumpkin Joe Nedlee were at each other's throats at the commission hearing over that condo project."

"Oh. And why's that better news than an earthquake?"

"The earthquake didn't happen. This did. Henspeter had a hangman's noose—"

"Dee-de-dee! Now that catches my fancy!"

Eldon delivered the coup de grace. "I took a picture of it, too."

"Dee-de-dee!" Fiske held out greedy hands for Eldon's camera. "Knew an old reporter had a collection of hangman's ropes—little snippets of rope from executions he'd covered. Had 'em mounted on a board—"

"Sidebar, too, Jimbo. Revealing interview with the environmentalist."

"Eldon, you're my boy." Fiske pulled the film roll from the Nikkormat and gloated over it. He looked at the clock. "Can you get it all done in time?"

Without waiting for an answer, Fiske yelled toward the production area: *"Wally!* Move the Jimmy Carter story inside somewhere. Good copy comin' through!" In the back-shop area behind the news desks, the production foreman started peeling the lead story from the day's Page One pasteup.

"Get on it," Fiske told Eldon. "Like I said, each and every one of the ropes in this reporter's collection had stretched a neck. He knew all the details, used to describe how they'd twisted and flopped. The way you talk about your fishing flies. The old geezer was from El Paso, he's up in Portland now. . . ."

Eldon dropped in front of his typewriter. One of these days he'd get to Portland, too. To some big newspaper somewhere. But he wasn't worried about that now. He was too relaxed. Enola Gay had wrung him out on the molecular level. Eldon rolled paper into his Royal and began writing:

PREACHER'S HOLE—A hearing on a controversial con-dominium project yesterday was disrupted by an environmental demonstrator, flourishing a hangman's noose, who read the Declaration of Independence to the Nekaemas County Board of Commissioners.

John Henspeter's impromptu demonstration brought him eyeball-to-eyeball with Joseph "Pumpkin Joe" Nedlee, county board chairman. Nedlee halted the land-use hearing after a shouting match with Henspeter.

Nedlee said later that the hearing would resume when the board "isn't being heckled by crackpots."

Henspeter contended that the Forest Vista Estates condominium project south of Port Jerome would endanger old-growth timber in the area. Henspeter tried Tuesday to stop construction work at the project site, at the same time that a desiccated human foot was found in nearby Schumacher's Landfill. . . .

Eldon felt as if he were driving tent pegs with his tired fingers as he hit the keys, but the words flowed as always. He could still weave a good one. As he wrote, his mind worked on another level: He thought about lunch. Good sex and good appetite! It reminded him of Berkeley days, when things were still good with Bernice.

Famished after a hard bout of love, they would go for cheeseburgers at a lunch counter down the street from their apartment. What was that place called? It had disappeared by the time he'd revisited Berkeley in '77. Time was passing, no doubt about that. But today he was in love.

But love meant that he was corrupted. He was sleeping with a source. It just happened, he thought. Eldon's fingers sped up, seemingly of their own will. He couldn't just drop the woman; it might be years before the pitying gods tossed him another such gift. But Commissioner Nedlee was her father! What if he found out? Eldon imagined Pumpkin Joe's steely fingers closing against his throat.

He jumped when he felt Fiske's pipe stem poke his neck.

"Take 'controversial' out of the lead," said Fiske. "It's a buzzword."

"Lemme get on with this, dammit. Who are we going to offend?"

"Common sense, for one thing. One tree-hugger with a noose ain't a 'controversy.' "

"Not even if his cause is just?"

"Not unless he hangs somebody with it." Fiske put his pipe in his mouth and began to orbit between Eldon's desk and the news desk, humming tunelessly, one eye on the clock.

Eldon shuffled through his notebook, found a Keith Howell quote: *We could simply cut down the trees there and get on with it. But environmentally responsible development can enhance the livability of our state . . .* Political cant—but on deadline it would have to do. The words had sounded smooth enough when Howell spoke them, but now they rang about as true as lead pennies. Thirty minutes. Eldon felt as if the clock's sweep hand were pushing him along.

He typed out the quote and followed with three paragraphs describing the encounter in the hearing room. He had to chuckle as he wrote about Henspeter and the commissioners swapping places. He added background on the condo proposal. That led naturally to a paragraph about Jasper and Paavo picketing the courthouse. For good measure, Eldon again credited Bouncer with discovering the foot in the landfill and typed "30" at the bottom of the story. He paper-clipped the pages together and pitched them toward the copy basket on Fiske's desk.

Fiske was still walking in circles. His trajectory intersected with that of the pages through the air; he caught them on the fly, whirled to the news desk, grabbed a pencil, and began editing the story. Fiske swiftly reached the bottom of the first page. *"Copy!"*

Someone seized the marked-up page and rushed it to Wally, who sat at the keyboard of a Compu-Graphic typesetting machine. Wally typed furiously. Punched yellow-paper tape, like tape from a stock ticker, trickled from the machine. As Wally reached the end of the page, an assistant hit a key that cut off the tape and fed the segment into another machine.

Fiske waved the second page of Eldon's story. *"Copy!"* The page was passed off to Wally. More punched tape curled from the Compu-Graphic. Meanwhile, the contents of the first page emerged from the second machine on shiny white paper, set in columns. A printer trimmed the curling strip, waxed its reverse to make it tacky and slapped it into the waiting gap on the pasteup.

"Copy!" Fiske finished the last page of the story. "C'mon, c'mon," he snapped at Eldon as the page was snatched away. "Let's have the sidebar."

Eldon pounded his typewriter. He ripped each newsprint sheet from his typewriter when he reached the bottom of the page and threw it over his shoulder. Eldon did not notice Fiske retrieving the sheets from the floor; there was nothing now but the words. The deadline.

JACKKNIFE CREEK—John Hensepeter is on guard among the trees.

The one-eyed environmental activist is camping in a stand of Port Orford cedar that he says is endangered by a condominium project in the area. He says he will do what he must to protect the old-growth trees.

Henspeter has a taste for dramatic confrontations. In recent days, the rangy former logger has tussled with construction workers at the condominium site and has bearded Nekaemas County Commissioner "Pumpkin Joe" Nedlee.

Henspeter says that's just the beginning. He believes that "an army" will soon rally to his cause—to preserve what is left of Nekaemas County's forests.

"This area is changing—and not for the better," Henspeter said. . . .

Eldon kept grinding, describing Henspeter's camp among the tall cedars, the tortuous path to the grove, the road up the slough to the house. He salted the descriptions with provocative quotes. He was coming into the stretch as Fiske came up in front of the typewriter and hovered there, eyeing the clock.

"Two minutes," said Fiske.

Eldon typed "30" and threw up his hands. Fiske snatched the sheet from the typewriter roller, swore as it tore in half, and rushed off with both fragments. He pasted them sloppily together onto a third sheet, swiftly proofread them, and handed the sheet to the typesetters. He rolled a half-sheet into his typewriter and punched out two headlines. A printer trotted it back to Wally.

Fiske rocked back in his chair, sucking his pipe. "Dee-de-dee! Made it! Clears the pipes, eh?"

Eldon nodded. "I guess I can still meet a deadline."

"Yes, you can. Just remember—I still want you to talk to that developer."

"Okay. . . . But I've got to get back to that foot."

"Keep on that, too." Fiske went into the production area to approve the modified page.

Eldon watched from his desk as the pasteup was carried away to the camera area, where an offset press plate would be shot. He felt as if he might melt and dribble out of his chair.

Fiske returned and pulled a cellophane-wrapped sandwich from his desk. He held it up like a preacher flourishing a Bible. "Tuna. Keep ya strong. Like prunes t' me."

Eldon was hungry again, despite his whopping breakfast. It was the sharp, happy appetite that comes after pleasurable haste. The story was done and the deadline past. Now he could stuff his face. But Eldon remained until he heard the alarm bells in the pressroom signal the start of the pressrun. The sound gave him goose bumps. Only when he felt the thudding of the press through the soles of his feet did he rise and head for Pop's.

Eldon ordered the Logger's Cheeseburger and fries in honor of having scored with Enola Gay. But when the cheeseburger arrived, greasy and steaming in its seeded bun, Eldon knew: He had been slacking off. Deadlines were there so the presses could roll on time, not to give him a benchmark for his sex life. You just as easily could've missed that one, he thought as he lifted the top of the roll and poured ketchup over the meat and melted cheddar. I've got to get back on track.

Eldon chewed French fries and thought about the mummified foot. Gotta keep that in the news, he thought. I'll give the county medical examiner a call after lunch. What's-his-name, the mushroom freak. Rosenak. I can't miss if I write another foot story.

But this condo-verses-trees nonsense is turning out to be pretty good, too, he thought. Nothing like a crank with a cause for good copy. I'll have to be careful, though, or I'll never be able to shake the son of a bitch. He'll be in every day with something or another, insisting that I write a story. I'll have to talk with the condo developer—maybe do a profile on him. Ask Howell if he really does intend to cover Nekaemas County with condos.

Who *does* own that cedar stand, anyway?

Eldon chomped more rapidly through the burger. A *Sun* delivery truck pulled up outside Pop's, and the driver climbed out and loaded the curbside newspaper dispenser with copies of the day's edition. CONDO PROJECT MEETS HANG-UP: Eldon read the headline through the window with pleasure. He hoped that Enola Gay would enjoy the profile of her ex.

I've got to slow down when I eat, Eldon thought, finishing off the cheeseburger. He tried to suppress a belch and decided that time was too short to order ice cream to clear his palate. That inspired a fantasy of Enola Gay licking ice cream off his intimate parts. No, that would be rather cold. Make it strawberry jam. . . .

When he returned to the *Sun*, Eldon called the sheriff's office and asked for Art Nola. The dispatcher told him Nola was still out at the landfill and no, the deputies had found nothing. So I'll check up on the foot, Eldon decided. He called Dr. Rosenak, who also was not in. He left a message with the medical examiner's secretary.

"Probably hanging out at the landfill, too," Eldon said.

"Then why aren't you out there with 'em?" Fiske asked.

"I can't camp out there while they sift a hundred acres."

"Dee-dee-de, you're right. How'd any work get done around here, then?" Fiske dropped a pile of press releases on Eldon's desk.

Eldon sighed. The releases were basic grist for the news mill—announcements of meetings, vacancies on public boards, school plays, flower shows, and all the social humdrum that formed a large part of a newspaper's stock-in-trade. Releases arrived in a steady flow. Each day, Fiske joined editors the world over in sorting through them, discarding all too few, and parceling the rest out to reporters, with instructions scrawled in red in the corner of each.

Fiske had scratched "ELDON—BRIEF" on each release in the pile. Eldon was to write one- or two-paragraph stories that would be used as needed to fill odd spaces on the pages of the *Sun*. Some of the fillers would lead to full-fledged stories in their own right. A flower show, for instance, might later be the subject of a feature with photos. Writing briefs was easy but it was dull, part of journalism's inescapable tedium.

On the top of the stack was the announcement of a Finnish dance at the Sons of Eiden Hall, the Scandinavian lodge, union hall, and, as jest had it, gladiatorial school. Eldon thought of Paavo and frowned. Then he thought of Enola Gay and smiled.

He called her. There were two and a half rings at the other end and then Enola Gay's voice: "Hi. This is Atomic Car and Truck Repair—" Eldon started to reply, then realized that he was talking to an answering machine. The recording continued: "We can't come to the phone just now, but if you'll leave your name and number and the time you called at the sound of the beep, we'll get back to you. Thanks!" *Beep!*

"Hi, ah, wow, ah, what do I say? This is *Eldon* at 2:15 P.M. You remember me. How about a date? My place or yours? Call me at the paper. Or at home tonight." Eldon recited his unlisted home number and, smirking, hung up.

The afternoon passed without incident—or result. Eldon called Keith Howell's office. The developer wasn't in, either.

"I've got calls out to everyone you want me to talk to, Jimbo. No one's around. I left messages."

"Sometimes it goes like that. Keep after 'em, dee-de-dee." Fiske was scrutinizing the latest issue of *Sasquatch and UFO,* one of his favorite publications; it seemed to have a calming effect.

Eldon churned out briefs. The afternoon took on the unplugged, timeless quality special to newsrooms and Third World villages. Marsha disappeared. Frank was nowhere to be seen. Ambrose

McFee, the sports editor, wandered in for the swing shift. McFee was five feet tall and and looked like a shaggy tree stump with buggy blue eyes. He wore a purple baseball cap with a yellow Q, the livery of no known Oregon school or team. Ambrose did not have his usual affable, tipsy grin—he was sober.

"How're you, Ambrose?"

"Better. Clearer. I'm cuttin' back. Goin' to confession and Mass and not chasin' women." Ambrose blinked. "Not sure I like it."

"Keep it up. It's better for you."

"Save me some lumps, anyway." Ambrose usually haunted the bars, pursuing tall women who inevitably had even taller husbands or boyfriends.

Ambrose's arrival signaled the end of Eldon's shift. He made the round of calls again, left more messages, decided to call Enola Gay in the privacy of his home, and left for the day.

For once his house didn't seem so lonely. Eldon lived atop a high ridge in the village of Regret, in a green stucco cottage with a view of Nekaemas Bay and the forested slopes across the water on the bay's northern shore. His spirits danced as he drove the van up the pitted road to the top of the ridge. The sun glittered on the distant bay.

He strolled through his book-lined living room, patted his fly-tying bench in the corner, and went into the kitchen in a celebratory mood. He got down the tub of French vanilla ice cream, put three big scoops in a bowl, and doused them with cognac. He returned to the living room, put on his lucky album of Bach lute suites, and sat back in one of the worn, comfortable easy chairs, tossing aside a pornographic magazine that now seemed superfluous.

She's someone who could change my life, Eldon thought as he slurped ice cream and savored the music and the view. The idea filled him with serenity. I hope she likes to go fishing, he mused.

He decided to call Enola Gay after dinner. Surely she would be home by then. In the meantime, he returned to Villon, translating the Old French easily as he read along: *Let us each find the guilt in his own heart, Let us each take revenge but be patient* . . . Jeez, François, thought Eldon, you ought to lighten up.

Time to call Enola Gay. But once again, the recorded message.

"This is me again," Eldon replied, getting into the swing of the thing. "I don't want your robot, I want you. I can't live without you. Gimme a call." He recited his home number again, added some heavy breathing for good measure, and hung up.

The evening went by without a call. Eldon considered calling yet again, fighting the jealousy that now churned in his gut. You don't own her, he told himself firmly. The situation is touchy up there. Better take it easy for now.

The thought comforted him more than he had expected. Anticipation of victory overrode uncertainty. Eldon played music and read distractedly until bedtime, drained a snifter of cognac, and corked off.

He did not think he was dreaming. He was floating in the water, splashing toward a telephone on a raft of logs bound for the mill. The phone was ringing. He had to reach the phone before the logs got to the mill.

Eldon grabbed the receiver, opened his eyes in his bedroom. It was morning. "Yeah? Who's that? Enola—?"

"Yeah, this is Art Nola."

"Yeah? Art?" Eldon had never given Nola his home number. "What the hell? Did you find something at the landfill—"

"I'm at the home of Ms. Enola Gay Hansen. I want you to come over right away."

Eldon felt a rush of terror. "What? Why—?"

"She said to call you. She's too upset to talk." Art paused. "Your number was on her machine."

"What's happened, Art?"

Nola lowered his voice, as if Enola Gay was in the same room with him. "Her boyfriend John Henspeter's up the hillside in the forest—spiked to an old-growth tree."

Eldon brought the van to a skidding halt before Enola Gay's house. Gravel sprayed from beneath the wheels onto the parked patrol cars and Detective Art Nola.

"Take it easy," said Nola as Eldon scrambled from the van.

"She's okay. She's in the house." Nola's voice was professionally calm yet commanding. "Now, before you go in there, let me tell you the situation."

"Henspeter's dead."

"Murdered. And where were you last night?"

"I was at home. What do you mean?" A cold hand seemed to clamp Eldon's heart. "I didn't—"

"I listened to your phone messages," Nola said. "We know you're involved with her."

Eldon was embarrassed. "I was home all night. I kept calling her."

"So you did," Nola said.

"You don't think *I* did this, do you?"

"I don't know. Did you? I hope not."

"Christ, Art, how could you think that?"

"Same reason you think things about me—business. Nobody's above suspicion."

"My 'business' is covering the news. Not offing Enola Gay's old boyfriend."

"That's why I don't think you'd write a story about the man and then come back later and kill him." Nola's smile was brittle. "You'd have killed him right then. Go ahead in and talk to her."

Eldon headed for the house. A sheriff's deputy at the door let him in at Art's signal. Eldon found Enola Gay sitting on the living room couch, pale but composed. Her eyes were hot and dry.

"I felt sorry for him," she said without preamble. "I took some hot coffee and rolls up to him for breakfast—and found him nailed to that tree. To that fallen tree."

"At least you're all right."

"I wasn't home last night," Enola Gay said. "Of course, you know that—you called and called."

"Yeah." Eldon looked around the room, noticed that the eel tank was empty.

"I got home this morning and saw that John had been in the house," Enola Gay said. Her voice had a flat quality suggesting suppressed terror. "He'd picked up some more of his things. So I thought I'd take him something to eat. You don't shut someone off like an appliance after living with him for two years."

"Of course not."

"But *someone* shut him off," Enola Gay said.

"It's a good thing you weren't here last night. That might've saved you."

"I was visiting Ronnie and Joline Endo. I've known them for years. I rebuilt a Harley engine for Ronnie and took it back to him."

"A motorcycle engine?"

"They're bikers. Ronnie was pleased. Then they started throwing crockery at each other—"

"What?"

"Ronnie and Joline break a lot of plates. But they don't mean anything by it. It's just the way they communicate. The fight went kind of late. I wound up sleeping on their couch. To think I was asleep while John was—" Anger and nausea crossed Enola Gay's face. "Go up there," she said fiercely. "Take a picture. *Put this in the paper!*"

Eldon nodded. "I'll be back in a while."

As Eldon left the house, the cool, protecting sense of abstraction that he always felt when covering violent death came over him. He knew exactly what to do and how to do it. The familiar feeling barely masked another—an appetite, almost a salivating sensation. A wolfish instinct that told him . . . *good copy.*

Art was leaning against a patrol car, jotting in a leather-bound pocket notebook. I mustn't let him mess with my head, Eldon thought, and went to his van and got the Nikkormat and his own notebook. "Take me up to the scene."

"You're on the job now?" Art said. "All right. Maybe you can answer some questions."

"Sure, Art. Anything. Ready when you are."

"No pictures, Eldon."

"I can't promise that."

"What's she going to think about his picture in the paper?"

"What does anyone ever think? If you don't put something in, you get anonymous calls about how you 'covered it up.' I've been accused of covering up a Cub Scout jamboree. But if you put something in that disturbs somebody, it's 'bad taste.' You can't win for losing. As a matter of fact, she told me to get up there and cover the story."

Art glanced dubiously toward the house. "Always nice to meet a woman who admires your work. How long have you been seeing her?"

"Ah, about forty-eight hours. Not exactly long enough to get in a killing rage over her old boyfriend."

"Long enough in these parts," Nola mused as they started across the yard toward the trees. "Do you have any rivals for her affections? Ones with fiercer dispositions?"

"Not that I know of," Eldon said. "Anyway, this couldn't have been a passion killing. This was *political*. He threatened to spike trees. It was a bluff but—"

"I think so, too," said Nola.

They reached the trees and Nola led the way up the steep path. Yellow plastic crime-scene tape marked the way, tied around tree trunks in big incongruous bows like birthday ribbons.

"Talk to those workmen who were at the condo site the other day," Eldon said. "That's when Henspeter made the tree-spiking threat. I warned him that was killing talk."

"And what did he say?"

"He shrugged it off. The foreman told Henspeter he'd kill him for tree-spiking. A pack of 'em might've held him down while they—"

"We talked to the workmen. They're clean. And that is off the record for now. All right?"

"Sure. I wouldn't accuse anybody."

"You're in no position to," Art said. "What's the *Sun*'s circulation?"

"Huh? About eighteen thousand daily, six days per week."

"But don't a lot more people actually read the paper?"

"The rule of thumb is that three people read each copy sold. We call that the 'penetration.' Why?"

"So fifty-four thousand people read your story about Henspeter. Ninety percent of the population of this county. Many of whom rely for their living on logging. Plenty of 'em might have done it."

Eldon prickled. The implication was monstrous—that his story in the *Sun* had led to Henspeter's murder by pinpointing the environmentalist's location—and perhaps by provoking the killer. "Crap," Eldon said as they continued to climb. "My business is information. I don't keep things out of the paper."

"Not even dangerous things," Art said.

"Henspeter reveled in the publicity."

"He made a mistake," Art said as they reached the campsite.

Henspeter's campsite was marked off with more of the yellow crime-scene tape. Sheriff's deputies walked carefully among the great cedars, stretching tape measures and taking flash pictures. Spokes of golden morning sunlight gleamed above their heads, faintly marbled with mist. The scene was much as Eldon had last seen it. The fire pit smoked. The sagging tarp was still pitched against the fallen tree. The deputies' industry was centered there, on something Eldon could not see because of the angle of the bole.

A big, plump man about fifty years old sat before them on a tree stump, rummaging in a big black medical bag. He had white hair and whiskers, but his eyes had a youthful glitter behind wire-rimmed spectacles. He wore a blue-plaid bow tie and a loud checked sports coat with unstylishly wide lapels. He looked like Santa Claus dressed for a Rotary convention.

The man looked up brightly as Eldon and Nola approached. "Hi-ho, Art Nola."

"Dr. Rosenak," Art said, "this is Eldon Larkin from the *Sun*."

Donald Rosenak was the county medical examiner. Eldon had never met him before, although they had spoken on the telephone.

"Oh, say, you've been calling about the foot," Rosenak said. "Sorry I haven't gotten back. Things have been hectic."

"It's okay," Eldon said. "I've been out of the office."

"Eldon has a few questions, Doc," Nola said.

"I'll bring him up to speed." Rosenak dug in the medical bag like a child seeking a favorite toy. At last he found a garden trowel and a little plastic box. "Glad to. First, let me take this specimen."

Eldon felt a chill. "A specimen of what?"

"This is a good spring for mushrooms." Rosenak climbed off the stump and squatted behind it. He dug for a moment with the trowel and flourished a mushroom as big as his fist. *"Galerina autumnalis."*

"Good eating?"

"No! Deadly!" Rosenak shuddered. *"Galerina's* the one dope hunters mistake for psychedelic mushrooms. But you eat these, you *die*. The longer I study mushrooms, the happier I am eating the ones I get in the supermarket."

"Doc, you should've been born five hundred years ago," said Art. "You'd have made a great poisoner."

"If the Borgias lived now, they'd stick with the supermarket, too." Rosenak placed the mushroom in the box and the box in his bag. "That fellow up the slope wasn't poisoned, that's for sure. Go on over, if you like; we're pretty much finished. Just watch where you step."

Nola led Eldon over to the fallen tree where Henspeter had camped. Eldon looked away. He had covered nearly every murder and fatal traffic accident in Nekaemas County for six years, but he did not want to look at Henspeter's face.

He gazed instead at the ground. There lay a wet, shredded paper bag, its pathetic contents scattered across the ground at their late owner's feet—old clothes, a blue toothbrush, a dented spoon, a staple puller, an old traveler's clock radio, an empty fountain-pen case and other junk. Henspeter's heels had churned up the wet, dark humus of the forest floor. His legs were askew, the knees cocked. It was as if someone had tossed a huge, grotesque doll against the tree and . . . Eldon forced himself to look. "Oh, shit."

Henspeter was arched back against the bole. His head was thrown sharply back and to one side; Eldon did not have to look at his face after all. Henspeter's beard pointed skyward, exposing a waxy, pale neck. His arms dangled stiffly. Investigators had encased the corpse's hands in brown paper bags that were taped closed around the wrists. A gray plastic body bag had been unzipped and neatly laid out nearby.

A dark steel spike protruded from Henspeter's chest. Blood spattered his shirt and jeans and spattered the tree trunk.

"There's not that much blood," Eldon said, mastering his queasiness.

"It's all inside him," Rosenak said.

A pinch-faced deputy with enormous arms squatted nearby, carefully pouring white plaster into a footprint to make a mold. "Justice for a tree-spiker," he said, deadpan, ignoring Art's swift, disapproving scowl.

"He swore to me he'd never do something like that," Eldon said.

"Looks like somebody didn't believe him," the deputy said.

Rosenak came up and pointed at the corpse with his trowel. "He took the spike right through the heart."

"You mean he stood there and let someone do it?" Eldon had a sudden image of Henspeter offering up his life to redeem the trees.

"I guess *not*," the medical examiner said. "There's evidence of a struggle. Things are in disarray. He was overpowered. You can't see his hands but they were slashed when he threw them up to defend himself—that's common in homicides."

"He was attacked with a knife?"

"For starters, I think so. He was thrown against that tree, maybe stunned. And then—wham! Right through the sternum with a hammer blow."

"There were several attackers, then," Eldon said.

Art cleared his throat. "Doc—"

"I'd better not comment," said Rosenak.

"The killer must've been strong as an ox," Eldon said.

"Well, he knew how to drive nails," said Rosenak.

"So you will confirm this is foul play?"

"Oh, yes, obviously. That's official."

"When did he die?" Eldon asked.

"Say between 10 P.M. and midnight last night. That's an estimate, of course, based on the rigor of the body, its lividity, and so forth. It's always hard to say without an autopsy."

"When will that be?"

"I'll let you know tomorrow."

"What's that footprint there?" Eldon said.

"That's what we hope to find out," Art said. "Don't get your hopes up—things like that often don't lead anywhere."

"Someone went through his pockets and scattered his things," Rosenak said, "which could suggest a motive of robbery."

"He didn't have anything worth stealing," Eldon said.

"We don't think it was a robbery," Art said.

"Is that a railroad spike?" Eldon asked.

"Naw, a railroad spike's not long enough," Rosenak said. "This is driven right through him into that tree. It's a pry bar, like you'd use in an auto shop or a logging operation."

Eldon feared for a moment that his stomach would betray him at last. But he knew it wouldn't do any good—Henspeter would still be dead when he'd finished throwing up. And what would Art think?

"Suspects?" Eldon got out at last.

"The investigation is continuing," Art said.

"I've got to have something I can use."

"You've talked to the medical examiner."

The detective's tone was matter-of-fact, but Eldon felt a sudden resentment. He opened his mouth and closed it with an effort. He was about to stride indignantly away when the huge-armed deputy stepped to Henspeter's corpse and drew on heavy work gloves.

"Yank it out now, Doc?"

"Thanks a heap," Eldon said abruptly. "I'll be in touch." He turned and headed down the hill, not looking back, although he was certain that Nola and Rosenak were staring after him.

You shouldn't have done that, he thought, stumbling down the slippery path. They were being helpful. And you know you've got to show some spine at gruesome scenes like these. Otherwise, the cops won't take you seriously.

Eldon realized he had not even tried to take a picture at the crime scene. Maybe it's time to find another line of work, he thought. He was weary of the constant need to grind out copy, the necessity to cajole sources, the ignorance and rudeness of the population, the isolation and violence of the South Coast. He loved the fishing—but how could he catch enough fish to make up for the rest of it?

He reached the back door of Enola Gay's house and knocked gently. Through the window in the door he could see her at the kitchen table, staring into a cup of coffee. She stood at his knock and let him into the kitchen. "Sit down. There's coffee."

Eldon accepted the steaming mug she poured for him. He wanted to embrace her but settled for curving his palms around the cup's warm ceramic. That was the worst thing I've ever seen, Eldon thought, and waited for his heart to stop drumming.

"Did you take a picture up there?" Enola Gay demanded.

"No, I didn't take a picture. 'Bad taste.' " Before she could respond, Eldon said, "He was killed by someone who knew him."

"What? Who? The cops told you that?"

"That's exactly what they didn't tell me when I asked them. I think it was a single killer."

"Nobody could have sneaked up on John. He knows—knew—the woods. And he would've been alert."

Eldon nodded. "That's why it had to be someone he let get close."

"Why do you think that?"

"A gang of people would've trampled the ground. As it was, the cops were happy to find one good footprint. Which may or may not provide a clue." Eldon sipped the strong coffee. His stomach was empty; he could feel the caffeine's lift. He concentrated on the heady sensation and stared at Enola Gay's drawn face. "Who might've done it? Who were his friends?"

"John didn't have a lot of those."

"How about enemies? They'd be just as good."

"He wasn't the kind of person who picked fights."

"That's not the impression I got the first time I met him."

"That was new. He was different when it came to the trees. He became that way, I mean. It was like he'd finally found something worth latching onto."

"He lived with you and didn't think he had something worthwhile?" Eldon asked. "Hooboy."

Enola Gay smiled a little. "Well, that was one of the things that came between us. Though I think he regretted it."

"I think so, too. Who's his next of kin?"

"No one I ever heard of. I'll have to do, I guess."

"Where'd John hang out?"

"Nowhere in particular and not very much. At Buster's. Or the Dead Man's Hand. Or even the Timber Topper. Any of the usual bars. He knew a lot of guys from when he worked in the forest and later in the mills."

"How well did he get along with 'em? After this tree-hugger stuff started, I mean."

"Don't call him that."

"Okay. Sorry."

"Good question, though. John went to the bars a lot less after that."

"So how'd he get onto this environmental trip?"

Enola Gay shook her head. "Damned if I know. Like I said, it was one of the things that came between us. You know—when one person in a relationship makes a very radical, important decision all on their own? Like getting religion? And then springs it on the other one?"

"Yeah, I do know."

"It was after that condo project started getting talked up."

"What'd you think about it?"

"Eldon, I love the forest. But it was like we were agreeing on different frequencies. We should've tuned in on this together . . . but we didn't. John was just too fierce about it."

"You weren't into chaining yourself in trees."

"I don't mean that. There was something behind the whole business that I didn't understand. Something else was driving him. I never got to the bottom of it. But it was something nasty."

"Oh? Such as what?"

"Have you ever driven a car and started hearing a sound that wasn't right but that nobody else could hear? And you took it to the mechanic, and the mechanic said nothing was wrong because he couldn't hear it either?"

"Yeah, I had a Citroën once—"

"I get cars in like that. And it was that way with John. I knew that if I didn't call it quits with him, I'd regret it."

"How *did* he lose that eye?"

"He almost lost it in Mexico. He got drunk and tried to emcee a cockfight. They kept telling him to get out of the way, but he couldn't understand Spanish. One of the roosters got him." Enola Gay shook her head. "He was always interfering."

She rose, folded her arms and walked into the living room. When Eldon followed, she nodded toward the empty eel tank. "John let the wolf eels go yesterday," she said. "He said it was time to give them their freedom. I helped him put them in the slough."

"And you still have all your fingers?"

"Well, it was touchy. But I didn't want to have to take care of them. We put them into a crate lined with wet cloths and took them down to the water, out behind the landfill."

"They're back in the bay by now, then. Maybe already out to sea."

"Not necessarily. They can hang around up in the slough as long as the water salinity is right. That ebbs and flows with the tides, of course. He found them in the slough and they might stay there— they're quite territorial."

Eldon eyed her. "First you told me that John didn't drink much. Then you said he lost his eye in Mexico when he got drunk."

"Well, he tapered off after that."

"I suppose so. He wasn't drunk when I talked to him," Eldon said, and waited. Enola Gay looked uneasy. Finally Eldon said, "You're going to have to be franker about John than you've been."

"How do you mean?"

"If you want me to write a story, then you have to talk about him. Do you want to talk about him?"

"Yeah. It feels better to talk."

"Look—I want to stay friends with you," Eldon said. "But I've probably been a reporter at least as long as you've been a mechanic. I notice slips, like what you said about the drinking. It's part of my work. You can't steer what I write about this any more than I could fool you with a wooden spark plug."

"I'm not trying to hide anything," Enola Gay said.

"So, how long have you known him? Really? And surely you didn't meet him in a tree."

"It seemed that way sometimes," Enola Gay said. "I've known him—knew him—seven years or so, on and off. Though we only lived together for the last couple of years. I came back down here from Astoria in '75, looking for work."

"You met him here?"

"No, but he was one reason I came back. And stayed. Mexico is where we met. Nineteen seventy-three."

"At the cockfight?"

"Yeah, in Mazatlán. I was young and wild in those days. I went down there during spring break from Arizona State. You can take the train from Mexicali to Mazatlán for next to nothing. It's customary to stay loaded the whole time and to do as you will.

"Anyway, we met in a bar where tourists go to dance. My girlfriends weren't too sure about him because John was kind of seedy even then. But we hit it off together. He said, 'Let's take a walk.' "

"And then?"

"We got busy out on the beach." Enola Gay's voice warmed with the memory. "Somewhere along the line we ended up at a cockfight."

"And John tried to stop the cockfight? Like he
condo work?"

"John never gave a damn about chickens, except
had this thing about *taking over* that would surface ev
usually in some impossible situation."

"I bet you loved that."

"He did a lot of that after he lost his eye," said Enola (we
got him to a Mexican hospital. John was so wasted that they gave
him a shot and he passed out. They barely saved his eye."

Large tears ran down her cheeks, but she continued, speaking
steadily. "I stayed with him while he was in the hospital. My
girlfriends said to leave while he was still unconscious but I couldn't
do it. Somebody had to bring him food, you know? Have you ever
done something for somebody who probably was unacceptable,
something you knew could change your life and probably not for
the better? Because you felt sorry for them? Because you didn't
have the guts not to do it? I imagine a lot of marriages get started
that way. Anyway, I went home on the train with John and not
with my girlfriends. He acted as if he'd had the time of his life."

Eldon waited.

Enola Gay resumed. "He lost the eye later, working in the
woods here. A choker chain snapped. That was one rooster he
never had a chance against. John worked in the mills after that. He
did more and more of that *taking over* stuff after he lost the eye. He
kept alienating more and more people."

"It doesn't sound as if he ever got over it."

"Would you?"

They sat silently. An ambulance rolled into the driveway, lights
flashing. White-shirted medics climbed from the vehicle and unfolded a gurney.

"His things were scattered all over up there," Enola Gay said.
"Do you think they'll let me pick them up?"

"The police will want to keep them for a while," Eldon said. He
watched the medics push the gurney to the edge of the trees, lock
its brakes and begin climbing the hill. "Evidence."

Enola Gay took a big breath and exhaled. "I appreciate your
being businesslike, Eldon."

"No charge. Look, I think you should come over to my place

couple of days. Just until things settle down." Eldon didn't
want Enola Gay to watch them bring down the body bag. "It isn't
as if you have to take care of the eels."

"John said you inspired him to let the eels go."

"You mean my story?"

"He said he'd got you thinking about the slough, that you had
a very open mind. About how development might threaten the
fishing. He thought that would get you to write some more."

"I'll cover the story regardless," Eldon said.

"If it hadn't been for your article the other day—"

"I already heard that suggestion once this morning. Please don't
say it."

"I was going to say that John loved your article. I think he'd have
given up that stupid camp up there if it hadn't been for your
publicity. It was why he died."

"It wasn't why he died," Eldon said. "It was just an article in the
newspaper."

"Do another article. With a picture. Show them." Enola Gay's
voice was brittle, her gaze slightly unfocused but hard as metal. "Go
back up there and take a picture."

"No." Eldon looked steadily back into Enola Gay's hard gray
eyes. "You're upset, and you are not going to tell me how to do
my business."

"I . . ." Enola Gay's expression grew solemn and curiously
patient. Determined. Eldon wondered if she had capitulated or
merely retreated to fight another day.

He looked out the window to see the medics struggling down
the hillside with the body bag.

Enola Gay also saw them. "It's too late for the picture now. How
are we going to flush out John's killer?"

"What do you think a picture in the paper is going to do?
Embarrass him?"

"It's a newspaper. That's special. A big story would keep the heat
on the case."

"It's a *murder*. The heat *is* on the case. It *is* a big story."

"It's more than a murder, Eldon," Enola Gay said, watching the
medics push the loaded gurney back across the grass to the ambulance. Rosenak followed the gurney, swinging his bag, chatting
with Art Nola and the other policemen; they looked like a band of

absentminded mourners. "And it's a bigger story than you think," Enola Gay continued. "I'll prove it to you."

She beckoned him into the bedroom. The bed had been made with fresh sheets. The compass-rose quilt was spread flawlessly across it.

"I didn't intend to show you these," said Enola Gay. "I thought John would take them away. But I have to be straight with you."

She threw up the hinged lid of the cedar chest at the foot of the bed and stepped back.

Eldon looked in and tried to whistle. He tried again after a moment, but his throat was too dry.

The cedar chest was full of guns.

Eldon stared at the black jumble of weapons. Finally he managed to whistle. Then he thought that whistling was a ridiculous, trite thing to do while confronting his professional ruin.

Suddenly he was privy to a secret cache of firearms owned by a murder victim. And he had slept with the woman who'd revealed them—the victim's ex-girlfriend.

He had slept with a news source.

Eldon forced himself to calmly examine the contents of the box. Maybe this was innocent. Homes in Nekaemas County traditionally were redneck arsenals, equipped with shotguns, hunting rifles, Magnum pistols for "home defense." The cedar chest was in another league. Eldon recognized an AR-15, the civilian version of the Army's M-16 rifle; a Soviet AK-47 assault rifle; an ancient German Mauser pistol; and a short, olive-drab tube, capped at either end, with a push-tab trigger assembly and wires.

"That's an Army LAW," Enola Gay said quietly. "Light Anti-Tank Weapon."

"He didn't need that for hunting. Where'd John get all this?"

"I don't know," Enola Gay said. "He wouldn't say. He collected it gradually. He'd bring home a gun at a time. Sometimes one part at a time. There's ammunition and grenades, too."

"Grenades?" Eldon looked deeper into the chest. Cardboard ammunition cartons were in the bottom, next to gray cans lying on their sides. Eldon resisted the impulse to touch the cans. "Those are smoke grenades, thank God. Not fragmentation."

"So you recognize them."

"We have identification books at the office."

"Are you going to write about these?"

"This is why you threw John out," Eldon said.

"I was afraid he'd *shoot* you with one of these guns. That was why I was so hard-nosed with him at breakfast yesterday."

She's a source, Eldon thought again. He pursued the terrible thought as doggedly as if he were trying to pin down a sleazy politician in an interview. You've slept with one of your sources. You're compromised for this story, at least. Maybe finished for good, if Jimbo finds out.

Would Fiske fire him? No, Eldon decided, Fiske would not. He would do worse. There would be no more good copy for Eldon. There would be nothing but safe, dull assignments.

Enola Gay dropped the lid of the cedar chest. "We've got to get rid of these."

"No," Eldon said. "It might be illegal."

"Eldon, I don't know if these guns *are* illegal in Oregon. John told me you can even own a machine gun here without a permit, if you like."

"Just wait a second. I've got to think."

"Shall we tell the cops?"

"Don't do that. We don't know that these are connected to John's murder, do we?"

"What else could they be connected to?"

"It might be coincidence."

"John never said what he wanted them for," said Enola Gay. "He had that fantasy about defending the trees, but he never—"

"He'd have needed an army to use all that stuff. Who else knows about them? Did he have accomplices? Anybody who came around or who he talked about?"

"No. That's what was so creepy." Enola Gay hugged herself. "I'd have felt better if he'd had friends—even scary friends."

"Drugs. Did he deal drugs?"

"No."

Car engines started outside; the police and the ambulance were driving away. Enola Gay grimaced and twisted her head away, but Eldon was relieved. Now he had time to plan. "I've got to get to the office and file a story."

"About John."

"About John. But I won't mention the guns for now."

This may be a big scoop, Eldon thought. I can't tip my hand yet. The guns are the angle that will pull the fat out of the fire with Fiske. "I want you to pack a bag and go to my place for a few days. You can't stay here—it's not safe."

"Right." Enola Gay got up, at once all competence, and dragged a suitcase from the closet. Eldon's heart melted as he watched her put clothes into the suitcase. That frightened him almost as much as the guns in the cedar chest. He felt moved to say something coldhearted, even self-destructive. "This murder is a big scoop. Good copy."

A tremor ran through Enola Gay's features. Then her reddened eyes shone and she smiled. It was a clear, firm smile, with no calculation in it. Yet it had about it a sense of . . . appetite. Eldon realized that Enola Gay was attracted to power. "Time you understood about me," he said.

"I understand you, Eldon." Enola Gay slid across the bed and buried her face in his lap.

When Fiske asks if I got a body shot, I'm going to tell him to go to hell, Eldon decided while Enola Gay fumbled with the zipper on his trousers. And I'm going to dog this story until they find the son of a bitch who killed Henspeter.

By Eldon Larkin
Sun *Staff Writer*

JACKKNIFE SLOUGH—Environmental activist John Henspeter was found murdered Tuesday in the grove of old-growth cedar he had sworn to protect. He was nailed to a fallen tree with a crowbar.

Sheriff's deputies said Henspeter was slain late Monday night.

Henspeter's body was discovered by Enola Gay Hansen . . .

91

"So what's the address of the house?" Fiske said.

"It's not safe to put that in," Eldon said. "The murderer might come back and threaten her—"

"The murderer goes all the way up in the forest to get Henspeter, and he needs to read our newspaper to find his way back?" Fiske's expression was bland. Eldon cringed, waiting for the inevitable.

"So what about the earthquakes?"

"What?"

"Earthquakes are the angle on this whole thing."

Eldon stared at Fiske. The editor's expression was serious. "John Henspeter has been murdered," Eldon said.

"That's right," said Fiske. "Finally, the landfill is a story."

"Finally?"

"A mummified foot is old news," Fiske said. "Like King Tut. Good for a slow day, but next day what's the angle? The condo project and the old-growth trees is okay, but that's just a bureaucracy story—they'll work it out at a land-use hearing.

"But now we've got a murder!" Fiske massaged the bowl of his pipe between his palms, like a man taking private pleasure. "Deede-dee! The very lad who opposed the condo project near where the foot was discovered."

Fiske leaned close, nearly overwhelming Eldon with the smell of burned tobacco. "What if that tectonic plate under the landfill shifts now? We're talking *good copy*—a national story."

"Don't you want to know if I took a picture of the body?" Eldon asked.

" 'Bad taste,' " Fiske said. "We've been getting complaints about your picture of Bouncer and the foot. We'll lay off body shots for a while. You coordinate with Frank on the earthquake angle. Get comment from the developer."

"About the possibility of an earthquake."

"No, about the *murder.*" Fiske shook his head. "Talk to Pumpkin Joe Nedlee, too."

That was close, Eldon thought as Fiske wandered off. Then his desperation returned at the idea of speaking to Nedlee again. Would he have to shout his questions over the sound of the commissioner hammering nails?

Eldon went to Frank's desk and twirled through the Rolodex.

The Board of Commissioners office was listed in the telephone book, but Eldon wanted the number of the phone on Nedlee's desk. Sure enough, Frank had it.

Eldon dialed the number. Nedlee answered immediately. "Hope you'll vote for Pumpkin Joe. This is Pumpkin Joe Nedlee. How can I help *you?*"

"Commissioner, this is Eldon Larkin at the *Sun.*"

"Yeah?" A low growl.

"Commissioner, John Henspeter was murdered last night—"

"I'm aware," Nedlee said.

Fast work by the sheriff's office, thought Eldon. "I'd like to get a comment."

"On what?"

"Your reaction to the murder."

"What the hell's it got to do with me? You think I killed him?"

Eldon felt his heart speed up and his ears heat. "You and Henspeter argued publicly—"

"What's that supposed to mean?"

Eldon began taking notes on his typewriter. Hammering began on Nedlee's end of the line, as if in retort.

"Is there anything you'd like to say?" Eldon asked.

"What do you think? It's senseless. Tragic. How's that?"

Eldon typed. The hammer went bam-bam-bam! Nedlee continued, his voice a little more settled. "Mr. Henspeter and I had our disagreements. I can't imagine who would want to do such a terrible *thing!*" Bam!

"How does this affect the condominium debate?"

"What debate?" Bam! "Mr. Henspeter seemed to be the only opponent. Likely the project will proceed." Bam-bam-*bam!*

Eldon typed it out. A surge of charity—or perhaps a desire to establish rapport with the father of his new beloved—impelled Eldon to say, "Your daughter's safe."

The hammering stopped.

"I talked to Enola Gay this morning," Eldon said.

"You aren't going to mention my daughter in the story?" Nedlee asked after a moment.

"Well, she discovered the body."

Nedlee made a sound of pain. "I didn't know that! What's the need to put that in the paper?"

"It happened."

"It's private!"

"It's part of the story—"

"It's private, what do you mean?" cried Nedlee.

"She lived with him for a couple of years."

"That's a family matter. That has nothing to do with me as a commissioner! How can you people ask someone about things like finding a body spiked to a tree and then put it in the newspaper—"

"She didn't mind talking to me," Eldon said.

"Wait—how did you find out she's my daughter?"

"She told me, Commissioner. Haven't you talked to her?"

Nedlee's voice rose to a scream. "I'd like to nail your stupid hat to your head! I'd better not catch you snooping around the county offices! This is the last comment of any kind *you* will *ever* get from this *office!*" BAM-BAM-BAM!

Eldon hung up.

What an asshole, he thought as he waited for his heart to slow down. Baloney about "tragedy" until I mentioned Enola Gay. He's afraid she'll embarrass him politically. He's probably worried people will think *he* killed Henspeter. But that probably would win him some votes. . . .

Eldon smiled, recalling his vision of Pumpkin Joe strangling Henspeter. His smile froze as he reflected on Pumpkin Joe's threat to nail his hat to his head.

It's not a *stupid* hat, Eldon thought. It's my *lucky* hat. It saved my life and I've caught lots of fish while I was wearing it, too. He pulled the hat from the desk drawer and inspected it, turning it by its floppy brim, bringing favorite fishing flies into view. Typical headgear on Oregon's South Coast included scarred hard hats, crumpled Stetsons, and the ubiquitous bicolor baseball caps silk-screened with idiotic mottos. A BAD DAY OF FISHING IS WORSE THAN A GOOD DAY OF WORK. Eldon's hat certainly was no less dignified than those—or was it? I could never wear this if I worked in Portland, he thought, they'd say I was eccentric. Or would they? He realized that he no longer could evaluate how the hat looked.

And then came the unbidden thought, popping to the surface of his mind like a cork on a casting line: Suppose Pumpkin Joe did kill Henspeter? Who'd suspect? Nedlee has the temperament, Eldon thought. He put on his hat and shook his head. The Board of Commissioners chairman—wouldn't that be a scoop?

He called Keith Howell. If talking to Nedlee had reminded Eldon of a visit to the dentist, asking Howell for comment was like falling into a feather bed.

"I'll miss John," Howell said at once. "John had a conscience and he had a heart. He was the sort of person that guys like me, who are focused on making money, need to hear from sometimes. It keeps us honest."

"But you're not going to cancel the project in his memory?"

Howell chuckled. "No. But I am going to change it. I'm going to build fewer units near the slough, to better protect that wetland. John had a point there. And I'm going to put up a stone in his honor in the park."

"What about the old-growth cedar?"

"Maybe I should put the stone up there."

"You don't intend to cut it?"

"No."

"What was Henspeter talking about, then?"

"Beats me. John had quite a head on his shoulders, no matter what some people say. But sometimes he led with his heart."

That's good, Eldon thought, typing out Howell's words. It'll go well in the obituary.

"How's that little dog?" asked Howell.

"Bouncer? Last I saw, he was safe in the hands of the man who raised him up."

"That's a very special little dog."

Eldon was puzzled by Howell's earnest tone. But not for long. "You don't credit that 'miracle,' do you?" he asked.

"Let's just say the Lord works in mysterious ways, Eldon."

There it is, thought Eldon with a mental shrug. Odd theologies sprouted like mushrooms from the rain-soaked humus of Nekaemas County's rustic culture. They flourished cheek by jowl with mainstream beliefs in a region where stormy weather and isolation drove thought inward, making religion an implicit obsession, if not an active hobby. Eldon was nothing more unusual than a lapsed Catholic. Fiske was a Lutheran. Art Nola belonged to a sect that predicted the future through dreams, and he wasn't considered odd in the least. Eldon decided that Keith Howell's brand of religion must hold with faith healing, not excluding the resurrection of dogs.

At least Howell didn't pound nails while talking. Still, it was time to change the subject. "Let me ask you about something else, Keith. Kind of a funny question."

"Sure."

"The University of Oregon says there's an earthquake fault around here. Maybe right under your condo site."

Howell chuckled. "I hadn't heard that, but I'm going to keep building."

"Aren't you afraid of an earthquake?"

"In Oregon? Nekaemas County is solid country, Eldon. Forest Vista Estates will stand."

"Good quote," said Eldon. "Thanks a lot."

"Don't mention it," Keith said. "Say, I have an invitation for you. I'm having a get-together at my house Sunday night. Why don't you come? I'll have some news for you."

"Like what?"

"I'm unveiling a model of Forest Vista Estates. Sure, it's a promotion gimmick, but you write business stories, don't you?"

"As a matter of fact, I'm supposed to do a story about you."

Howell laughed. "Just so you spell my name right."

"I will. So when's the party?"

"About eight. I'm going to unveil something else, too. Something special."

"What's that?"

"That's a surprise," said Howell. "You'll be impressed."

"Well, okay, you're on."

"I'll see you then."

Eldon hung up and gave himself over to fiery thoughts about Enola Gay. He glanced at the clock. Plenty of time to finish the murder story. Then he'd drive home for lunch.

Frank Juliano came briskly into the newsroom.

"Thanks for the phone number," Eldon said.

Frank pushed his glasses up his nose. "Which phone number?"

"Pumpkin Joe Nedlee's."

"What's up? More on that land-use beef?"

"John Henspeter was murdered last night."

"What, did Nedlee do it?"

"He'd have liked to. I called him for comment. Because of their argument at the hearing."

"And Joe pasted your ears back, eh? You've got to keep your wits about you with Nedlee."

"I also got a quote from Howell, the condo developer. He's not afraid of an earthquake."

"Well, he shouldn't be." Frank waved his notebook. "I just interviewed a seismologist. There's no earthquake fault up there."

"That's not what the wire story said."

"The university has refined its data. The tectonic plates meet off the coast, not beneath Port Jerome. One of the plates is pushing under Oregon, under the North American continent. Subduction, they call it. That's probably what the wire story meant to say."

"Have you broken it to Fiske? I guess we're back to Bigfoot stories."

"It doesn't rule out earthquakes. But we're probably safe for a few more centuries." Frank picked up the first page of Eldon's murder story. "Lemme see your copy—yow, spiked to a tree! You get pictures?"

"It was too horrible."

"You were there? And you didn't take a picture? That's not the Eldon I know."

"I was there this morning. Probably done in by someone who knew him."

"That'll play well when they catch him." Frank scanned the page silently, then said, " 'Enola Gay' is the name of a rather famous airplane."

"It's also the name of Henspeter's ex—the topless horse-woman."

"That's who she was? You talked to her?"

"Yeah, well . . ." Eldon had to boast to somebody. "I got laid."

Frank was delighted. "No shit? I thought you looked perky."

"It just happened—before I knew she was Henspeter's ex." That was a lie but Eldon let it ride. At last he was in the running with Frank, the newsroom Casanova.

"She just swept you off your feet, huh?" Frank asked. "Isn't this a little touchy? After all, she's in your story."

"That's not her fault. Anyway, you did a feature on that librarian you were seeing."

"That was about the library microfilming program."

"Which she was running," Eldon said. "Are you still seeing her?"

"That's cooled off. She's interested in a guy works for the Bureau of Land Management. Anyway, I met another girl at the myrtlewood shop—"

"But are you still on speaking terms with the librarian?"

"Yeah, sure."

"Could you have her dig up a book with current state firearms regulations?"

"Sure. But we could get them from the sheriff."

"That's just who I don't want to ask."

"Why don't you go to the library and ask her yourself? Good way to meet women."

"I have a woman." Eldon savored the words.

"So what's with the guns?" asked Frank.

"I can't tell you just now. But I think it's good. When I break this one, it'll get earthquakes off our backs forever."

"What kind of guns do you want to know about?"

"All kinds. Just something that tells what you need a permit for and what you don't. State and federal both."

"Okay. Get your story finished and let's go eat."

"I'm going home for lunch today," said Eldon with pride. "I have a houseguest."

"No! Not—" Frank was openly admiring.

"Enola Gay is lying low at my place. Whoever's crazy enough to nail Henspeter to a tree might come back after her."

"For Chrissake, what makes you think that?"

"Okay, look—don't tell this to anyone. Especially Fiske. Henspeter had a trunkful of guns in the house."

"That *is* good."

"We don't know if the guns are connected with the killing."

"What do the cops say?"

"The cops don't know about them."

"Ah, I begin to see. But the cops are your best bet for tracing weapons."

"Are they? And will that flush the killer or chase him away?"

Frank became thoughtful. "You're going to catch the killer yourself?"

"Correction—I'm going to trace the killer. Art Nola can do the catching. That's what he's paid for."

"Are you out of your gourd?" said Frank. "Reporters don't solve crimes—they report the news. That's all they know how to do. You think these guns are a clue? Everybody owns guns around here."

"Not rocket launchers."

"Henspeter had a bazooka—?"

"Keep your voice down. Of course not. It's a LAW."

"Same difference," Frank said.

"And Enola Gay doesn't know why or how."

"He must've been serious about defending those trees, all right," Frank said.

"So are you going to interview Eco-nut High Command?"

"Henspeter didn't have any brother nuts, according to Enola Gay."

"Are you sure she's being straight with you, Eldon?"

"Yes," Eldon said firmly. "Absolutely. No question." And the voice in his head warned him, *You're getting in awfully deep with her.*

That's why you're doing what you're doing, Eldon reminded himself. *I can't just hang around Enola Gay and get laid. I've got to respect myself in the morning.*

"Respect is what it's all about," a reedy male voice said.

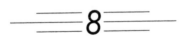

Eldon gave a guilty start. A dog barked. Eldon looked across the newsroom to see Cap'n Jasper at the front counter, his white ensemble topped off with a cheap yachtsman's cap. Bouncer sat on the counter before him. Paavo the Finn loomed at Jasper's side. Behind them, One-Square, Wheelie, and Beanpole formed a wary, defensive ring.

Jasper waved a forked stick. Eldon sighed and started to get up.

"I'll deal with him," Frank said. "You're on deadline."

As Frank started toward the counter, Fiske came out from behind the news desk, moving swiftly across the room like a hound after meat.

"That's a dowsing rod," Jimbo said. "Frank, get your notebook. Eldon, keep typing."

Eldon returned to his story but kept an eye on the scene at the counter. It was not difficult to follow events there. The ensuing drama was conducted at a volume suitable for a raucous bar.

FISKE: I'm James O. Fiske, the editor here.

JASPER: We wanta see Eldon.

PAAVO: Yeah. You're an atheist.

FISKE: You mean a Lutheran. Call me "Jimbo."

JASPER: What have we got to talk about?

ONE-SQUARE: You don't believe in the risen dog.

FISKE: Dee-de-dee! Is this is the famous little feller? [*ruffles BOUNCER'S fur*] OW! Bit my finger!

ONE-SQUARE: Bouncer doesn't like you.

FISKE: I put his picture on page one. That's a mighty snotty dog.

PAAVO: He's a miracle dog.

BOUNCER: [*barks and wags tail*]

JASPER: You gave our church that good publicity? Maybe we've misjudged you.

PAAVO: I was a Lutheran once. How's your finger?

FISKE: I think he broke the skin—

ONE-SQUARE: Naw, he didn't, ya big no-hair!

FRANK: You'll need rabies shots, Jimbo. In the stomach.

BEANPOLE: B-b-bouncer d-don't got r-r-rabies! [*bursts into tears*]

JASPER: Everyone calm down. I'll cure that finger through the laying-on of hands.

FRANK: You'd do that even with a Lutheran's finger?

JASPER: Everyone's welcome at the Church of the Rising Dog. [*He seizes FISKE'S index finger and clamps his eyes shut. JASPER'S lips move soundlessly as he prays with enormous concentration.*]

JIMBO [*puffs his pipe*]: Dee-de-dee. . . .

[*FRANK gets a camera. PAAVO, quick to seize a cue, produces his concertina and swings into "Rock of Ages." BOUNCER yaps and dances atop the counter on his hind legs.*]

That dog learns fast, thought Eldon as he typed "30" at the bottom of his story. He proofed the pages, tossed them into Fiske's copy basket, and went to the counter as Jasper's drama of faith built toward its climax.

Fiske beamed and smoked his pipe while Jasper prayed and Frank snapped away with the camera. The bustle of activity in the *Sun's* office died away as Paavo's music and Bouncer's dance claimed the attention of advertising salesmen, secretaries, typesetters. "They're ready for the miracle," said Paavo as he wielded his concertina.

Jasper released Jimbo's finger with a flourish. "Amen!" Paavo stopped playing.

"Well, dee-de-dee!" Fiske held his finger high. "Not a mark on 'er!" Scattered cheers and applause, perhaps sarcastic, came from the *Sun's* staff. Jaded by years of deadbeats, four-flushers, and crazies, the newspaper's employees returned to their work.

"Finally got your attention," Jasper said to Eldon.

"I was on deadline," Eldon said. "Jimbo, you're on deadline, too."

Fiske squinted at the clock. "Gad, look at the time! Frank—gimme a hand!" Fiske shot to the news desk and snatched up Eldon's murder story.

"The presses will roll in a minute," Eldon explained to Jasper.

"You gotta rush if you want to get that miracle picture in the paper," Jasper said.

"We don't put pictures of staff members in the paper," Eldon said.

Jasper gaped. Paavo made a gloomy, dangerous sound. One-Square, Wheelie, and Beanpole emitted cries and wheezes of distress.

"You wanted photographic proof," said Jasper. "Now you've got it."

"Healed your editor," said Wheelie in his hoarse whisper. "And him a Lutheran atheist."

"You think we told the dog to bite 'im?" One-Square said.

"I have a lunch appointment," Eldon said. "What've you got

here? A dowsing rod? The last thing we need to find on the South Coast is more water."

Jasper held the stick by its forks and flexed it, making the point bob. "It's not for water. It's to find the body."

Eldon wondered whether Jasper hoped to raise John Henspeter from the dead. Then the pressroom alarm bell sounded and the muffled, slowly escalating thump of the press vibrated through the floor. Eldon realized that with the day's edition not yet on the streets, Jasper might not know of Henspeter's demise.

I'll sock it to him and shut him up once and for all, he thought. "Which body?"

"The one in the landfill," said Jasper. "The Church of the Rising Dog supports our community. We want to help out the sheriff and save taxpayers' money."

"But not raise him up?"

"He's past the point, don't you think?" Jasper said.

"You saw his foot, the shape it's in," Paavo said.

"But a dowsing rod to find a body?" Eldon asked.

"In this climate, even a mummy's got to have taken on some water," Jasper said. "We'll look for the concentration, like."

"That's worth a story for sure," Paavo said.

Eldon knew by the vibration that the press had reached full speed. "Come with me for a minute, Jasper."

He beckoned Jasper around the counter and led him across the newsroom, into the vestibule separating the offices from the press-room, and beyond a heavy door into the pressroom itself.

The wind and enormous sound of the Goss Community press hit them. It was a roar that blurred the senses. Jasper clapped his hands over his ears. But Eldon stood drinking it in, feeling gooseflesh run over him in the cool wind.

The press consisted of eight big offset printing units lined up and locked together by a framework, four on either side of a folder unit. Each unit was about six feet high and six feet wide, and a twelve-foot-high maintenance scaffold something like a submarine's conning tower rose from the folder into the gloom of the high-ceilinged room. Huge, squat rolls of blank newsprint hung spinning in the framework as paper fed through the press in intricate zigzag webs. The webs picked up images as they sped from either end of the press into the folder. There, complex machinery slashed and creased the printed sheets into finished newspapers that streamed away on a conveyor belt.

Ink-smeared pressmen snatched early copies from the conveyor, checking ink density, alignment, clarity of photo reproduction, and other details. They pitched the earlies into fifty-gallon refuse drums and clambered over the thundering press, twisting knobs to adjust ink flow and roller pressure.

"You do this every day?" Jasper yelled with delight.

"Every day." Eldon guessed that the old man saw every copy of the *Sun* as a potential propaganda leaflet. Pity he can't afford to buy some ads, he thought dryly.

A busy pressman discarded a newspaper by their feet. Eldon picked it up and thrust it in Jasper's face: CONDO FOE SPIKED TO TREE.

Jasper's eyes bugged and his face grew pale. He snatched the paper, smearing the fresh ink. "Oh, no!" Jasper's voice was drowned in the noise of the press.

Eldon ushered Jasper back through the door, into the relative quiet of the vestibule. "He was killed last night," Eldon said.

Jasper scanned the story in dismay. " 'Mr. Henspeter seemed to be the only opponent. . . . Likely the project will proceed.' " His eyes glistened. "What's going to happen to us now?" Jasper turned and rushed back into the newsroom.

Eldon followed and found Fiske leading the three invalids and Paavo around the newsroom floor. Frank had vanished; presumably he had gone to lunch while the getting was good.

Wheelie held the dowsing rod's forks in his feeble, upturned hands while Paavo pushed his wheelchair across the carpet in Fiske's direction. Fiske dashed from spot to spot, pointing eagerly with a rolled-up magazine. "Try here!"

Paavo swiveled the wheelchair and rolled Wheelie along, leaving a line of muddy boot-tracks.

Jimbo watched the dowsing rod critically. "Not a twitch."

"You're not holdin' it right," One-Square told Wheelie.

"Sure I am," Wheelie whispered. "You think you know everything just 'cause you can walk."

Bouncer dozed beside Eldon's desk, muzzle on forepaws.

Eldon reflected that it was a scene well worthy of Fiske. The editor's body came to work each day at the *Sun,* toting its sack lunch, but his mind roved far afield. Fiske's pursuit of the elusive ideal of "the truth" had become so attenuated in the course of his long career that it now resembled astral travel. Eldon knew without asking that the rolled-up magazine in Fiske's hand must be the latest issue of *Sasquatch and UFO*. Its irregular arrival in the mail set Fiske's imagination soaring.

"Try over there," said Fiske, pointing between Eldon's feet.

"We're looking for the plate," Paavo said.

"The plate?" asked Eldon.

"The tectonic plate," said Fiske. "Those colliding plates way down below are lubricated by water. With dowsing rods, maybe we can trace the fault line where the plates come together."

"Why doesn't it point at the water fountain?" Eldon asked. "Or up at the sprinklers in the ceiling?"

"Never mind that!" Jasper cried. "John Henspeter's been murdered!"

Beanpole and One-Square rushed to Jasper's side while Wheelie squawked weakly from his wheelchair.

"Hell of a story, hey?" said Fiske.

"Spiked to a tree—I told ya we got enemies," One-Square announced in a voice rich with paranoid satisfaction. "I want a pistol. I'm askin' the sheriff for a carry permit."

"Me, too," Wheelie whispered.

One-Square snorted. "You'd do better to wire dynamite to that chair."

"You ain't so steady on the draw yourself," Wheelie said.

Beanpole burst into tears. "I d-d-don' w-w-wanna get spiked! Cap'n Jasper—wha-wha-what're we g-g-gonna do?"

Jasper whimpered and shifted nervously from foot to foot. His eyes darted. He pawed his chin with one hand. His other hand trembled, still clutching the newspaper.

Paavo stepped over and laid a comforting hand on Jasper's shoulder. The Finn took the newspaper, his eyes gleaming like lamps. "Just as well this happened."

"Why?" demanded Eldon.

Paavo threw the newspaper to the carpet. Deliberately, he kicked it aside and kneaded his misshapen knuckles. An ugly smile spread across Paavo's face.

"Because now there's going to be a damned good fight," he said.

Jasper steadied at the words. He stood no higher than Paavo's collarbone, and that only because of his peaked yachtsman's cap. Now Jasper straightened the cap and seemed to take on stature. His expression hardened. The blue of his wide eyes became the blue of steel. He seemed again to be captain of a South Coast tugboat with a raft of precious logs in tow.

" 'No more opponents'—that's wrong," Jasper said. "There's me and my congregation. They're not going to take away our church. They'll build those condos over my dead body."

So Paavo's the brains, not Jasper, Eldon thought. I should've realized Jasper didn't have anything left to think with after all those years swilling hooch.

"Like I said, I'm his Saint Peter," said Paavo, as if in confirmation. "Peter cut off ears with a sword. But I just tear 'em off with my hands. It's easy."

"Like the cap'n says—they'll build those condos over our dead bodies," said One-Square.

"Then you could resurrect yourselves," Eldon said.

Jasper held up a hand, now completely back in form. "We've got to find that body," Jasper said, "to keep the media's fickle attention and head off that damned county commissioner."

"Dee-de-dee." Fiske bobbed his head agreeably.

"Let's get out to the landfill. We've got work to do." Jasper turned and began a progress toward the front door, One-Square and Beanpole in trail.

"You want to talk to Detective Nola," Eldon called. "Tell him I sent you."

Jasper waved his cap in acknowledgment.

"Bouncer, c'mon," Paavo said.

Bouncer rose and trotted over. Paavo scooped the dog into Wheelie's lap and pushed the wheelchair after their comrades.

Eldon watched Paavo push Wheelie out the door and then stared down at the Finn's muddy footprints. Cold excitement stole over him. What had the footprint at the scene of Henspeter's murder looked like?

No. Impossible. But Paavo the Finn certainly had the strength and disposition to drive a pry bar through a man. And Paavo had been strangely composed at the revelation of Henspeter's murder.

I've got to get a look at the cast of that footprint, Eldon thought.

He took his camera from his desk drawer and snapped a series of exposures of one of the blurry cleat patterns on the carpet.

"What're you doing?" Fiske asked.

"Probably nothing." Eldon wound up the film roll and removed it from the camera.

"That's obvious. Good story walks in here and you're taking pictures of the carpet. Get out to the landfill and get me that story on dowsing."

"Aw, Jimbo, that's stupid."

"How can you say that?" Fiske unrolled the magazine. It was a new issue of *Sasquatch and UFO*, all right. "It was all right in your Henspeter feature."

"What d'you mean?"

"About his wolf eels," Fiske said. "Eels prove plate tectonics. Look at this article."

" 'Dowsing and Lost Continents.' "

"Right," Fiske said. "The reason that European eels swim so far to their ocean spawning grounds is that it wasn't quite so far when they started. Europe's moved, because of the plate tectonics. Now they have to swim all the way to the Sargasso Sea."

"That's what tradition gets you," Eldon said. "I'm going home for lunch."

"Not to Pop's?" asked Fiske, entirely too swiftly. "Dee-de-dee. Getting our protein at home now."

"I'm tired of chili. And I want to lose weight."

"You'll sweat off some weight at the landfill," Fiske said. "It's good and hot out there. Suppose the dowsers find that stiff?"

"This afternoon, Jimbo. They're not going to let Jasper and his friends tramp over the crime scene with a dowsing rod."

"That's a point. It'd be like that murder I covered in '58, when the old sheriff stepped in the brains at the murder scene and scrambled up the case. Hm . . . Jasper could stand outside the tape."

"I doubt if dowsing rods work at a slant," Eldon said. "He'd have to be right over the body to get a hit."

"We'd better be there when he does."

"I will—that's a promise. I'm going to go see the medical examiner after lunch. I'll check in at the landfill afterward."

"What's the M.E. got to do with it?"

"He can tell me about feet."

Eldon drove to his ridgetop home expecting to find Enola Gay wan with grief. She greeted Eldon at his door with a wet, open-mouthed kiss. She wore nothing but cowboy boots and her aviator glasses. "Lunch is ready."

"I'll say." Eldon slid his arms around her supple waist but Enola Gay slipped free, plucked Eldon's hat from his head, and put it on her own.

"Oh, don't start getting dressed," said Eldon.

"Okay, just the hat." Enola Gay crossed the living room, smiling over her shoulder. Eldon followed hungrily but was suddenly uneasy that his lucky hat rested on another's head.

A white tablecloth had been spread over the worn oak table in Eldon's kitchen. Two places were laid. At each was a bowl of steaming vegetable soup and a hunk of dark bread. Eldon's mouth watered at the sight and scent of the food. God, this was better that he'd ever imagined.

Enola Gay pulled out a chair for Eldon and stroked his neck as he sat down. Eldon caught her fingers and kissed them. Enola Gay went to the other place and sat down. She adjusted her glasses and put her elbows on the table and her chin on her hands. "So what have you found out?"

Eldon fumbled with his spoon. "Ah?"

"About John's murder. You've had all morning."

"Enola, I just got the murder story done."

"It's 'Enola Gay' at all times. 'Enola' sounds like an old maid from Indiana."

"Yes, ma'am. Enola Gay."

Steam from her soup bowl clouded Enola Gay's glasses. "I thought reporters worked fast. Aren't you drumming up clues, talking with police, grilling sources?"

"You'd be as good an editor as Fiske," said Eldon, enchanted by the sway of her breasts. "And you're prettier."

"I'm not going to stand for another loafer. John was a loafer."

"Am I going to enjoy this soup in my own house or what?"

"Sorry."

"Don't tell me how to do my business. All right?"

"All right."

"Actually, I do have a lead. A footprint."

"Whose?"

"I have to look into it. It's probably nothing."

"Who do you suspect?"

"Let it ride for now," Eldon said and took a mouthful of soup. "This is great! I don't want you, oh, running off and killing someone who might be innocent. Especially dressed like that."

Enola Gay smiled. It was a slow, sweet, calculating smile. She tugged at the brim of Eldon's fishing hat. Without that hat, he felt almost as naked as she.

"I don't think I'm capable of killing," said Enola Gay. "Even dressed like this."

"Give me my hat."

"Perhaps I'll hold onto your hat. As a guarantee of performance."

Eldon rounded the table and seized her. "What kind of performance?"

Enola Gay mumbled, "Eat your soup," as they kissed and toppled slowly to the floor. Enola Gay fell on top of Eldon and Eldon found himself expertly pinned, Enola Gay's strong thighs clamping his knees together and her hands pressing his shoulders to the floor.

"I talked to the medical examiner," Enola Gay said. "He didn't say anything about a footprint."

"He doesn't know about this footprint." Eldon tried to buck her off, though not too hard. "Why were you talking to Rosenak?"

"To find out when he'll release John's body for the funeral."

"There hasn't been an autopsy yet."

"That's what Dr. Rosenak said. The autopsy will be at one P.M. tomorrow. He was very kind. Offered his condolences."

"You're naked and planning a funeral."

"Someone's got to bury him, Eldon."

"His next of kin—"

"He didn't have any, I told you. So I said I was John's wife."

"You what?"

"His significant other, anyway. So they'll release the body to me. 'Wife' is how I want you to list me in the obituary."

"The hell I will. That's putting false information in the newspaper."

"I'm not going to let them toss John in a pauper's grave, no matter how sour things went between us."

108

"The editor won't allow it," Eldon said.

"Don't tell your editor. Rattle the killer's cage. Flush him from cover." Enola Gay pressed down, probed Eldon's mouth with her tongue.

Heat swept over Eldon's face as he returned the kiss, but a chilly feeling rushed into his gut. An inaccurate obituary and then what? Eldon managed to grab his hat and got a fishhook in his palm; he hissed.

Enola Gay pulled back. "What's wrong?"

"Everything. Get off me."

Enola Gay complied, looking worried. Eldon sat up and tried to pull the fishhook from his palm. Enola Gay clucked, gently took his hand, and worked at the hook.

"Ouch," Eldon said. "It's in deeper than I thought."

"Do you have needle-nose pliers?"

"In my fishing box. It's on the fly-tying bench in the front room."

Enola Gay got the pliers and returned to kneel beside him. "Now, tell me what's wrong."

"One should not be naked when one is racked with grief."

"I like going naked. I thought you'd like it, too." Enola Gay's lower lip quivered.

"I do like it," Eldon said. "You're the sexiest woman I've ever known. Just don't turn on the tears." He squirmed with distraction, his attention divided between the naked woman and the naked hook in his palm. What could he tell her? He didn't want to lose the girl or his job.

At last he said, "I ought to boot you out."

"All right—" Enola Gay's jaw set.

"But I'm not going to do that. It wouldn't solve anything. The only way now is to follow the story all the way through."

Enola Gay took Eldon's palm again. "Keep talking. And hold still." Expertly, she pinched the bend of the fishhook with the pliers and twisted the hook around and upward so that the barb broke through the skin. She snipped off the barb and backed the hook out of the little wound in Eldon's hand. "Got some iodine?"

"In the bathroom. But hold on a minute." Eldon pinched the meat of his palm to make it bleed, carefully mastering his feelings. "Shall I be frank?"

Enola Gay sat up. "Yes. Frank and earnest."

"You think this is a game."

"You're having fun so far, aren't you?"

"You think this is how you get things from men."

"Isn't it?" She grinned. "You gotta keep smiling."

"I'm going to cover the story whether you're dressed or not. Because covering the news is what I do. If I didn't feel that way, I'd have quit last year, when I almost got my head blown off."

"I see." Gravely.

"I am not playing reporter out here in the forest," Eldon said. "I'm serious about it. I'm not here just because of the fishing. Or you. You don't need to stick around or do anything for me. One way or the other, I'll get the story."

Enola Gay knelt silently, hands on her knees. Tears sparkled for a moment in her eyes.

"I'm staying," she said.

"Good." Eldon pulled Enola Gay to him again and kissed her. "Now make yourself useful."

She giggled and squirmed. "How?"

"That way later," Eldon said. "For now, tell me more about John."

"What do you want to know?"

"Just more about him. You say he didn't have any friends, but that can't really be true. Surely there was someone besides you who knew him as more than just a guy at work or a drinking acquaintance."

"Well, there's Ronnie and Joline Endo. I fixed Ronnie's bike engine."

"Right, I remember them. Where can I find them?"

"They'll be at the funeral. They'll talk to you if I tell 'em to."

"Good. Who else?"

"There's my father, I guess."

"Pumpkin Joe hated him," Eldon said. "He hates me, too. I'll have to get him in a friendly mood."

"What about that footprint?" asked Enola Gay.

"Did John have any friends who were, ah, Finnish?"

"Not that I know of. . . . Was it a Finnish footprint? With opposable toes?" Enola Gay snickered.

"Racist."

"Name's Hansen."

"That's not Finnish."

"Oh, it could be," Enola Gay said. "There are Swedish-speaking Finns. My name is Danish, however."

"Scandinavian promiscuity," Eldon said with relish.

They kissed until Enola Gay came up for breath. "Soup's getting cold."

"Let it."

"It's homemade. I brought the stock from home." Enola Gay looked furtively up at the table. "I made it for John." Suddenly tears glistened behind her glasses. Her face contorted. The tears rolled down her cheeks as she exploded into racking sobs and clutched Eldon in a bone-cracking grip.

Eldon was terrified. "It's all right. Just hang on now." He held her until her wailing subsided. Then he said, "Why don't you put on some clothes?"

Enola Gay pulled off her glasses and wiped her eyes. Eldon handed her a paper napkin from the table. "Feel better?"

She blew her nose and nodded. "You act like you knew that was coming."

"No. But I did think you were acting . . . pretty self-possessed."

"For someone whose ex was just murdered?" Enola Gay dabbed at her eyes and got up. "Eldon, that's life. You laugh or you crack."

"It's kind of that way with newspapermen, too."

"I'm going to get dressed."

"Okay." Eldon sat down at the table as Enola Gay went into the bedroom. His appetite was gone. Maybe it *was* the same way with newspapermen, but he didn't feel better. He dunked some bread in the now-lukewarm soup and forced himself to chew it.

Enola Gay returned, clad in a cowboy shirt and jeans with embroidered cuffs. She had a squeeze bottle of Bactine and a Band-Aid from Eldon's medicine cabinet.

"We used to wear jeans like that in my Berkeley days," Eldon said. "Back when I was married."

"Ah. I hope those are good memories. Give me your hand." Enola Gay squirted Bactine onto the cut in Eldon's palm and pressed the Band-Aid over it.

"This same misfortune saved my life once," Eldon said. "Except it happened to somebody else. He grabbed my hat and got a hook in his hand at just the right moment. That's why this is my lucky hat."

Enola Gay examined the fly. "A March Brown. You'll have to retie it. You must go after a lot of trout."

"Sure do." Eldon felt the pleasure he always felt when someone expressed interest in fishing. But then he flinched slightly, thinking, Bernice liked fishing, too, and look where that landed me. Here in Port Jerome.

"What's wrong?" Enola Gay asked.

"I was thinking about my ex-wife."

"Where is she?"

"In Australia, I think. I haven't heard from her in a long time. Just the notice that our divorce was final, back in '76."

Enola Gay sighed. "Eldon, I've got to go buy a coffin."

"It's a good thing you got dressed, then. Do you need any money? Any help?"

"No. It's okay. Really. And I think I want to do this alone. I'll be back later."

She kissed him and went out to her truck. Eldon watched from the doorway as she drove off. Just puts on her clothes and heads out to buy a coffin, he thought. As easily as she repaired my car.

Here atop the ridge, from his front door, he could see the shining bay, framed by birch trees at the edge of the lawn. Eldon stared at the fine view. It would be hot at the landfill. He longed for the cool spatter of rain on his face.

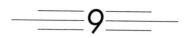

9

"Yeah, it's a human foot, all right," Dr. Rosenak told Eldon, pulling open a deep lower drawer of his cluttered desk. "Hell of a thing to find in a landfill. I'll show you."

Rosenak paused to straighten the checked bow tie that he wore today with a pink striped shirt and suspenders. He reminded Eldon of a large, lively birthday present. Then Rosenak lifted a lumpy, foot-sized object wrapped in butcher's paper from the desk drawer. Eldon watched with a prickly feeling as the medical examiner carefully placed the parcel atop the files and medical books on the desk.

Rosenak's eyes twinkled with the eagerness of a man happy in his craft. He unbuttoned his shirt cuffs and turned them back, flexed his fingers. "Since this is between friends, I'll dispense with the rubber gloves. I just washed my hands."

Eldon stared. Wouldn't the county buy Rosenak a refrigerator? Why didn't the package smell?

Rosenak hummed as he scissored the tape holding the bundle together. Eldon imagined him at work during an autopsy. He leaned forward a little as Rosenak unfolded the layers of paper, and now the smell hit him—the rich scents of mayonnaise, Dijon mustard, and fresh bread.

In the center of the paper was an enormous Dagwood sandwich, a regal ziggurat of thick-sliced vegetables and sourdough bread. Rosenak gestured like a genie revealing treasure to Aladdin. "Take half, why don't you? I was just going to dig in."

Eldon sighed and nodded. Maybe solid food would settle his worried stomach.

Rosenak tore a sheet of yellow paper from a legal pad. He plopped half the sandwich onto it and handed it to Eldon. "Entirely vegetarian," he said proudly as Eldon chomped down. "I've lived off these at the office for years. My wife bakes the bread."

"Good stuff. Avocados."

"And good Bandon cheddar and fresh lettuce from our greenhouse," Rosenak said. "And how about those onions? I grew those, too. I got the mushrooms at the murder scene the other day."

Eldon chewed more slowly. "You said that one was poisonous—"

"Not the ones in the sandwich! *Galerina autumnalis* is over there on the shelf. I found these for the sandwich after you left. *Boletus mirabilis,* very common. Not the most exciting species, but eatable and good. That's a good mushroom area up there." Rosenak gave a happy wink. "I like to collect mushrooms at murder scenes."

"I thought you stuck to supermarkets."

"Usually do. But there's something about wild mushrooms springing up in the forest that still whets my appetite. The hunter's instinct. And at a crime scene—well, I couldn't resist." Rosenak took a big bite of the Dagwood. His beard waggled as he chewed and swallowed. "It was a rare pleasure. You'd be surprised how many people are murdered indoors."

Eldon scanned Rosenak's tiny office as they ate. A diploma from Yale University Medical School and a certificate of membership in the Oregon Mycological Society shared the wall with a three-barred Eastern Orthodox cross. Eldon turned his attention to the bookshelf. He always examined personal libraries, possessing an extensive one himself. Eldon believed that a person's worth could be plumbed by the books they owned.

The titles suggested that for all his twinkly exterior Rosenak was dedicated to his job. *The Pathology of Homicide,* by Adelson. *Anatomy of the Human Body,* by Lockhart, Hamilton, and Fyfe. *Medicolegal Investigation of Death,* by Spitz and Fisher. A handsome edition of *Gray's Anatomy* bound in maroon leather with black trim. And several big picture books devoted to mushrooms.

"There are wonderful pictures in those mushroom books," Rosenak said, acknowledging Eldon's interest. "They're beautiful books. And they're mostly wrong."

"Why?"

"Until about ten years ago, much of what we knew about mushrooms was based on European folklore. The books still haven't caught up. There are mutations. A mushroom that looks safe can be just different enough to be deadly. There's no way to know every tiny variation. The rule of thumb is that there's no rule of thumb. In the shadowy world of mycology, all bets are hedged."

Eldon looked at his half-eaten portion of sandwich. "You're sure of these?"

"These, absolutely. Eat up. Then we'll do business." Rosenak shook his head. "They're fun to pick and study, but if you're going to put one inside you, take along an expert. Better yet, pick a second mushroom so we can identify it when they bring you in. Even experts make fatal mistakes."

"Sure." Eldon chewed, wondering about the symptoms of mushroom poisoning.

Rosenak wiped his hands on a tissue from a box on the desk and pulled a mushroom book from the shelf. He opened it, displaying page after page of vivid color plates. "Really beautiful organisms.

I'd much rather look at mushrooms than dead people. Dead people look like hell."

"Henspeter sure looked like hell."

"His autopsy's tomorrow at one. Want to come?"

"Uh, no. Thanks."

Rosenak appraised Eldon. "Now I *know* you're a professional. Never attend an autopsy unless you need to, and you don't need to. You're smart."

"Thanks."

"I'm glad you came around, though," Rosenak said. "I was worried I did something to offend you, up on the hill. You took off kind of fast."

"No, no. Deadline, you know. Now, about the foot—"

"Finished? Come on to the lab." Rosenak rose and led the way down the hall, through a door marked NO ADMITTANCE.

They stepped into a cool, white-tiled room that smelled of formaldehyde. In the center was a stainless-steel autopsy table. To Eldon's relief there was no corpse; Henspeter's body must be in a cooler somewhere. There was a big surgical light over the table and a microphone hanging from a ceiling boom. On the floor was a foot pedal with a cable running to a wall outlet. Eldon knew it was the switch for the microphone and for a telephone speaker box in the wall; Rosenak could dictate notes or talk on the telephone while his hands were full.

Counters lined the walls, laden with racked bottles, loose-leaf binders, and medical paraphernalia. They were scrubbed and modern. But the sight of them plus the formaldehyde smell irresistibly called to mind Dr. Frankenstein's laboratory. A small refrigerator stood in a corner. Eldon read the hand-lettered sign on the door: DON'T PUT FOOD IN HERE.

Rosenak opened the refrigerator. It was empty except for something on a stainless-steel tray covered with a white cloth. The doctor brought the tray to the autopsy table and whipped off the cloth with a flourish, unveiling the mummified foot. A morgue tag was tied to the big toe. "As I said, it's a human foot."

Eldon wrinkled his nose. But the foot didn't seem so bad, displayed as a scientific specimen. "There was doubt?"

"Nah. No other animal has a foot like ours," said Rosenak.

"Hands are more difficult. I had a case where they brought me a chimpanzee hand, as we finally decided. We had to send it up to the primate center in Portland to be positive."

"A chimp on the South Coast?"

"Presumably it escaped from a circus. We never did pin it down. They don't keep very good records on chimps." Rosenak shrugged. "They don't keep very good records on people, either."

"So we can't know whose foot this was?"

"I need more than a foot to make an identification. I'd really like a mandible, a lower jaw. Teeth will last."

"And there'd be dental records."

"Maybe there'd be dental records," Rosenak said. "I'm not giving up on trying to trace the owner, however. We're looking for things that make this foot unique."

He went to a file cabinet and plucked out a large manila envelope. He behaved with the same ceremony with which he had unveiled the Dagwood and then the orphaned foot. Clearly, Rosenak was a man who enjoyed revealing things. "X-ray is the way to do it." Rosenak slid a big gray sheet of X-ray film from the envelope and slipped its top edge under the clips of a view box on the wall.

Eldon stepped closer as Rosenak flipped the box on. There were two images on the film. One was the distinctive profile of a human foot; ankle bones, arch, and metatarsals were clear to see. The other image puzzled Eldon for a moment. "This view is looking up at the sole of the foot."

"Very good." Rosenak pointed with a ballpoint pen. "Now check out the metatarsophalangeal joint of the fourth toe. For you tourists, that's the third joint back. What do you see there?"

"The oval shadow?"

"Yeah. That's a sesamoid bone. Vestigial. They're not common, but they do occur."

"Making this foot unique."

"All feet are unique, Eldon. Your feet and my feet. As every mushroom is unique." Rosenak made a tune of the words and danced a brief jig, his belly romping as he marked time with the pen.

"But there's something else that makes this foot even more unique." Rosenak stopped dancing and spoke once more in normal tones, but his excitement was plain. He thrust the pen at the profile image. "That's part of a severe fibular fracture. A nonunion fracture, as we say in the trade."

Rosenak returned to the autopsy table and indicated a point on the foot's ankle with his pen. Eldon looked closely, saw a dirty ivory bone fragment sticking out of the outer side of the ankle. It was about one-quarter inch long and attached by tissue that looked like a wrinkled scrap of masking tape.

"That is a distal fragment of the fibula, the thinner of the two bones in the lower leg."

"What's the brown stuff?"

"Dried ligament," Rosenak said. "The fibula is a bone that doesn't necessarily heal well. It's a pain in the ass to treat. This break was fairly well along to being healed. But it still would make it much easier to disarticulate the whole joint."

"Easier for Bouncer to pull the foot off the rest of the mummy."

"Yeah. But more likely it was pulled off by some other animal in the past—a cat or a raccoon, and the dog picked it up. Otherwise, they'd have found the rest of the body right away."

"If an animal didn't bring it to the landfill from somewhere else."

"That would have been quite a distance. Let's assume not. We won't find all of it if animals have been at it."

Eldon put his elbows on the autopsy table and considered the foot. "How long's it been in the landfill?"

"Spitz and Fisher say mummification's possible after fifteen or twenty years."

"Even in this climate?"

"The corpse would have to be protected from the weather."

"We assume it's buried. How would it get dried out?"

"Things decay in a landfill," Rosenak said. "When they decay, they generate heat. Heat would keep the body dry—if there's something to take the moisture away. If the moisture didn't go away, it would just cook."

"Nineteen sixty or sixty-five," Eldon said. "Recall any disappearances then?"

"I was in Chicago."

"No way to tell if it's foul play, I suppose?"

"Not with what we've got here," Rosenak said. "But what else would it be? She was just getting over a serious injury to her foot. She wouldn't be out taking a walk, wandering in a landfill."

Eldon rose off his elbows. " 'She?' "

Rosenak tugged merrily at the ends of his bow tie. "Let's go back to the office and I'll give you my diagnosis."

The doctor tossed the cloth back over the foot and returned the tray to the refrigerator. He paused to wash his hands, then snatched the X ray and whirled through the laboratory door like a quick-change artist making a fast exit. Eldon hurried after him.

Behind his desk once more, tapping his fingers on the arms of his worn swivel chair, Rosenak said: "The following is an educated guess. The foot belonged to a woman about twenty-five years old. Murdered under circumstances unknown."

"We're on the record here?" Eldon asked.

"Sure, put it in the paper. Maybe someone will remember her."

"Tell me more."

"The gender is just an old M.E.'s hunch, based on the size of the foot. The bones are rather light, and it would wear a seven-medium woman's shoe size. I think it belonged to a rather small person."

"But not a child."

"Not a child. Sesamoid bones don't develop until after adolescence. On the other hand, the foot's quite desiccated. Maybe it just shrank."

"Or belonged to a shrimpy male. What do you need to be sure?"

"Gimme hip bones. You can tell with a skull, too, though that's less reliable." Rosenak rattled the X ray that lay on his desk. "I'm more confident about the age."

"How so?"

"That sesamoid bone. They develop in the tendons after the teenage years. The victim was at least twenty." Rosenak's expression of pleasure intensified. "Probably twenty-five."

Eldon realized that the doctor was waiting for him to ask the next question. "Why twenty-five?"

"Sesamoid bones develop from use of the hands or feet, and that takes time. They can get painful and require surgery, but they're usually not a problem in a young person. No evidence of surgery here."

"But what's 'young'?"

"You're only as young as you feel, Eldon. How old are you?"

"Thirty-three."

"You could be full of sesamoid bones waiting to cause you agony. Say she was thirty years old and split the difference. Twenty-five."

Eldon frowned. He worried enough about his teeth. Now he had to worry about his skeleton, too. It could betray him in the same way as cars and women did. "But if the sesamoid bone didn't bother her, there'd be no records—"

"Of course there are records! That nonunion fracture had to have been X-rayed before. The sesamoid bone just gives us another point of comparison."

"Yes, you're right. . . . But where are the records?"

Rosenak raised a hand to make his crowning revelation. "That is a very peculiar fracture. A general practitioner isn't likely to have handled it. I know I wouldn't fool with it. The G.P. would've sent her to an orthopedic surgeon."

"Who would that be?"

"There isn't one around here. The closest one would be in Coos Bay. We'll have to find the right orthopedist. If he's in this state. If he's still alive."

"What about footprints? Aren't they as good as fingerprints?"

"I don't know anyone who takes that seriously, much less does it," Rosenak said. "The practice of footprinting newborns was dropped. It was technically useless and misleading." The doctor shook his head. "They say that in a few years, they'll be able to do amazing things with computers, checking records. But even then, there won't be any science-fiction solutions."

"No chance that pertinent records might turn up?"

Rosenak shrugged. "Records turn up fortuitously all the time. But you can't count on it."

"And there's no one in your 'missing' files who might conceivably fit this situation."

"Naw. I only became M.E. in '73."

"Who was M.E. before you?"

"A doctor who moved to Vermont. He was M.E. from 1971 to 1973."

"Still not early enough. Before him?"

"Wasn't one. There was a county coroner. Oregon scrapped the coroner system in '71 and came into the twentieth century. There wasn't any physician before then—it was a local undertaker, and he's dead."

"His records?"

"Don't dignify them with that term. They're long since destroyed, anyway, except for summaries. Nothing in the summaries fits this. I checked. There aren't any unexplained disappearances around here in that time frame. And none at all that fit this case."

"None that fits your theory, you mean."

"This foot may never be connected to anyone. But sometimes this job is more like an art than a science. Like mycology."

Eldon returned to the *Sun* and went to the big closet jammed with disorderly shelves of telephone directories. New and old, they covered most of Oregon and much of Washington and Idaho. There were odds and ends of directories from elsewhere, as well, brought back over the years by *Sun* employees as trophies of enviable vacations. Eldon wasn't sure why a vacation in Salt Lake City or Minot, North Dakota, would be enviable; but perspectives mutated after a few years in Port Jerome, and one never knew which directory might prove useful. The directory that caused him to burn with hatred was the one from Jamaica. Marsha had brought it back two years ago. She still told swooning tales of Rasta men.

Eldon spitefully doodled a stick clown on the Jamaican directory's cover and chucked it aside. He wanted the directory for Coos Bay. When he found it, he saw that it was quite new. He opened the Yellow Pages, seeking "Physicians—Orthopedic." There were a half-dozen listings under the category. Eldon wrote the names and telephone numbers in his notebook and went into the newsroom to make calls.

To his relief, Fiske was not around. "He went home for lunch," explained Frank, who was seated at the news desk, sorting wire copy. "He said the desk was shaking too much. Said he couldn't digest his food."

"He's got plate tectonics on the brain."

"He said you went to the landfill."

"To the M.E.'s office. I'm going to make some calls about the foot. The M.E. thinks it's a woman's foot."

"Well, that's something. I checked out the state gun regs for you. Basically, Oregon doesn't restrict firearms."

"Not even machine guns?" Eldon asked. "Nothing?"

"And betray the traditions of our pioneer forefathers?" Frank asked. "You just need federal permits for automatic weapons. A lot of local jurisdictions in Oregon require concealed-weapon permits. And in a lot of places you can't carry a loaded firearm inside the city limits. That's about it. No registration requirement."

"Crap—there's no paper trail, then. You don't think Henspeter had a federal permit for a LAW, do you?"

"No, but it doesn't hurt to ask," Frank said. "You might find out from the sheriff if he had a permit to carry concealed."

"That's just what I don't want to do. I don't want them to know about those guns."

"Why not?"

Eldon opened his mouth, then closed it. Finally, he said, "I've just got a hunch."

"What kind of hunch?"

Eldon was silent.

Frank continued, "I'm all for your getting laid, but you're letting the little head do the thinking for the big head."

Eldon's ears burned. You should talk, he started to say, then thought of a better squelch. He pulled out the roll of film he had shot of Paavo's footprints. "I'm going to soup this. Then we'll talk about which head's doing the thinking."

"And that is—?"

"Maybe it's the footprints of Henspeter's killer."

Eldon went into the darkroom and closed the sliding door before Frank could reply. He turned out the lights and wound the film into the developing canister while he brooded about Enola Gay.

He closed the canister lid and switched on the light, poured in developer, set the windup timer and began gently agitating the can. Suppose Paavo's footprint looks like the footprint at Henspeter's murder, Eldon thought. What have I got? Circumstantial evidence. He changed chemicals. That means I have to connect Paavo and Henspeter.

Finally the timer chimed. Eldon yanked the negatives from the rinse and examined the strip. Good, clear exposures. He went back out into the newsroom, trailing the negatives from one hand to let them dry.

"Well?" Frank asked, irritatingly at ease.

"Footprints, all right."

"Whose?"

"Paavo the Finn's."

Frank exploded with laughter. His glasses nearly flew off his face. At last he stopped for breath. "Talk about a little head—"

"There was a footprint at the Henspeter murder scene. The cops took a cast of it. Maybe Paavo's—I flashed on that when Paavo was in here today. He left muddy footprints on the carpet."

"Yeah. I swept them up to mollify Fiske. Sorry."

"You know Paavo's disposition. And you should've seen him in here with Jasper. He's the brains behind this Rising Dog Church—"

"That doesn't take any brains! Why on earth would Paavo kill John Henspeter?"

"To get control of the church, somehow," Eldon said.

"That 'church' is all in their heads."

"It still makes sense. And Paavo's the only person strong enough that I know of to have run that pry bar through Henspeter—"

"Premeditation is not the style around here. It's sure not Paavo's style. Smash and crash, that's him. Anyway, he's turned loving Christian."

"He said he'd tear ears off for his church," Eldon said. "Paavo wanted to make an alliance with Henspeter."

"So why kill him?"

"Paavo goes to see Henspeter. He wants Henspeter to use his ecology campaign to help the Church of the Rising Dog. The proposal isn't pure enough for Henspeter. Paavo's offended. They argue—"

"Let's see those footprints." Frank inspected the negatives through a plastic viewing lens. "You better hope the shoe sizes match."

"That's a good thought."

"Yeah. Ask Paavo his shoe size."

"You'd be surprised what people will tell a reporter." A thought blossomed in Eldon's mind. "The guns. They argued about the guns. Paavo knew about the guns."

"The guns? Say, now . . ."

"It's worth looking into. What if some of the guns have federal licenses in Paavo's name?"

"Then you'd have something," Frank said. "Get the serial numbers and I'll try and check 'em for you. What's Paavo's last name?"

"Wikkula. And I'll get his shoe size," Eldon said. He went to his desk and opened his notebook to the names and phone numbers of the orthopedists.

Eldon began calling. The calls to Coos Bay were long-distance, and he carefully listed them on a card, because the newspaper would claim them as a business expense at tax time. Shortly, Eldon knew the money had not been well spent. None of the orthopedists had been in practice on the South Coast earlier than 1970. That was the first thing he asked the receptionists; it was unnecessary to go further.

"Dead end," he told Frank. "Nothing to do for now but write the latest foot story and then head out to the landfill."

Batting out the Rosenak interview improved his mood somewhat. When Eldon left the office, he saw clouds gathering in the sky. There was a sharp smell in the air. It was going to rain. Suddenly things seemed markedly better. He sped out of town and down the highway to the landfill.

A sheriff's patrol car blocked the road at the trailer park. There Jasper's raggle-taggle band confronted a sheriff's deputy who looked like a beet with a handlebar mustache. Jasper and Paavo were arguing with the deputy. Jasper clutched Bouncer while the three acolytes wandered uncertainly back and forth in the road. Paavo looked menacing—swollen with anger until he seemed even larger than he was. The deputy, whom Eldon knew slightly, was unintimidated. "No admittance beyond this point," he told the zealots as Eldon drove up.

It was time to unleash the power of the press. "Hi, Bobby," Eldon said. "Can I go through? I'm supposed to talk with Art Nola."

"Hi, Eldon. Okay, he's up at the crime scene. Stay this side of the tape." The deputy waved Eldon through.

Eldon beamed and eased the van past the patrol car. It was too much for One-Square, who snatched the dowsing wand from Wheelie's lap and jabbed the deputy in the ass. The deputy snatched the dowsing rod as Eldon left the brouhaha behind.

The scene at the landfill was much the same as on the first day. Down the road, work was progressing at the condo site; Eldon heard the whine of power tools and the snarl of a chain saw. Off behind the houses another tree came down. He parked and climbed up the slope to the landfill, to see Art Nola knee-deep in a broad pit, peering intently into a sifting tray.

Eldon stopped at the yellow tape and called, "Find the rest of her yet?"

" 'Her'?" Nola looked up. "News travels fast."

"I've been talking with the M.E."

"Be surprised if you hadn't." Nola shook the sifting tray, and dirt trickled through the screen.

"Got something there? Teeth, perhaps?"

"Dream on. But I did find something." Eldon pulled out his notebook. Nola produced a plastic bag.

"That plate you found," Eldon said with a sigh.

"Yessiree," Nola said happily. "Properly bagged and cataloged. Crime scene and all that, I always follow procedures. But I can't wait until I get it out of the bag. That's Royal Vienna."

"What's in the tray?"

"Parts of a ballpoint pen. *They* might be relevant."

"You mean someone *is* buried there?"

"Not that we've found. But a pen is the sort of thing that might be in someone's pocket. Not so with a china dish, obviously. That's for me."

"What about other stuff?"

"Miscellaneous junk, though we do keep a list of what we find. Just now we've hit a vein of old newspapers."

"It's the tomb of an ancient editor," Eldon said. "The papers provide him with copy to proofread in the afterlife. How're you doing on the Henspeter case? Anything jell?"

"No. I'm stretched thin, with this case and that one."

"Surely, Henspeter is more important."

"Let's just say that word from On High is that this case is equally important."

Oh, ho—the condo land-use ruckus, Eldon thought. "Listen, what became of the cast of that foot—the one from the murder scene?"

"No comment."

"This is not for print."

"It's a common brand of logger boot," Nola said. "I've got a pair myself. Worthless as a clue without something to compare it to."

"What's the shoe size?"

Nola shook his head. "It's pretty big."

"I thought so. I'd like to know the size."

"What do you mean, 'I thought so'?"

"It just looked that way to me up there on the hill."

"I see." Nola's eyes locked on Eldon's like twin radar arrays. "I'll let you know." He looked like a fox spotting chickens.

"Did Henspeter have a criminal record?" Eldon asked.

"Not that we're aware of," Art said.

"What about Enola Gay?" Eldon asked on impulse.

"That's not the sort of question I'd usually answer. But she's clean, Eldon. Take it from me."

Eldon felt a rush of relief. In gratitude, he almost told Nola about the guns, then realized that the scrap of information was bait. Did Art already know about the guns?

But what about Paavo and the footprint? Eldon gazed at the pit. The sky suddenly darkened as rain clouds rushed across the sun. As the first drops hit Eldon's face, it came to him: The two murders were connected—the woman in the landfill and John Henspeter.

10

Eldon sneezed. The sneeze raised clouds of dust and he sneezed again. And again. He gasped for air as the dust settled on moldering volumes of the *South Coast Sun.*

The huge, badly cared for books lined the walls of the storage room. The collection began in the 1870s, with the *Sun*'s forebears, the *Port Jerome Times* and the rival *South Coast Chronicle.* These earliest volumes were bound in rotting maroon leather. The years beginning with 1906 were those of the *Times-Chronicle,* bound in what once had been rich blue cloth, now torn and faded to gray.

Eldon wiped his nose and mustache with the back of his hand and turned another brittle page in the volume in his lap. April 1961.

It was one of the latest generation, stamped *The South Coast Sun* and bound in an ugly shade of green cloth that was only growing more putrescent with time.

The Bay of Pigs. John F. Kennedy. Yuri Gagarin orbits Earth.

Eldon was tempted to linger over Gagarin's yellowing photo and the columns of faded text about the world's first spaceman. But instead he scanned the page for local stories about disappearances, murders, or similar incidents that might conceivably relate to the foot in the landfill. The stories in these dusty volumes also had once been filed in the *Sun*'s library; but those clippings were gone, purged years before to make room for newer ones. Eldon was searching the seventy-two monthly volumes covering 1960 through 1965; he could always look further. He had paged through sixteen volumes so far, grimly faithful to chronological order. Nothing. Eldon looked around the windowless room and sighed, then turned the page. More about Yuri. You'll be dead by 1968 but Castro will stick around, Eldon thought, feeling like a weary visitor from the future.

Despite his resolve, he began reading the theater ads—*Posse from Hell,* starring Audie Murphy. *Stranglers of Bombay.* A horror double bill—*The Man Who Could Cheat Death* and *13 Ghosts,* the latter filmed in something called Illusion-O. Eldon shook his head. Theater admission prices had risen dramatically since 1961; Port Jerome's cultural standards had not.

"Dee-de-dee! Read all about it!"

A copy of the *Sun*'s latest edition sailed through the air and landed on the page with a smack and an explosion of dust. Coughing, Eldon looked up to see Jimbo Fiske swagger through the door.

"I can still hit the bull's-eye," Fiske said. "Started as paperboy and worked my way up. Not like you kids."

Eldon picked up the paper. His story describing Rosenak's theory about the origin of the mummified foot screamed across the top of the page. Frank's story about the South Coast's creeping tectonic plates was on the lower half of the page—"below the fold," in newspaper jargon.

"An edition for the ages," Eldon said.

"An embarrassment of riches," Fiske said, "and you're my major embarrassment, Eldon, if you get my meaning."

"Not bad for a guy who's slacking off, eh?"

"You had to come up with this scoop today, of all days. I wanted to run Frank's story above the fold, but your story bumped it down. Well, that's the newspaper business."

"Jimbo, you're an ungrateful old bastard."

"Dee-de-dee," Fiske replied. " 'What did you do for me tomorrow?' That's the editor's motto."

"I'm trying to find something in these old editions that might relate to an appropriate disappearance."

"But what does Howell have to say about tectonic plates?"

"I'll find out Sunday," Eldon said.

"Sunday?"

"I'm going to a party at Howell's house. He's going to unveil a model of his condo development. It's perfect for the profile. I'll interview him there."

"The man in his world. I like it." Fiske peered into Eldon's open volume. *"13 Ghosts*—I remember that movie."

"So what was Illusion-O?"

"They gave you a plastic filter that was half red and half blue. You had to watch the movie through the blue side to see the ghosts."

"What?"

"If you watched through the red half of the filter, you couldn't see the ghosts. The red was for people who were too scared to look at them."

"Oh. And what happened if you didn't use either filter?"

"You just saw the ghosts faintly in red. Dee-de-dee, that was some show! Reminds me of the time that—"

"What was your point?"

"The point is that Sunday's a long time to wait," Fiske said. "Tectonic plates start rocking and rolling, that's the end of the South Coast real-estate boom. Maybe the end of the whole South Coast."

"There's no real-estate boom."

"I'll bet Howell would like there to be," Fiske said. "Before you go to that party, you want to find out just how much of the county he owns."

"I hadn't thought about that," Eldon said.

"You should watch *13 Ghosts,*" Fiske said. "Teach you something about covering politics."

With or without the filter? Eldon wanted to ask. But he let Jimbo wander from the room.

Just above the movie ad was a news brief reporting the opening of the South Coast Pioneer Clinic by Dr. Clifford Smith. An orthopedist. The address was on the nearby street where Eldon's dentist had her office, but neither the name of the old clinic or the doctor's name sounded familiar to Eldon. Long gone. He jotted the name and address down. And sneezed again. That's enough dust for today, he decided and went back to the newsroom.

Marsha sat at her desk looking smug, her hands folded in her lap. She gave a malevolent smile as Eldon beat the dust from his sleeves with his hat. "Well? Did you find anything?"

"No."

"I did."

"You what?"

Marsha held up a sheet of paper with a yellowed news clipping pasted to it. "I don't know why you roll around in that dirty storeroom when everything you want is on file."

"Where'd you get that clip? Why're you horning in on my story?"

"Jimbo said to help you out—"

Eldon snatched the clipping. " 'Congregation Quits in Political Feud.' This is from the 1950s. Those clips were trashed years ago—"

"They tried to throw them out when I first came to work here, Eldon. But I rescued most of them and took them home. You never can tell when you might need them."

"All right. Thanks." Eldon examined the clipping, hiding his chagrin and then his pleasure. The congregation in question was none other than the Fearless Faith Lutheran Church, in those days a going concern. The story reported that the congregation's board of directors had voted to disband the church and liquidate its assets because of an irreparable political rift among the worshipers. The nature of the quarrel was not explained. Probably it had been described in earlier stories.

The next paragraph gave the names of the church's directors. Several of the names were Finnish. They meant nothing to Eldon. But one of the directors was Ellis Weems, the late county commissioner, and another was Joe Nedlee.

"I assume that's Pumpkin Joe," Marsha said. "The age is about right."

"You know, Marsha, there is something to be said for your reverence for the past."

"Thank you, Eldon."

"Are there any other clippings about this? Like what they were fighting about?"

"That was the only story I could find," Marsha said, a little sadly. "I didn't save them all."

"I can find them in the bound volumes if I need them," Eldon said. "Nedlee told me he voted to rezone the property for development, but he never mentioned he'd been connected with the church. I smell a conflict of interest."

"State law doesn't bar him from voting on a matter if he has a conflict," Marsha said. "All he has to do is declare the conflict at the time of the vote."

"I know that."

"Did he do that?"

"I don't know. It may not have been illegal, but it was mighty cozy."

"It's an interesting thing to omit. What now?"

"See if you can find any stories in those old files about a Dr. Clifford Smith. Orthopedist. Opened the South Coast Pioneer Clinic in April '61. I want to know what happened to him."

"Was he connected with the church?"

"No, but he might have medical records pertaining to the foot. If there's anything about him at all, it's probably filed under business stories. Or the obits."

"Or maybe under medicine." Marsha jotted the name in her notebook and rose, shouldering her purse. "This is interesting. I like piecing things together."

Eldon watched as Marsha headed out the front door with a businesslike stride. She has nice long legs, Eldon reflected and suppressed that line of thought with a shudder. What pound of flesh would Marsha eventually extract from him for these favors?

It's useful she's such a snoop, he thought, and decided to call another good snoop—Loretta Starbuck, Nekaemas County assessor. He dialed the assessor's office at the county courthouse in Preacher's Hole. Loretta's trademark hearty laugh battered Eldon's ears when she heard his voice. "Eldon, I've been thinking about you! There are stirrings in my crystal ball."

"Good ones, I hope." Eldon visualized Loretta sitting like a chubby queen bee among her ledgers and property records, a crystal ball on her desk, her spectacles gleaming and her fingers adorned with rings.

"Can't tell until we peer more deeply, babes," Loretta said "I loved your stories about the foot. And man, that tree-hugger's murder was *ugly."*

"There might be more stories, if you can help me out."

"I'm always ready for that." Loretta laughed again.

"I need some ownership history on the church land down by Schumacher's Landfill. And on the condo site down there, too."

"The one Keith Howell is developing."

"That's it. Sounds like you know it."

"Sure do. I've always got an eye out for rising assessed values, Eldon. That's the law. What're you after?"

"I'm not sure yet. An ownership tussle."

"How far back are we talking?"

"The fifties. The church was the Fearless Faith Lutheran Church. And I need to know who owns some old-growth cedar up on the hill above the condo site."

"Got tax-lot numbers?"

"No—"

"I'll check my maps. An owner's name?"

"Try Ellis Weems for the condo site and the church property. I don't know about the cedar. Weems is dead."

"Don't hang up." There was a thump as Loretta put down the receiver. Eldon heard her voice in the background giving orders. Then she came back on the phone. "I'll tell your fortune while my staff earns its keep. I don't tell too many fortunes over the phone, you know."

Eldon chuckled. Loretta's fortune-telling act was famed at school benefit carnivals and the county fair. "You ought to go professional," he said.

"Then it wouldn't be fun," Loretta replied. "But my, my! The crystal ball says *you're* having fun! I see a lady in your life. Is that right?"

"You're right." Eldon was pleased.

"Anyone I know?"

"Ah, not really."

"Is she pretty? Is she nice? Of course she is. I can see that in my crystal ball. But there's something else, too." Loretta's voice dropped. "I see danger."

"Too much party?"

"You're going to a party, all right—and there will be danger," Loretta said. "You gotta watch your step."

"Well—I won't drink too much."

"No, I mean it, Eldon. I see something dangerous. Something to do with the lady."

"Like what?"

"It's not clear. Something about mushrooms—"

"Mushrooms? Sure you're not seeing Doc Rosenak in that crystal ball?"

"The M.E.? I'd hardly mistake him for a beautiful woman. Your lady wears glasses, doesn't she? But enough of this superstitious nonsense. One of my elves respectfully approaches. She hands me a hoary file. And the winnah is . . . Ellis Weems, an ancient county commissioner."

"The late Ellis Weems. That confirms what I already know."

"Funny about that 'late' part," Loretta said. "There's a bunch of stuff stuck in this file about probating the estate."

"Is that usual?"

"No, this sort of stuff is filed with the county clerk. But every now and then we get copies. Somebody decided the tax-lot file was the place to stick it; I must lash my elves. But let's see . . ." Eldon heard pages rustling. "There's a lot of transferring of title back and forth between Weems and the church—obvious maneuvers to avoid taxes. Anyway, Weems wound up with the property—and he's dead. In effect."

"In effect?"

"That's what's interesting—Weems was declared dead in 1967. He'd disappeared ten years before. The property went to Scott Weems, who subsequently died—"

"That must be the cousin."

"—and Keith Howell bought the property in '71."

"Ellis Weems disappeared how?"

"Vanished. Evaporated. I was in high school at the time, but I remember that he disappeared after he was recalled from the county board. There was talk that he ran off with a woman, now that I think about it."

"Why was he recalled?"

"Beats me. I wasn't old enough to vote. It was something juicy, I remember that."

Eldon thought suddenly of the foot in the landfill as Loretta went on. "As for Keith Howell, why, it would be an exaggeration to say he owns half the county, but he owns many of the parts worth owning. His father left him well fixed in property."

"Such as?"

"Scads of prime developable land. Land for houses and apartments, land for seaside retirement cottages. D'you want the tax-lot numbers?"

"All I really need to know is that it's valuable."

"You bet it is. Keith'll be in very good shape if this place ever catches on as, say, a retirement community for people from California. His old man acquired most of it—including that stand of cedar you asked about. Keith owns all the land around that landfill."

"Good stuff. I'm writing a feature about Howell."

"Go to it—I love to read gossip!"

"It's not gossip, Loretta, it's news. But let me ask you something that's got to stay between us."

"Everything we talk about stays between us," Loretta said. "If it didn't, I wouldn't be one of your best leaks."

"Thanks. Is Pumpkin Joe Nedlee's name anywhere in that file on the church property?"

"Joe?" Loretta sounded surprised. "Not anywhere that I see. Why Pumpkin Joe?"

"Just a wild thought I had."

"The only property in the county I know of that Joe owns is the land he lives on."

"Well, thanks. I gotta go now. Remember—let's keep this between us."

"Always. Say hello to your lady for me, babes. And remember, watch your step."

Eldon felt uneasy as he hung up. How had Loretta known that Enola Gay wore glasses? How had she known about Enola Gay at all, for that matter? Eldon put little stock in fortune-telling, but even so he uneasily massaged his stomach.

I hope I don't get an ulcer, he thought.

He returned to the storage room and hauled down the volumes for 1957. After another thirty minutes of turning pages and sneezing, he found it: A front-page story about the successful recall of County Commissioner Ellis Weems in May 1957. There was a grainy photograph of a tall, sour-looking man with wide shoulders.

The foot in the landfill probably doesn't belong to Weems, then, Eldon thought. Rosenak said the foot was too small to be a man's.

He read the story, which was bylined with the name of a reporter he had never heard of. Weems had been recalled in a controversy over whether to recite the Pledge of Allegiance *twice* at Board of Commissioners meetings. He had favored reciting the Pledge at the beginning of meetings but had balked at reciting it again at the end. He said that reciting the Pledge once per meeting made everyone loyal enough.

Apparently that had triggered a recall campaign, and when the question had reached the ballot, Weems had lost his job. The story included a nasty comment by the ousted commissioner, and Eldon suspected that there was a good deal more to the recall—possibly the consequences of an arrogant manner had come home to roost. The gloating comments of the chairman of the recall were included, too. He had a Finnish last name that meant nothing to Eldon. The rest of the story was devoted to the outcome of other issues in the primary election.

In six years in Nekaemas County, Eldon had never heard of the rise and fall of Ellis Weems. He reflected that the reputations of politicians were as ephemeral as those of reporters; he could look up the details of Weems' fall later. But wasn't that interesting about Pumpkin Joe and Weems and the church?

I wonder if Joe had a hand in that recall? Eldon thought. There's nothing like a recall for shooting down the competition if you want to become a commissioner yourself.

11

Keith Howell lived on the western heights above Port Jerome overlooking Nekaemas Bay. Here swank contemporary houses stood along winding, landscaped lanes. Every house had a view of the bay, yet was protected by the spine of the ridge from Pacific Ocean storms. The neighborhood's low-slung lines were in contrast to the weathered clapboard Victorian houses that comprised most of the town.

Howell's house was on a promontory and had curving picture windows facing the bay. A circular driveway was full of late-model cars and new pickup trucks. Music reached Eldon's ears on the evening breeze as he parked his van and climbed out with his camera and notebook.

He followed a walkway of round flagstones to the house. The flagstones were still damp from the recent rain. The walk wound through a rock garden with a stone tiki-god statue and low bristle-cone pines pruned to resemble bonsai trees. Wind chimes tinkled at the door.

Keith Howell answered Eldon's ring. He had a drink in a heavy square crystal glass.

"Eldon! Glad you could come." Keith motioned him into a plushly carpeted hallway. The walls were hung with the mounted heads of large ruminants—deer, bighorn sheep, pronghorn antelope, and others. Shining plaques hung among the trophies. The plaques were construction industry awards, chamber of commerce citations, and the like. Animal trophies were not uncommon decorations on the South Coast, but Eldon had seldom seen such a variety. "You must hunt a lot," he said.

Keith winked as he accepted Eldon's hat and dropped it on the head of a stuffed beaver squatting near the door. "Nope. My hobby's taxidermy. What'll you have to drink?"

"Same as you, if that's bourbon. On the rocks."

"It is and it's coming right up."

"This is some neighborhood."

"It should be; I built most of it." Howell led the way into the crowded, noisy living room. There was a wet bar to one side. Near it a scale model of Forest Vista Estates rested on sawhorses. Eldon looked over the crowd as Keith stepped to the bar to fix his drink.

Many of Nekaemas County's movers and shakers were present and having a great time. Eldon was acquainted professionally with many of them—business people, a judge, a prominent doctor and his wife, and the white-haired president of the community college in Coos Bay. There was a state representative, dark of beard and bald as an egg. There was the portly owner of the Oldsmobile franchise in Preacher's Hole and a passel of realtors and their wives. The guests wore expensive leisure suits and stylish dresses, gleaming shoes, glittering watches and rings. Eldon felt frowzy—he was wearing his best tan polyester slacks, his blue shirt with the frayed collar, and a newer clip-on necktie from the thrift store. His shoes needed a shine.

Everyone had a drink and a rosy glow. Well, drinking is the glue that holds South Coast society together, Eldon reflected as he accepted a hefty glass of bourbon from Keith. He began greeting people. He admired the magnificent view of the bay as he exchanged pleasantries. It was an Olympian perspective. The water glittered in the waning light. Ships looked like toys in a bathtub. Port Jerome's buildings were like child's blocks. They were scattered along the water's edge and back into the forest, which was growing darker and more indistinct as the sun descended. Lights were coming on below; Eldon thought, as he often did, that they looked like discarded stars. He looked across the bay to the ridge where he lived, but of course he couldn't pick out his house. Keith and I live at about the same altitude, only he pays a lot more for it, Eldon thought.

He settled into a soft chair and sipped his drink. There certainly was something to be said for moving in this stratum. A gas fire burned in a circular metal fireplace with a cone-shaped hood. A majestic elk's head dominated one wall. A golden eagle with spread wings perched on a tree bole on the wide windowsill. Keith wasn't

135

kidding about being a taxidermist, Eldon thought. That'll be good for the profile.

Keith came over. "Come take a look at my baby. First development of its kind on the South Coast."

Eldon went to examine the subdivision model. Another Olympian perspective. Little white blocks representing condominium buildings were scattered among tiny abstract trees made of green fuzzy plastic stuff, shaped like lollipops and cones. An expanse of the same green plastic replaced Schumacher's Landfill. The model was merely conceptual, but for some reason Eldon was struck with its phoniness. It's those crazy little trees, he thought. They look like ugly candy.

Jackknife Slough was represented by a blue-painted strip winding through the forest at the layout's rear. Eldon studied the slough's course, saw that the development cut in close to its banks. There was a tiny plastic rowboat in the painted water. The slough will make a nice backyard for the few people who can afford it, he thought.

Eldon got out his camera, attached the flash unit, and cajoled Keith and some of the realtors to pose with the model. That was a crowd-pleaser. So was the plump, tipsy blonde who plucked up one of the little trees and put it in her drink. "Just saving the old growth!" That brought laughter.

After the picture came hors d'oeuvres and more jokes and chatter. Eldon found he was enjoying himself. He had a pleasant buzz on from the bourbon, and the snacks were great—little open-faced pâté sandwiches, barbecued chicken wings, raw vegetables with creamy dip. He picked up some tips for possible business stories, although there was also a lot of chaff. The realtors especially treated Eldon as if he were a free advertising service who would promote their ventures on demand. Eldon reminded himself not to let it annoy him. He had never knuckled under to their patronizing entreaties and didn't intend to start now. He sipped bourbon, munched chicken wings, and said he'd relay their suggestions to Fiske. That set off the inevitable complainer, a red-faced chamber of commerce luminary who began a harangue about how the *Sun* wasn't doing enough to promote the community. Eldon nodded gravely but grew irritated. Keith Howell intervened with a smile:

"I've never known Eldon to do anything but cover his beat honorably. Eldon, let's go talk."

They went through the house. Animals and birds were mounted throughout. It was like walking through a paralyzed zoo. Eldon wondered if it wasn't all a bit much, but the workmanship was superb. It was nice to find someone in this town who was passionate about something. "A regular wild kingdom," he said.

Keith grinned. "I want to show you something because you seem interested in taxidermy. But just between us. No photographs, okay?"

"Okay, long as it's not a mummy."

Keith opened a door. "My private office." They stepped inside. A Danish-modern rosewood desk faced a window with a view of the town and the bay. A coyote pelt was spread on one wall. On the corner of the desk was a mounted bald eagle, wings spread, perched on a tree bole. Clearly it was a companion display to the golden eagle in the living room.

"I see what you mean," Eldon said. Bald eagles were protected.

"It came from Alaska," Keith said. "I keep it in here. Not many people have seen it."

"I won't say anything," Eldon said.

"Thanks," Keith said. "I knew you wouldn't." He touched the eagle's head. "I like special animals in my collection." He nodded at the pelt on the wall. "I'm getting interested in smaller projects again. Especially the canines. Red fox, coyote—"

"Where's your workshop?" Eldon demanded. "I want to take some pictures."

"I converted the garage. We'll go down there in a bit. Let's get the interview out of the way."

"Good idea."

Keith pulled up a captain's chair and sat down. Eldon saw that the chair was constructed from deer antlers cleverly woven together. The chair's legs ended in fetlocks and hooves.

Eldon got out his notebook. "That's some model out there."

"Like it?"

"The development crowds Jackknife Slough, doesn't it? That might hurt the fishing."

"You're a fisherman?"

"Yeah. Tie my own flies."

"The county planners were worried about that, too, and I think they had a point. So we compromised. I won't build as close as the model suggests. Landscaping and wild cover will buffer the slough from the development." Keith slid a bright brochure across the desk to Eldon. "Here's the specs. No need to write all that stuff down."

"Thanks," Eldon said. "While we're talking specs, how old are you?"

"Thirty-four."

"Almost the same as me," Eldon said and thought that Keith looked more like forty-four. "No wife, I gather?"

"I never have married. Don't get me wrong, I don't rule it out. I'm not queer," Keith said, with a sort of ha-ha laugh. "But it takes a long time to separate the nice girls from the gold diggers."

"And you do have a lot of gold to dig," Eldon said.

"Dad left me pretty well fixed," Keith said. "And business is good. I'm continuing the family business. I take family very seriously."

"Mother? Brothers? Sisters?"

"My mother's long dead, and I'm an only child. My father and stepmother are dead, too."

"You've got a reputation as an environmentally conscious developer—"

"I intend to keep that reputation, too," Keith said. "I want to build an economically viable community integrated with the environment."

"John Henspeter didn't see it that way," Eldon said.

"I knew John when he was a logger—before he came around to that way of thinking. He brought me the beaver that's wearing your hat. He was one of the guys I used to drink with. I don't drink as much anymore." Keith looked thoughtful. "As I've said, John was sincere and his murder is a tragedy. If I could've stopped it, I would've. But he was wrong about my project and I intend to prove it."

"By building Forest Vista Estates."

"By building Forest Vista Estates," Keith echoed.

"What about earthquakes?" Eldon asked. Keith's expression

138

darkened and Eldon quickly added, "My editor told me to ask you."

Keith's nostrils flared like a bull's as he pulled in a deep breath. There was a puzzling expression in his eyes. Eldon thought at first that it was the glint of anger. No—it was something else. Panic? He peered intently at Keith, who returned a sudden broad smile.

"I guess you've got a job to do. But when have we ever had an earthquake on the South Coast? Nothing in recorded time. No Indian legends that I've heard of, either."

The smile widened. Selling his project seemed to put Keith on firm ground once more. The firm ground of the tennis court, Eldon thought, noticing an almost subliminal swing of Keith's right shoulder. It reminded him of a man returning a tennis serve. "My project is sound, Eldon. I'd hate for your article to suggest that Forest Vista Estates is snakebit before it even gets built."

"That's not our purpose. The story's about you."

"That article you wrote about John—"

"That was John's side. Now I'll give yours. But tell me more about the taxidermy."

"I started when I was a boy," Keith said. "Preserving nature always fascinated me. Taxidermy is like rescuing these animals—like grabbing hold of something that's on its way to nowhere."

"You mean, everything dies?"

"Yeah. You might say that bald eagle has a new lease on life."

"What was the first thing you stuffed?"

"A squirrel," Keith said. "It wasn't a very good job, but my dad really liked it. 'You've got hold of something at last,' I remember he told me." He gazed out the window into the darkness that was speckled with Port Jerome's lights. "My father was a very strong-willed man. Possessive. I looked up to him. My hobby pleased him, so I stuck with it. And I found that it pleased me, too."

Keith's voice warmed as he described taxidermy technique—carefully skinning the dead animal, readying the hide, the scissors, the needles, the thread for the mounting. Preparing the wooden form with chisel and sandpaper. Arranging the mounted creature in a way pleasing to the eye.

"It's a construction job," Keith said. "It's a lot like building a house, when you think about it. Beauty made permanent. You can see the captured power in the eagle here."

"Like Forest Vista Estates."

"I hadn't thought of it that way, but yeah, that's good. Sure you don't want a job writing advertising copy for me?"

"Naw, thanks." Eldon scribbled notes, thinking that he ought to ask Keith to mount a fish for him sometime. But then I couldn't eat the fish, he thought, and I'd rather do that. He looked at the eagle. "It's beautiful, but isn't it going to waste? It's not in the wild anymore."

Again the twitch of Keith's right shoulder. A twitch of the whole arm? Keith's right hand grasped the antlers that formed the arm of his chair. "Forest Vista Estates won't be an embalmed community. It will be a living use of the beauty of the wilderness."

"I see." Eldon jotted that down.

Howell waited for him to finish writing. "I rescued that eagle, in a way. It was going to die, sooner or later."

"Why not let it die later, then?"

"This way we have the benefit of its beauty now."

"At least you do."

"Everyone will be able to enjoy Forest Vista Estates."

"If they can afford it, you mean."

"That's business. But the prices will be reasonable."

"You think you'll get buyers? This area is pretty depressed."

"Buyers will come from outside. Vacationers and retirees from California."

"You think so?"

"This eagle's my lucky charm." Keith rose from his odd chair and nodded solemnly. "Every one of these animals represents some good luck for me, Eldon. Good luck in the hunt, you know."

"Did you bag them all?"

"Very few. But they represent good luck for somebody. I can't shoot worth a damn. It used to make my father mad as hell. Dad had a thing about hunting and fishing. He thought that being good at them was the mark of a man. You would've impressed him." Keith's shoulder twitched. "I wish he could be here to see Forest Vista Estates."

"The project's a monument to his memory?"

"He'd always wanted to see that land developed, but he never was able to acquire it. It galled him. Dad and the owner were not friends."

"I understand that you bought it from an estate."

"That's true; the opportunity was there and I took it. Dad would've been proud. But that was a while ago. How'd you find out about it?"

"Commissioner Nedlee told me about it after the hearing."

"Ah, Pumpkin Joe." Keith smiled and shook his head. "Henspeter sure got him going that day, didn't he?"

"Joe does have quite a temper."

"He's a passionate man," Keith said. "Sometimes too passionate for his own good. Do you know that Joe and my father were once rivals for the hand of a woman? But I'd better not go into that."

"They were?"

"Hey, now—I can't have old hatreds getting into print."

"Oh, hell, I wouldn't use something like that, Keith. It's irrelevant."

"Maybe I'll tell you about it sometime," Keith said. "Right now it's time to head downstairs to the workshop and show off the real reason for this party."

"A new taxidermy project?"

"Just finished. I hold a party this time every year and unveil something new. The subdivision model was ready so I put that out, too. It seemed fitting."

"Okay. Before we go down, is there anything else I should ask you about or that you want to tell me?" It was Eldon's standard way of wrapping up an interview.

"Just that the ground is rock-solid beneath Forest Vista Estates," Keith replied.

"Other hobbies? You play tennis, don't you, Keith?"

"No. I work out with weights." The shoulder twitched. "And I like to read." To Eldon's astonishment, Keith recited:

> " '. . . if it be your design
> To find out death, turn up this crooked way
> Towards that grove, I left him there today
> Under a tree and you'll find him waiting.' "

"That's Chaucer," Eldon said with delight. *"The Canterbury Tales."*

" 'The Pardoner's Tale,' " Keith said. He opened a lower desk drawer and pulled out a bottle of bourbon. "Freshen your glass?"

They returned to the living room a short while later to find that the party was growing lively. Loud music played and some couples were dancing the samba.

Eldon sipped his drink and decided to add some ice. He looked behind the wet bar but didn't see any. He wandered into the kitchen with his glass asking, "Ice?" of various guests. He decided to simply get ice from the refrigerator. He opened the capacious freezer compartment. Something fat and cylindrical wrapped in silver foil blocked the way to the ice trays. Eldon pulled out the heavy thing and read the hand-printed label: "Great Horned Owl."

A future taxidermy project, Eldon thought. I hope it doesn't affect the taste of the ice.

Keith's voice sounded in the living room: "It's time for the unveiling!" Eldon returned as Keith herded the guests from the living room with jests and good-natured threats.

They made their way downstairs. There was a door at the foot of the heavily carpeted stairway. Eldon, at the head of the crowd, opened it. Something huge and indistinct dominated the dark room beyond. Eldon found the light switch and flicked it on. A massive, canvas-shrouded figure stood in the center of the workshop. The partygoers surrounded it immediately.

"You've outdone yourself this year, Keith!"

"It's huge! What could it be?"

"I bet it's a gorilla."

"Too tall."

"Then how about Bigfoot?"

"No peeking!" Keith said.

Eldon looked around. The workshop was well-appointed, quite the gentleman's hobby setup. There were work tables with tools, rolls of chicken wire, and wooden animal forms. On one table a tanned fox skin was partially stretched over a wooden form. Heavy needles and thread lay nearby. On another table a smaller wood form for a canine was in early stages of preparation.

Keith grasped one corner of the canvas shroud that covered the great figure. "You know I'm always trying to be bigger and better.

Build bigger, better housing developments with bigger, better beauty—"

"Aw, you just like those bigger, better awards!" the drunk from the chamber of commerce said.

Howell smiled modestly. "They're appreciated, too. But I've never forgotten that I've got to earn my way. It's a hard world out there, and you've got to earn your place in it. Am I right, Eldon?"

"Oh, ah—right," Eldon said.

There was a titter from the other guests.

"Thanks," Keith said. "Since most of you have been coming to these parties of mine year after year—"

"We like the booze," said the judge.

"Thanks. You know they've been getting bigger and better, too—"

"When ya gonna do a whale, Keith?" a realtor asked, to more laughter.

For reply, Keith yanked the canvas away.

Gasps and then applause. Eldon stood amazed. Keith had stuffed and mounted a Kodiak bear.

The bear was chillingly lifelike. It stood on its hind legs nearly ten feet tall, immense, hairy, and snarling. It had teeth like ivory railroad spikes, and its glass eyes looked meaner than many living ones Eldon had seen. Each of the bear's claws was as long as a man's finger. One paw could have covered—and torn off—Eldon's face.

The guests crowded forward, stroking the bear, congratulating Keith. Eldon recovered his self-possession and shot a picture. Then Keith stepped to one side, still gripping the canvas and looking curiously deflated while his friends admired his handiwork.

Eldon sidled up. "It's a hell of a job. Where'd you get it?"

"Alaska, like the eagle. I'm not satisfied."

"That's the artist in you speaking."

"Well, it's some teddy bear—but what am I going to stuff next?" Howell asked. "Bigfoot? A hippopotamus? A whale? No, I started with small animals and I'm thinking small again. Small animals are like magical little clocks. All that life, all those things inside them, packed into so little space. The small animals are where you learn, Eldon."

"Got something in mind?"

"Maybe. It'll be something special. But I'm talking too much, as

Dad used to say." Keith flicked a wall switch. Suddenly there was music in the workshop. "I've got speakers through the whole house. I built 'em right in. I think I'll do that in the condos, too."

"I'd say you have a nose for marketing—"

"It's not that," Howell said impatiently. "I want folks to *have nice homes*. Does that sound stupid?" He considered Eldon. "I didn't have a happy childhood. I want to give other people the chance to be happy. To have something they really want."

The party guests began dancing around the bear. The blonde who had dunked the plastic tree in her drink swept Keith away before Eldon could question him further.

Eldon decided to leave. Let's see, did he have everything? Camera and notebook were in hand, and his hat was in the entry hallway, sitting on the beaver's head. But there was something he'd forgotten . . . the Forest Vista Estates brochure. He'd left it in Keith's office.

Eldon slipped out the door and went up the stairs. The brochure lay on the office desk. He pocketed the folder and paused to examine the antler chair and to admire the bald eagle once more.

He saw that there were two red squirrels mounted as bookends on a shelf. Eldon chuckled at Keith's whimsy and went over to peruse the books. They were titles about real estate. He had hoped to find Chaucer or something else in the medieval line, but of course nothing compelled Keith to keep pleasure reading in his office.

A vivid pamphlet on the shelf caught his eye. It was yellow with diagonal black stripes. Even though it had been shelved backward and upside down, hiding the title, Eldon recognized it—one of the Cliffs Notes series of crib booklets known to desperate students of literature everywhere. He remembered the distinctive covers well from his days at Berkeley.

A suspicion formed instantly in Eldon's mind and was just as instantly confirmed when he pulled out the pamphlet and turned it over. *Cliffs Notes on Chaucer's Canterbury Tales.*

=12=

It was raining again on the afternoon of John Henspeter's funeral two days later—raining with the kind of vengeance Eldon loved. That good old South Coast weather, he thought as he strode into the funeral-home chapel near the boat basin and watched rain drum on the windows. The weather made the town beyond the windows agreeably remote, its weathered buildings soft gray silhouettes smeared on a flat white sky.

Eldon felt good. The weather suited him, and Enola Gay was a very merry widow. Last night's bout had been better than ever. She had become more sexually ravenous as the funeral approached, returning each day from the preparations to fall upon Eldon without mercy. Eldon's every joint ached as he shook rain from his fishing hat. But he felt sharp and alert. Was there a limit to his endurance? Certainly he was in far better shape than Henspeter, who lay at the front of the chapel in a plain open coffin surrounded by fir boughs, like a gift under a Christmas tree.

The motif was somehow in keeping with the decor. The chapel was furnished in myrtlewood, purported to grow only on the South Coast and in the Holy Land. The light brown, marbled-looking wood was mainly used for making salad bowls. There was a citation from Isaiah that supposedly proved its biblical pedigree posted in the shops that sold the salad bowls to summer tourists. The chapel was redeemed in Eldon's eyes by a mounted fish on one wall—a real beauty of a Chinook salmon.

Eldon was admiring the fish when a big, tubby blond man stepped from an office off the chapel. He was younger than Eldon, with a high forehead and a cheerful, self-satisfied face fringed with close-cropped, reddish-blond whiskers. Round, metal-framed spectacles gave him a clerkish aspect. He wore dark suit trousers and vest and a crisp white shirt but was coatless. "Hi. Caught that salmon up in southwest Washington, couple of years ago. Can I help you?"

"It's a beaut," Eldon said. "I'm here for the Henspeter service. I'm kind of early." Eldon and Enola Gay had agreed to arrive discreetly separate.

"That's okay," the man said. "Make yourself at home. I've got coffee in the office."

"Eldon Larkin from the *Sun*. I'm covering the funeral."

"Reuben Amick of Stephen Amick and Son. I'm the son. Dad's dead."

They shook hands. Eldon pulled his camera from beneath his wet coat. "You don't mind if I take pictures during the service, do you?"

"It's okay with me if it's okay with the family. Can't beat the free advertising."

"I know the widow," Eldon said. "It'll be okay. The fir boughs are nice."

"Thanks. They were her idea. She wanted things simple. I'm to deliver a homily and that's it. Private cremation."

Eldon knew this. "Very appropriate," he said.

"She haggles like an Arab," Amick said. "That's our cheapest coffin. She found it in the back of the storeroom. She found a scratch on the lid and made me give her a discount."

"Well, you're going to cremate him," Eldon said and went up for a closer look.

Henspeter was laid out in a dark suit and somber tie. He wore an eyepatch like some suave pirate. Other than the uncharacteristic apparel, the dead activist looked very much like himself, Eldon decided. But of course there was something missing. Henspeter was gripped by a rigid serenity, all his tension and energy at an utter and final halt.

Eldon smelled a faint, cloying odor, like distant ripe flowers. Amick stepped behind the coffin and touched a wall switch concealed by drapes. Drafts of cold air blew up through floor vents and the odor abated at once.

"How long will he keep like that?" Eldon asked.

"Oh, three or four days."

Eldon searched in vain for the faint line across the corpse's forehead that would indicate where Dr. Rosenak had sawed off the top of Henspeter's skull. "He looks good."

"Thanks," Amick said. "We took care because of the autopsy. He was easy, though. You should see some we get. Especially some murder victims."

"I have seen 'em."

Amick glanced at the coffin with a pleased expression. "It's the family business. You know, I feel—well, superior, to corpses. Smarter, somehow."

"Me, too," Eldon said. "I'm here and they aren't. 'If you're so smart, how come you're dead?' "

"Right," said Amick. "Of course, we'll become corpses ourselves, but that's a problem for another day. Come have some coffee."

He led Eldon into the office. A suit coat hung from a hanger on the back of the door. Lying on the desk, partly disassembled on a cloth next to a National Rifle Association ashtray, was a stainless-steel .357 Magnum revolver. A cigar box contained gun oil and cleaning implements.

"A Ruger Security Six, for home defense," Amick explained. "I was just putting it back together."

"It's a beauty," Eldon said.

"Double action." Amick slipped the pistol's cylinder into place. "It's got an adjustable rear sight and a fixed-blade front sight. Pachmayer 'Gripper' grips on it, to help absorb the shock of firing Magnum loads. I just keep it loaded with .38 rounds unless I'm going to the range. Plus-P loads—liability, you know."

"How so?" Eldon accepted a Styrofoam cup of coffee.

"A Magnum round could pass through a household intruder and go right on through the wall," Amick said earnestly. "It could ricochet around the neighborhood."

"A great way to drum up business."

"They'll be along in their own time, Dad always said." Amick nodded in the direction of the chapel. "Dad would've been interested in that one. He was county coroner back in the sixties."

"You don't say? Did he ever talk about any odd cases, back about 1960 or '65?"

"He had lots of great stories," said Amick. "But I was just a kid. What did you have in mind?"

"The foot in the landfill. Did your father deal with missing persons cases?"

"Say, I read about that! Dad didn't tell any stories about mummies." Amick's eyes glittered behind the glasses. "You're an investigative reporter, then?"

"Every reporter is an investigative reporter," Eldon said. "Did your dad issue death certificates? For persons missing and presumed dead?"

"Yes," Amick said. "These days, the state medical examiner in Portland does it. But back then, the coroner issued the certificate."

"Your father kept copies, surely. You wouldn't by any chance still have them?"

"You know, I think we might."

"Can I see them?"

"If I can find 'em," Amick said. "It's been years. Let's see . . . I think all that stuff is in a trunk in my mother's basement. Let me get back to you."

"I'd appreciate it." Eldon handed over his business card.

"I'll—" Amick sprang up at the sound of the chapel door opening. He snatched his coat from the hanger and slipped it on. His expression fell into formal, unctuous lines, and his posture stiffened. The undertaker stepped into the chapel with measured tread.

Eldon heard him murmuring greetings and went to the office door to see whether Enola Gay had arrived. She hadn't. It was Art Nola, hatless, his dark overcoat dripping.

Amick glided from the chapel. Recorded organ music filtered into the room as Nola removed his coat and sat down in the last pew. Nola's hair glistened with moisture. "Howdy, Eldon."

Eldon sat down next to him. "Hi. You ought to get a hat."

"I won't melt," Nola said.

"What brings you here?"

"Business. Besides, it's too muddy to dig."

"What business?" Eldon said.

"It's good practice to attend homicide victims' funerals. Interesting people turn up."

"Like who?"

Nola gave a broad, slow yawn, like a sleepy fox. "You can tell a lot about someone by who attends their funeral. Sometimes a killer comes to his victim's funeral. Or visits the grave."

"That's crazy."

"Is it? Murder's crazy. But murderers and their victims know one another in at least half the cases. Not that I expect someone to throw himself on the coffin and confess."

"Henspeter didn't have many friends," Eldon said.

"When they don't appear to know one another, it's often because we haven't guessed the link," Nola said.

"Tell me, Art—could the person who killed Henspeter have killed the woman in the landfill?"

"Maybe *that's* what I dreamed," Nola muttered and then went on in a normal voice: "There's no evidence of that. The crimes are years apart." But clearly he was intrigued by the idea.

Eldon watched him. Sometimes Nola's dreams were uncomfortably prescient. Eldon believed it was because detective work was like writing—the subconscious processing of material continued even during sleep. But Nola believed that his dreams were hints from God.

"So what did you dream, Art?" Eldon asked.

"Something about writing. You might have been in it."

Eldon started to press him but there were footsteps in the vestibule beyond the chapel door. The door opened and Enola Gay entered, coat on her arm, dignified in a high-collared black dress complete with black gloves and a veil. She wore high black boots against the rain.

Eldon stood, trying to appear nonchalant. Nola rose and nodded courteously, glancing at Eldon with raised eyebrows. Enola Gay stepped to the pew and silently squeezed Eldon's hand. There were flecks of rain on her aviator glasses behind the veil. She allowed Amick to take her coat and escort her down the aisle. She stood silently before Henspeter's coffin for a few moments and then sat down in the front pew.

"Did you get that shoe size?" Eldon asked Art.

"Oh, that. Fourteen."

"A man's shoe, then. A big man. Any distinguishing marks on the cleats?"

"No. It could've been anyone."

"Anyone big, you mean."

"Or a little man with great big feet," Nola said. "Or a woman. I need more than a shoe size. I need probable cause."

The wild roar of a motorcycle outside blanketed the noise of the storm, then shut off abruptly. The chapel door banged open. In the doorway stood two fat, hairy people clad in rain-streaked biker leathers. They had eyes like wild pigs'.

"Ronnie and Joline Endo," the man blared as Amick glided up.

The Endos were holding hands. They wore identical dark-brown motorcycle suits with laces up the legs and sleeves and huge boots.

Amick bowed them into the chapel. Ronnie and Joline clumped down the aisle as if they had rocks on their feet. Both had long black hair streaked with gray that fell past their shoulders. Ronnie had a sodden beard that spread across his chest like a hirsute cravat.

Ronnie glared at Art Nola as they passed. Art stared back coolly while Eldon fought down a snicker. Ronnie carried a motorcycle helmet under one arm—a Viking helmet with horns. Joline had no helmet; apparently she preferred to let her hair stream in the breeze as they rode. It hung in lank, wet strands around her face. The Endos threw themselves into a pew. Ronnie began punching his right fist into his left palm, over and over.

For a time there was only the thrum of the rain, the droning organ music, and the smack of Ronnie Endo's fist. Then Jasper and his followers arrived, looking as if they had been blown in by the storm. All were soaking wet. They must have walked, Eldon thought. Paavo seemed aggrieved as he pushed Wheelie's wheelchair, as if he had been prevailed upon by a superior force of nature. The others merely looked bedraggled. Paavo's concertina was in a leather case in Wheelie's lap. Jasper clutched Bouncer like a wet rag doll. The chair left wet tracks on the carpet as Amick led them up the aisle.

Eldon cocked an eye at Paavo's feet. Yes—Paavo was still wearing the boots.

Beanpole was enthralled by the chapel. "It's b-b-byootiful." Then he saw the open coffin and fell silent.

Paavo sat down like a huge gloomy mountain in the middle of a pew, taking up the space of two persons. Jasper, Beanpole, and One-Square wedged in around Paavo while Amick parked Wheelie in the aisle.

Bouncer squirmed in Jasper's grip. Eldon had never seen a dog at a funeral. Bouncer's wet fur smelled rank, and the animal's farts threatened to supplant all breathable air in the chapel. Eldon wished that Amick would speed up the blowers. The atmosphere had reached nearly one-hundred-percent intestinal gas when Pumpkin Joe Nedlee entered the chapel. Keith Howell was just behind him. Eldon stared as they stood in the doorway warily sniffing the air. Had Nedlee and Howell come to gloat together over the fallen nuisance?

If so, they were a striking contrast. Pumpkin Joe's face was a nauseating hypertension-scarlet, almost the color of fresh liver. The commissioner's complexion clashed horribly with his cherry polyester blazer and wide turquoise tie. Nedlee's breathing was ragged, and his eyes bulged as he scanned the scene, as if he were ready to fire his eyeballs from their sockets like missiles.

Howell was composed as he removed his raincoat to reveal a rich, dark suit, complete with a flower in the buttonhole. He smiled at Eldon and Nola and made his way to a pew, something imperious in his posture. Eldon decided that Howell and Nedlee had merely arrived at the same time.

Enola Gay rose when she saw her father and turned back her veil with an expression of tearful surprise. Nedlee lurched up the aisle and stiffly embraced her, then seemed to remember he had an audience and relaxed. His embrace became warmer, his scarlet face more cordial. The consummate politician, Eldon thought contemptuously. He'd probably like to nail the coffin lid shut himself.

They all sat listening to the dolorous music and the rain. Eldon felt hungry. He always grew hungry at funerals. After all, I'm still here, he thought, staring at Henspeter's coffin. We can all go out for a bite to eat after this is done.

The music faded at last. The only sounds were the rain and the faint whir of the blowers. Reuben Amick entered the chapel, carrying a Bible reverently before him. He strode up the aisle to a myrtlewood lectern near the coffin, placed the Bible on it, and straightened his glasses and the knot of his tie. Then Amick gave a wide smile and opened his coat to expose his Magnum pistol in a shoulder holster.

He drew the gun.

"Life is like a pistol," the undertaker began, as the dozen mourn-

151

ers sucked air. "It can go off when you least expect it. This is what happened to our brother John Henspeter . . ."

Eldon remembered to exhale as the sermon continued. He glanced at Nola. The detective was leaning sharply forward, watching through slitted eyes.

"He loads it with .38 rounds, because of the liability," Eldon whispered. "Plus-P loads. Home defense, you know."

Nola's glance slid to Eldon for a moment and then back to Amick. Eldon got out his notebook and cocked his camera. With Tri-X black-and-white film and the 28mm lens, there was plenty of available light for pictures.

"That can't happen with this pistol," Amick continued. "It's equipped with a floating firing pin. It acts like a safety. If you drop it, you can't set it off, because there's a transfer bar that comes up between the firing pin and the hammer, in order to fire. The only way it can come up into position is to pull the hammer back. My friends, life is like the hammer and the transfer bar is like faith; and Jesus Christ is like the floating firing pin . . ."

Amick flourished the pistol and rain pounded the windows. Yessiree, Eldon thought as he snapped a picture, it's a fine South Coast day.

Amick's homily was a variation on the theme of We Know Not the Day nor the Hour, embellished with ballistics lore and tips on buying liability insurance. Eldon learned more in thirty minutes about the supposed relationship between Christianity, firearms, and the insurance market than he had ever wanted to know. He felt that Amick glossed the Fifth Commandment somewhat, but there were some pretty good quotes. Especially one likening Henspeter to "a Magnum load in a Plus-P world" and another about "the tracers of righteousness that flash like the light of Christ."

Eldon took many notes. He was cheerful, if relieved, when the sermon ended and Amick returned the pistol to its holster. It was amazing how long a man could talk while waving a pistol, Eldon thought.

"Let us now pay our last respects," said Amick. "Please file past the coffin before it is closed."

Paavo stood up, lugging his concertina from the leather bag, and announced, "First our church wants to dedicate a hymn to John Henspeter—if it's all right with his lady."

Nedlee clenched his teeth like a Japanese devil mask, but Enola Gay said, "Oh, please, go ahead."

The Church of the Rising Dog struggled to its collective feet. Jasper stepped up before the coffin, arms raised, to lead the hymn. Let me guess, Eldon thought. Sure enough, it was "Rock of Ages." One-Square, Beanpole, and Wheelie struggled uncertainly through the words. But it didn't matter. Paavo drowned them out with his bellow, and the Endos rose and joined in loudly.

Bouncer toddled down the aisle on his hind legs when Jasper raised his arms. The dog yapped and twirled in a circle. Howell stood and joined the singing, a misty expression on his face as he watched the dog.

Amick seized the moment to usher Enola Gay and Pumpkin Joe up to the coffin. Still singing, the others lined up behind them. Eldon and Nola hung back, watching. Eldon continued snapping pictures.

Pumpkin Joe shuffled up to the casket and stared at the corpse with an expression somewhere between hatred and horror. Enola Gay gazed at the body with a tender expression. Nedlee looked up at Eldon's camera and began, "Take that away—" He stopped when Enola Gay tugged his wrist, and then he merely turned away.

The Endos clumped up in their massive boots and assumed stalwart postures for the camera. Ronnie carried his horned motor-cycle helmet under his arm.

"We'll get the bastards that didja, John," Ronnie declared while Joline dabbed at her eyes with a lace hanky. "We'll smack 'em around. I know ya put up a good fight. I'm uppin' the voltage on my electric workouts in yer memory."

They stomped over to hug Enola Gay and shake hands with Pumpkin Joe. Ronnie loudly pledged Nedlee both their votes in the next election.

"He can't vote; he's a felon," Nola whispered to Eldon. "First-degree assault."

Electric workouts? Eldon wondered. It's going to be some interview with this pair.

Jasper picked up Bouncer and led his friends past the coffin.

Wheelie and One-Square were silent, One-Square nodding know-ingly as he passed the body. Eldon watched Paavo closely, searching for something that might betray guilt. But the big man merely seemed sad. Beanpole brought up the rear, weeping. "I d-d-don't w-w-wanna get s-spiked!"

"Nobody's gonna spike ya, kid!" Ronnie said. "I won't let'em! C'mon over here!"

"We gotta stand our ground now, Beanpole," said Paavo. "You gotta have hair."

Beanpole huddled with the others as Keith Howell approached. The developer rested his hand on the lip of the coffin and gazed solemnly at Henspeter. Then Eldon's attention was pulled away by Bouncer's snarl. He looked over to see Pumpkin Joe yank his hand away from the dog's head. Bouncer farted. Pumpkin Joe wrinkled his nose and backed up as Jasper cackled with satisfaction.

Howell went to Enola Gay and took one of her hands in both of his. "John and I had serious differences, but I think we could have worked them out. His death is a terrible tragedy. I just wanted to say that."

"Thank you," Enola Gay said.

Bouncer yapped and wagged his tail, and Enola Gay smiled. Howell walked over and petted Bouncer without concern, mur-muring quietly to the dog. Bouncer whined and licked Howell's hand.

Jasper hugged Bouncer. "This is the Rising Dog. Don't you lay hands on him."

Howell was unoffended. "But he likes me. Don't you, boy?" He stroked Bouncer again. "What a fine little dog, good pal, I'm glad you're my pal." Bouncer barked once more and wriggled with pleasure, squirming out of Jasper's arms to drop to the floor.

"You can't fool us," said One-Square. "You want to pull down our church."

"I'd like to talk that over—" Howell began.

But Jasper cut in. "We'll fight you. You and that commissioner there. We owe it to John. The Church of the Rising Dog is taking up his cause."

Howell gave Eldon a broad wink. "Are you getting all this, Eldon? By the way, thanks for the story."

One-Square looked at Eldon with disgust. "Scab."

154

There was an almost subliminal rumble that Eldon realized was Paavo, growling. Would the Finn pull off Howell's ears? Reuben Amick slid smoothly in from one side like a maître d' about to bounce an unruly drunk. Eldon suddenly thought of the Ruger Security Six under Amick's coat and the tracers of righteousness.

"Thank you all for coming," said Enola Gay firmly, stepping into the middle of the group. "John would have been pleased."

Paavo looked abashed. Everyone glanced at the coffin. The crisis had passed. Amick began maneuvering people out into the vestibule. Art Nola nodded to Enola Gay and Eldon and joined the exiting crowd.

Enola Gay sighed. "I thought we were going to lose it there. Thanks, Eldon."

"Thanks for what? I didn't do anything."

"Thanks for being here."

"I'm on the job."

"I know. But you'd have come anyway."

"Yes, I would've. I'll come back and get you after I write my story."

"No, go home," Enola Gay said. "I'll be along later. I want to spend some time with my father. It's been a while. I'm going to ask him to stay here with me while they . . . you know."

Eldon nodded, slightly relieved. He had been unable to think of a convincing excuse for being present as press for the cremation. But he had felt as if he would betray Enola Gay by leaving. Pumpkin Joe's going to find out about us someday, he thought, and then things will get awkward, especially with that temper of his. "See you tonight."

"Oh, *yes,*" Enola Gay said.

"I'll make a nice dinner," Eldon said, "and a fire."

Eldon put on his hat, slipped his camera and notebook under his coat and went out into the rain. The promise in Enola Gay's *yes* made him feel frisky despite the gloomy occasion and the cold beat of the rain. And he had a pretty good story, of course. Even John Henspeter's enemies had come to mourn him. Good stuff.

Then he saw that the story was going to get even better.

Five youthful protesters stood in the rain with cardboard signs. The signs had wilted in the downpour, but one young man with strands of wet hair in his eyes was handing fliers to the departing mourners. Eldon took one. "You need a hat," he told the kid. The flier denounced the Forest Vista Estates project and demanded the recall of Pumpkin Joe Nedlee. This is why Nedlee was upset, Eldon thought. He didn't give a damn about Henspeter.

He was interested to find an excerpt from his profile of Henspeter in the flier's text. His article had gone out on the state wire, and apparently the *Register-Guard* in Eugene had picked it up. Eugene was a university town and a hotbed of environmental ferment. If Henspeter had had few friends in life, he certainly was accumulating them in death.

Keith Howell politely accepted a flier and strolled off down the street. Paavo took a leaflet and passed it to Jasper. They held a whispered conversation and quickly shepherded their followers onto the picket line. The kids looked surprised and then nervous, as if they expected to be ambushed and eaten by loggers. I know the feeling, Eldon thought.

Back at the *Sun* office, writing for the next day's edition, Eldon laid it on thick. He found he had taken a good picture, too, shot at the climax of the sermon—Amick with the pistol, the coffin, the little group of mourners, Keith Howell and Pumpkin Joe prominent among them. The 28mm lens had pulled it all in.

Fiske praised the copy. He pronounced it the most moving funeral story in the *Sun* since one he had written himself in November 1963, about the burial of an old bum who had suffocated while sleeping in a mountain of wood chips at the wharf. The chips were loaded into the holds of freighters with huge suction hoses, and the bum had been sucked in. The angle was that the bum had been buried on the same day as John F. Kennedy, and Jimbo had contrived a grotesque tie-in. . . .

Eldon got out before Fiske in his ramblings could work around to the idea that there was time today for one more assignment. That was another victory. Eldon stopped at the market to get dinner fixings—something light and dignified and cozy.

Crab casserole, Eldon decided. He would have to splurge on canned crab at this time of year, but what the hell. The funeral was over; it was time to get on with the business of living. Whistling, he collected ingredients—crab, a lemon, cream cheese, green onions, capers, and Oregon cheddar cheese. He added a loaf of fresh

French bread and a bottle of crisp Washington Riesling. He would serve his favorite dessert—French vanilla ice cream laced with cognac. He kept his freezer stocked with French vanilla ice cream.

He put the groceries into the van and drove homeward through the rain-lashed streets. He whistled as he drove over the bridge to Regret and up the hill. The rain beat on the old gas station and the stucco municipal utility shed and on the bungalows and rusted trailers encrusting the hillside. The rain gusted in sheets across the ruins of the mill across the slough.

Eldon was chuckling with anticipation by the time he parked the van in front of his house. He would serve dinner by candlelight with Mozart on the stereo. What elegance! He picked up the grocery bag and trotted to the front door, keys in hand.

There Eldon stopped chuckling, lost his appetite, and dropped the groceries on his foot.

A bullet hole decorated the center of his living room window.

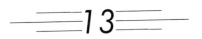

13

Eldon threw himself off the porch and belly-flopped onto the swampy lawn. He hit hard; his teeth clacked and the wind went out of him. He crawled, gasping, across the grass to crouch beside the van, shuddering and gulping air. Eldon had faced gunfire once before in his career, and that had been enough.

But there was no gunfire, only the sound of the wind through the trees and the patter of rain on the asphalt of the deserted municipal tennis court across the street.

There's no ambush, Eldon realized as breath came easier and rain dripped from the brim of his hat and down his collar. That bullet hole was there when I drove up.

He rose and walked slowly to the house, glancing around. The front of his coat and pants were sodden now, and there was water in his shoes. He had almost knocked out his teeth—was one of his caps loose? Eldon found his keys by the door, near the woodpile under the eaves. He grabbed the grocery bag. The bottom disintegrated. He smelled the tang of Riesling and heard the sludgy sound of crushed glass as the groceries slid out onto the lawn in a wet lump.

I broke the goddamned bottle of wine, he thought. The bread's ruined, too.

Eldon threw down the bag and unlocked the front door. The living room was as he had left it—his many books, the stereo, the worn armchairs flanking the Franklin stove, the cluttered fly-tying bench in the corner, his mounted news photographs on the walls.

But wait. His eye went to the portrait of the 1977 Nekaemas County Fair queen surrounded by children as she read them a story. Eldon had lusted after her in vain. The picture hung opposite the front window, on the wall dividing the living room from the kitchen. A round, black bullet hole now obliterated the queen's face.

Eldon went into the kitchen. There was a little bulge in the Sheetrock where the bullet had almost punched through. Eldon got an awl from his fly-tying bench and dug into the Sheetrock. This was ruining evidence, but Eldon was seized by a need to have the slug safely in his hand.

Eldon broke the Sheetrock away. The bullet had grazed a stud and was lodged there. He prized it out with the awl's point and weighed it in his palm.

This was fired through the window after both of us left for the funeral, Eldon thought as he placed the misshapen lead pellet on the table. Somebody doesn't like my stories. Jesus Christ.

He got the telephone from the living room and brought it back into the kitchen on its long cord, safely away from the front window. He tried to dial the sheriff's office but couldn't remember the number, although he had called the sheriff each weekday morning for six years to make cop checks. He went back into the living room, skin crawling, got the telephone book, and looked up the number.

"This is Eldon Larkin from the *Sun*. Someone took a shot at my house. I want a deputy, please. . . . I'm there now. No, I'm not injured."

Eldon gave the dispatcher his address and hung up. It would be several minutes before a patrol car arrived from downtown Port

Jerome. They need a substation in Regret, he thought. I ought to write an editorial about that.

He should leave town at once. But what about Enola Gay? She'd bite the gunman in half if she met him, Eldon thought. And then she'd bite me in half for running away.

There it was. He didn't want to look bad in front of his girl. Eldon sat staring at the bullet. He spun it on the table and watched it wobble to a stop.

There was a knock at the door.

Eldon jumped and peeked into the front room. Had the patrol car come so quickly? Through the front window he saw a familiar green 1965 Chevelle parked next to his van. It was Frank.

"You're alive," Frank said when Eldon opened the door. "Looks like you dived for it."

"Yeah."

"We heard on the police scanner that someone reported shots fired at his house and then your address. Fiske said to get up here."

"If I wasn't alive, who made the call?" Eldon asked snappishly. He got the bullet and tossed it to Frank.

"Wow." Frank dropped into an armchair and examined the slug, adjusting his glasses. "How close was it?"

"It was imbedded in the wall when I got home."

"You weren't here when it happened? I thought you had to dive for cover. I thought this was going to be good copy."

"Come away from the window—"

"Why? They're not shooting at me. And who says anyone's shooting at you? Could've been some kid out potshotting."

"That's no .22," Eldon said. "Somebody doesn't like my stories about Henspeter."

"Well, maybe they'll be happier when they read your coverage of the funeral," Frank said. "I never heard of a newspaper story making anyone shooting mad, even in Port Jerome. We just get phone calls about 'bad taste.'"

"Someone didn't bother with the telephone."

"Here's the sheriff's car."

It was Bobby, the beet-faced deputy who had argued with Jasper's congregation at the landfill the day the rain began. He examined the slug and dropped it into a little manila envelope.

"Looks like a pistol slug," said Bobby. "We'll have to check that, natch. A pistol probably would have been fired at close range, straight at the window."

"A warning shot across my lawn," Eldon said. "Great."

"Might be," said Bobby, his handlebar mustache wagging as he talked. "You writing the life story of that environmental fanatic and all. Lumber is this town's bread and butter, Eldon."

"Most of the mills have been down for years," Eldon said.

"Lots of people don't want to think about that," Bobby said. "My brother-in-law, for instance. He's typical."

"Does he own a pistol?"

Bobby smiled. "I doubt it was him—he's still got work. Say, you shouldn't have dug this bullet out of the wall. It makes our job all the harder if someone screws up the evidence. Like the time the sheriff stepped in the brains—"

"I know about that."

"I'll check for tracks on the lawn."

The telephone rang while Bobby was outside. Eldon grabbed it, thinking he might as well take any threatening calls while the law was on hand.

"Frank? Is he dead?" It was Fiske.

"I'm still alive, Jimbo," Eldon said.

"Well, dee-de-dee! What'd you do, catch the round between your teeth?"

"Somebody shot at the house while I was at the funeral. Put a hole through the front window and through that nice picture I took of the fair queen."

"You still got the negative, don't you? Make another print," Fiske said. "You got great pix of that crazy undertaker today."

"He might have old records that could help us identify the body in the landfill—"

"That'd be good copy. If they ever find a body. Where's Frank?"

"He's right here. You want him?"

"Tell him there's no story," said Fiske. "We'll treat this like a bomb scare, unless you want to proceed otherwise."

"No." Eldon was grateful. The *Sun*, like many other newspapers, didn't run stories about bomb threats in the belief that publicity encouraged them. The *Sun* would not report this shooting incident, lest Eldon draw more fire. "Fiske says no story, Frank."

160

"Jimbo?" Frank took the phone and listened. "Okay. I'm coming back, then. Yeah? I'll tell him. He'll love it."

Bobby came back inside as Frank hung up. "If there were tracks on the lawn, the rain's obliterated 'em," Bobby said.

"What do I do now?" asked Eldon.

"Call if there's any more trouble. We'll run a car past here now and then for the next few days."

"Tell Art Nola about this, will you?"

"Natch."

After Bobby left, Frank and Eldon gathered up the remains of the groceries. They carried the mess into the kitchen and dumped it into the sink.

Eldon looked at the hole he had chipped in the Sheetrock. "I want that slug back. I want to make a sinker out of it. For fishing."

"You have a more pressing problem," said Frank. "Fiske still wants a story about dowsing rods."

"That moron! I nearly get my face blown off and—"

"They missed," Frank said cheerfully. "Didn't even come close. You have deprived the newspaper of good copy. Therefore, you owe copy. Can't weasel out of it."

"You're a crackerjack moral philosopher, Frank. You ought to join Jasper's church."

"A couple of years ago you'd have hit an assignment like that with both boots," Frank said. "You'd have had a good time with it."

"Not now," Eldon admitted.

Eldon saw that the rain had stopped. Late afternoon sun gleamed behind rolling, sooty clouds, throwing off glaring light but no heat. Frank drove away. Eldon stared at the sky awhile and then went into the kitchen and got the tub of French vanilla ice cream from the freezer. He ate ice cream from the tub with a soup spoon and stared mournfully at the heap of cans, vegetables, and broken glass in the sink. Dinner was irretrievable.

He needed to think.

He returned the ice cream to the freezer. Then he got his fly rod from the closet, went to the fly-tying bench, selected a fly he had recently constructed from his tackle box, and attached it to his line. It was black and lime-green, with metallic striping and white-and-purple feathers. Eldon had learned the design from a Portland cop

161

he had met while fishing on the Rogue River, and now he found the bright colors somehow comforting.

He got the red plastic cup that he used for a casting target and went out into the yard.

Eldon looked around suspiciously. It didn't feel like his lawn anymore; an invader had trod here. But now he would take the lawn back. He placed the red cup before the salmonberry bushes at the lawn's far edge and took up position across the yard in front of his van. He flicked the rod, feeling its familiar spring. He brought the rod upright, eyeing the cup as he stripped line from the reel with his left hand. He whipped the rod back—then snapped it abruptly forward in a short, sharp cast like a jab to the chin.

The fly sailed across the lawn and into the grass just short of the cup. Close enough for a first try, Eldon thought, but I've got to stop hammering. It's got to be more like uncoiling a punch.

How many times had he scolded himself about that? He backed up and bumped into the van's wet fender. I need a higher vantage point, he thought.

Eldon went to the rear of the van and climbed the chromed ladder onto the roof. He picked his way carefully across the rain-slick metal, braced his feet, and prepared to cast again. He could almost see down into the cup. Eldon cast. The line hummed out. The fly plunked into the cup.

"Bingo!" But this was cheating. Or was it?

Eldon turned carefully, surveying the world around him. A dangerous one. He smelled the fir needles and the damp humus and scanned the ranks of Douglas fir on the bay's north rim. To the west were the ruins of the mill and Port Jerome beyond, on the far lip of the bay. On the western horizon was the grayish shine of the Pacific. It was a world Eldon had thought he knew all too well—until now. Nekaemas County was a rough-and-tumble place, but in six years as a reporter he had never been personally threatened. Well—he once had been jumped and beaten, and Paavo once had been about to tear him limb from limb in the Dead Man's Hand bar, but neither incident had been premeditated. And the Finn had paid the price—literally through the nose.

He's capable of this, Eldon thought. He's still got a temper like a wounded skunk under all that newfound piety. He didn't just up and shoot me at the funeral because he knew he couldn't get away with it. Not like killing Henspeter—

Another thought followed, clearly and disconcertingly: Paavo had been at the funeral.

So he couldn't have been up here shooting at your house, Eldon thought. Or could he? When did Enola Gay leave the house? He might've had time to take a potshot on the way to church.

But how long would Jasper and the others have let him out of their sight? Eldon wondered. He could not envision Jasper, let alone his three enfeebled followers, countenancing an armed attack on Eldon's house. Not and keep their act together afterward. Beanpole alone would babble about it all over town.

Eldon frowned and prepared to cast again. Were there any other suspects? He might as well suspect the entire town, the entire county, as Bobby had suggested. Uneasily, he recalled Art's suggestion that his story about Henspeter might have precipitated the man's murder. Christ, what do you do? Stop writing? Keep the readers in the dark? That's when murders start happening. . . .

Eldon cast again. Another hit. Very good. He was sure of one thing—the warning of the bullet seemed to support his notion that Henspeter's murder and the mummy in the landfill were connected. But *how?*

Eldon practiced casting for another hour, shivering a little in the cool breeze and losing himself in the repetition. Although it was spring and the days were growing longer, the roily clouds dulled the light. Finally Eldon heard the sound of an engine and looked down to see Enola Gay's truck swing into the driveway. She parked and climbed out, looking tired.

"Up here," Eldon said.

"What the hell are you doing?"

"Thinking. We've got something to think about now." Eldon pointed to the window and tried to appear unconcerned as he worked his way back to the ladder and limbed down to the ground. "It must've happened while we were at the funeral. All in a day's work for a reporter."

Enola Gay went to the window and peered at the hole. "Did you call the sheriff?"

"They think it was a pistol." Eldon put his arm around Enola Gay's shoulders. "How'd it go?"

"Well—it's done."

"I'm sorry I wasn't there."

"It was just as well. You didn't really know him. And Joe's in a bad way because of the whole business—the fight with John and all. He feels guilty. About a lot of stuff."

"Guilty? I'd have thought he'd be glad."

"Joe takes being county commissioner very seriously, no matter what you think of him, Eldon. I'm glad I got to spend some time with him."

"But you went your separate ways afterward."

"Yes, we did."

"This wasn't the time to tell him about you and me, I'm sure." Eldon knew at once that he had committed a gaffe, for Enola Gay gave him a curious look. He realized unhappily that he was moving too fast. "Let's go out to eat. My treat."

"No time for that, Eldon. We've got to act." Enola Gay's eyes flashed behind her glasses.

"What do you mean?"

"John's guns. We've got to get them out of my house." Enola Gay headed for the front door, pulling off her coat as she went. "We've got to hide them."

Eldon followed her into the house, carrying his fly rod. "Why? Where? We can't bring them here."

Enola Gay threw the coat aside and unzipped her dress as she went into the bedroom. "It should be obvious—that shot wasn't meant to warn you, Eldon. It was meant to warn *me.*" She let the black dress drop to the bedroom floor and stepped out of it. She wore black underwear. "Whoever fired through your window knows about the guns."

Eldon licked his lips; black underwear and black boots made an arousing combination. He gripped his fishing rod and forced his mind to grapple with Enola Gay's assertion as she pulled her camisole over her head and stepped gracefully out of her half-slip. "How could they know about the guns?" he demanded.

"The guns must be why John was murdered."

"He was murdered for threatening tree-spiking."

"So the guns are connected. They have to be. That's the only thing that makes sense—the only way the stakes would be high enough for someone to kill John."

"You mean before John killed them?" Eldon stood blinking as Enola Gay removed her bra—it was the type that unhooked in front—and stood regarding him in black bikini panties and boots, her hands on her hips. Finally, Eldon got out, "Why didn't I think of that?"

Enola Gay smiled and moved into Eldon's arms. She took away his fishing rod and tossed it on the bed. "Maybe because you're thinking about something else."

She gave Eldon a wet, openmouthed kiss. He returned the kiss. Enola Gay's kissing became ravenous and she shoved him backward onto the bed. He managed to push his fishing rod aside as Enola Gay landed on top of him. She tore open his belt and fly and jerked down his pants, then squirmed out of her panties and mounted him.

It was a rough ride and a quick one. Eldon loved every moment. The bullet hole in the front window added the spice of danger.

Afterward, Enola Gay lay with her cheek against his, her face covered with her damp hair. "I needed that. Thanks."

"Wow," Eldon said. "I think I'll shoot a hole in my front window every day."

Enola Gay snickered, then gave a deep sigh. "The guns."

"Forget the guns! What's the point of moving them, anyway?"

"For safekeeping. And to throw 'em off balance."

"Let's have dinner and think it over. Where are we going to disappear them to? We're not bringing them here."

Enola Gay pushed herself up on her arms and regarded Eldon through her tangled hair. She still wore her glasses, and they sat askew on her nose. "I suppose not. Too obvious."

"I won't have 'em here," Eldon said. "I can't afford to."

"Relax. I know just the place—Ronnie and Joline Endo's."

"They'd hide them for you?"

"Sure. They're tough customers."

"Maybe we'd better just tell the sheriff."

"No. I need to find out for myself what this is all about. Then maybe I can bury John for good. Let's get going."

They showered quickly together and drove to Enola Gay's house in Eldon's van. It was twilight when they reached the house. Its darkness and silence gave Eldon a chill. "Go on inside," Enola Gay said. "I've got to put away some tools while we're here."

Eldon walked carefully through the empty house, looking at the silent eel tank and the picture of Test Bravo on the living room wall. He went into the bathroom and got a washcloth, then entered the bedroom and opened the cedar chest. The weapons were undisturbed. Eldon quickly copied the serial number of each into his notebook, using the washcloth to handle the guns. He was finished and had the washcloth back on the towel rack and the notebook put away before Enola Gay came in. They lugged the chest into the van. Eldon moved carefully because of his sore groin.

Enola Gay clearly enjoyed the intrigue. "Careful, Eldon, don't scratch the chest."

"Maybe we should put the guns in a different box."

"No—the cedar chest is perfect camouflage. Innocent. You worry too much."

You should talk, Eldon thought, but his thought was a fond one. Enola Gay cut a romantic figure in her boots, tight jeans, and denim shirt. He liked the way she left the top two shirt buttons open. This was a superior way to do an investigative story, no doubt about it. You're going to have to put out some copy pretty soon, to justify all this fun, Eldon thought as he turned on the van's ignition and seized the eight-ball gearshift.

"Which way?" he asked.

"South of town. Not all that far from the landfill, actually. We'll take back roads."

Enola Gay directed Eldon up the road that ran along the slough. The Endos lived in a shabby ranch house painted some dark color that Eldon could not discern in the fading light. Moss clotted the shingled roof. Two motorcycles stood in a carport beside a woodpile and two overflowing trash cans. A porch light threw pale highlights onto the bikes' chrome. The yard seemed to be covered with a white encrustation. Huge mushrooms? Pieces of pale slate? They climbed from the van and walked closer. Eldon saw that the debris was broken porcelain.

Ronnie Endo came out of the house, shirtless, carrying a big box. He poured more shattered china onto the lawn with a crash. Ronnie squinted into the darkness. "Who's that?"

"It's me, Ronnie," called Enola Gay.

"Hey, hi! We were just cleaning up. Who's that with ya?"

"Eldon Larkin." Enola Gay led Eldon through the slippery sea of broken plates, cups, and saucers. "He was at the funeral."

"Hey, right." Ronnie crunched through the debris to meet them. The hair on his chest and shoulders was so thick that in the twilight he looked as if he were made out of hair. "You're that newspaper guy. Shake." Ronnie seized Eldon's hand and gave a surprisingly flaccid handshake. "The *Sun*'s a cool paper, I don't care what everybody says."

"Thanks," Eldon said. "Sorry I didn't introduce myself at the funeral."

" 'Sokay. We all had a lot on our minds."

"Eldon especially," Enola Gay said. "He wants to talk to you."

"For the paper?" Ronnie said.

"Eldon's after John's killer," Enola Gay said.

"No shit." Ronnie gaped happily. "You're an investigative reporter! Like in that *President's Men* movie."

Eldon winced inwardly. "I just need some background. Don't worry."

"I'm not worried," Ronnie said with a growl. "They may've got the drop on John, but *nobody's* gonna fool with me and Joline."

"Amen," said Enola Gay. "And I'm gonna ask a favor, Ronnie."

"Sure." Ronnie kicked aside a broken gravy boat and started for the house. "HEY, JOLINE! COMPANY!"

The Endos' living room was furnished with worn thrift-store furniture. A cartoonish portrait of a big-eyed waif hung on the wall behind the sagging couch. A Venus de Milo lamp stood on an end table next to a vinyl recliner. The figurine had a clock in its stomach. Ronnie's horned Viking helmet rested on the mantel of a sooty fireplace. Battered French doors closed off what Eldon presumed was the dining area.

The Endos were unpacking an enormous set of china. Gleaming stacks of new plates, cups, and saucers were everywhere. Cardboard boxes spilled shredded packing onto the nondescript shag carpeting.

"Two hundred pieces," Ronnie said with pride.

"Pardon?" Eldon said.

"The china setting." Ronnie displayed a saucer with a floral pattern. "Fine china really makes a meal, I always say."

"It was a peace offering." Joline Endo came out of the kitchen and hugged Enola Gay. "I didn't expect you back so soon. Who's this? You were at the funeral."

"Eldon Larkin from the newspaper," Enola Gay said. "He's a friend of mine."

"Friend of yours, friend of ours," said Joline.

"Thanks," Eldon said.

"Hey, siddown," Ronnie said and threw himself into the recliner. "Just move the dishes any old where. Sorry I can't offer you a beer, but no alcohol is a condition of parole."

Eldon and Enola Gay sat together on the couch.

"A 'peace offering' for what?" Eldon asked.

Enola Gay grinned and told Ronnie: "Reporters are always asking questions. Get used to it."

"*This* isn't for the paper, is it?" asked Ronnie.

"Oh, gimme a break!" said Joline. "Ronnie and I had a argument the other night and broke some plates. Enola Gay was here."

"You broke *all* the plates!" Enola Gay said delightedly.

"Every plate in the house!" cried Joline. "Next morning Ronnie had to eat breakfast off the floor!"

Ronnie looked solemn as the women laughed. "That was the morning we found out that John got killed," he said.

There was silence. Then Enola Gay said, "John's why we're here, Ronnie."

"Just a second, then," Ronnie said. "I need to clear my mind for this important discussion." He rose and threw open the French doors. Eldon squinted in puzzlement. The dining room looked like a cross between a machine shop and a gymnasium wired for sound. Electrical wiring draped a press bench and a set of barbells. There were a couple of car batteries on the floor. Wires ran along the walls. A big high-voltage knife switch was mounted on the wall. The switch hung open.

Ronnie stepped into the dining room, grabbed the poles of the knife switch with the outspread fingers of his right hand, and swung his elbow onto the switch contact to complete the circuit.

There was a *snap!* and a flash. The muscles in Ronnie's arm rippled like crazed snakes and Ronnie grimaced like a gargoyle. His hair stood on end and his beard bunched out. Eldon watched in astonished horror as Ronnie grunted through clenched teeth: "UHN! OOH! UHREE! UHORR—!" Eldon realized that the noises were numbers; Ronnie was counting upward from one. At "UHIVE!" Ronnie wrenched his arm free of the switch. "Ah! Good! Fuck!"

Ronnie flexed and massaged his arm as Joline applauded. "Electric workouts," he explained and stamped back into the living room.

"So that's what you were talking about at the funeral," Eldon said. "How are you still alive?"

"Low amperage," Ronnie said. "It's amps that kill a guy. But I've gradually learned to take more and more volts."

"Why the hell—?"

"Keeps the muscles loose," Ronnie said. "You get into a fight, nobody can hurt you—when they grab ya, your muscles just pull away from the bone. Learned about it when I was a kid, in the fifties."

"I told you they were tough customers, Eldon," said Enola Gay.

"When I was a kid, I used to wind electrical coils for this Hawaiian," Ronnie said. "He had a machine shop down on the boat basin. Sam Santiago. Looked like a mahogany brick. He's been dead for years, so I guess that didn't save him. Sam was into this kind of Oriental fighting where they plucked each other's muscles."

"How do you mean 'pluck'?" asked Eldon.

"Y'know—grab and yank," Ronnie said. "Twist and shout. I think it was some weird kind of jujitsu. You had to be able to stand the agony. That's why the electric workouts. The looser your muscles were, the better. It was illegal as hell, of course. They used to hold secret bouts in Sam's garage."

"There was a secret jujitsu cult here in Port Jerome?"

"Sam came from L.A." Ronnie shook his head at the memory. "He could pluck arm and leg muscles like fucking harp strings. Nobody could beat him at his own game. But one time a guy came to town whose specialty was grabbing *butt muscles*. The old glutes!" Ronnie slapped one buttock. "Sam got conned into fighting him. What a mistake! The guy literally had Sam by the ass. Old Sam Santiago was in ag-oh-NEE!"

Ronnie and Joline roared with laughter. At last Ronnie said, "Hey, someone at the funeral really took me back to those days. Guess who?"

"Art Nola," said Joline with a laugh. "He's a real pain in the ass."

"She's kidding," Ronnie said. "I mean Keith Howell."

"You know Howell?" asked Eldon.

"When we were kids," said Ronnie. "Haven't talked to him since high school. And then he shows up at John's funeral, solemn and self-important as ever."

"You didn't get along when you were kids?" Eldon asked.

"We got along okay," Ronnie said. "Keith was one of the kids who hung around Santiago's machine shop. He used to sell Sam scrap wire from the landfill, to get candy money."

"I thought he was a rich kid."

"His father used to make him work for his allowance. Anyway, Keith was fascinated by the electric workouts. We all were."

Enola Gay shifted impatiently. Eldon laid a restraining hand on her thigh. Instinct honed by six years of reporting told him that this might prove relevant. He couldn't guess why; you just kept piling up facts until some of them connected.

"Keith's been quite a success," Eldon said.

"He's a big-time developer and I'm an ex-con," Ronnie said. "He got a head start, thanks to his father's money. But you know where *I'm* the successful one?"

"Where?" Eldon asked.

"The electric workouts! Keith didn't *have the hair.*"

"Sam Santiago let little kids—"

"We'd sneak a spark when Sam wasn't lookin'," Ronnie said. "Keith couldn't take the juice the way I could. He really wanted to, though, to impress his old man. His father was pretty fierce. And really strong, I remember that. He was one hard-nosed bastard. Keith was desperate to please him.

"This was a broken-home thing," Ronnie continued. "Something about a wife who ran off. Maybe she wasn't even Keith's mother. I never got the details—you didn't talk about that kind of stuff in the fifties, it's not like now." Ronnie eyed Enola Gay. "You know, it seems like Pumpkin Joe was involved, somehow."

Enola Gay sat up. "Where'd you hear that?"

"I don't remember," Ronnie said. "It's been years."

"What did you hear?" Enola Gay said.

Ronnie frowned in concentration. "Just some story I heard. This was back when I was in grade school. It's real hazy."

"A lot of things are said about Pumpkin Joe, but I don't recall anything like that," Enola Gay said in a troubled way.

"There's probably nothing to it. Now, what's this favor?"

"Come on out to the van," Enola Gay said.

They all went outside. Eldon slid open the van's side door, climbed inside and switched on the dome light.

Joline laughed when she saw the paintings on the walls. "Dig the muscle men!"

"Pretty, aren't they?" said Enola Gay. "But don't get the wrong idea about Eldon. He's a real stud. Ronnie, flex those electric muscles of yours and help Eldon carry this chest into the house. And be careful."

Eldon and Ronnie manhandled the cedar chest out of the van, across the broken porcelain, and into the house. Ronnie certainly was strong, electric workouts or no; Eldon let him carry most of the load.

"Set 'er down there," Ronnie said, indicating a clear spot on the living room floor. "What's in this trunk? Another corpse?" He grimaced at his own joke.

"I almost wish it was," Enola Gay said.

"It's a pretty chest," Joline said.

"It's yours," said Enola Gay, and pulled open the lid.

Ronnie and Joline stared at the contents for a few moments. Then Ronnie said quietly, "Shit, you know I'm on parole."

"You've got to hide them for me," Enola Gay said. "You're the only ones I could come to."

"What about *him?*" Joline poked a finger at Eldon.

"Eldon knows too many cops," Enola Gay said.

"Yeah, I saw him sittin' with Nola," Joline said.

"I won't say anything about this," Eldon said quickly.

"I sure hope not," Ronnie said. "So what's the score?"

"John had these guns," said Enola Gay. "I don't know why. I'm staying with Eldon for a while—and today somebody put a shot through his front window, while we were at the funeral."

Ronnie eyed Eldon. "Not some kinda beef with another reporter, was it?"

"It was meant to warn *me*," Enola Gay said. "I think it was a warning from John's killer. And if he knows I'm at Eldon's, he probably knows about the guns."

"They catch me with this shit, they'll put me away," Ronnie said.

"I'm trying to find out if the guns are hot," Eldon said.

"Of course they're hot," Ronnie said. "Why else would John have had so many? Like, what's that there—a LAW?"

"What's a LAW, Ronnie?" Joline asked.

"A baby bazooka. You don't hunt rabbits with that."

"We can't hide 'em here," Joline said. "I don't want Ronnie behind bars again."

Ronnie waved dismissively. "We'll figure out something."

"Like hell we will," Joline said.

"Ya help your friends," Ronnie said. "That's the biker code."

"Oh, bullshit," Joline said tearfully, "what good can you do if you're back in prison?"

"We'll hide the box," said Ronnie. He glared at Joline and looked as if he were sending roots into the floor. Joline looked ready to spring at him.

"This was a dumb idea," Eldon said. "We'll take the chest away. I'm sorry." He looked to Enola Gay for support, but she only watched, bright-eyed behind her glasses.

"No, leave it," said Ronnie, still glaring at Joline. He tipped the chest lid shut and put his foot on it.

"Yes, you will take it," Joline said.

"No, you won't," Ronnie said.

Joline took a brand-new serving plate in both hands and broke it over Ronnie's head. Ronnie grimaced and hunched his head down between his shoulders like a turtle pulling into its shell. Joline threw a saucer. Ronnie dodged, snatched up a sugar bowl, and hurled it past Joline's head. The bowl shattered against the wall. The painting of the big-eyed waif fell off its nail and hit the floor with a bang.

Eldon and Enola Gay ran out the door as more crockery flew.

"Good job!" Enola Gay said as they dashed across the grass and scrambled into the van. "They'll hide the box for us, no sweat."

"Joline'll kill us," Eldon said.

"Nah, she's happy to help. She just gets these anxieties." She gripped Eldon's arm like a silent-movie heroine. "My hero!"

There was an enormous crash of glass as a soup tureen shattered the picture window. The next thing through the window was Ronnie. He hit the ground in a somersault, china showering down around him. Had Ronnie jumped or been thrown? Ronnie's Viking helmet sailed out after him.

Ronnie climbed to his feet and jammed the helmet on his head. He gathered up a double handful of china shards and stumped back toward the window as plates, saucers, and cups shot through the hole and bounced off his helmet and shoulders. Ronnie planted his feet deliberately and started hurling china back through the hole.

"They love each other so much," Enola Gay said as Eldon backed the van down the driveway and out onto the road. "Did you see how she threw him his helmet? They'll work it out. But I'm glad you and I don't communicate like that."

"But where'll they hide the guns?"

"Let's not ask. You didn't get to talk with them about John."

"That stuff about Keith Howell is better."

"But why—?"

"You've got to learn to pay attention," Eldon said with satisfaction. "Didn't you get that bit about Keith selling scrap wire from the landfill when he was a kid? Keith knows all about that landfill."

"So?"

"This is just a hunch—but anything I can find out about that landfill might be important. Because I think the foot in the landfill and John's murder are related."

"*What?* Why?"

"I don't know why. Yet."

Enola Gay sat quietly as they sped down the road. At last she said, "Jesus. You really do know what you're doing."

"Everybody takes me for a chump," Eldon said. "I may need to lose weight but I'm not a chump. I'm going to dig a story out of this if it kills me. Now, where do I turn?"

"At the next intersection," Enola Gay replied. "It's kind of hard to spot in the dark."

She fell silent once more. Finally Eldon said, "I was a little hard on you there. Sorry. But I feel a responsibility."

"It's not that," replied Enola Gay. "It's what Ronnie said about my father."

"Aw, the electricity's cooked Ronnie's brain," Eldon said, but he remembered what Keith had told him.

"But Pumpkin Joe *did* philander," Enola Gay said. "He chased everything in a skirt in Nekaemas County. That's why he and my mom broke up." Enola Gay grinned and slid her hand along Eldon's leg. Her grasp was hard and her smile feral in the darkness. "He set a hell of an example for his kid to live up to—don't you think?"

14

"You're walking funny this morning," said Fiske.

"No, I'm not," Eldon said.

"Stiff and slow," Fiske said. "Like I did right after I got married. Dee-de-dee! Sure wish I walked that way now!" The telephone on the news desk rang and Fiske picked it up.

Marsha looked across her typewriter like a triumphant school-marm who had caught a child at some odious practice. Eldon knew she was about to deliver a moral judgment. "Don't say it," he told her.

Eldon went tiredly to his desk and picked up the stack of press releases that Fiske had placed on his typewriter.

Frank came over to Eldon's desk, frowning.

"What?" Eldon demanded.

"Bad news," Frank said quietly. "Federal firearms records aren't public."

"Damn." Eldon glanced at Fiske and saw that he was still on the phone. "What can we do?"

"Do you have the serial numbers?" Frank asked. "I'll try some of my sources in the state police."

Eldon tore the sheet with the serial numbers from his notebook and handed them to Frank beneath a press release. "I don't want Fiske to see."

"I think you're making a mistake, sitting on this."

"What am I gonna do if I can't trace them? Write that Henspeter owned a bunch of guns?"

"At least tell Fiske what you're working on."

"Not yet."

Frank shrugged. "It's your story. I'll get back to you."

"Thanks, Frank."

Eldon was bleary and his muscles ached. He had slept with one eye open, fearing more sniper fire—when he had slept at all: The night had passed quickly and strenuously, thanks to Enola Gay. The woman had fire; her revelation about Pumpkin Joe had only stoked her blaze. Now, in the cold glare of morning, Eldon felt like a charred log. The unsettled feeling in his gut was horribly familiar. He had felt the same sensation in Berkeley while his marriage was coming apart. Then he had wound up in Port Jerome.

Something bad is going to happen, Eldon warned himself.

Fiske hung up the telephone and said, "Eldon. Come here."

This is it, Eldon thought, getting up and trying to walk normally.

"Dee-de-dee," said Fiske. "I wanted to see you walk again, to be sure. I want to talk to you about your efficiency."

"Do we have to do it here?" Eldon glanced at Marsha; she looked intently at her press releases, obviously straining to catch their every word.

"I like to see my reporters getting some," Fiske said expansively, like a king dispensing largess from the throne. "It improves worker efficiency. That's a well-known Management Fact. Take our prim Marsha there. Ever since she met that Coast Guard officer Beamish last fall—"

"Jimbo!" Marsha squealed and flounced off, bright red.

"Little pitchers have big ears," Fiske observed. "The puzzle to me, Eldon, is that you're slacking off."

"How can that be? Readers are shooting at me."

Fiske raised his pipe. "This reminds me of the time I covered the boy who stole the dynamite . . ."

"You've told me before," Eldon said.

"Not about this one," Fiske said. "This was a different boy and different dynamite. He tried to use it to hunt bats . . ."

Eldon realized that he hadn't heard this story after all. Fiske probably had thousands of stories that Eldon had not yet heard, and there were long years ahead in which he would have to listen to them. Eldon feared that gradually, against his will, the stories would grow fascinating as he became more and more like Fiske. Fiske had been a newsman for so long that reality and lies and lunch and *good copy* had fused into a continuum in his mind. Nothing was irrelevant anymore. Fiske turned over all stones alike. He sniffed everything, like a dog nosing a pile of garbage. Eldon realized that he had to throw the old dog a bone.

"I think the murders are related," he said.

Fiske looked up. "Oh? Which murders? Do we have more murders?"

"Henspeter and the body in the landfill."

"You're sure the one in the landfill's a murder?"

"You read what the M.E. had to say."

"That was a good story," Fiske said. "How are the cases connected?"

"There are noises in high places."

"Oinks? Grunts? Barks? What?"

"Commissioner Nedlee is interested in both murders."

"So what? I don't imagine Pumpkin Joe approves of murders in Nekaemas County. Not without his permission."

Eldon had to smile. "Joe would have liked to have murdered Henspeter himself—" He broke off, thinking again of Nedlee's hammer and nails and ferocious temper and the pry bar driven through Henspeter's chest. Or maybe Nedlee had hired it done. . . . Eldon thought of Ronnie's story about the long-missing Howell wife and the old rumor about Nedlee.

He opened his mouth to tell Fiske about the guns but Jimbo said: "What's going on at the landfill? Are you keeping on top of that?"

"They were still digging when I made cop checks this morning—"

"I'm talking about something else, dee-de-dee." Fiske gave a hungry smile. "Guess what that phone call was about. Jasper's occupied the condo site. Raising a ruckus."

"Eh?"

"I just got a hot tip. Jimbo has sources, too."

"I'd better get out there—"

"I thought breaking news would get you humping," Fiske replied. "Of course, you've *been* humping—"

"I've got to check on those undertaker's records, too," Eldon said to shut Fiske up.

"Don't worry about that now," the editor said. "You get out to Schumacher's."

Fiske lit his pipe and sucked its contents to a glow with a sound like a defective air pump as Eldon rummaged after his notebook and camera. "This situation is a lot like that boy who stole the dynamite," Jimbo said. "After the dynamite went off, the boy was all around us. The deputy turned and said to me, 'There's more to him than met the eye.' "

Eldon rushed for the door. He was going to miss the scoop.

"And be sure to get me a dowsing shot while you're out there," Fiske called.

Eldon drove to the landfill as quickly as he dared. But when he turned onto the access road he immediately suspected that Fiske had been had. He looked in vain for signs of barricades, a flag, smoke from rebel bonfires, anything that would signal occupation and riot. He parked the van by the trailer park and walked down near the construction site. There the ham-faced foreman who had confronted Henspeter was cutting down another tree with his chain saw. Other men were at work framing condominiums. Everything seemed routine.

The foreman stopped sawing for a moment and fixed Eldon with an unfriendly eye. Eldon waved, stepped through the hole in the landfill fence, and went up the slope.

Ah, there were the putative occupiers—a line of familiar figures moving in single file over the landfill, well away from the condo site. White-clad Jasper led the line with the dowsing rod. His apostles followed, each gripping the shoulder of the one ahead as they weaved slowly across the rough terrain. Paavo brought up the rear, pushing Wheelie. Bouncer yapped and raced around them as the line made its slow progress. It all reminded Eldon of the final scene of Ingmar Bergman's movie *The Seventh Seal*. Except for the risen dog, he thought. And the yellow tape. For Eldon saw that the sheriff's deputies were still digging.

Eldon trudged forward resignedly, readying his camera. Beanpole saw Eldon and broke out of line, waving a greeting.

"W-w-we h-h-haven't f-f-found anything yet," Beanpole said

177

as Eldon came up. "B-but you c-can bet we will." He saw Eldon's camera and whirled back toward his comrades, yelling happily. "P-pi'ture! He's gonna take a pi'ture!"

Paavo parked Wheelie's chair and stalked up to Eldon. Eldon watched him approach with a shiver.

"Why're you staring at my feet?" demanded the Finn.

"Oh, nothing!" Eldon said. "I was . . . just thinking about how the fault line might be right under where you were walking."

"No need to worry about that," said Jasper, joining them. "There's no earthquake fault around here. No sign of one at all." He flourished the forked stick by way of explanation. "Somethin's in the breeze, though. Look how she quivers."

He raised the stick in the turned-out dowser's grip. The tip waved up and down. Jasper pivoted slowly in a circle. The divining rod began to jerk sharply when he faced the evidence dig.

"Probably zeroing in on water in the cops' canteens," Eldon said.

"But we found out something important," Paavo said, sensing Eldon's indifference.

"Right," Jasper said. "It's gotta be off the record, though."

"I need stuff I can use," Eldon said.

"Soon's you've got something off the record, you can always figure out some way to get it *on,*" Jasper said.

"True," Eldon admitted and reminded himself not to underestimate a professional prophet. "So what have you got?"

"We've been doing some research about the church," Jasper said. "Talking with old-timers."

"The old-timers say the same man once owned our church property and the timber stand where John was murdered," Paavo said.

"Gives us a right to it, morally," Jasper said.

"Oh. And is the owner still around?" Eldon asked.

"We heard that he's been dead for years," Jasper said.

"And who owns them now?"

"Well, Howell owns the church. And the trees. But there's more to it—"

"Thanks," Eldon said, mentally adding "for nothing." "I'm going to see how the digging is coming."

"W-w-what about the p-p-pi'ture?" Beanpole asked.

"All right, I'll take a picture." Eldon shoved the bunch of them into a wedge, taking special pleasure in manhandling the Finn. At the front, Jasper beamed with the dowsing rod in hand and Bouncer at his feet as Eldon banged off several frames.

"Thanks," Paavo said. "When will this be published?"

" 'In the near future,' " Eldon recited wearily.

The wail of a siren drifted through the air behind them. Eldon turned to see flashing red ambulance lights moving down the gravel road in a cloud of dust.

"It's headed for the condo site," Eldon said. "Must be a construction accident." He started across the landfill, leaving Jasper and Paavo behind. A couple of sheriff's deputies at the evidence dig started in the same direction.

The ambulance was parked, lights flashing and rear doors flung open, by the time Eldon reached the edge of the landfill. There was activity that Eldon could not see because of the ambulance. Eldon rushed down the slope, clutching his camera as he stumbled in the soft earth.

He rounded the ambulance to see three medics in dark blue jackets working on a bloody man who lay on the ground next to the partly sawed tree. It was the foreman, eyes glazed and complexion pale. There was blood on the tree trunk, blood on the foreman's dungarees, blood on the folded gray blankets that elevated his feet against shock.

One medic held high a plastic IV bag. A line ran from the bag into the foreman's left arm—the uninjured arm. The medic's partners were wrapping the right arm in layers of gauze. The right hand looked like a bloody white mitten. Blue and white bandage wrappers littered the blood-splashed ground. Eldon was amazed, as he always was at accidents and murders, by the quantity of blood.

A broken chain saw lay nearby. Its blade was horribly bent, its shattered chain strewn loosely on the ground like a charm bracelet. The sharp shine of metal glinted in the tree's fresh-cut wood. A spike.

Eldon moved in, focusing the camera.

"What the hell are you doing?" a workman demanded. He was too close.

"It's my job." Eldon clutched the camera and backed up.

"You're not taking a picture of that—" The man reached for the camera.

One of the sheriff's deputies who had come from the dig was at the workman's elbow. "Why don't you step over here?"

Eldon nodded a quick thanks as the deputy guided the man away. The familiar detachment came over him as he started snapping pictures. He quickly burned through the rest of the twenty-frame roll, shooting different angles and exposures. When the film was expended, he rewound it and popped it from the camera. By now, the medics were preparing to lift the injured man onto a gurney with its jointed chrome legs collapsed to bring it to ground level.

As Eldon reloaded, he heard One-Square's squawk: "The newspaper's here! You'll get exposed now, ya bastards."

The angry voice of the workman who had confronted Eldon replied: "Let's get those sons of bitches—"

Eldon looked up. Jasper's congregation formed a ragged line atop the landfill. Paavo lurched down the slope and planted himself at the edge of the gravel road with a meat-eating expression. Jasper stood above, straddle-legged and arms crossed with his divining rod, looking like a kid who had brought his big brother to cope with the school bully.

The three cripples were bunched nearby, Bouncer snuffling unconcernedly at the ground around their feet.

Eldon realized that Jasper did not know what had happened; the ambulance blocked his view as it had Eldon's. But to the workmen it looked as if Jasper was gloating. They moved toward Paavo, faces tense. A man picked up a hammer. The two sheriff's deputies stepped in, gesturing the men back.

One deputy plucked the hammer from the workman's hand. The other pulled his nightstick and pointed it at Paavo. "Get out of here now. Get the hell back up that hill where you came from."

"I'm not doin' anything," Paavo said, in a tone that made it clear he would love to do something.

The deputy stepped up and laid the tip of his nightstick on Paavo's chest. "I'll be glad to discuss it with you—*after you get up that hill.*"

Eldon snapped a picture.

The medics hoisted the injured man onto the gurney. They unfolded its legs, raised an aluminum support for the IV bag and pushed the gurney into the middle of the gravel road, maneuvering it to the ambulance.

When Jasper saw, he called, "Paavo, somebody's hurt."

The Finn nodded grimly as the gurney rolled into his view and started back up the hill. Eldon got pictures of the injured man being loaded into the ambulance. He didn't like the looks he was getting from the workmen but he needed information. "How'd it happen?" he asked the nearest hard hat.

The man seemed glad to take his attention away from the confrontation. "He was cuttin' and he hit that damn spike." The man glared up the hill. "If those bastards with the dog had anything to do with—"

"They don't know shit," Eldon said. "What's his name?"

"Ask Howell. He's comin' out here. I don't want to talk to you. That man lost his fingers. He'll never work construction again. Four kids. And we'll still cut down that goddamn tree." The workman's eyes glistened as he stared up at Jasper and the others on the edge of the landfill. "Aw, who wants to fight a bunch of cripples? Just look at 'em."

The medics were about to close the ambulance doors when Keith Howell rolled up in a new burgundy Buick LeSabre. Howell slid from the sedan and climbed into the ambulance. Eldon got pictures of him speaking to the injured man. Finally the medics shooed Howell out.

Howell beckoned his workmen around him as the ambulance rolled away. He spoke to them in low tones that Eldon could not overhear. A couple of the men argued, equally quietly, gesturing at the tree and toward the spectators on the landfill. Howell shook his head firmly. He pointed at the condos. Finally the crew drifted back to work.

Howell stared at the gory, half-cut tree trunk as the hammering and sawing resumed. His features were composed but Eldon could see muscles work in his jaw. Howell nodded as Eldon walked up. "Now we've got *this* to deal with. Christ."

More sirens sounded on the road. Eldon saw approaching cars with flashing blue lights. "That must be the sheriff's crime team. Did your company receive any spiking threats?"

"No. Whoever did this didn't want to stop the work; they wanted an accident to happen." Keith gave a twisted smirk. "Somebody definitely wanted to create a monument to John Henspeter's memory."

"Maybe Henspeter did it, before he died."

Howell looked startled. "I don't think so. No."

The patrol cars rolled up. Plainclothesmen with toolboxes scrambled out. Eldon was surprised to see Dr. Rosenak, clutching his medical bag. Usually, the medical examiner came only to scenes of homicide or unexplained death.

Today Rosenak wore a pale yellow shirt and trousers, a puce bow tie and matching suspenders. He was coatless; Eldon noted that Rosenak carried a snub-nosed .32 revolver in a waistband holster. The doctor pulled on a maroon baseball cap decorated with the letters M E and headed for the landfill with the others, ignoring the tree. Eldon realized that their arrival was coincidental—that Nola and his men must have found something in the landfill. He rushed after Rosenak without another word to Howell.

"Hi-ho, Eldon," said Rosenak, puffing with his medical bag as they climbed the slope. "Jackpot today. With any luck, we'll find out if my theory was right."

"I bet it is," Eldon said.

"How much you wanna bet?"

"I owe you a sandwich, regardless." Eldon stuck close to Rosenak as they crossed the landfill, allowing the doctor to escort him under the yellow evidence tape that blocked off the dig. Art Nola waited in the pit, which now was nearly chest-deep. Jasper and his followers were some distance to one side, standing at the tape. Eldon squinted; was Jasper's dowsing rod pointing toward the hole?

"I'll take you up on that," Rosenak said. "How'd you beat me out here? You reporters certainly find out things fast."

"Someone spiked a tree."

"Down there? Anyone hurt?"

"A guy lost some fingers."

"A real jackpot day." Rosenak tugged an assistant's sleeve. "Hey, Mark, did you hear that? Go back and check out that tree."

They stopped at the edge of the pit. Rosenak reached down and shook hands with Nola, who frowned at Eldon. "Stay up there, Eldon," Nola said as Rosenak dropped carefully into the hole.

Eldon looked through his camera viewfinder. The 28mm lens pulled in the whole pit. He focused on pale slabs sticking out of the sandy soil. They looked like giant pieces of tree fungus. Eldon lowered the camera. One of the slabs waved and crackled under Rosenak's touch: the stacks of discarded newspapers that Nola had mentioned, preserved through long interment in the landfill.

"A ton of discarded advertising supplements from the *South Coast Sun,*" Nola said. "Somebody ran out of birdcages to line."

Eldon took a picture. "They're bone-dry, too."

Nola directed Rosenak's attention to a spot on the pit's floor. The doctor squatted, opened his bag and took out a camel-hair whisk brush. Eldon scooted along the lip of the pit, snapping pictures as Rosenak gently worked the brush. Part of a little ivory arch became visible, imbedded in the dirt.

"Hot doggy, it's a mandible," Rosenak said softly.

"Just a jawbone?" Eldon asked.

Nola gestured for silence but Rosenak said, "There's more bones, but teeth are what we need for an I.D."

"I thought there'd be a compete mummy, to go with the foot," Eldon said. "It would've made a hell of a picture—"

Nola made a noise of disgust.

"These newspapers probably provided insulation, but the whole body needn't have become mummified," Rosenak said. "You just can't depend on mummification, except with ancient Egyptians."

"No King Tut here," Nola said. "The newspapers are about twenty years old."

"What's the date?" Eldon asked. "Can you still read it?"

"Sharp questions from this fella," Rosenak said.

"Too sharp for his own good, sometimes." Nola drew out his magnifying glass and peered at a newspaper scrap. "April 22, 1963."

"Fits my theory," Rosenak said. "Wha'd I tell ya, Eldon?"

"You get a sandwich with everything on it," Eldon said.

"Maybe I'll even have meat," Rosenak said.

"This doesn't date the murder," Nola said. "The newspapers were dumped here after the corpse had been buried. And we don't know when."

"It wasn't too long after," Rosenak said. "Maybe a few years. Look at the strata on the side of the pit."

"Extra advertising stuffers wouldn't have been thrown out until after the ads had expired," Eldon said.

"How long after?" Nola asked.

"Within a couple of weeks after that date. Those things take up space."

"Anybody at the *Sun* who remembers those days?"

"Fiske, maybe, and a couple of guys in the back shop," Eldon said. "But they wouldn't remember a particular advertising supplement."

"They might remember a story about a disappearance at about that time, though," Nola said. "The *Sun* keeps bound copies, doesn't it?"

"The public library has the whole run on microfilm, too."

"That's even better," Nola said. "We'll keep sifting here for other stuff, too—bracelets, buttons, anything that might aid in an I.D."

"Be great if she wore a locket with her name on it," said Rosenak, busy with the camel-hair whisk. "I like getting paid for doing nothing."

"Still think it's a female, Doc?" Nola asked.

"If we find a pelvis, we'll know for sure," Rosenak said.

"What was that ambulance doing down at the condo site?" Nola asked. "My guys who went down there haven't come back."

"Somebody discovered a spike in a tree—with his chain saw," Rosenak said. "Mark's looking into it. They're with him."

Nola gave a low whistle. "Damn greenies."

"We don't know who did it," Eldon said.

"Except maybe Henspeter," Art said.

"He told me not, before he died," Eldon said.

"Then who, except more tree nuts like him?" Nola said.

"Damn it, Art, be fair," Eldon said. "That's like blaming every logger in town for killing Henspeter."

"It makes the same sort of sense," Nola said. "We may have a vendetta on our hands. Somebody took a shot at your place, didn't they?"

"Yeah," Eldon said uncomfortably. "That's a point."

Rosenak looked up. "Does that happen a lot in your line of work?"

"Well, not a lot," Eldon said.

"Maybe they ought to stop work on those condos, at that," Rosenak said. "They're not worth blood."

"This is supposed to be an earthquake zone anyway," Eldon said.

"An earthquake is the least of our problems if this gets out of hand," Nola said. "Eldon, you've got a talent for getting into the middle of dangerous trouble."

"Just call it a nose for news," Eldon said.

Rosenak displayed what looked like a finger bone; he clearly was too pleased to be distracted by the debate.

"Hold that bone up and let me get a picture," Eldon said.

Rosenak complied. " 'Dem bones, dem bones gonna rise.' Let's try to find all the bones we can today, Art."

"I'd better get down and see what's what with the tree-spiking," Eldon said. "Gotta deadline. I'll keep in touch."

Eldon turned away from the pit to see Keith Howell standing at the tape, watching. His mouth was open, suggesting an uncharacteristic dishevelment.

"Is that what I think it is?" Howell asked.

"A skeleton," Eldon said, ducking under the tape. "The rest of whoever belonged to the foot."

Howell shook his head. "I used to play out here when I was a kid. Knew every inch of the place."

"You don't remember any rumors about buried bodies, do you?"

"Just pirate treasure," Howell said. "And trolls that lived underneath. . . . This is very bad for business. And now one of my men is hurt."

They walked back toward the edge of the landfill. With a bark, Bouncer darted under the yellow tape and across the forbidden square to squirm happily around Howell's ankles. Howell knelt and rubbed the dog's head. "The Rising Dog, the Rising Dog, and a very good dog is he, oh, yes . . ."

Eldon was anxious to be away. But he had to smile as Jasper and his congregation hurried around the tape with cries of dismay to retrieve their miraculous mascot. Jasper led the way with the dowsing rod outthrust. It still quivered eerily. Trick of the grip, Eldon thought.

"Our dog finds the foot and our dowsin' rod finds the rest,"

Jasper declared when they reached Eldon and Howell. "Lucky for you ya took our picture." The dowsing rod's tip fluttered as Jasper clutched it, bobbing down to point at Howell.

"I must be standing on water," Howell said.

"Or on an earthquake fault," Eldon said.

"Nonsense," Howell said pleasantly. "Jasper, let's powwow."

"Nothing to powwow about," Jasper said. "We don't even know what happened down there."

"Somebody spiked a tree," Howell said.

Jasper lowered the dowsing rod. "We didn't do it. We wouldn't do that!"

"These condos are still going to be built," Howell said. "Folks need homes. I'd think a minister would favor that."

"I do. But not here."

Bouncer ambled over to Wheelie's chair. Howell whistled and the dog returned to him at once. "Some of my boys wanted to beat the tar out of you. I told them to leave you alone."

"Much obliged, sir," Paavo said with his sharklike sneer.

"I could ask the sheriff to run you off," Howell said. "But I'm not going to."

"You sure aren't," Jasper said. "The newspaper's here."

"You know what they say about publicity—'as long as they spell my name right.' " Keith grinned at Eldon. "Anyway, chasing you off wouldn't solve anything."

"Sure wouldn't," Jasper said.

"You know I wanted to build a memorial to John up here—"

"On a garbage dump," Paavo said.

"You're right," Howell said, "that wouldn't be much of a monument for what John believed in. For what you believe in. And I think that what you believe in is good. So . . . I'm going to let you rebuild the church."

Eldon let the camera swing loose around his neck on its strap and yanked out his notebook. Bigod, he thought, you never can tell what you'll get if you hang around.

Paavo's eyes expanded to the size of half-dollars. Jasper's jaw flapped up and down, as if he were masticating air. One-Square, Wheelie and Beanpole did not react at all. The crusaders suddenly had no one to fight.

"You're going to rebuild the church," Jasper got out. "For us?"

"That's right," Howell said.

"What's the catch?" Paavo demanded.

"Only that you make a go of it," Howell said. He scratched Bouncer between the ears. "And that you let me come by and play with the dog."

Howell stood and offered his hand. Jasper took the hand cautiously.

"W-w-we're g-g-gonna have a church!" Beanpole cried. He lunged down the landfill slope and ran down the road toward the church, windmilling his arms. Bouncer took off after him.

Jasper watched them, then looked back to Howell. "I guess you win," he said in a puzzled way and started across the landfill, dragging the dowsing rod.

One-Square made a disgusted noise and tossed his cane in Wheelie's lap. He took the brake off the wheelchair and pushed it after Jasper.

"I guess you think you've bought us off," Paavo told Howell.

"You've got me wrong," Howell said. "I just want folks to be happy." He turned to Eldon. "Now I'd better get back to my crew—and the sheriff probably has questions about that tree." He moved away across the landfill.

"That asshole," Paavo said.

"Give it a break," Eldon said. "You got what you wanted."

"Howell can't buy us off just because Bouncer feels sorry for him."

"Hasn't he? Jasper thinks so."

"The cap'n sees it plain enough and I do, too," Paavo said. "Who'll go to that church? Not humble people, not real people like us. It'll be *Howell's* people—the kind of people who'll buy his condos. How long d'you think we'll last with that crowd? 'Make a go of it.' Howell knows his condo people will run us out. They won't want to listen to my squeeze-box and watch Bouncer dance. They'll think we're stupid. There's not a lot of call for miracles from people who live in condominiums."

Paavo's tiny eyes, set deep on either side of his smashed nose, glowed with the sore-loser expression that was a Port Jerome trademark. "You wrote about his party," the Finn said in a jealous little voice.

"I've got to get all sides of the story," Eldon said. "That's the way a newspaper works. It's nothing personal."

"Then come to my party, too," Paavo said. "I can go that bastard one better—"

"Paavo, I've got a deadline—"

"—and give you a chance to check up on what we told you about the church. I want you to come up to the Sons of Eiden Hall. There might be old people there who'd remember what went on."

"I don't know if—"

"It's the monthly Sons of Eiden dance," Paavo said. "It's on Saturday night."

"Oh, yeah, we got a press release—"

"It's better than any developer's tea party. There'll be lots of Finnish food and Finnish girls. And some good fights. You'll know you've been to a *party.*"

"Okay, okay, I'll come," said Eldon, anxious to get back to the office.

"Good." Paavo dropped a hand on Eldon's shoulder, making Eldon list. "I guess you're right about having to check what we told you. A reporter can't trust anybody."

"I'll bring somebody along, if you don't mind. A Dane."

Paavo grinned. "Even Danes are welcome. As long as she's pretty."

"Oh, she's pretty, all right," Eldon said.

Paavo stared at the point where Howell had disappeared over the side of the landfill. "I'll never give up. I'll beat that S.O.B. somehow."

"You're supposed to be a Christian now," Eldon said. "But you didn't even flinch when they rolled that poor bastard that lost his fingers into the ambulance."

"I've seen lots worse on fishing boats and in the mills. Every workin' man around here has. It's too bad Howell wasn't runnin' that chain saw himself."

Eldon allowed himself another glance at Paavo's feet. Size fourteen, eh? Won't it be *good copy* if your boot size matches that print they found near Henspeter, too? Eldon thought. I'm going to get your size somehow at the Sons of Eiden Hall, and if it matches my photo, Enola Gay and I will have quite a party ourselves, afterward.

=15=

Back in the newsroom, Eldon thought: If I can implicate Paavo, I'll take the evidence to Art Nola. He'll owe me big after that.

Eldon imagined the headline over his story about the Finn's arrest. He could see the page layout, complete with a shot of a scowling Paavo, safely handcuffed. He'd write a first-person sidebar about how he had cracked the case, too. The wire service certainly would pay him a few bucks for that—he'd take Enola Gay to dinner in Eugene.

But if that left one murder down, there was still one to go. No matter what his intuition had suggested, Eldon could not conceive of a link between Paavo's killing John Henspeter and the mummified foot in the landfill. The discovery of the foot and Henspeter's murder were merely a sad coincidence in a violent community. Unless, of course, Paavo had buried a victim in the landfill as a homicidal child.

Eldon smiled at that and decided to call Reuben Amick. Perhaps the undertaker had found something in his father's papers.

"You won't like this," Amick told him jovially.

"Won't like what?"

"A pipe burst in my mother's basement a couple of years ago. The basement flooded. The trunk with Dad's records in it sank."

"Oh, shit."

"I forgot all about it. After you and I talked, I went and opened that trunk up for the first time since then, and man, what a smell! Like a month-dead client. When mold gets started around here, it really goes to town. Nothing's legible."

"Damn. Why didn't you open it and dry it out back when it got wet?"

"I didn't know about it," Amick said. "I was on a fishing trip when the basement flooded. It was when I caught that big Chinook, as a matter of fact. My brothers hauled stuff out of the basement and helped Mom clean up. I guess the trunk just got shoved aside. If I'd realized—"

"At least you caught a fish," Eldon said.

"Sorry. But listen, thanks for putting my picture in the paper. Have I been getting calls! Every N.R.A. member on the South Coast wants me to bury 'em! What kind of booze do you drink? I want to send you a bottle."

"Couldn't accept it," Eldon said. "But thanks."

"You've got to let me do something for you," Amick said.

"Just keep digging through that mold. If you find anything useful, give me a holler."

"Will do—"

"Wait a second. When your dad was coroner, he knew a lot of doctors, didn't he?"

"Sure." Amick chuckled. "He used to tell 'em that every doctor's patient winds up in a funeral home, sooner or later."

"Can you find out if your dad knew a Dr. Clifford Smith? An orthopedist?"

"Sure he knew him. Uncle Cliff taught me how to shoot."

" 'Uncle Cliff?' "

"That's just what I called him. He and Dad were lodge brothers in the Moose. Cliff was quite a character. He was something of an artist; he used to draw nudes, which was pretty scandalous back then. He was pretty good. Uncle Cliff was big in the N.R.A., too. He started me out on a .22 rifle and squirrels—"

"Where is he? Is he still alive?"

"I haven't talked to him in years. He's in a nursing home in Coos Bay."

"Still savvy?"

"Savvy enough to send my mother a Christmas card every year."

"What's his address?"

"I'll get it from Mom. I'm sure she got a card from him last Christmas—"

"Never mind, I'll look it up. Coos Bay couldn't have that many retirement homes."

"What's cooking?"

"A long shot. It's possible that your Uncle Cliff treated the ankle of the lady in the landfill. His records could help identify her."

"He'd have 'em, too. Cliff never threw anything away. He taught me how to reload spent ammo, to save on brass."

"You've just repaid me, Reuben. Thanks."

Eldon went to the *Sun*'s repository of telephone books. He got the current Coos Bay directory and lugged it back to his desk and turned to "Retirement Homes" in the Yellow Pages. Only three were listed. Eldon started calling. The first two rest homes had never harbored a Clifford Smith. Eldon dialed the number of the third and asked for Smith.

The receptionist switched him to the manager's office. The manager said that Dr. Smith had died the previous January.

No more Christmas cards for Amick's mother, Eldon thought. Suddenly he was frantic. Relatives had a way of cleaning house after a death. They might've thrown the records out. "Are there any relatives I could talk to? This is important."

Yes, there was. Dr. Smith's nephew was an actuary in Grants Pass in southern Oregon. Since the nephew was executor of the estate, it would be proper to give Eldon his telephone number.

Eldon wrote the number down on his telephone log card. He found himself staring at it for long moments before he dialed, wondering: Will Enola Gay have any use for me once I've solved the crime? His thought made Eldon indignant. By God, that's *her* problem. At least I'll get the scoop.

He dialed Grants Pass. The telephone buzzed three times at the other end. A fourth time. A fifth. Eldon was about to hang up when a man answered. "Peter Smith." His voice sounded gravelly and hung over.

"You're the Peter Smith who had the Uncle Clifford in Coos Bay? You're the actuary?"

"That's me. He owe ya money? Tough luck."

"No, I—"

"He's dead. Too much Christmas cheer. At his age he shoulda laid off the Cutty Sark."

"I know he's dead," Eldon said. "I'm a reporter for—"

"He choked to death—"

"—the *South Coast Sun*—"

"—on a rubber surgical glove," Smith said. "The old goat got so he'd eat anything when he was drunk. You say you're a reporter?"

"Yes. I'm working on an investigative story. Maybe you can help."

"Sure. How?" Smith said. Now his voice was interested.

"I'm trying to identify an old skeleton that was found over here."

"Yeah? Go on."

"Your uncle might've treated this person, years ago when he was an orthopedist here in Port Jerome."

"Wow, think so?"

"The skeleton had an ankle injury," Eldon said. "I want to look through the records of your uncle's medical practice and see if anything matches up."

"Aw, I can't help you—"

"Look, I'm not trying to embarrass you or anything. I'm sure your uncle would say this is a good cause—"

"I'm all for it," Smith said. "But you're too late. We burned that stuff, oh, just a couple of months ago. I couldn't go the storage charges anymore."

"You burned it all?"

"All that we had."

"There's more?"

"Not that I know of. We burned boxes and boxes of stuff. Uncle Cliff had been in practice since the thirties. If there was anything else, God knows what became of it."

First the burst pipe and now this, Eldon thought. Not twice in one day.

But he knew as he thanked Smith and hung up that he should not be surprised. This was all too common a story. Time passed, sources and witnesses died or forgot, records disappeared. He was merely confronting time's accumulated consequences. There was nothing to do for now but go to Paavo's party.

===16===

The Sons of Eiden Hall loomed like a troll's lair in the night fog as Eldon and Enola Gay parked the van among the pickup trucks and approached. The lodge was near the Nekaemas Bay boat basin, where many of its Scandinavian-American membership toiled on the fishing boats.

Eldon considered the stories about fighting "Scandahoovians" to be sentimental Oregon folklore, at least in modern times. Then he remembered a story of Fiske's about the Finn who had found the Eiden Hall locked on a Sunday and had sawed the door off with a chain saw. He smiled and told himself sternly to forget the ethnic jokes for tonight.

"That music is loud," Enola Gay said happily.

"You Scandahoovians sure know how to have fun," Eldon said.

Enola Gay poked him in the ribs. Eldon thought she was teasing him in return until he saw something shining in her hand. "Earplugs," Enola Gay said.

"Good thinking. Thanks." The earplugs were in a tiny clear plastic box. Eldon opened the box and twisted the bits of plastic foam into his ears.

"There can be too much of a good thing," Enola Gay said, brushing back her hair to insert a pair of her own.

The music sounded like a thundering meld of Jimi Hendrix and polka. Eldon knew it was played by a live band called the Sons of Eiden. The band's membership was as ecumenical as that of the lodge. The saying went that anyone who wanted to could come to the Sons of Eiden Hall and fight.

Sure enough, the Eiden Hall's door burst open and two men were pitched through like bowling balls. They rolled off into the fog. A huge man stepped into the doorway, blotting out the light within. It was Paavo.

"Chickenshit Norwegians!" Paavo knotted his fists for further battle as Enola Gay and Eldon approached.

"Peace, Paavo—it's us," Eldon called.

"Eldon! Glad t' see ya!" Paavo's eyes lit up at the sight of Enola Gay. *"Tervetuloa!* Welcome to you."

"This is Enola Gay Hansen," Eldon said proudly. "She's the Dane I told you about."

"I remember you from the funeral," Paavo declared. "Hey, weren't you the one on the horse—?" He gulped and reddened and clumsily pumped Enola Gay's hand. "I'm just clearing out a few Norwegians."

Enola Gay gave Paavo a dazzling smile. "Give 'em a good toss for me!"

"With pleasure!" Paavo lunged back through the door. *"Nähdään vielä!"*

"That means, 'See you later,' " Enola Gay said. "I know a few Finnish and Danish expressions. It works wonders."

"I hope so," Eldon said. "Do the different Scandinavian groups fight for possession of this place?"

"That's about the size of it," Enola Gay said. "Those Norwegians must've trespassed on a night reserved by the Finns. Or maybe they just showed up looking for a fight."

"At least Paavo didn't tear off their ears."

"Oh, never at a party."

They entered the hall and found themselves in a lobby paneled with dark wood. The trim was painted with Scandinavian flags and folk decorations. There were faded black-and-white photos on the walls of people in archaic clothing—the Knights of Keleva, the Finnish Socialist Federation, the Finnish National Temperance Brotherhood, the Norwegian Temperance Brotherhood, and others. Eldon noted with interest the framed front page of an ancient Finnish-language newspaper called *Toveri,* published in Astoria. There was a case of bowling trophies, too. A real chalice of coastal culture, he thought. The trophy case stood next to a flight of stairs leading to the second floor. The din upstairs was tremendous, even with earplugs. The band blasted away with amplified instruments, and scores of dancing feet thundered on the floor above. Eldon felt the vibrations through the banister.

Another man was bowled down the stairs and out the door. Eldon jumped back. "Another Norwegian—"

"Looked like a Finn to me," Enola Gay said, straight-faced.

"I thought Norwegians were the enemy tonight."

"It depends on your brand of Finn," Enola Gay said. "The church Finns, for instance, are mostly Lutherans. A lot of them are dry Finns or temperance Finns. Opposing them are the labor Finns, who are anything but dry and mainly shy away from church activities. That's the tradition, anyway."

"You know a lot about Finns, for a Dane."

"You don't know the Oregon coast unless you can keep your Scandinavians straight," Enola Gay replied. "I'd guess that the one who just rolled out the door was a church Finn. Maybe he got into a fight with a labor Finn."

"How could you tell?"

"He didn't smell of liquor. He might've started preaching temperance and a socialist polished him off. Or a monarchist. Or a hard-line pacifist. There are a scad of splinter groups, or used to be."

"I'm with the socialists," Eldon said as they went up the stairs.

Two large, heavily built Finns stood guard at the head of the stairs. They had stereotypical square, snub-nosed faces, icy blue eyes, and blond hair. It was anyone's guess whether they were socialists, although they obviously had given the latest human bowling ball a helping hand. They sized up Eldon while a pleasant middle-aged woman, also blond, also snub-nosed, sold him two tickets to the dance. The woman had to root through the cash box to break his twenty-dollar bill; Eldon grew uneasy. Had the bowling ball lacked exact change? Then one of the bouncers caught a high sign from Paavo, who was up on the stage with the band. The bouncer flashed thumbs-up, and Eldon knew he would be allowed to live.

Eldon and Enola Gay made their way around the edge of the dance floor, which was packed with people of all ages dancing to the band's vigorous beat. Eldon saw no drunkenness, just people having a good time. Old folks paced decorously, while teenagers writhed to the music. Couples of intermediate age fox-trotted and jitterbugged. Some girls and young women wore dark, full-skirted, flowered jumpers that Eldon assumed were traditional styles. Many of the women were classic Scandinavian blondes, but there also were slighter, dark-haired women with more delicate features.

Enola Gay saw him ogling and explained, "The blond Finns are Tvasts. They're the more typical kind. The dark ones are Karelians and people from Savo province. They're supposed to have the better sense of humor."

"You're as beautiful as any of them."

"I envy these people," Enola Gay said, speaking loudly over the music. "It must be great to *belong*."

"You're Scandinavian. You belong."

"Not like this, Eldon. I was raised about as Scandinavian as you were."

"You know a lot of the traditions."

"That's just what it is—tradition. This stuff is dying out, and too bad, too."

"Not as long as we have Paavo," Eldon said.

Paavo was pumping his concertina as if crushing heads. Eldon strained to pick out the squeeze-box's contribution to the band's thundering mongrel tune. Sure enough, it was the opening bars of "Rock of Ages," played over and over like a bass riff.

Paavo stomped time with his right foot, reminding Eldon of what he had come for. He inched toward the stage, wondering how to get an imprint of Paavo's boot, when Enola Gay grabbed Eldon's hand. "Let's dance." She pulled him into the crowd.

Enola Gay was not a particularly good dancer, but she was an enthusiastic one. Eldon, who could barely dance at all, let her lead as they took off in a rapid, disorganized polka. Her enthusiasm was infectious. Eldon got with the rhythm. They dodged and collided with other dancers. Enola Gay laughed and Eldon laughed, too. He hadn't had this much fun for a long time. They reached the other side of the dance floor as the music ended, and things got even better—Eldon's nostrils were filled with wonderful smells.

A buffet table was covered with food. His mouth watered at the sight, a truly titanic repast. There was spiced herring and salted herring, herring in aspic, and herring in tomato sauce; cold cuts; salads and cheeses, pastries and vegetables; breads scrolled, twisted, and knotted into intricate shapes. Soup bubbled in heavy iron pots. There were stuffed meat rolls, casseroles, a sliced pork roast, and plates of whole salmon. An entire table was covered with desserts. The rich scent of cardamom coffee bread dominated everything. Tonight I'll eat until I die, Eldon thought.

A heavy hand clamped his shoulder. It was Paavo, down from the stage, leaning over to speak in Eldon's ear.

"*Voileipäpöytä*—Finnish for smorgasbord," Paavo said. "That's *lipeäkala*—lutefisk. That over there is *uuni juusto*—custard made from the first milk of a cow after she's calved. And that's *kala-kukko*—bread pie stuffed with trout. The soup is *seljankakeitto*—fish stew . . ."

"Like a bouillabaisse." Eldon's mouth watered as Paavo identified each course. He reflected that he was getting a lesson in Finnish cuisine from someone who might have run an iron bar through a man's chest. The thought enhanced Eldon's appetite. The gourmet crowbar-killer—what an angle that would make!

Enola Gay was enthralled by Paavo's gastronomy lesson. She nodded eagerly as she absorbed the information. When the band struck up a 1940s dance tune, Enola Gay coaxed Paavo onto the dance floor. Eldon was dismayed—but suddenly he saw his opportunity as Enola Gay pulled off her shoes, the better to prance on the polished wood floor. Paavo whooped and followed suit. Eldon grabbed their shoes and hurried to the sidelines. He looked for the size stamped inside Paavo's well-worn boots. But there was only a faint silver smudge in the ankle of the right boot. The numeral had been worn off.

"Damn." Eldon lowered the shoe. The killer giant was dancing around the floor with his girl—and acquitting himself well. Good grief, they were *waltzing*. Where had Paavo learned to waltz? Eldon watched jealously as a beaming Enola Gay followed the Finn's lead with artless grace. Soon they were lost in the crowd, except for the top of Paavo's head.

Eldon spied an empty cardboard cake box in a trash can. He tore off the box's top, slapped the right boot onto it on the floor, and traced the outline of the sole with his pen. Now he would compare it with the photograph he had taken in the *Sun* office.

Then he realized that the photograph wouldn't show scale. The footprint would be whatever size he printed the negative. Shit, he thought, I've got to get to a shoe store—

"You like those boots, eh?"

Eldon looked up into the face of an aged man—not the square, blond face that he expected but a narrow one, with gray eyes and lined, sharply defined features. The man's hair was iron gray. He was dressed in a dark suit and white shirt and narrow old tie. He leaned on a cane.

"I was, ah, thinking of buying some," Eldon said, getting to his feet. "I wanted to see the brand name."

"You can get those most anywhere." The old man had a slight accent. "They wear like iron."

"Yeah, that's what I heard."

"I don't think I know you," the man said. "That's a mighty pretty girl you came in with."

"Isn't she?" Eldon thrust out his hand. "I'm Eldon Larkin, from the *Sun*."

"Erho Saarima," the man said as they shook hands. "Are you writing about us Finns?"

"Oh, kind of. Paavo Wikkula invited us."

"Ah, Paavo. I knew his grandfather—there was a fighter! Paavo, too, though he's different these days. Paavo is temperance now, you know."

"Yeah, that's what he told me," Eldon said, wondering whether Erho was a socialist and would hit him with his cane.

Erho spoke in Finnish to a grandmotherly woman in a light blue dress who was arranging cakes. She was round-faced and somewhat stout. Her hair was a faded silvery yellow and her hands were knobby with arthritis, but her smile was quick and her blue eyes lively. Eldon caught his own name and the word *sanomalehti,* because the woman repeated it.

"I told my wife that you write for the newspaper," Erho said. *"Sanomalehti* means 'newspaper'?"

"Very good." Erho spoke to his wife and she addressed Eldon in Finnish, with excited approval.

"Ida likes your paper," Erho said.

"Tell her thank you . . . or does she speak English?"

"She reads it okay, though I translate a lot for her," Erho said fondly. "She's never talked English worth a damn, and we've been in this country a long time."

"You speak it perfectly."

"I hope so! Young folks think it's funny that Ida doesn't speak much English. But when we were young, you could live on the coast just fine and only know Finnish. That was until, oh, the 1950s. Not that long ago." Erho patted his wife's gnarled hand. "Old habits die hard."

Ida, smiling, handed Eldon a piece of cake on a paper plate. Eldon dug in with a plastic fork. It was a delicious almond cake. "Tell her this is great! One of my favorites."

Erho complied and added, "My wife's a good cook and an educated woman, even if she doesn't speak English. She speaks Russian, which I do not, and French, which I barely understand."

"*Français?*" Eldon said. "*Donc, vous parlez français, Madame Saarima? Il n'est pas nécessaire que votre mari traduise.*"

Ida Saarima laughed again. "*Comment aimez-vous mon gâteau aux amandes?*"

"I like your almond cake very much, madame," Eldon replied, in French.

"You're right—it is not necessary for my husband to translate; you speak French very well. But please call me Ida. How did you learn French?"

"In school," Eldon said. "I traveled in Europe. I was in Paris. I never got to Finland, though."

"We fled to Paris during the Winter War,—the Russo–Finnish War," Ida said. "We were very poor in Paris, though we managed. French is an excellent language. But I regret not learning English."

"There is always time."

"Oh, I am too old now. I started once, but that did not work out."

"For one as gifted in languages as you? How so?"

"I took lessons years ago. At church. But the congregation broke up and I never continued." Ida's eyes flashed. "The tutor and I were not speaking to one another by then. *Le fils de putain! Il ne se prenait pas pur une merde.*"

Eldon blinked as he reached for more cake. Had this grandmotherly lady just said that the son of a bitch thought his shit didn't stink? Yes, she had. "Uh, why do you say that?" he asked.

"There was a terrible political argument."

Eldon became alert. "When was this?"

"Perhaps twenty years ago. Please try the fig butter cake."

"*Oui, merci. C'est bon!* Not by chance the empty church at Schumacher's Landfill?"

"Yes, that's it," Ida said. "Where they found that foot and then the body the other day. How did you know?"

"The congregation was Finnish?"

"Not entirely, but many were," Ida said. "Of course, the Finns started fighting. About Senator McCarthy. *Quel déconnage!*"

That was something like saying, "What bullshit!" Eldon hadn't heard such French since his coffeehouse days in Paris. He pressed on, puzzled for a moment. Senator Eugene McCarthy had run for president during the Vietnam War, years after the congregation had dissolved. Then he realized that Ida meant Senator Joe McCarthy, the infamous red-baiter of the Cold War.

"Some of the people liked Senator McCarthy's hunting down communists," Ida said, her expression darkening. "*Je l'emmerde!* I shit on him! The temperance Finns liked McCarthy and so did the monarchists. They said the socialists in the congregation, like Erho and me, were communists. 'That's just bullshit!' I told them. '*Va te fair enculer!*' they replied."

Meaning, Get the fuck out of here, Eldon thought, sorting through the gutter French in his mind as Ida filled in Erho with a rapid burst of Finnish.

Erho nodded vigorously. "There was more to it than that, though. It was really about the church's land."

"*Continuer, s'il vous plaît.*" Eldon listened intently, for the band was playing loudly.

"The land was owned by a man named Weems," Ida said. "Oh, what was his first name—"

"Ellis Weems. He was a county commissioner."

"Ellis Weems," Ida said, nodding. "I can see him plainly. He was a big man. He had a falling-out in business with another church member, Harmon Howell. They had a terrible argument over the land. Harmon Howell split the congregation, trying to get the land. He sided with the people who liked McCarthy and persuaded them that he should own the property. He called Weems a traitor because he was a Democrat. I told him not to talk bullshit."

Eldon wondered if Ida was as foulmouthed in Finnish but decided it was just as well that he would never know. He said, "Was Harmon Howell related to Keith Howell?"

"He was Keith's father, of course," Ida said. "I don't have anything against the son. He was just a little boy then, but now he has a shitload of money. He is going to have his father's way with the land, after all these years, if Erho correctly translated your newspaper to me."

"He is going to develop the land, if that is what you mean."

"Yes. Old Howell wanted that land to build on, and the church would not sell it to him."

"Why did he not buy some other land instead?"

"Getting that property was a point of pride with the old son of a bitch," Ida said. "Money owned him. And if you take the business back far enough, the Howell family laid claim to the land in the nineteenth century. They lost out to the Weems family then, in what they always claimed was a shady deal. *Quel déconnage!*"

"What happened then?" Eldon asked.

"Things became so bitter that the church broke up. So much for Christian love! The bitterness spread to the community, too— that's the kind of time it was. Ellis Weems was recalled as a commissioner; Old Howell was behind that, too. Weems was so disgusted that he left town. Howell died before he could get the land himself, and I am still glad."

"You have few happy memories of that church," Eldon said.

"There were some good people in the church, too," Ida said. "Our county commissioner, Monsieur Nedlee, was on our side. He always gets our vote at election time."

"Pumpkin Joe?" Eldon expressed it in French as *Joseph le Potiron,* and Ida laughed.

"Very good," she said. "That is he."

"How did he get involved with you Finns?"

"He was a friend and business partner of Weems. He succeeded Weems as commissioner."

Now doesn't that put the condo project in an interesting light? Eldon thought. Two pioneer families at each other's throats. Keith talks very kindly, but maybe he's getting revenge for something that happened in the nineteenth century. Or maybe that he just thinks happened.

201

Revenge in the name of something that had incubated like fungus in the rain for generations. It was like a Faulkner novel. And it had left Nedlee a commissioner? Now Pumpkin Joe, once a friend and business partner of the former owner of the land, was about to sanction its development. That was more interesting still.

How could Paavo possibly fit in? Eldon wondered. Well, he could always figure that out if he placed Paavo at the scene of Henspeter's murder. . . .

"It must be interesting to be a reporter," Erho said.

"It's fun," Eldon said. "What do you do?"

"I'm retired. I was a shoemaker."

Eldon nearly dropped Paavo's boot. He thrust it at Erho Saarima. "What size is this boot?"

Erho examined the boot. "Ten-B or C. Gonna try 'em on?"

"A ten? You're sure it's not a fourteen?"

"Too small for you? I still know a size-ten boot when I see one!" Erho translated the exchange to Ida and both laughed.

"But Paavo's a giant," Eldon said.

"He has small feet," Erho said. "Like his father and grandfather—I repaired their shoes. All Wikkulas have small feet. But they can kick like mules! Wikkulas have *sisu!*" Erho reverted to Finnish and flourished the boot, making kicking motions while wobbling on his cane. He and Ida found this tremendously funny.

Eldon grimaced and tossed the top of the cake box back into the trash. He looked around for Enola Gay and Paavo, didn't see them, and decided to have some more food. After all, he had their shoes.

"Harmon Howell!" Ida said. "I have not thought about him for a long while. He was a real *pisse-froid*. I had customers like him in Paris. I charged them whether they could perform or not—"

"What?" Eldon blurted in English.

"*Alors*, I have said too much," Ida said. She eyed him for a moment, then continued. "We were very poor in Paris, as I told you. We had to make ends meet." She was quite unself-conscious. "War brings hard times." Ida's blue eyes flashed. "Men who tried to abuse me were sorry—Erho was a magnificent fighter in his day!"

"I am sure he was." *Le souteneur*, Eldon thought. That was the word for pimp.

"I have shocked you," Ida said.

"Oh, not really, I—"

Ida glanced around and looked relieved when she saw that Erho was at the other end of the smorgasbord, sampling food. "My husband will be embarrassed that I have told you this. He will say I am indiscreet."

"I will tell no one, Madame."

"Thank you. That was a long, long time ago." She smiled mischievously. "I have not talked like that to a young man in years."

"Oh, ah—"

"I must not amuse myself at your expense," Ida said. "You will want to dance with your beautiful young lady. Meanwhile, try this dish. It is *lasimestarin silli,* which means glassmaster's herring, although this is trout, which works just as well. It is delicious."

"Merci." Eldon accepted the plate with relief. "You can teach me a Finnish word. What is *sisu?"*

"Oh. It means 'Finnishness,' I suppose. It has no exact translation in any other language." Ida called Erho back and spoke in Finnish.

"Sisu?" Erho said. "That's something like—solid. Patient. Stubborn. A Finn must have *sisu*—a good head on his shoulders, and maybe even a streak of downright cussedness." Erho thought about it. "The closest thing in English might be 'guts.' Or 'balls.' You've been talking about Finland?"

"Your wife says you have balls."

Erho smiled. He still had all his own teeth.

The music ended and the band took a break. Enola Gay and Paavo came up laughing. Enola Gay was flushed with enthusiasm and Paavo was grinning. Eldon fought off dark imaginings and forced a helpful smile as he returned their shoes. He felt relieved that Paavo could not be Henspeter's killer. But a mean streak in him thought it was too bad that he would not be able to bring down a lout with whom Enola Gay had enjoyed dancing.

"Have a good time?" Eldon asked her after Paavo had moved down the smorgasbord, lustily inhaling food.

"He's a good dancer," Enola Gay said, brushing the hair back from Eldon's ear. "But I came here with you."

Eldon's heart melted. "We'll dance some more when the band comes back. Uh, what was so funny?"

"Eldon, you have green eyes."

"Can't help it."

"We were talking about his 'occupying' the condo site."

"How did you know about that? That wasn't in my story."

Enola Gay smiled. "I told the newspaper about it."

"You're the one who called Fiske?"

"Was that his name? I wanted to talk to you, but he answered the phone and so I told him."

"What the hell do you mean, doing that?"

"Steady there, Eldon. I'm not answerable to you—for anything."

"You sure as hell are answerable when it's something I'm writing about," Eldon said. "What's the idea?"

"Fiske answered the phone and said he was the editor. I decided there was a better chance of a story if the editor got a mysterious tip."

"Mysterious tips are a dime a dozen in the news business. You didn't tell Fiske who you were?"

"I already said I didn't." Enola Gay grasped Eldon's hand. "I didn't mean to make you angry."

"I got a good story out of it—no thanks to you. What possessed you to go to bat for those loons anyhow?"

"They're not loons," Enola Gay said. "I talked to them. They're trying to do something admirable, trying to rebuild that church. It used to be a Scandinavian church, you know. And they're trying to save those trees like John wanted."

"That cedar grove's days are numbered. Your father says so himself."

"I don't have to agree with my father, Eldon. And I don't have to agree with you."

"I thought nothing would do except that I catch John's killer. I've already dodged a goddamn bullet—"

Enola Gay fixed Eldon with a look of such determination that he had to laugh. "Let me tell you why we came to this party. It wasn't because Paavo invited me."

"It wasn't?"

"If you'll look over in that trash can—*don't* gawk, just glance over slowly!—see the box top with the footprint drawn on it? Proof that Paavo didn't kill John."

"What?" Enola Gay gave a start.

"There was a footprint at the murder scene. But it wasn't Paavo's size."

"You checked his boots while we were dancing!"

"I had to find out. I saw my chance and took it."

The band left the stage and the dance floor cleared. Clicks and hissing came over the sound system and then recorded classical music. Eldon recognized Edvard Grieg's Opus 17, a suite of Norse folk tunes and country dances arranged by the Norwegian composer. This particular section was called "The Pig." Girls in traditional garb began a folk dance. No one here knows how to play the old music anymore, Eldon thought.

A drunk weaved onto the dance floor and began declaiming:

> "I am driven by longing,
> And my understanding urges
> That I should commence my singing
> And begin my recitation.
> I will sing the people's legends,
> And the ballads of the nation—"

The bouncers yanked him away. The dancing continued. There were sounds like a bowling ball receding down the stairs and a distant bang as the bowling ball hit the door.

"That was from *The Kelevala*," Enola Gay said absently. "What now?"

"Tonight let's enjoy ourselves," Eldon said. "We're guests of a kindly giant Finn who runs with a faith healer and a risen dog. Have something to eat."

Enola Gay sighed. "I'll bet the food is good."

"Sure is. I learned a lot about Finnish cuisine." And had a very informative conversation, Eldon added to himself as he escorted Enola Gay toward the smorgasbord. He was not about to tell Enola Gay about her father's connection with the old church or the theory taking shape in his mind.

=17=

"No dice on the federal firearms records," Frank said around a bite of his lettuce-and-tomato sandwich. "They're not public. I tried my state police sources and everyone else I could think of."

"They've helped you before," Eldon said. "Why not now?"

"Seems that NCIC keeps a record of who asks for the hit. Unauthorized queries can be traced right back to the source."

"Goddamn police state."

They sat in Pop's on Saturday afternoon, talking in low tones in the nearly empty restaurant. Eldon jabbed his fork into his potato salad, lifted the gooey yellow mouthful, and, for once, didn't want it. He put the fork down. "I want to know more about those guns. Henspeter knew he might have to defend himself."

"Then why wasn't he armed on the night he was murdered?"

"Because he didn't think he needed to be," Eldon said. "The killer had to be someone Henspeter knew."

Frank shrugged. "You've said that from the first."

"Look, Frank, I want to bounce something off you."

Frank took another bite of his sandwich.

"Pumpkin Joe Nedlee murdered John Henspeter," Eldon said.

Frank stopped chewing. He pushed his glasses up on his nose, resumed chewing, and swallowed. He smiled. "Nedlee? Last I heard, the killer was Paavo the Finn."

"I told you on the way over here why it's not Paavo. It was a stupid idea."

Frank snickered and almost choked on his sandwich. "Tiny feet."

"Henspeter claimed that Nedlee had an interest in the property around the landfill. I thought he was blowing smoke, but Nedlee's an obvious suspect when you think about it. He's viciously impulsive."

"An old stick like that? A county commissioner? Come on."

"He's not that old. And that thing he has about driving nails into his desk—that's what got me thinking." Eldon shuddered. "He hated Henspeter. Anyway, politicians are capable of anything."

"Even murder?" Frank said. "Just because he's mean?"

"No," Eldon said. "That was my mistake in suspecting Paavo—I assumed Henspeter's murder really was just another South Coast crime of passion."

"Henspeter asked for it, if he spiked that tree."

"If he did, that just shows how high the stakes were." Eldon sketched Nedlee's connection with the church land. "Where was Pumpkin Joe on the night of Henspeter's murder?"

"Don't know."

"You're the county government reporter and you don't know where your commissioners are?" Eldon asked.

"I don't sleep with *my* sources," Frank said. "Where's Enola Gay, anyway?"

"At her place, repairing a car," Eldon said. "She's gotten behind in her business." He shifted in his seat and winced a little. Last night in bed, after the Sons of Eiden dance, he had gotten a real going-over to something like a polka rhythm. "I told her I had to catch up on work at the office. I'm glad you were here."

"Well, let me think," Frank said. "On the night Henspeter was killed, all three commissioners were supposed to be at a town-hall meeting out in the sticks. Pumpkin Joe didn't show—and it's not the sort of thing he would miss. Voters, you know."

"Did you ask him where he was?"

"He claimed the next day that he was hung over."

"Sounds lame."

"If Nedlee and Harmon Howell had a feud over the land years ago, why is Nedlee helping the guy's son now?"

"Pumpkin Joe was a friend and business partner of Ellis Weems'," Eldon said.

"That's my point," Frank said.

"That's my point, too," Eldon said. "Take it a step further. Nedlee's connection with Weems means he once had a piece of the action, right? What if he still does? And he's trying to cover that up?"

"Henspeter was blackmailing him about this?"

"Nedlee misled me about the history of that land," Eldon said. "His connection with the property must be in old records somewhere. I think Henspeter knew about it, too—that's why he owned a trunkful of guns."

"Nedlee was going to sweep Henspeter aside with a couple of land-use hearings," Frank said. "Why would he bother to kill him? And Pumpkin Joe wouldn't exactly be the visitor that Henspeter would welcome into his beleaguered camp."

Eldon decided to spring it. "Nedlee is Enola Gay's father."

Frank drank some cola. "You *are* in deep."

"That's why Pumpkin Joe hated Henspeter."

"For shacking up with his daughter? She's a grown woman. These are modern times."

"Pumpkin Joe wasn't a very good father," Eldon said. "He feels guilty and that didn't keep him calm about Henspeter. I think he went to see Henspeter under the guise of patching up the family quarrel. But he really went up there to kill him."

"That was a big risk," Frank said. "Henspeter might've been armed."

"Nedlee had the best chance of getting close to him under those circumstances."

"But what about the blackmail? Henspeter wasn't much into money."

"Henspeter's price was saving the trees."

"That still seems extreme."

"Not if Henspeter upped the ante," Eldon said. "Maybe he started out just wanting the Port Orford cedar preserved. Okay, says Joe, I'm a politician, we'll deal. But then Henspeter gets his nose full of power and starts trying to block *all* the development around there. Henspeter loved playing the monkey wrench in official gears. Good way to jab at his girlfriend's father, too."

Frank finished his sandwich and began cleaning his teeth with a red-tassled toothpick. "Maybe Keith connived with Joe in the murder."

"Eh?"

"If what you say is true, Henspeter blows the whistle on Joe, he blows it on Keith."

That was something Eldon hadn't considered. He weighed the idea. "That's too complicated. Anyway, Keith apparently has clear title—there's no mention of Joe in the property records. So the connection goes deeper. Maybe Nedlee *didn't* plan to kill Henspeter. Maybe they quarreled and he seized the opportunity. Grabbed that crowbar and spiked Henspeter right to that tree the same way he drives nails into his desk."

"What does Enola Gay think about this?"

"I haven't told her."

"You're going to let her read about it in the newspaper?"

"I'll think of something," Eldon said.

"You'd better tell Fiske what's going on," Frank said. "Cover your ass. He'll forgive you. He understands manly appetites."

"Not these appetites."

"You don't cover the Board of Commissioners. Screwing a commissioner's daughter is not a conflict of interest for you."

"Jimbo will want to know why I didn't tell him about the guns."

"Tell him there's no angle yet."

"He might take the story away from me, give it to you."

"I won't take it," Frank said. "Let's get back to the office. Jimbo's probably there now, checking the wire service machines."

Eldon nodded and pushed away his potato salad. They left the restaurant and headed back toward the newspaper. It had rained and the sidewalk was still dark and wet. The smell of rain hung in the air, but Eldon was not comforted as he trudged down the street. He felt as if he were marching to his execution.

Fiske sat at the news desk, sucking his pipe and poring over a large book. He looked up as Eldon and Frank entered.

"Glad you dropped in, Eldon. Didn't know you had a cleaning lady."

"What? I—ah—"

"I called you at home. Your 'cleaning lady' said you were downtown." Fiske rolled his eyes. "I recognized her voice from the other day. She's a good one for news tips, eh?"

"Jimbo, I—"

Fiske spun the book around. It was an atlas. Brightly colored Mercator projections of the world gleamed on the facing pages. The continents looked strange.

The map on the left-hand page showed a massive, irregular blob of land in the middle of a single great ocean. It was captioned, "The World as It Was 200 Million Years Ago." The map on the right-

209

hand page showed modern land masses and oceans. Red arrows pointing in various directions were superimposed on the continents. Jagged black lines cut through the ocean beds. The caption read, "The World As It Is Today."

Fiske tapped the left-hand page. "Pangaea. The original supercontinent. Before those tectonic plates took off hell-bent for leather." He tapped the right-hand page. "Here's the world today, with the bolts all shot. The arrows show how the plates are still slipping."

"I don't think it happens like that, Jimbo," Frank said.

"They could pull apart at any time," Fiske said.

"It's kind of late for repairs," Frank said.

"We've run your interview with that crackpot professor," Fiske told him. "Now we've got to tell the other side."

Eldon said, "Jimbo, I've got to talk to you."

Fiske glanced at Frank. "You mean talk private?"

"I'm in on this, too," Frank said.

"Dee-de-dee," Fiske said expectantly.

"I think Pumpkin Joe Nedlee killed John Henspeter," Eldon said.

Fiske merely moved his pipe from one side of his mouth to the other. "Oh? He confessed to you? I sense some hesitancy there, Eldon."

Eldon took a deep breath and spilled his guts. Relief rushed through him. It was like going to confession as a small boy, pouring out his absurd, petty sins to the priest. Frank's presence made his self-abasement all the more satisfying. Fiske regarded Eldon steadily as he told of the affair with Enola Gay and Enola Gay's relationship to Nedlee. Then Eldon told Fiske about the guns and explained his suspicions about the land.

"I didn't say anything about the guns because I—I didn't want to bother you. I didn't think there was an angle. I don't have anything solid yet."

"You didn't want to embarrass your girlfriend, is what you mean," Fiske said.

Eldon nodded.

"I tried tracing the guns but I couldn't get zip," Frank said. "I'm not going to tell Eldon how to do his job, Jimbo."

210

"Where are the guns now?" Fiske asked.

"Stashed with friends of Enola Gay, for safekeeping."

Fiske lit his pipe and puffed out smoke. "Zero on the guns, and my hardest hitter has compromised himself with a good-looking woman." Fiske regarded Eldon through the smoke. "I've misjudged you, Eldon—"

"Jimbo, I'm sorry—"

"—I didn't know you were such a stud!" Fiske's smile stretched across his face like a crooked, gold-edged fence. "I love the newspaper business. Just when you get bored, it surprises you. This is like the old days, when men were men! When Lyman Dunthorpe was publisher and not this Johnny-come-lately corporation."

"Lyman Dunthorpe was crazy," Eldon said.

"He never let a little screwing around get in the way of a good story, though," Fiske said. "I remember when he ran the entire proceedings of his divorce case in the paper—"

"You've told us," Eldon said.

"Dee-de-dee. Too many prima donnas in the business today. Let's see—we still have to trace the weapons."

"This new police computer system has dried things up," Frank said. "It makes queries too easy to trace."

"You got serial numbers?" Fiske asked.

Frank brought the sheet. Jimbo looked it over. "I'll give these to Marsha, see what she can do."

"Marsha!" Eldon said.

"Can you think of anybody who's happier when it comes to doing this kind of bookkeeper stuff?" Fiske said. "After all, she connected Nedlee to the land out there in the first place."

"By accident! She'll embalm the story!" Eldon said.

"She'll have a little more distance on it than you do." Fiske fixed Eldon with a gaze that was all the more wilting for its out-to-lunch amiability.

Frank pulled Eldon away. "You got off light."

"Marsha!" Eldon sat down at his typewriter. "*Marsha!*"

"She'll never trace the guns," Frank said. "And if she does, we can always brighten up her copy. Listen, I'm going to bow out."

"Cut and run, you mean—"

But Frank was heading out the door.

Jimbo was engrossed in *Sasquatch and UFO*. "More proof about plate tectonics, Eldon. Says here an Egyptian scarab's been found carved on a rock on Guam."

"I have an idea for a story—"

Fiske laid a metal pica stick on the floor by the news desk. "This desk is further from the wire machine than it was the other day. Just by a few picas, but I can tell."

"The janitor moved the wire machine when he vacuumed the carpet," Eldon said. "I want to write about—"

"Then how do you explain the scarab?" Fiske asked.

Eldon realized that he had to take his medicine—exile from breaking news, just as he had feared.

"If this story is as big as you say it is, we've got to cover every angle," Fiske said. "But we've got to play it straight. If you're going to accuse a county commissioner of murder, it helps not to be sleeping with his daughter."

"I guess so. But I'm going to write a story about Nedlee's conflict of interest."

"Oh? And what will you say?"

"That old story Marsha found said he was one of the church directors. I can connect him to the property."

"I don't know if I'd call it a conflict."

"But it *is* news. The property is the focus of public controversy. Once Joe McCarthy, today land use. And a county commissioner has been less than frank. It lays the groundwork for later, when we pin Nedlee for killing Henspeter."

"When and if. Okay." Fiske puffed his pipe. "I know you'll redeem yourself, Eldon. Be good if you can work earthquakes—"

"—into it, right."

Eldon drove home. It was an effort not to bypass the Regret turnoff and continue south on the highway to Schumacher's Landfill. He wanted to stay close to the story. At least Fiske didn't send Marsha there, Eldon thought.

His palms were moist as he gripped the steering wheel. He needed to think and that meant he needed to go fishing.

Eldon smiled. Fishing to get closer to the landfill, by way of the creek that ran down behind the condo project and fed into the slough. Development might affect the creek, I can't overlook that angle, Eldon thought, rationalizing fiercely.

That was it—a fast reconnaissance. He and Enola Gay could follow the back roads that had taken them to the Endos' house. They could get up on the high ground above the landfill, where he could at least look down with binoculars. He would feel like an urchin staring in the window of a candy store, but it would be better than nothing.

He saw with pleasure when he arrived home that Enola Gay's truck was parked before the house. He entered the house and felt a thrill when he heard the shower running and Enola Gay singing wordlessly. He imagined her in the shower, sleek and wet and naked. Eldon took off his hat and jacket and crept into the bathroom like Anthony Perkins in *Psycho*. Enola Gay continued singing. He could see her trim figure moving behind the pink plastic shower curtain. The curtain was decorated with cartoonish patterns of tropical fish and seaweed. Eldon had bought it at a garage sale.

He moved stealthily up to the curtain, heart pounding with childish pleasure. He seized the shower curtain and yanked it aside. *"Boo!"*

Enola Gay screamed and punched him in the mouth. A hard left, lots of knuckles. Eldon yelled and sat down hard.

"Eldon!" Enola Gay cried. "Holy shit, I didn't know it was you!"

Spray from the shower coated Eldon as he writhed on the bathroom floor, clutching his mouth. Enola Gay shut the water off and climbed from the tub. "Oh, you damned fool, what did you think you were doing?"

"I was just playing. Oww—!"

"Let me see," Enola Gay said. "Sit up. Did I hurt you?"

"I think one of my front teeth is loose. Ow! They're capped."

"Don't be such a baby. I didn't draw blood."

"Ow. Ow."

"You idiot. I'll get some ice." Enola Gay kissed his forehead. "Sorry. But you scared me."

Eldon sat moaning. Wasn't this the way his life always went? His teeth had been capped to begin with because Billy Vogel had punched him out in grade school. He wanted to pound Billy's head against the side of the bathtub right now. He felt like shouting at Enola Gay. But he was filled with gratitude when she returned from the kitchen with an ice cube wrapped in a hand towel.

Eldon put the ice cube to his mouth. "Thanks. Want to go fishing?"

"I've never been asked that by someone I coldcocked when they tried to mug me in the shower."

"I'm a special kind of guy."

"Yes, you are."

"This is just a quick trip up the slough. There's another ruckus at the condo site and I want to see the lay of the land."

"What's going on?"

"More environmental fuss."

"We're going fishing at a demonstration?"

"Frank's out there now. Fishing rods will give us an excuse to hang around. Anyway, fishing helps me think."

"How's the tooth?"

Eldon tested it and decided that his tailbone hurt more than his mouth. "I guess it's okay."

He got up with Enola Gay's help. Eldon went to his fly-tying bench and got his binoculars, tackle box, and fishing rod.

Enola Gay followed him into the living room, toweling her hair. "Do you have a spare rod?"

Eldon smiled even though it hurt. If there was one thing that always won his heart, it was fishing. "You and I will go far," he said.

"Farther than you think," Enola Gay said.

Soon they were driving along the back roads that followed the creek. They came fairly quickly to an ideal spot, a turnout in the road that provided a natural viewpoint. Below, a big creek rushed downhill through the woods, a glittering thread weaving down to join the slough behind the condo project. The building frames were clear in the evening light. Eldon parked the van among the trees. Through binoculars he could readily see the crime scene and men moving around the pit.

"There's Frank—there's no mistaking him. And there's Rosenak."

"You can see the church steeple, too," Enola Gay said.

Eldon studied the scene. It was obvious from here that the condo project was right on top of the slough. It would turn the slough into a private stream, and that was no good for fishing. He imagined well-heeled condo dwellers skimming off the slough's bounty, fishing from their backyards, barbecuing their catch, and tossing the bones into the water afterward.

They got out the fishing tackle and sat by the water preparing their equipment. Eldon experimentally wiggled the tooth again.

"Is it loose?" Enola Gay asked.

"I'm not sure."

"Maybe you'd better see the dentist."

"I hate dentists."

"I am sorry I poked you."

"It's okay. I'm sorry I scared you."

"There I was, soaping away and jeez—"

"I miss my Citroën."

" 'Scuse me?"

"I don't know why I started thinking about it," Eldon said. "I just did. It was an old Deux Chevaux. I drove it for years. I drove it up here from Berkeley."

"They're interesting cars to work on. What happened to it?"

"Killed in action last year," Eldon said. "I let the Vietnamese up in Muskrat strip it for parts. I think it was originally slipped into this country illegally in the 1950s; I read somewhere that some of that model were. I bought it when I was a student at Cal and it was ancient then. Somebody had rewired it with a keyed ignition like an American car."

Enola Gay nodded. "The old Citroëns didn't have keys, just starter buttons."

"That car gave me all kinds of trouble but I miss it."

"I'd like to have gotten my hands on it," Enola Gay said. "I could fix it up for you. But you've got a nice van now."

"Yeah. It runs perfectly." Eldon felt melancholy. The stream, the view, the lost Citroën, the fist in the mouth: All were gathered together in his mind like a cloud of gloom. And the thunder in the cloud was his suspicion about Pumpkin Joe Nedlee.

He tried to tell Enola Gay about it but could not make himself say the words. He told himself that it was because his mouth was sore, but he knew that really it was just like the times in Berkeley when he couldn't bring himself to tell Bernice he thought it was all over.

"My first car was a '32 Ford roadster," Enola Gay said, smiling. "The classic American hot rod, real low and real cool. It was

'Cadamera red'—kind of a metallic wine color—and had a drop top. And fenders and running boards and lots of carburetors. I put a later-model engine in it and hydraulic brakes. It was a lot easier to forget my first guy than my first car."

She plucked Eldon's fishing hat from his head and examined the brightly colored flies. "Let's see—it's spring and we're fishing for— oh, trout, wouldn't you say?"

"Yeah, this is a good stream for native rainbows."

"Saul Alinsky and Emma Goldman—I wonder if they're still around," Enola Gay said.

"The wolf eels? They might be."

"I think a Bucktail Coachman will do just fine." Enola Gay slipped the fly from Eldon's hat and began tying it on the leader on her fishing line. Eldon got the fly that the Portland cop had shown him how to make and displayed it proudly.

"The guy who invented this called it a Code Three," he said. "I never have tried it out. You learn a lot of things from other fishermen."

"You know, John taught me how to fish," Enola Gay said.

"He did? Do you like it?"

"Yeah. I learned it to please him, to begin with. I started out sitting on the bank watching him cast. John liked to be watched—"

"Yeah, he did."

"Then I realized that *I* could fish just as well as John could." Enola Gay gave a wry mile. "John didn't like me fishing. He felt threatened. Competed with. I told him that it just meant there would be more fish to eat, but I think that's when things started to go sour."

"Well, nothing can go sour with me over fishing," Eldon said. "You've come to the right place."

He pulled Enola Gay close and kissed her, and she returned the kiss with a laugh. The kiss hurt Eldon's mouth and he thought, Yeah, I'd better see the dentist. But he didn't care about that just now.

They fell back on the bank, kissing lustily, still holding their fly rods. After a while, Enola Gay plucked Eldon's rod from his grasp and carried both rods down to the edge of the slough. She threw the lines into the water and wedged the rods upright among rocks. "Let's see what we catch."

Eldon lay back with his hands behind his head. "That's no way to fish."

"It is when I've already got something on my line." Enola Gay returned and jumped astraddle Eldon. They rolled over and over along the bank, kissing feverishly.

"Let's make love in the van," Eldon said. "I've never made it in the van before."

"No?"

"Just unlucky, I guess. Until now."

"I'll have to take you out of pity, then." Enola Gay sprang up, pulled off her shirt, and bowed toward the van. "After you."

Eldon yanked open the sliding door and sprang into the vehicle. Enola Gay climbed in after him. "Leave the door open so we can hear the stream," she said.

They sat in the doorway and pulled off their shoes.

"Positively your first time in this van?" Enola Gay said.

"An entirely new place for me," Eldon said.

"Not even with the woman you got it from?"

"Sadly not."

"What about her?"

"Well, yeah, she certainly used it. And then there was the gay she bought it from in California. He's the one who outfitted it like this in the first place."

Enola Gay ran a fingertip over the velvet biceps of one of the muscle men on the walls. "Ah, the things these walls have seen."

"You probably wouldn't want to see some of 'em." Eldon tugged at the button on Enola Gay's jeans.

She kissed him and then her tears started. "I'm glad John and I let the wolf eels go," Enola Gay said. "I think maybe that was John's real funeral service, but of course we didn't know that. There are so many things in life that you don't know about—that have a significance you don't understand."

"Yeah." Eldon stroked her breasts.

Enola Gay kissed him again. It hurt Eldon's lip but he returned the kiss eagerly. They struggled under the covers. Eldon squirmed out of his pants and tossed them aside. Enola Gay did the same. She threw a leg around Eldon and began kissing his neck from where she lay beneath him.

Eldon lifted his head to let her continue and admired the view

217

through the van door. The stream, the trees, the fishing rods on watch. He could see the church steeple far below, the landfill, and even a glittering hint of the bay. He was king of the world and his world was perfect.

He looked down at Enola Gay and then heard a footfall. Eldon looked up again, into the face of Pumpkin Joe Nedlee.

Nedlee's face was florid. "Are you going to have a stroke?" Eldon asked. It was all he could think of to say.

"I don't think so," Pumpkin Joe said.

Enola Gay yelped when she heard her father's voice and wrapped herself in the sheets.

Nedlee was wearing old jeans, a red checked flannel shirt, and a green-and-white baseball cap commemorating the 1972 Port Jerome Pioneer Days Festival. He could have been one of his own redneck constituents. The ensemble looked odd to Eldon, who was used to seeing Nedlee in a coat and tie. Pumpkin Joe watched as Eldon dragged on his pants.

"Hello, Joe," Enola Gay said levelly. She had swiftly regained her self-possession.

Nedlee didn't reply. Neither did he turn away. His eyes kept swiveling, sizing up the situation. His neck got that banty-rooster stretch and his face began to darken.

He's got a clamp on his temper like a hydraulic vise, Eldon thought.

"Fishing, I see," Nedlee said. The words were bitten off.

Eldon looked around for a means of defense if necessary. His hands, seemingly of their own accord, snatched up his pen and notebook. "I was going to call you, Commissioner. Let's take a walk while Enola Gay gets dressed."

"All right." Nedlee whirled and stomped toward the water. But he kept his eyes on Eldon. His head seemed to stay in place while his body rotated. Eldon climbed from the van and hurried after Nedlee, deliberately crowding him to put him on the defensive.

Pumpkin Joe merely smirked. "You may have bitten off more than you can chew with her. Your lip looks like you surely did. Believe me, she has a way of living up to her name."

"I've got a few questions."

"Oh, you're not off duty?"

"Reporters never sleep. We're a lot like politicians. How come you're up here?"

Nedlee's color began to subside. Eldon thought that Pumpkin Joe was letting his years of political experience take over in this confrontation with the press. The effect was sinister.

"Official business," Nedlee said. "I'm viewing the locale for purposes of making an informed decision about the Forest Vista Estates proposal."

"I thought the fix was in for the condos."

"The 'fix,' as you put it, young man, is never 'in.' Not with Pumpkin Joe Nedlee. And there are two other votes on the commission. A decision has yet to be made."

"But you know this county like the back of your hand."

"It's important to avoid even the appearance of impropriety."

"Then why'd you lie to me about that church land?"

"What lie?" Nedlee demanded, outraged.

Eldon got ready to run. "You were one of the directors of that old church down there. You were tight with Ellis Weems."

Nedlee blinked. "Ellis Weems? Why, that was years ago. Where'd you hear about—?"

"It's my job to find out things, Commissioner."

They reached the creek's edge. Nedlee looked at the fishing rods. "Enola Gay set these up, didn't she? She has a way of making things work for her." He picked up a rod and tested its spring, stripped the line, and made an expert cast. Eldon noted that it was the rod with the Code Three fly. "Nice rod," Nedlee said. "The fishing is good along here."

"It won't be so good if Keith builds those condominiums."

"So that's what you're worried about. I might've known. Everybody's got a wild hair about something." Nedlee's eyes measured Eldon like precision instruments.

"Why didn't you tell me about your connection with the church?" Eldon asked quickly, for he wanted to avoid a debate about his objectivity. "Don't you think that's a conflict of interest if you're voting on the disposition of the property?"

"I never had an interest in the property. The church is long gone. The issue is moot."

"You were a business partner of Ellis Weems'."

"We were partners in a kitchen-supply business. I ran the store and Ellis was the bankroll. The business went under after Ellis disappeared."

"What happened to him?"

"No one knows—as I'm sure you're aware." Nedlee reeled in the line and examined the fly. "What the hell's this?"

"It's called a Code Three. I'm trying it out."

"Might do for these native rainbows." Nedlee stripped the line again, whipped the rod, and cast. The line sailed out in a graceful arc and the fly plopped into the rushing water. "I'm trying to drop it into that deep pool by those rocks," Nedlee said. "It was Ellis disappearing that first got me appointed to the county board. State law said another Democrat had to succeed him and the party turned to me. I certainly needed a job; the kitchen-supply business had failed." He grinned. "I've been reelected every four years since. I think I worked out real well, for a pinch hitter. We have better roads."

"What happened to Weems?"

"It's said he ran off with a woman." Nedlee started reeling in line. He kept glancing at Eldon; each time they made eye contact Nedlee jiggled the rod, playing the line as if Eldon were the fish Nedlee was trying to hook.

"Who was the woman?" Eldon asked.

"Well, you see, Eldon, the woman was Harmon Howell's wife."

There's the real reason for the feud, Eldon thought. The land was secondary. Or was it? "Where'd they go?"

"She was from Louisiana," Nedlee said. "I always thought they went back there."

"Funny you're helping out your enemy's son," Eldon said. "I got the lowdown about the fight that Harmon Howell picked to get control of the property."

"Who told you about that?"

"A source friendly to you." Eldon remembered what Enola Gay

had said about her father's proclivities. Joe and Ida Saarima might have been very close friends indeed, he thought.

"Harmon wasn't my enemy," Nedlee said. "A good politician doesn't make enemies—not like you mean. He can't afford to. He may be on one side of an issue one day and on another side the next, that's all. That's something Ellis never understood; he took everything personally and made a lot of enemies, and one day they got together and got him."

"Did you mention your connection to Ellis Weems when you voted to rezone the land for development?"

"I guess I didn't. Maybe that was an oversight but Weems didn't own the land anymore and everybody knew it. He was legally dead. And I'm not doing anything special for young Howell. I'm considering his development application, same as I would yours."

"You might say his father ruined you, though. The kitchen business collapsed because Weems took off."

"But I wasn't ruined, was I? It launched my political career." Nedlee cast once more and looked out over the water. "Maybe I do owe something to Keith. And maybe you do, too."

"Like what?"

"Like not drafting him into an old war that was none of his doing. We've got other things to think about now, like building this county up."

Enola Gay, now dressed, climbed from the van and came down to the water's edge. "Well, Dad, now you know," she said.

"He's smarter than the last one," Nedlee said. "Got two eyes, too. Though I can't say he's any better favored."

"Eldon is special," Enola Gay said, like a high-school girl assuring her father of the character of her prom date.

Nedlee cackled. "At least he has a job. He's been doing it, too, while you've been getting decent."

"We've been talking about the condos," Eldon said. "Bet you didn't know that Pumpkin Joe was a member of the old church, years back."

"The church at the landfill?" Enola Gay asked. "No, I didn't."

"You were so young you wouldn't remember," Nedlee said.

"I remember Mother giving you the boot," Enola Gay said.

"I'd do that differently if I had it to do over again," Nedlee said. "But it's old sorrow, same as the business with the church."

"Your connection to the church is worth a story," Eldon said.

"I stand by my actions," Nedlee said. "There was no conflict of interest to declare."

"I'll put that in," Eldon said.

Nedlee's face grew redder once more. He's like a barometer made of raw meat, Eldon thought. When the barometer hits the top he may do anything. Including spike John Henspeter to a tree trunk. Eldon's skin crawled. Nobody knows we're up here, he thought. We're in danger.

Enola Gay touched Nedlee's shoulder. "Dad, calm down."

Nedlee's temper flared as if Enola Gay had touched a match to tinder. "He's trying to hang me politically, and you want me to calm down?"

Enola Gay stepped back. "Eldon's not trying to hurt you."

"He's trying to hang me for a scoop! It's what a reporter does!" Nedlee flourished the fly rod as he might have his gavel, stared at it, and abruptly thrust it at Eldon. "Here."

Eldon grabbed the rod before Nedlee could club him with it. "I didn't make this stuff up. It may have happened a long time ago, but it's back in the news now." He wondered what to ask next. Old records—if he could find them—would verify or give the lie to Nedlee's contention that he did not have an interest in the property. But he couldn't just ask, Did you kill John Henspeter?

"I came up here because I needed to think," Nedlee said. "About the whole ball of wax. About John's death, and the land case—and about Enola Gay."

"What about me?" Enola Gay asked.

"You and I will talk about that."

"Nothing we can talk about that Eldon doesn't already know, Dad."

"You never were very discreet," Nedlee said.

"I never was a hypocrite, you mean. What the hell, it never cost you any votes."

Eldon expected Nedlee to flare up again. Instead his expression crumpled, as if he were a paper figure that Enola Gay had crushed in her hand.

"I worked hard at being a good commissioner because I wasn't a very good father," Nedlee said. "There, it's said. I've admitted it. In front of Larkin."

"If you'd worked less hard at being a commissioner, you'd have had something to come home to now," Enola Gay said.

"I could be recalled because of this Forest Vista nonsense," Nedlee said. "The developers and the unions will be after me if I don't let Howell build. The tree-huggers will be after me if I do. It's unholy. So many years in office, and you take your finger off the button for just one second—"

"Someone's talking recall?" Eldon asked.

"Those rising dog crackpots," Nedlee said. "They think if they block the condo project by recalling me, they'll save that junker church. Of course, they claim they're worried about the cedar over yonder."

So Paavo found a way to stick it to Nedlee and Howell both, Eldon thought. *Good copy.*

He knew that Nedlee was a long way from losing his job. Several thousand signatures would be needed to put Nedlee's tenure to a countywide vote, and recall movements often were more talk than action; in the end, two-thirds of them failed. But recall was a sword of Damocles over every Oregon politician. Which was as William Simon U'ren had intended.

"Nobody's going to recall Pumpkin Joe Nedlee," Eldon said. "It won't even make the ballot."

"All margins erode," Joe said dolefully. "I've been in office a long time, and my reelection last year was pretty close."

"You won by fifteen percentage points against a nobody."

"Land-use issues are political dynamite. And if the *Sun* starts beating the drum about the fishing—"

"Relax. I'll bet they haven't even taken out a petition yet."

"But you'll report it when they do. Them and their nasty little dog."

"You didn't complain when we reported you'd won another term."

Nedlee made a sour noise. "Looks as if Henspeter will have the last laugh."

"John wanted you to like him," Enola Gay said.

"He threatened to *recall me!*" Nedlee cried. "Over those damn trees!"

Bingo, Eldon thought. "What's your shoe size, Commissioner?"

"What? Fourteen-C," Nedlee said. "Why?"

"John threatened to recall you?" Enola Gay interrupted. Her face lit with angry understanding. "Wait a minute—some of the things he talked about just started making sense. I thought you and John were at loggerheads over my living with him. But it didn't really have anything to do with me, did it? You and John were just trying to see who was toughest. Who could come out on top." She surveyed Nedlee and Eldon with equal disgust. "You never can tell with men."

"It wasn't that at all," Nedlee said. "I wanted to do what was best for the people—"

"You might've done what was best for Mother and me," Enola Gay said. "Then you wouldn't be in this fix!"

"Maybe not." Nedlee looked out over the vista before them. "I wish that clown Jasper really could heal and raise the dead." He looked at Eldon's notebook. "Put that in your story, too."

Nedlee walked back up the slope, past Eldon's van, and into the trees across the road. After a few moments they heard a car start and drive away.

Eldon felt a tug on his fishing line. He reeled it in to find that he had caught a nice little rainbow trout.

"Here's dinner—Joe was right about the fishing," Eldon said, then saw that Enola Gay was scowling at him.

"My father is a very lonely and unhappy man, Eldon," she said. "I may not get along with him, but I don't like what you're trying to do to him."

Eldon took a deep breath. This is it, he thought. "Your father is a public official. The people pay him money to do his job—"

"Don't lecture me. You're trying to get him! For a . . . a scoop!"

"I don't 'get' anybody. If someone digs a hole and falls into it, and I write a story about the hole the guy dug for himself, I didn't 'get' him. People get themselves."

"You're never responsible, are you?"

"Only for the story."

Enola Gay still glared. But she was listening. Eldon pressed ahead. "I don't think I ask very important questions. I don't think what I write makes much difference. But when someone doesn't

224

ask those questions, that's when it makes a difference. That's when things start happening that shouldn't. Like John getting killed."

Enola Gay's eyes glistened. She snuffled and self-consciously wiped her nose. "I know that you're just trying to find out who killed him. But it just seems like we've wandered away from that. You're down to heckling Joe about his clodhopper shoe size."

"I wasn't heckling. A size-fourteen footprint was found near John's body."

Enola Gay fixed Eldon with a piercing gaze that was frighteningly like Pumpkin Joe's. Then she put her hands to her mouth. Tears glittered in her eyes. "Oh, God. Dad said that John was trying to blackmail him."

"Threatened him with recall. Over the trees."

"That would do it. That's the one thing that would make Joe kill—because he wouldn't have anything to lose. The one thing. Because if he's not a commissioner anymore, he's nobody. He's just a busted-out kitchenware salesman."

"He probably put the bullet through my window as a warning, too," Eldon said.

Enola Gay dropped her hands. "It got you moving on the case, though, didn't it?"

"I'd have written the story regardless."

"It would be like Joe," Enola Gay said wonderingly. "You never can tell with men. Yeah, it would be like Joe."

"We have to prove it."

"But we're going to, now that we know. Oh, yeah." Enola Gay stared in the direction that her father had gone. "You don't have to like someone you love, Eldon—but now I know why I didn't like Joe, all these years. You know why? Because he'd do anything to feel happy."

Enola Gay's ferocity was so like her father's that Eldon shivered. You're just like him, he thought, uneasily touching his sore lip. You'd even pin this on your own father, to pin somebody.

Then he felt even colder and thought, And so would I.

=19=

"How much of the skeleton have you found?" Eldon asked the next day.

"Oh, nearly all of it," Nola said. "No I.D. yet, so don't bother asking. Our records don't match any known case. Neither do Rosenak's."

"NCIC?"

"No hits."

Nola had his feet up on his desk in the sheriff's office in the county jail in downtown Port Jerome. There was a community college diploma and a small picture of Jesus on the wall over the desk. The chipped Royal Vienna china saucer that Nola had found in the landfill stood on a plate stand in the center of the desk. The desk seldom had anything on it, and there had never been anything else on the wall that Eldon could remember. Nola wore a faintly exasperated expression.

"There are crimes we just never solve," he said. "That doesn't ride too well with detectives or reporters. But that's the ride, sometimes."

"How can someone wind up dead in a landfill and nobody know about it?"

"Because maybe they weren't from here," Nola said. "Maybe Nekaemas County is where they disappeared *to.*"

"I hadn't thought of that," Eldon said. "It's a great place to disappear to, isn't it?"

"I'd have picked somewhere with more sun, like Palm Springs," Nola said. "Or Hawaii. But who knows? Do you have any idea how long it would take to comb records in fifty states? And their records wouldn't be any more complete than ours. It's hard enough to run down a fresh killing, like Henspeter's."

Eldon ran his tongue over his front teeth, which only reminded him that the cap might be loose and that his lip was still sore from Enola Gay's punch. "Look Art—I'm going to do something I normally wouldn't do. I'm going to tell you about something I'm working on. Because I think I'm right up on something important but I can't connect."

"And that is—?"

"It's—got to be off the record."

"You're using that line on *me?"* Nola smiled. It was as if his face had broken open to let out his teeth. His features folded into myriad new wrinkles, and his teeth sprang out of them. The effect was remarkably foxlike.

Eldon felt like a cornered chicken. "You've got to promise not to tell."

Nola waited, still smiling.

Eldon squirmed. At last, he got out, "I think Joe Nedlee killed John Henspeter."

Nola took his feet off his desk and sat up, no longer smiling. "Sit down here." He pointed to the gray metal office chair next to his desk. Eldon realized that he had become the sort of person that the chair was intended for.

Nola got out his leather-bound notebook. Eldon realized how intimidating a notebook could be. Nola got out a pen. Eldon felt doubly intimidated, as if he were about to confess to the murder.

"Now," Nola said softly, "why do you say Pumpkin Joe is the killer?"

"He had a motive."

"What motive is that?"

"Blackmail." Eldon pushed out each word as if forcing pebbles from his throat. "Henspeter tried to blackmail Nedlee about the church property out by the landfill."

"The land that Keith Howell owns? The land that Jasper's up in arms about?"

"Nedlee was a business partner of the original owner of the property, the guy who owned it before Howell, years ago. Nedlee never made that fact public when the county board voted to rezone the land. So Henspeter threatened to start a recall against Nedlee if he let Howell go ahead with his condo project."

Nola nodded thoughtfully. "Who knows, I might sign a recall petition myself."

"I'm not kidding about this, Art."

"You don't sound like you're kidding. Why do you think this?"

"Stuff Nedlee told me." He sketched the conversation at the slough.

"Very interesting," Nola said. "And what else?"

"Nedlee's shoe size is fourteen-C."

Nola remained expressionless. Eldon knew that he had hit home. He could see Nola visualizing the footprint in the mud near Henspeter's corpse.

Eldon felt sweaty and slightly nauseated. He did not want to mention Henspeter's guns. I could phone in an anonymous tip about them, he thought. There was no reason to jeopardize Ronnie Endo's parole.

But once exposed, Ronnie would have little reason not to say that he had gotten them from Eldon and Enola Gay—especially if it meant beating jail.

Maybe Ronnie won't tell, Eldon thought. But if he doesn't, Joline will.

I can pretend to discover the guns after Nedlee is arrested, he thought. I'll find out where Ronnie hid them and write a story about them, say I found out about them from anonymous sources. There was an appealing recklessness to the thought, and Eldon realized why some people committed crimes—to get away with them.

"Find any more antiques out there?" he asked Nola.

"No more porcelain. We'll keep digging—I've got a feeling."

"You had a dream?"

"I dreamed I found pirate treasure in that hole. If I strike it rich, I can retire early."

Eldon could not tell whether Nola was joking or not. "Gold and jewels and stuff," Nola continued. "Might be something to it, the way old Jasper's witching stick keeps pointing at the hole."

"Jasper's still running around out there?"

"He acts like he owns the landfill. Claims he's just walking the miracle dog. He never gives up. I'll let you know when we get to China. Or strike gold."

"D'you think he really raised that dog up?" Eldon said with a smile.

"To be raised you have to have faith. How can a dog have faith? What happened to your lip?"

"I walked into a door," Eldon said. He probed his tooth with his tongue. He couldn't tell whether it was loose or not. Dread filled him. Being arrested for obstructing justice was nothing compared to visiting the dentist. "I'm going to see the dentist now." He made himself speak calmly.

"Toothache?" Art asked.

"I think one of my caps is loose."

"Walking into a door will do it."

"You believe what I told you about Nedlee, don't you?"

"It's certainly a serious accusation. I like tips from responsible sources."

"Thanks, that's nice of you to say." Eldon felt formality creeping into his speech as he thought about visiting the dentist. "Keep me posted, will you?"

"I can't comment too closely on an ongoing investigation."

"You know what I mean. If a county commissioner is arrested for murder, it'll go statewide. I don't want to find out about it by reading the *Oregonian.*"

"Don't worry—you'll be the first to know. And thanks."

"You're welcome."

Eldon's spirits lifted a little as he left the building. Art did not suspect that he was holding something back. A clever criminal could walk around for years undetected, Eldon thought. Like whoever buried the body in the landfill.

But now he had to face the dentist. Eldon turned back to face the county jail instead, like a man looking at the world for the last time. The jail was another modern California-style building plunked down in the heart of moldering, rain-warped Port Jerome. It had been built with a federal grant, the latter-day answer to the WPA. Eldon knew that in another generation the jail probably would look as bad as the county courthouse in Preacher's Hole. And I'll probably be here to see it, he thought. Still working for the *Sun.* I'll have false teeth. Or maybe by then they'll be able to grow new teeth in your head when you need them.

He walked to the dentist's office because that way it would take longer to get there. He trudged past Pop's, past Amick and Son, past the bank where cashiers from the downtown stores came and went with paper sacks filled with cash from the day's business. You could pull off a reasonably lucrative robbery just running around downtown Port Jerome grabbing paper bags away from women. Eldon had considered doing a story on the topic but had rejected it. No sense tempting fate.

He walked more slowly now, for he had reached his dentist's street. Eldon registered the scene with abnormal clarity. He was struck by minute details—the green of crabgrass growing through cracks in the sidewalk, the textures of peeling wood and dented aluminum siding on buildings. He shuffled past a building that he realized had housed the late Dr. Smith's South Coast Pioneer Clinic. Now it was an auto parts store. Car parts reminded him of Enola Gay.

Eldon reached his dentist's door.

CLARA ADAMS, D.M.D., the sign read.

Eldon shuddered. The name made him think of a nurse in a dark Victorian dress and bonnet like Florence Nightingale, from before there was Novocaine.

Dr. Adams actually was a small, trim woman with fair skin, dark hair, and flint-colored eyes, who kept up-to-date issues of *National Geographic* in her waiting room. She had a triangular face with high cheekbones, a small jaw, a straight nose, and an expression like a businesslike elf. Today she wore an open white lab coat over a gray sweater and charcoal slacks. She was about Eldon's age, smart, unattached and, he had to admit, not bad-looking. But she was a dentist.

"Okay, Eldon, up in the chair." Dr. Adams waited patiently while Eldon crept into the chair and clutched the padded plastic arms. She put a white bib on him. For the blood, Eldon thought. She tilted the chair back. "How many years have I been seeing you now, Eldon?"

"About . . . six years. You had just opened your practice."

"Then you should know by now that I'm not going to hurt you. Now what's the problem?"

"I think one of my caps is loose. Right front tooth."

"Open up." She touched Eldon's swollen lip. "Who popped you?"

"My—girlfriend."

"Hm. I'd like my ex to meet her. In a dark alley. But let's take a look. . . ." Dr. Adams adjusted the chair's overhead light and tipped a little dental mirror into Eldon's mouth. Eldon tightened his grip on the chair arms, waiting for the pain. He feared dentists more than anything. He had transferred his primal hatred of Billy Vogel, whose punch in the mouth in elementary school had led to agonizing root canal work and finally to caps, to the entire dental profession. Eldon knew it was unjust, but he couldn't help it.

"Huhwl?" he asked. He meant to say, "Well?"

Dr. Adams removed the mirror. "Bite down for me. Gently." Eldon did so. "Now open again." Eldon obeyed. Dr. Adams picked up a dental pick. Eldon whined.

"Don't be a baby," Dr. Adams said tolerantly.

"Careful."

"I'll be careful. Open up again." Dr. Adams tugged and prodded the tooth, ignoring Eldon's now-stertorous breathing. "Looks sound to me, Eldon. But how long since you've had your teeth cleaned? You've got some plaque in there." She used the pick to scratch determinedly at a molar.

Eldon's fortitude withered. He twisted his head away. "I always floss—"

"I can tell that you do. Your gums are nice and pink. Buildup of plaque is natural."

"I'm awfully busy just now."

"I guess so. I've been reading the paper. A murder. Skeletons in landfills. Recalls. Gigantic stuffed bears. Pretty amazing stuff."

You have no concept of human pain, Eldon screamed in his mind. But he kept silent. He did not dare alienate his dentist. Once he had ruined a weekend in Eugene by unwittingly going to see the thriller *Marathon Man*. The scene with the drill was with him yet. Or most of it was. Eldon had fled the theater. He had been too shattered to ask for his money back—it would have meant explaining the problem, living the scene all over again.

"Open again," Dr. Adams said. "I want to check the rest of your teeth."

Eldon inched back into position and opened his mouth. If she found a cavity, he would beg for gas. Anything but that mile-long needle . . .

Dr. Adams moved her dental pick over Eldon's teeth, gently

probing fissures and fillings. "You have good dentition, Eldon. I don't know why you worry."

Eldon rolled his eyes down and watched the metal butt of the dental pick. Treat this like a traffic accident or a murder, he told himself. Be detached.

"You see some horrible dentition in this town," Dr. Adams went on. "I had an Okie kid in here this morning, twelve years old—his teeth were rotten green stubs. I'll have to pull what's left and fit him with dentures. You should've heard *him* whine. He was worse than you." She put the pick down. "Okay. No cavities. You're fine."

Eldon burned with shame. He had to prove his courage. "Are . . . are teeth in Port Jerome getting better or worse? That might make a health story."

"Oh, I don't know. I'd have to go through my records, make a real study. Six years of practice doesn't really give you enough data, though. It's not enough time."

"Maybe you could compare notes with other dentists."

"Actually, I do have enough records, from before. But I don't have the time to—"

"Records from before what?"

"I purchased this practice from a dentist who retired. I kept his records; a lot of his patients carried over."

"You kept all his records? Dental charts? X rays? The works?"

"Yes."

"How far back do they go?"

"Back to—gee, decades."

"Where are they?"

"They're in the storeroom. Along with records from—"

"Let me see. Now."

"What for?"

"It's for a story."

"Come on, then." Dr. Adams led Eldon through the office and into the back of the building. She unlocked the door to a big, cool storeroom that had deep metal shelves filled with dust-filmed boxes. "Why're you so interested in these?" she asked.

"These might—*might*—help identify that skeleton in the land-fill." Eldon eagerly pulled a couple of boxes down from the shelf, intending to open them. There were more boxes behind the first rank; they were of a different size and were differently labeled. "What're those?"

"Back there? Those belong to a retired doctor. They've been stored here for years. Records from the clinic where the auto parts store is now. The two offices were part of the same practice. I wonder if he hasn't died. He's months behind on his rent—"

Eldon leaned into the shelf and dragged out one of the boxes. The cardboard tore and manila files bulged out. Eldon wiped away dust and read the yellowing label on the box. *Dr. Clifford Smith.* "Oh, baby!" He pulled out more boxes. *Dr. Clifford Smith.* And there were the names of patients, grouped alphabetically and by year.

By Eldon Larkin
Sun *Staff Writer*

PORT JEROME—The skeleton of a woman found in Schumacher's Landfill is that of Isabel Mulford, who apparently died in the late 1950s, the county medical examiner said.

Dr. Donald Rosenak said Mulford was identified by means of old medical records stored in a Port Jerome dental clinic. Deputies dug up the woman's skeleton in the landfill after a dog discovered Mulford's mummified foot. The foot had become separated from the rest of her skeleton.

Rosenak said he could not immediately establish the cause of death and that the investigation was continuing. Rosenak thinks the woman was murdered. Sheriff's deputies are treating the case as a homicide.

Mulford was born in 1937, according to her medical records. She is thought to have been in her middle twenties at the time she disappeared. She lived in Port Jerome, according to an address in the records.

The records that identified her belonged to Dr. Clifford Smith, an orthopedist who died last January in a Coos Bay nursing home. Smith treated Mulford for a broken ankle in . . .

"Pretty good copy," Fiske said.

Eldon stopped admiring the *Sun*'s front page and eyed the editor warily. He had never heard Fiske qualify the term *good copy* before. "What's 'pretty good' about it?"

"She's been dead kind of a long time."

"For God's sake, Jimbo, I've cracked a decades-old missing-person case."

"Be even better if you find out who killed her. And if you crack the Henspeter killing, too. Now, a double-header like that would be good copy. I'd put you in for a journalism award."

"I thought I was off the story."

"Dee-de-dee. Looks as if you've muscled your way back on. I knew I couldn't hold you back, Eldon. You're my hardest hitter."

"Thanks, Jimbo."

"All it took was finding the medical records, hey?"

"They were incomplete, but it didn't take Rosenak long to winnow them down. There's no doubt—the records included X rays of the ankle break. They matched the foot perfectly."

"Are you working on the follow-up? Who the hell was Mulford?"

"I'm checking that now. She didn't go to high school around here or anything like that. No Mulfords in the phone book or voter records."

"The medical records don't list her next of kin?"

"That part's blank."

"Place of birth?"

"It wasn't filled in."

"An out-of-towner," Fiske said. "Like you. What do the fuzz say?"

"There's nothing about her in sheriff's records. They're running NCIC queries. Something might turn up out of state."

Eldon admired the paper again. His story was illustrated with his photograph of Art Nola and some uniformed deputies carrying boxes of records out of Dr. Adams' office. Nola was grimacing at the camera, like someone who had just lost a grueling foot race. Dr. Adams was staring at Nola's grimace as if she were evaluating his teeth.

"The cops took all the records?" Fiske asked.

"Everything for the relevant time period. They took old dental records, too, to see if they could make a cross-check."

"Dee-de-dee. Nothing left to chance."

"The readers will learn some forensics," Eldon said.

"I'd be happier if they learned who Isabel Mulford was," Fiske said. "Get on it. Find out about her life. No stone unturned."

"Right."

"And speaking of stones, don't forget the earthquakes."

"What?"

Fiske leaned down. "I plan to write something up for *Sasquatch and UFO*. Now, *what else* could be buried in that landfill?"

"Nola says pirate treasure," Eldon retorted.

Fiske gave a big smile. "Dee-de-dee. You're so busy hitting hard you can't see the forest for the trees."

"And what trees are those?"

"Murder victim in the landfill. Conflict of interest on the part of a county commissioner, who doesn't mention his connection to the land thereabouts. Resurrected dog. Earthquake fault. Suggest anything to you, Eldon?"

"No—"

"County commission's gotta decide about Keith Howell's development. Recall talk in the wind. Ancient McCarthy-era ugliness. Woman missing from that time. Dee-de-dee."

"Holy Christ—you don't mean *Nedlee* killed her?"

"Now that's a thought," Fiske said. "He's mighty anxious to get that land built over and a park put down on that landfill. That would've covered up a lot of evidence."

Fiske's idea was nutty, Eldon thought, an instinctual leap by a diseased mind. He remembered his own hunch at the landfill—that the old murder and the new one were connected. He said cautiously, "There's no reason to think that, unless Nedlee killed Henspeter."

"There's probably no reason to think it at all," Fiske said and lit his pipe. "But everything connects. Like that scarab on Guam." He wandered off, puffing his pipe.

What would Enola Gay say if I pinned her father for *two* murders? Eldon wondered. Hell, maybe Nedlee's a serial killer, done every murder in Nekaemas County since he took office. Being a politician would be the perfect cover.

Frank burst into the room.

"Jasper and Paavo have filed a recall petition against Nedlee," Frank said. "They've started collecting signatures. I got some pictures at the courthouse. People with picket signs."

"Good man," Fiske said. "That's tomorrow's lead story."

"Eldon, you'll like this." Frank, grinning, unfolded a sheet of paper. Eldon saw that it was another photocopied leaflet. It bore a snapshot of Bouncer with a crudely drawn word balloon in which the dog declared, "I didn't come back from heaven to put up with Pumpkin Joe Nedlee!"

There also was some childish stuff about how there wouldn't be any trees for a little dog to water when Nedlee carried out his plans for Nekaemas County. It was typical nitwit populism but the message was plain and potent. Eldon was sure that it would get under Nedlee's very thin skin.

"Joe's stepped in it, all right," Eldon said.

"I'll bet you lunch that he won't be recalled," Frank said.

"What if he's arrested for murder?" Eldon asked.

"Then I'll buy you two lunches. I'm going to soup my film."

Eldon hummed merrily. He was in his place, the newsroom, grinding copy. That the newsroom was on Oregon's South Coast was less of a problem than it had been—things were getting zesty.

Fiske rocked back and forth in his chair with glee when he saw Frank's picture of the recall pickets. It was a good shot. Paavo, Wheelie, One-Square, and Beanpole were followed by the kids from Eugene and—significantly—several other people whom Eldon recognized as locals. A smoldering resentment of Pumpkin Joe was beginning to take fire. The crowning touch was Jasper at the head of the column, bearing Bouncer aloft like an icon.

"Dee-de-dee!" Fiske said. "And the copy'll be in by five, too! Jimbo goes home at a civilized hour. The wife's fixin' liver and onions! Nice to have a day when everything wraps up nice and neat, isn't it?"

"Now and then, yeah." But Eldon thought his day was anything but nice and neat. There was still work to be done.

"I'm going to make some calls around and see if I can't drum up somebody who remembers Mulford. People should be getting home for dinner soon. I'll catch 'em then."

"Suit yourself. But don't work too late. Shouldn't keep your 'cleaning lady' waiting, dee-de-dee!"

Frank banged out his story and left with Fiske. At five, there was a sudden general exodus from the office. Eldon was left alone in the newsroom. He called Enola Gay's house but only got her answering machine. He tried his own home. No one answered there, either. Maybe she was with the Endos. He got the phone book and looked for a telephone number, but none was listed.

Eldon looked up the number of Erho and Ida Saarima. He could ask them about the past. Sure enough, they were home having dinner. But the name Isabel Mulford meant nothing to either one. Eldon chatted with them briefly and rang off.

He was hungry.

He closed his eyes and thought for a moment about Enola Gay's cooking. And about her body. But this evening he toiled in the newsroom in search of truth. He would wallow in the gritty realities of his profession. Eldon went out and bought a big sack of fried chicken at the franchise down the street. He would share it with Ambrose McFee when the sports editor came in to work.

Eldon returned to the *Sun* to see the incontestable sign that the night shift had begun: McFee's purple baseball cap with the yellow Q, which seemed to float in the air behind the counter. Eldon knew that the hat was on McFee's head. He simply couldn't see McFee behind the counter because McFee was so small.

He rounded the counter. McFee was at his desk, typing rapidly with a telephone to one ear. Taking sports scores, no doubt— McFee always wore the hat while taking scores. He had a vast network of informants who kept him tuned in to the high-school sports action that was his department's bread and butter.

Eldon put the sack of chicken on his desk, pulled out a drumstick and a handful of fries, and dropped them onto a sheet of newsprint. The drumstick was hot and greasy. Eldon used another sheet of newsprint to wipe his mouth and fingers while he ate. The fries were too salty. He could feel his arteries hardening as he ate. This is awful, he thought. Nothing like Enola Gay's cooking. God, you get used to a woman fast.

237

If I stay with Enola Gay, I might be stuck in Port Jerome forever, he realized. I can't see her moving to the big city.

The pragmatism of their arrangement dawned on him. I want to get laid, and she wants John's killer brought to justice, he thought.

It was a fine working arrangement, but what about the long term? Eldon fished around in the bag of fried chicken and found a thigh. He chomped away, watching McFee at his typewriter.

Ambrose slammed down the phone and rushed over with a sheaf of notes and a stricken look. "Eldon—this one's yours."

"Traffic accident?" Eldon swallowed and reached for his camera, remembering just in time to wipe the grease from his hands.

McFee looked into the sack, took out a drumstick, and bit into it as a big tear formed in each eye. The tears ran down his cheeks as McFee chewed and swallowed. Eldon stared.

"That was Jasper O'Shay," Ambrose said at last. "The Rising Dog's been stolen."

20

"*Good copy!*" Eldon said and laughed.

"It's not a joke," McFee said, distressed. "Jasper and his people moved into the old church today. They left Bouncer there for a while, and when they came back he was gone."

"Maybe he's in the landfill, digging more bones."

"He was locked in the building. Someone broke in and took him."

"Who?"

"How should I know? But what's this Jasper said about a recall?"

"Jasper and his pals are trying to recall Pumpkin Joe Nedlee. 'Save the old growth.' I wrote a story for tomorrow."

"Maybe it was someone against this recall," McFee said. "Nedlee has a lot of friends. People in these parts murder each other's pets over junior-high soccer."

"Damn fast work if it was Nedlee's friends," Eldon said. "They just filed the petition today."

Eldon wondered if workmen at the condo site had stolen

Bouncer in retaliation for what they saw as complicity in the tree-spiking. No, he decided, they'd have nailed the dog to the church door. "It's a put-up job, McFee. Jasper will do anything for publicity."

"Why now? They have the church." McFee wiped the tears from his fat cheeks. "You think how valuable that animal was. How unique. The canine Lazarus."

"Aw, it's a publicity stunt."

"Then Jasper filed a fake theft report with the sheriff, because I called them." McFee handed Eldon his notes. They were competently typed; McFee was displaying all sorts of hidden abilities since he'd gone on the wagon.

If the dog's been stolen, it's good copy, Eldon conceded. "Maybe you're right, Ambrose. Thanks for the notes."

"It's an incredible story. Jasper really might've raised that dog up, you know. Eldon, we've got to find that little dog."

"What we've got to do is write a story. Where's Jasper?"

"He didn't say." McFee's voice dropped. "I think he was in a bar. There was music. He sounded *drunk.*"

"There goes the recall campaign," Eldon said. Then the police scanner at the news desk came to life, reporting a disturbance at the Timber Topper, a bar just down the street.

"I'll bet that's Jasper right now," Eldon said. "I'll walk down there and see if I can get anything else out of him before the cops take him home to the drunk tank."

McFee stared at the scanner and nodded miserably.

"Buck up, McFee," Eldon said. "This is the news business. All prophets have feet of clay."

"I'm coming with you," McFee said.

"Sure. Okay. But what about the sports scores—?"

"It's only six. They won't come in until later." McFee got a notebook. His huge blue eyes were intent. "It's a risk for me, going into a place so full of sin and booze, but I'll do it. We're in a risky business."

Eldon got his camera. McFee took another piece of chicken, and they went out into the street.

Eldon had to admire McFee's courage as they hurried through the twilight. The Timber Topper had been one of the sports editor's main hangouts in his drinking days.

A sheriff's car was parked at the Timber Topper, its lights flashing. The door of the bar was fashioned with an ax imbedded in its wood. Eldon grabbed the haft and pulled the door open. He and McFee stepped into the dark, smoky bar.

All seemed as usual. The jukebox played bad country music. Ugly men and women drank and groped in the booths. Others loitered at the bar, complexions like slag in the neon glow of the beer advertisements. The room stank of cigarettes and flat beer. Then an all-too-familiar polka beat asserted itself. It was "Rock of Ages." Eldon saw through drifting cigarette haze that there was a confrontation at the back of the room.

One-Square, Wheelie, and Beanpole held two bemused deputies at bay. The three had formed a defensive ring around the towering figure of Paavo the Finn, who stood weeping at a corner table, pumping his concertina. Jasper was slumped at the table, his sailor's hat turned upside down beside him to receive donations. Both Paavo and Jasper were drunk.

Eldon caught his breath. The Finn in his cups meant that the Timber Topper was as dangerous as a minefield. At any moment, Paavo's temper might explode, and that would mean mutilation and ruin. Eldon heard a bellowslike sound over the noise of the jukebox—McFee, hyperventilating. Eldon remembered that Paavo had once tried to kill McFee in public.

"Get out of here," he told McFee. "Go back to the office."

McFee stared at the Finn. Sweat gleamed on his wide brow. He teetered on his heels, a man on the brink—like a sky diver poised in the airplane door with his hand on the rip cord and the Earth far below. Then McFee slapped his toes to the floor and said, "I'll see this through."

"He might tear off your—"

"It's a *story,* Eldon."

That's the only reason *I'm* staying, Eldon thought ruefully as they inched closer. One-Square was moving his cane in a wobbly circle, pointing at the deputies. Beanpole stood behind Wheelie's chair with a determined expression; he gripped its handles as if ready to use the chair as a ram. Wheelie clutched Jasper's dowsing stick and whispered over and over, "Stand back. Stand back."

"Let me help, Officer," McFee said in a hearty voice, like an athletic coach stepping forward to give a pep talk.

"You're McFee, from the *Sun,* aren't you?" one of the deputies said. "I recognize your cap. You know these guys?"

"The big fella's a friend of mine," McFee said. "Let me take 'em home."

"Just so they get out of here. They're bothering other customers."

"Right." McFee stepped around One-Square and up to the table. "Come on with us, Paavo."

Paavo stopped playing. Hostility smoldered for a moment in his eyes, then was quenched by a flood of tears. "Bouncer's gone—we're finished!"

"Where there's faith, there's hope," McFee said, patting Paavo's shoulder. He looked like a mouse consoling an elephant. "Help me with Jasper."

Paavo put the concertina in Wheelie's lap and pulled at Jasper's shoulders. "C'mon, Skipper, we gotta go." Jasper wept and keened, "Bouncer's gone, Bouncer's gone." He was limp as a rag doll. Paavo wept afresh.

"Get his arm over your shoulder," McFee said. "That's it—I'll take the other one." McFee and Paavo pulled Jasper to his feet, stretching him between them at a crazy tilt. Jasper's leg nearest Paavo barely brushed the floor, while the leg next to McFee folded under him. The three of them staggered for the door like a huge, misshapen crab.

One-Square grabbed Jasper's hat with its few coins while Eldon and Beanpole pushed Wheelie's chair.

"Thanks," Eldon told the deputies.

"Don't mention it," one replied. "McFee did a nice piece on my kid's swim team."

Outside, McFee headed up the street, pulling Jasper and Paavo with him. "We're going to the newspaper office," he declared. "We'll pour some coffee into you two and sober you up, then figure out what to do. It's disgraceful, men of the cloth, drunk in public—"

Jasper was incoherent. Paavo hung his head in shame.

"So the press is finally givin' us some attention," One-Square said to Eldon as they marched. "You're all hacks. But at least this'll get the story before the people."

"Don't get your hopes up," Eldon said. "I don't know I believe that the dog's been stolen."

"Not been stolen?" One-Square cried. "You callin' us liars? The crime of th' century an' you think *we* did it?"

"Got any *other* suspects?"

"Pumpkin Joe Nedlee hates our little dog."

"Maybe it was plain thieves. A dog raised from the dead is worth its weight in gold," McFee said.

One-Square peered morosely at the change in Jasper's cap. "Dollar eighty-nine cents. Not much of a ransom."

They got back to the newsroom just as a telephone stopped ringing. "Sports scores," Eldon said.

"They'll call back," McFee said. He and Paavo dropped Jasper into a chair. McFee brought Styrofoam cups of coffee and several packages of Twinkies from the vending machine in the coffee room. He started forcing the coffee into Jasper while One-Square and Beanpole gobbled the Twinkies.

Paavo watched uncertainly, his features pale and glistening with sweat. "Where is it?" the Finn blurted. Eldon pointed toward the men's room and Paavo rushed inside. Moments later came the sound of explosive vomiting.

McFee pulled up a chair and opened his notebook. "Now tell me what happened."

Jasper merely moaned. One-Square, Wheelie, and Beanpole all spoke at once. McFee sorted them out like a veteran conductor bringing order to an amateur orchestra. He walked them through the story of Bouncer's abduction, which was as Jasper had related it. The upshot was that there wasn't the slightest clue as to who had taken the dog. They had returned to find the padlock pried off the church's flimsy door and Bouncer missing.

"So Jasper and Paavo went out and got drunk as skunks," McFee said.

"Wouldn't you if somebody stole *your* miracle?" One-Square said. "That's not going to stop us, though. We three aren't drunk. We tracked Paavo and the skipper down in the bar. We'll find Bouncer. The Church of the Rising Dog will go on. Won't it, boys?"

Beanpole and Wheelie grunted in agreement. Eldon realized sheepishly that he now saw them as determined human beings and not merely as comical freaks. And he wondered whether One-Square would not be at the top of the church's minuscule hierarchy by morning.

Paavo emerged from the men's room, still pale. He lumbered over and sat down on the floor. "I'm so ashamed."

"Buck up," Eldon said. "We're going to write a story about this. Bouncer's more valuable to you dead than alive, anyway. Every church needs a martyr."

"You're a cruel bastard, Larkin, you know that?" Paavo said. "The whole point was that Bouncer was *alive*. You reporters are like vultures picking through trash. The cops are out in the landfill looking for bones. Keith Howell wants to build something that's dead. Pumpkin Joe Nedlee hates John Henspeter, a dead man— Nedlee looks half-dead himself. They want to cut down the trees and make them dead, too. All we want to do is make our church live."

"W-we've gotta f-find B-b-bouncer," Beanpole said. "That's all."

"How we gonna do that?" One-Square demanded.

"Offer a reward," McFee said.

Paavo snorted. "A reward? We don't have any money."

"Tickets," McFee said.

"Tickets?"

"I've got a stack of comps to the all-coast high-school basketball playoffs. I'll give the whole wad to anyone who has information about Bouncer. I'll put it in my column tomorrow."

"You would?" Paavo said.

"Sure," McFee said. "It's a righteous cause."

Paavo thrust out his hand, and he and McFee solemnly shook on it.

Other than money or beer, Eldon could think of few other offers that might so quickly drum up information. But the odds seemed long that it would do any good. Bouncer was probably dead in the bottom of a trash can or floating drowned in the slough. "It's worth a shot," he said, "but I wouldn't get your hopes up."

"Gotta get 'em up," One-Square said. "Otherwise, it's back to . . ." He let the sentence trail off.

He doesn't need to say it, Eldon thought. The only luck these three had ever had was hooking up with the Church of the Rising

Dog. No dog, no church. Keith will pull the church building down after all, and One-Square, Beanpole, and Wheelie will be living in packing cases at the boat basin.

One-Square's features hardened, as if he, too, foresaw the same hopeless future. "We've gotta get back and defend our church. Like we defended the Cap'n tonight."

"I'll stop the bulldozers with my bare hands if I have to," Paavo said hoarsely. "In Bouncer's memory—if that's the way it's got to be."

"His m-m-memory?" Beanpole began to snuffle. "If B-b-bouncer's—dead—Cap'n Jasper'll raise 'im up again. Won't you, Skipper?"

Jasper moaned again. No one else responded to Beanpole's question. Slowly the congregation gathered itself up.

"I'll drive 'em back out to the church," McFee said. "I want to have a look around. Put a 'reefer' line at the top of your news story saying to turn to the sports page. I'll rewrite my column when I get back."

"Okay. I've got your notes. I'll put on a joint byline."

"I don't care about that," McFee said. "Finding Bouncer is what matters to me. Okay, Jasper, let's get you on your feet. Stick with me, guys; everything will be all right." He led them out the door.

McFee may give One-Square a run for his money when it comes to becoming their new pope, Eldon thought. But right now he had a story to write. Wait'll Fiske finds this one in the basket tomorrow morning, Eldon thought. He rolled paper into his typewriter and began grinding out copy.

Eldon went home that night in excellent fettle. He was delighted to see Enola Gay's truck at his house and a light burning behind the drawn curtains in the living room. A piece of wood was bolted over the bullet hole in the window. That girl's quite a handyman, Eldon thought. Handy at a lot of things. Ho ho.

He tiptoed to the door, slid his key into the lock, and placed his other hand on his zipper. Let's see if I can time this right, he thought. One, two—"Three!" He turned the key and knob and yanked down his zipper as he stepped in the door.

Enola Gay had company. Ronnie and Joline Endo.

Joline was eating a bowl of ice cream; she waved her spoon in greeting. Ronnie grinned. Enola Gay simply stared.

"Uh—wait a minute—" Eldon, face burning, turned and fumbled his zipper closed. "Sorry—I—didn't know anyone else was here. I, ah, didn't see your bikes—"

"They're parked behind the house," Ronnie said. "Attract less attention that way."

"Something wrong?"

"The heat's on," Joline said. "We've got to move the guns."

"You mean the cops know about—"

"Not yet," Enola Gay said. "It's where they hid them."

"So where'd you hide them?" Eldon asked, closing the door.

"In the landfill," Ronnie said.

"In the landfill?"

"It seemed like a great idea at the time," Ronnie said. "Joline said we had to get the guns out of the house, and after we broke all those plates, I saw she had a point. Why not put 'em out in Schumacher's, where nobody'd think to look?"

"There are cops all over Schumacher's," Eldon said.

"That's what made it so perfect," Ronnie said.

"And it's why we've got to move 'em now," Joline said. "It's a big landfill. We went down there at night and buried the chest and dumped a load of broken plates on top. We figured no one would find it because no one was looking for it. But things are heating up out there. We can't take chances. Ronnie's fingerprints are all over those guns."

"What kind of action?" Eldon asked.

"We heard the sirens from our house, went out and looked."

"What time this evening?"

"About six," Joline said.

"Any idea what went down?"

"We thought you'd know," Enola Gay said. "I called the ne~ paper but no one answered."

"Damn," Eldon said, thinking of the phone call he had b missed. "The sports editor and I were down the street pulling out of a bar. If there was any police traffic on the new scanner, we missed it."

"What was Jasper doing in a bar?" Enola Gay asked.

245

"The rising dog's been stolen," Eldon said.

"That cute little thing?" Enola Gay said. "When?"

"Today," Eldon said. "I'm late because I was writing the story." He glanced at the clock on his fly-tying table. "McFee went out to check the landfill—he might be back by now." He picked up the telephone and dialed the *Sun*'s sports number. Sure enough, McFee answered.

"Ambrose—this is Eldon. What's going on at the landfill?"

"Something big," McFee said. "I was about to call you. At first I thought they'd found Bouncer murdered or something. That really gave me a scare. But then I saw the medical examiner. He wouldn't go out there for a dog."

"No. But what was it?"

"I don't know. By the time we got out there, they were just about packed up and gone, and I had my hands full with Paavo and Jasper. Man, can that little guy puke—"

"But you're sure you saw the M.E.?"

"Sure. Big fat guy, dresses like a clown. I know Rosenak—his kid's in double-A wrestling. Dresses just like his old man."

"Rosenak's home number is on my Rolodex," Eldon said. "Give it to me and I'll take it from here."

"Okay." After a pause, McFee read off the number. "I'll get going on my column about Bouncer. I read your news story—it's good."

"Thanks."

"You know what, Eldon? It's great to be back."

"Eh?"

"To have my head clear. And to have a crusade. A crusade is everything to a newspaperman, hey? It's a gift from heaven. Same as Bouncer."

"Yeah, right." Eldon hung up before McFee could talk any longer. He dialed Rosenak's home telephone number and was relieved when the medical examiner answered.

"Hi-ho, Eldon Larkin. How're you doing?"

"Curious is how I'm doing. I heard you were out at the landfill tonight."

"News travels fast." Rosenak chuckled. "But I owe you this one for finding those old records. Even though you probably won't believe me when I tell you."

Eldon waited. He knew that Rosenak was savoring the revelation he was about to make.

"Cross-checking those dental records turned out to be more important than we'd thought," Rosenak said.

Eldon's skin prickled. "You mean the foot wasn't Mulford's?"

"The foot belonged to Mulford, all right—but the mandible didn't. There were *two* skeletons buried in the landfill."

"Christ!" Eldon pulled his notebook from his hip pocket and fumbled for his pen. "Let me get this straight. You found Mulford's dental records, too? And the mandible didn't match them?"

"We never found Mulford's dental records. We matched the mandible to *someone else's* dental records."

"*Who?*"

"Ellis Weems, the long-lost county commissioner."

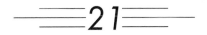

Eldon didn't feel anything. A tiny voice in his brain chanted Scoop-of-the-year, scoop-of-the-year. "I'd better call my editor," he said.

"He'll probably kiss you on both cheeks," Rosenak said.

"What now, Doc?"

"We dig for more bones, starting tomorrow."

"Both skeletons were buried at the same time?"

"I'm certain they were. Though I'll have to verify it with tests."

"It *was* foul play?"

"They sure didn't bury each other."

"No. Of course not." Eldon's mind raced, grabbing bits of fact and supposition and splicing them together. The picture firmed up quickly. The fight over the church land, Harmon Howell on one side and Ellis Weems on the other. The bitter recall that had been Howell's revenge.

Nedlee said that Weems' disappearance had kicked off his own political career, Eldon thought. The recall was the perfect cover for murder. Nedlee killed Weems to clear the political path for himself and buried Weems in the landfill. If anyone suspected foul play, they'd suspect Harmon Howell, not Nedlee. As it turned out, no one had suspected either.

"Thanks, Doc," Eldon said. "This is a hell of a story."

"Ask me how they were killed and it'll get even better," Rosenak said with glee.

"What? Don't hold out on me—"

"I won't. But you've got to sit on this part. It's got to be off the record. Promise me?"

"Okay. Okay."

"There's a crowbar in the hole. Looks like the same modus operandi as in the Henspeter case. The killer's still around."

"Doc, I could kiss *you* on both cheeks. Thanks."

"I don't want to see that part in the paper, Eldon. The killer can't know we know. I'm trusting you on this."

" 'No comment' on the M.O. It's a deal. Uh—no chance Henspeter was a copycat killing?"

"We're still off the record, right? A copycat doesn't seem possible at this remove. No one but Henspeter's killer knew about the two earlier murders."

"I think so, too. I just wanted to hear a pro say it."

"Off the record."

"Off the record. Thanks, Doc."

"Just don't forget that sandwich. You're welcome."

"Amen." Eldon hung up the telephone, his mind still racing.

Nedlee killed the woman, too, he thought, the woman that he couldn't have because Weems got her. Keith said that his father and Nedlee were rivals for a woman. That woman was Harmon Harwell's wife. If I look up the marriage records, her maiden name will be Isabel Mulford. When we run that story, Nola won't have to read more than a few paragraphs to head straight for the grand jury.

"What happened?" Enola Gay asked. "What's that about two skeletons?"

"I'll tell you later."

"Now. Ronnie and Joline are friends."

"Yeah," Ronnie said. "We've come a ways with you, you know what I mean."

"There are two people buried in the landfill," Eldon said. "Pumpkin Joe killed them just like he did John."

Joline gasped and grabbed Ronnie's hand. Enola Gay asked quietly, "Have they arrested him, then?"

"No. But it's only a matter of time."

Eldon sketched his theory of Nedlee's guilt. Ronnie jumped up and began to pace, slapping his fist into his palm. Joline shook her head. "And to think we voted for him. This is heavy shit."

"Eldon figured it out the other day," Enola Gay said in a tired voice.

"Are you going to put it in the paper?" Joline asked.

"Some of it," Eldon said. "Mostly I'm going to let events take their course, let the sheriff arrest him."

"Remember that story you told us about Dad being involved with Howell's mother?" Enola Gay said. "Looks like it was true."

"The skeletons in the landfill belong to her and a man named Weems, who was Nedlee's predecessor on the county commission," Eldon said.

"Christ, does Keith know?" Ronnie asked.

"I hadn't thought of that," Eldon said. "I guess the police will tell him. I'll have to get comment from him tomorrow—one of the unpleasant parts of my job."

Ronnie bit his lip. "I should've kept my mouth shut about that old story. I'm sorry I brought all this down on you, Enola Gay."

"You did right," Enola Gay said. "It was down on me already, in a lot of ways."

"But Pumpkin Joe is your *father*," Joline said.

"Joe's got a lot to answer for in my book," Enola Gay said.

"A lot of bad karma will be put to rest," Ronnie said, still pacing and slapping his fist into his hand.

"They're going to search for more bones tomorrow," Eldon said.

"We gotta get those guns out of the landfill or I'm sunk," Ronnie said. "The cops will tear that landfill apart."

"Let's get down there," Joline said, starting to rise.

"Not now," Enola Gay said.

"When, then, dammit?" Ronnie said.

"Where'd you bury the guns?" Eldon asked. "Not near where they found the bones, I hope?"

"They're out on the fringe by the slough," Joline said to Eldon's relief. "Near the condo development."

"We'll retrieve the chest tomorrow night, then," Enola Gay said. "We can sneak in through the construction site. Eldon and I will help you. It's risky but it's the only way."

"Good plan," Ronnie said.

"Count me out," Eldon said. "I can't—"

"We need you to help move them," Enola Gay said. "They're heavy."

"Ronnie and Joline didn't need my help to bury them," Eldon said but then thought, In for a penny, in for a pound. "And once we've got them back?"

"We bring them here," Enola Gay said.

"Why not just take them back to your place?" Eldon asked.

"If my father is arrested for murder, the cops could come around my place, asking questions."

"But they won't search—"

"Anything could happen. But *your* house won't enter into it."

"It entered into it for whoever blew a hole in my window," Eldon said.

Ronnie said, "With that arsenal of John's, you can blow a hole right back, in whoever gives you any more trouble."

"You're our eyes and ears," Joline said. "You can tell us what the cops are up to tomorrow, so we won't get caught."

"Just a minute." Eldon went into the kitchen and got the ice cream bucket from the refrigerator. The gouge in the kitchen wall where he had dug out the bullet stared blankly at him.

Eldon opened the tub, got a spoon, and swallowed several big mouthfuls of French vanilla. Odds were the four of them simply could slip down to the edge of the landfill, retrieve the trunk, and leave. Police attention would be focused on the crime scene, not on scavengers. But the trunk seemed bigger and heavier than ever in Eldon's mind. What the hell had Henspeter wanted with a rocket launcher? With automatic rifles? With smoke bombs? If he'd feared for his life, why hadn't he simply camped out with a pump shotgun?

That was one piece of the puzzle that didn't fit.

He put the container away and returned to the living room as

Enola Gay was saying, "We'll keep the guns here at Eldon's for a while until they cool off."

"Let's borrow a boat and dump 'em in the bay," Eldon said.

Enola Gay looked shocked. "Those weapons are valuable."

"I thought they scared you."

"Those pieces could be fenced," Ronnie said. "I know bikers who'd buy them with no questions."

"They aren't gonna buy them from *you*, Ronnie," Joline said pointedly. "Not if I have anything to say about it."

"Or from me, either." Eldon searched frantically for a way to change the subject. "I've got to call Fiske, then get back to the office. Two skeletons won't wait."

He took the phone into the kitchen, where he called Fiske and told him about the theft of Bouncer and the discovery of the second skeleton. "There's just one more thing to do—check out old marriage licenses. To definitely link the woman to Harmon Howell."

Fiske was delighted. "Nedlee's doom is sealed, dee-de-dee. This is lots better than a recall."

"I'll have to go to Preacher's Hole to check the marriage records—"

"Frank can do that," Fiske said. "And never mind about doing more writing tonight. I'm not paying overtime. Pull it all together in the morning, when you can add more details. Anyway, the dog story's already in the basket."

"All right." Eldon dropped his voice so that those in the living room would not overhear. "Has Marsha found anything on the gun registrations?"

"Nope. Why?"

"Just wondering."

"Don't worry, Eldon, she hasn't one-upped you yet."

"Damn right she hasn't. Two stories for two's not bad, is it, Jimbo?"

"Three for three would be better."

"I'll get something on the guns, too, don't worry."

"That would make it four for four, then," Fiske said.

"What do you mean?"

"Number three is the seismic shocks."

"Shocks? I didn't feel any shocks."

"Well, you've had a lot on your mind lately. The university detected shocks over in the Willamette Valley. What'd I tell ya? Those tectonic plates are slipping."

"Have Frank deal with it, for Chrissake."

"He'll have a story in the paper tomorrow. You must have enough material to bang out a sidebar, don't you?"

"About what?"

"Life at the scene of Nedlee's old crimes, of course. The tense vigil of the deputies as the earthquake approaches and the area's land-use future hangs in the balance. In case the whole place is swallowed up in a chasm that opens in the Earth."

"And me with it?"

"You're too resourceful for that, dee-de-dee."

Eldon returned to the living room. Ronnie and Joline were agitated but Enola Gay seemed cool. She's a lot like me when I'm covering an accident or a murder, he thought. She's got that same ability to disconnect. And there'll be the devil to pay when she finally plugs back in.

"All right, we'll do it your way," Eldon said. "We'll dig up the chest tomorrow night. But I'm not keeping the guns here for long. Any delays and I'll throw 'em in the bay myself."

"Any delays and I'll help you," Joline said.

"We're going to fade now," Ronnie said. "Come to our place tomorrow night, after dark. And bring that snazzy van. We're gonna need it to haul the boodle."

"Just stay away from the landfill until then," Enola Gay said.

"Don't worry," Ronnie said. "I've got to do some electric workouts. I'm upping the volts to get ready for this."

"Snap a spark or two for me," Eldon said.

"You're okay, Eldon, you know that?"

The Endos rolled their motorcycles from behind the house and blasted away into the night, the cycles' unmuffled engines thundering like the afterburners on jet fighters.

"Maybe Ronnie will fry his brain tonight and we won't have to go through with this," Eldon said as the noise dwindled.

"We have to go through with it," Enola Gay said. "My fingerprints are on those guns, too."

"But how'll we get rid of them?" Eldon asked. "I still say throw them in the bay."

"We'll think of something."

"Let's think of something now."

Enola Gay stepped up to Eldon and put her tongue in his ear. "Let's think of something else."

"This is not the time to—"

"I thought what you did when you came in the door tonight was *great*. You were so hot you couldn't wait." Her expression turned serious. "Eldon—I need this tonight."

His appetite was sharp when they got into bed. Enola Gay pulled him over on top of her. Then Eldon suddenly got the feeling that she wasn't really there. Her body worked briskly enough but she was silent, methodical. She had an air of fierce concentration, but he knew she was not concentrating on him. Her eyes were distant in the cold moonlight streaming in the bedroom window.

Eldon stopped. "What's wrong?"

"What do you mean? Nothing's wrong."

"What are you thinking about? Your father?"

A pause. "No. I was thinking about that poor little dog."

With that, Enola Gay wrapped her legs tightly around Eldon and threw her head back over the edge of the bed. Eldon realized as they resumed that she was looking out the window, her perspective now topsy-turvy.

"Isabel Mulford married Harmon Howell in 1955," Frank said over the telephone the next morning from the courthouse in Preacher's Hole. "I found it in the clerk's microfilms."

"Keith would've been about ten years old," Eldon said. "She was his stepmother."

"You going to talk to him?"

"I'll have to. He might shed light on the disappearance." Eldon glanced at the newsroom clock. There was plenty of time until deadline.

"You going to tell him what you suspect about Joe?"

"Hell, no."

"You going to talk to Joe?"

"Double hell no. I'm going to let the wheels of justice grind him up. It won't be long."

"Nedlee's not around the courthouse today," Frank said. "Maybe he's skipped town."

"That'd be good copy, too."

Eldon hung up. A grating voice called, "Larkin!" Eldon looked up and was annoyed to see One-Square peering over the front counter, waving his cane. Without waiting for an invitation, the hunchback rounded the counter and lurched to Eldon's desk. One-Square's top hat was cocked at a rakish angle, and he jabbed his cane into the carpet as he walked.

Eldon didn't offer him a chair. "You're the new pope, eh?"

"The Church of the Rising Dog doesn't go in for that Catholic crap," One-Square said. "We welcome all denominations and bow to none."

"I meant that you seem to be in charge."

"I'm Cap'n Jasper's loyal crewman. He's sober enough today."

"Then where is he?"

"Where he should be—out at the landfill, raisin' hell. McFee said to come down here and notify you."

"McFee's out there?"

"He's joined us. A fellow traveler, like."

"Good. Get him to do a story for the church page. We run church news on Thursdays."

"McFee said you'd want to know about this."

"Okay, what?"

"Bulldozers at the condo site are filling in the slough."

"Impossible."

"Saw it m'self. Shoving dirt right in the slough."

"That's illegal as hell."

"That's what we've been sayin' about the whole thing, ya chump."

"You want people to know Bouncer's been stolen or not?"

One-Square glowered and licked his teeth. Eldon said, "I'll make a call about it. Now I've got stuff to do."

"You're gonna tell people about what's happened to Bouncer?"

"Yeah, don't worry."

"That dog means a lot to us."

"I know. He's a cute mutt."

254

"What do I tell McFee?"

"Tell him to cover the news." Eldon watched One-Square hobble out and then called Keith Howell's office. Keith was there. First the little question and then the big question, Eldon thought.

"Hi, Eldon, what's cooking?"

"Couple of things. First off, I just got a tip that you've got bulldozers out at the condo project, supposedly filling in the slough."

"That's ridiculous. They're putting up a berm. It's part of the landscaping."

"Does that involve filling in the slough?"

"Eldon, why are you even bothering to ask? You know my policies."

"I have to ask."

"Okay, we're not filling in the slough. The county wouldn't allow it."

"Then what're they talking about?"

"Hell, I don't know. Maybe some dirt *did* spill into the water. But it's inadvertent. The whole county's hopping because of this Nedlee recall. Rumors run wild."

"I'll take your word for it." McFee can sort it out—he's on the scene, Eldon thought. "Now I've got something else to talk to you about. Have you talked with the sheriff today?"

"No. Is this about the bulldozers?"

"No. Keith, I've got some sad news for you."

"Sad news? It isn't about the little dog being stolen, is it?"

"Ah—no. Keith, the person in the landfill, the one the foot belonged to, I mean . . . it was your stepmother."

There was silence. Eldon waited for the reaction, preparing himself for an explosion of grief, curses, anything. At last, Keith said, "Well, after all these years, it's good to know what happened to her. Thanks." His tone was philosophical.

"I'm sorry to have to tell you, especially over the phone."

"That's all right," Keith said. "After all, it's been a long time since she left. One day she was—gone. I was pretty torn up about it."

"Never any explanation from your father?"

"He just said she'd gone away. That's how it was—one day she was there and one day not. No explanations. Believe me, Eldon, I knew better than to ask more. Later I figured she'd just left him."

"Maybe your father suspected something, didn't want to upset you—you know, telling a little kid that his stepmother's disappeared."

"Maybe. The old man had an odd way of caring. I'll do it differently if I ever have kids."

"I'm sure you will."

"How did you find out she was my stepmother?"

"We looked up the old marriage licenses in the courthouse."

"I just hope it was quick for her," Keith said softly. "And to think I used to play out there in that landfill. God, who could've done it?"

"There's more," Eldon said. "There was another skeleton buried with her."

"Do they know whose?"

"Do you remember Ellis Weems?"

"Dad's old enemy—it's *him?*"

"Yes, it is. Positive I.D.'s on both of them."

"Man, oh, man! I knew that thing was bitter, but I had no idea—"

"I guess no one did," Eldon said. "This was the rivalry you told me about at the party, wasn't it?"

"Yeah. I didn't want to get into details . . ." Keith's voice trailed off. "God! Both of them!"

"Do you remember anything about it?"

"Nothing more than I told you. I was a kid. Give me a break."

"I'm sorry. Of course you didn't. I didn't mean to press."

"That's okay. It's your job. I know you didn't mean it personally. But there's one funny thing."

"What's that?"

"This is just about the anniversary of when they disappeared. It was this same month, all those years ago—I remember very clearly. And now they find their bodies."

"The anniversary? Now, that's helpful."

"Helpful? Do you have a lead on whoever killed them—?"

"Keep reading the *Sun.* That's all I can say for now."

"You couldn't give me a hint about what you're up to?"

"I can't, Keith. Be patient."

"Well, you don't tell me how to build condos, so I'd better not tell you how to cover the news." Keith laughed and added, "Except when it comes to earthquakes."

"They had some tremors or something over in the valley."

"Really? Well, work at Forest Vista Estates goes on. You know what? I'm going to add my stepmother's name to that plaque I was talking about. And Ellis Weems' name, too."

"Let me know when that happens. It's worth an article."

"Sure. I imagine I'll be hearing from the sheriff pretty soon, about finding the bodies." Keith paused. "Thanks again for calling me. I'm glad I heard about it first from a friend."

"Thanks, Keith. Talk to you later." Eldon hung up and turned to his typewriter. Well, that went smoothly, he thought. And the anniversary—that was an angle.

A puzzling thought struck him. Could *Harmon Howell* have killed the two in the landfill? But that didn't square with the circumstances that pointed to Nedlee—and Harmon Howell certainly hadn't killed John Henspeter.

Eldon jumped as Fiske poked him in the shoulder with his pipe.

"That was Jasper's hunchback," Fiske said. "What'd he want?"

"Bulldozers at the condo site, supposedly defiling Jackknife Slough."

"Dee-de-dee—in the news business, when it rains, it pours."

"McFee's already out there."

"Dee-de-dee! Ambrose is showing some enterprise since he went dry. I read his column in pasteup this morning."

"I'll do the story about the second skeleton now. Frank verified that Isabel Mulford was Harmon Howell's wife."

"Did you talk to the sheriff?"

"I went to Art Nola with my suspicions about Pumpkin Joe a couple of days ago. When he reads this story, I'm sure he'll arrest Nedlee."

"Glad to hear you're a responsible citizen, Eldon." Fiske examined his pipe. "Just so the *Sun* breaks the story of the arrest."

Eldon felt queasy. That damned cedar chest full of guns was like Pandora's box waiting to spring open. But in a few more hours they would have the guns safe from official discovery.

Then I'll trace them, Eldon thought. A story about Henspeter's links to God-knows-what will give this fracas one final twist.

22

Storm clouds were blowing over the bay that evening when Eldon and Enola Gay arrived at the Endos' house. It was nearly dark. The lawn still gleamed with broken china. The living room drapes fluttered through the huge hole in the front window.

"The living room'll just have to get a little wet, is all," Ronnie said with a shrug. "I've replaced glass before."

"Are you ready to do it?" Enola Gay asked.

"Sure we are. Are you?"

"You bet," Enola Gay said. "If we run into somebody, Eldon's checking out a tip, okay?"

"What tip?" Joline asked.

"We want to see about the slough being filled in," Eldon said.

"What if there's trouble?" Ronnie asked.

"What kind of trouble?" Eldon asked.

"I dunno. Trouble."

"Just keep your eyes and ears open," Enola Gay said.

"They're not going to *shoot* us, you know."

"Hope not," Ronnie said. He put on his Viking helmet.

Eldon and Enola Gay wore jeans and dark shirts and jackets. The Endos had donned their biker leathers. Eldon thought they looked like barbarian commandos about to descend on some luckless village, especially when Ronnie flourished a collapsible Army shovel and thrust it in his belt. We'll get the damn guns out of there, and then I don't ever want to see the Endos again, Eldon thought.

They climbed into the van. Eldon drove to the lookout point above the condo site and the landfill where he and Enola Gay had encountered Nedlee.

Eldon drove most of the way using only parking lights. Now he killed even those and they looked down upon the condo site, a vague forest of scaffolding in the weak moonlight. The landfill beyond was dark save for a few lights at the far periphery. The trees all around them looked like a range of ragged mountain peaks. They framed the bay, which glittered dully under gathering storm clouds.

"Looks like rain tonight," Eldon said.

"Then 'Let it come down,' " Enola Gay said with a smile. "The road down to the site is just down the way. That's the road I took on my horse, first day you saw me."

They drove farther and came shortly to a dirt road. Eldon eased the van into low gear, thankful that the way was straight and the van wasn't giving him trouble. It's the best car I ever owned, he decided with the irrelevancy of one under growing stress. I hope Enola Gay will stick around and keep it in tip-top shape.

He slowed. Just ahead was a small temporary truck bridge across the slough.

"What's that dark stuff down there?" Ronnie asked as they crossed.

Eldon saw freshly mounded earth by the water. "That must be part of the new berm."

"He's digging mighty close to the water," Enola Gay said.

"Let's just get the damn guns and get out of here," Eldon said. "Ronnie—Joline—you're sure you remember where you hid 'em?"

"Of course we do," Ronnie said. "Over there. I took a sight on those two trees. It's in a depression near the edge of the landfill."

Eldon eased the van along and parked on a tree-rimmed rise. They were at the same elevation as the top of the landfill, but the trees cast the rise into a pool of shadow that concealed the van.

Ronnie settled his horned helmet more firmly on his head and slid open the van's side door. Immediately, the dome light flashed on.

Eldon swore and snapped it off. "Sorry. I should've disconnected that."

"No harm done," Enola Gay whispered. "Nobody's around."

"Let's get in and out while the getting's good," Eldon said.

They climbed quietly, single file, onto the landfill. Ronnie led the way, until a broken plate crunched under his foot.

"We're here," Ronnie whispered, drawing out the shovel. "Where is it?"

"Where the plates are the deepest. We buried it and then dumped on the plates." He started digging, grunting and gasping as he shoveled broken china aside.

Eldon peered nervously across the landfill. The breeze was in their faces, and he told himself that the noise would be carried into the woods.

Enola Gay started pacing. "C'mon, c'mon," she said after a few minutes. "Where is it?"

"It's deeper than I thought," Ronnie gasped, still excavating.

Eldon remembered games as a child in which he had buried toy soldiers or trucks, carefully marking the spot, except that he never found the toys again when he dug to retrieve them. Then he had imagined that they had sunk far into the Earth, maybe all the way to China.

Eldon was sweating despite the cool breeze. The smell of rain definitely was on the wind. His teeth began to chatter lightly. The ceramic crashing stopped; now Ronnie was digging through soft earth. "We're nearly there," Ronnie said.

"Eldon, keep watch," Enola Gay said, and she and Joline started digging.

Eldon scanned the landfill, trying to discern in the darkness the spot where the skeletons had been found. The crime scene was dark. Eldon had wondered whether a deputy might not be on watch there but apparently not; the landfill was too far from town to attract vandals or souvenir seekers. He decided that the distant lights burned at the trailer park, where Jasper and his friends doubtless prayed for Bouncer's safe return.

The lights gave a sense of scale, and Eldon relaxed somewhat. They were well away from the road, from the trailer park, from the old church. Darkness covered them like a cloak.

Joline hissed. "Shit! It's not here."

"Don't talk stupid!" Ronnie said. "We just haven't come to it yet."

"Try more over to the right," Joline said. "I wish you'd marked it a little better."

"What'd you want me to do?" Ronnie said. "Erect a fuckin' obelisk?"

"How deep did you bury it?" Enola Gay asked.

"Not so deep we couldn't find it," Joline said.

"I saw your car light," a man said.

Eldon's breath went out of him and his bladder nearly let go. He whirled in time to see Pumpkin Joe Nedlee step from the darkness.

"Dad!" Enola Gay said. "What the hell—"

Ronnie stood up and waved the shovel. "Stand back, you murdering son of a bitch!"

Nedlee waved his hands in annoyance. They were empty. "What the hell are you talking about?"

"What are you doing here?" Enola Gay repeated.

"Trying to vindicate myself," Nedlee said.

"A little late for that, isn't it?" Eldon measured the distance between Nedlee and himself; it was sufficient to give him a good head start if he had to escape across the landfill.

"Of course not," Nedlee said. "I've caught Keith red-handed."

"Red-handed at what?" Eldon asked.

"Illegally filling in the slough."

"The new berm?" Eldon asked.

"Your man McFee called me this afternoon at the courthouse," Nedlee said. "I was late getting in. 'Why are you backing this illegal fill?' he wanted to know. I thought he meant Keith's plans to plant a lawn on Schumacher's. I'd read Larkin's story today, the one about me and the old congregation, and I know the *Sun*'s decided to get on the recall bandwagon. 'Damned if you hacks will run me out of office,' I told McFee. But then he told me about the bulldozing, which I hadn't heard about."

Nedlee chuckled. "Naturally, I decided to drop by to check it out—'view the locale for the purpose of making an informed decision about the Forest Vista Estates proposal.' At night, before Keith could get everything tidied up." Nedlee chuckled again. "He thought he could fill in part of the slough before the commission voted. Present us with a fait accompli, which is political talk for rubbing someone's nose in shit. Figured we'd take the path of least resistance and give him the go-ahead anyway. Keith's just as stupid as his father was. The fix is *never* in with Pumpkin Joe Nedlee."

"Where were you today, then?" Eldon asked.

"Doing groundwork to fight the recall," Nedlee said. "You can't line up your ducks too early. And I'm going to line up the major duck when I vote to kill this condo project. That'll pull the plug on the whole business. Now—what are all of *you* doing down here? What's this digging?"

Enola Gay spoke in a voice cold with unforgiving fury. "Okay, Dad, since you're here, we'll tell you—"

A dog barked in the darkness.

"Bouncer?" Eldon said at once. He had no idea whether it was Bouncer, but he did not want Enola Gay to tell Nedlee what they were up to. He thrust his forefingers in his mouth and whistled. "Here, boy!"

A small, dark form scurried out of the darkness with a happy yap. It *was* Bouncer. The dog rushed up to Eldon, wriggling and whining. Eldon saw that a length of rope was tied around Bouncer's neck—and that another trailed from one paw. "It's our kidnap victim, all right, broken loose. You had him tied up, didn't you, Nedlee?"

"I did *not!*" Nedlee roared, readying himself for a lunge. "Now d'you want to recall me for dog-stealing?"

There was a sound like a sputtering lawn mower from somewhere across the landfill. Eldon turned, puzzled, as large bees buzzed past his head. A geyser of dirt sprang up to his left. Lights twinkled in the distance. "They're shooting!" Eldon dived head-first into the sea of broken plates. He yelled for Enola Gay to get down. More bullets churned the dirt, and bodies crashed down on top of Eldon. A piece of broken porcelain jabbed him in the cheek and he screamed.

"Are you all right, Eldon?" Enola Gay cried.

"I'm all right, I'm all right. Oh, Jesus, somebody's shooting. Anybody hit?"

No one was. Bouncer barked.

"We're getting out of here," Enola Gay said.

"If I had a gun, I'd charge 'em," Ronnie said.

"Fuck you, Ronnie," Joline said, gathering up the dog.

"Back to the van," Enola Gay said. "Stay low. Dad, you come with us."

"Okay," Nedlee said. "But who's shooting at us? And what are they shooting at us with?"

"AR-15 converted to full automatic," Enola Gay said. "A Finnish knockoff of an AK-47. Other stuff. Somebody beat us to the trunk."

"The trunk?" Nedlee asked.

"Later," Eldon said.

They scrambled over the edge of the landfill and started along the slope, only to be met with another crash of gunfire. Someone was in the construction site, firing wildly with a weapon that made a guttural punching sound. A red tracer sailed overhead like an immense, lazy firefly as they flattened themselves against the slope.

"That's the AK," Enola Gay said. "Back up."

They scuttled back to their starting point. Eldon's teeth were chattering insanely now, but Nedlee smacked his lips with zest. "Now Pumpkin Joe's gonna get you out of this."

"Let's just surrender," Eldon said.

"No, they'll kill us," Enola Gay said.

"I know this county like the back of my hand," Nedlee said. "One of the things I know are all the trails across this landfill and through these woods." He gave another raspy chuckle. "That's how I got down to the landfill tonight without attracting attention. You never know what might come in handy when you're an elected official."

There was another burst of gunfire from the construction site. Pumpkin Joe sprang off into the darkness. Eldon followed, the others close behind.

Eldon had thought of the landfill as flat but realized now that much of Schumacher's was rolling terrain. Nedlee led them down an inclined double rut that probably had been used by dump trucks. Quickly, their heads were below ground level. Someone started shooting again, sporadically, from across the landfill, but closer now. A bullet chewed the earth above them, harmlessly. They were being chased.

Nedlee moved in great striding hops like a man-size toad. Eldon kept close, breathing openmouthed. As they came to a turn in the sunken road, Eldon glanced back to make sure that Enola Gay and the others were still there, missed his footing, and went sprawling.

"Take a breather," Nedlee ordered as Eldon lay gasping for breath. "Everyone's here?"

"Yeah—" Joline said as Bouncer barked.

"Shut that cur up," Nedlee said.

"No need," a voice said. "And he's not a cur. Bouncer's a very special little dog."

Keith Howell stepped from the shadows, holding a weapon. It was the Mauser pistol from Henspeter's trunk; Eldon recognized the box magazine extending down the trigger guard. A dark tube hung by a strap in his other hand.

"Give him back to me," Keith ordered.

Joline hesitated, her eyes fixed on the Mauser. Bouncer whined. "Just hand me the rope," Keith said. "I'll deal with him."

He tossed the tube aside and held out his hand. Eldon saw that the tube was the LAW from Henspeter's trunk. Keith took the rope and Joline dropped Bouncer. Keith yanked up on the rope, hauling Bouncer up on his hind legs so that he began to choke.

"Don't do that," Eldon said.

"You have a big mouth," Keith said. "I'm going to close it in just a minute, before those cops out there catch up with us."

The gunmen weren't behaving like any police officers Eldon had ever met, but he decided not to disabuse Howell. At least they're coming closer, he thought, whoever they are, and prayed that they would come faster.

They did. There were shouts and then the ragged banging of guns. Keith sprang up the slope, still dragging Bouncer, and fired back with the Mauser. Confused cries rose in the darkness. Eldon didn't know how many shots the pistol held; he also knew that jumping an armed man was mere cinematic fancy. Maybe Ronnie will rush him, he thought, then looked over to see the leather-clad biker couple clinging to one another and trembling like rabbits.

There was a lull.

"The trunk's in the church—I found it there when I took the dog," Keith said. "I took these guns and that thing in the tube. Then Bouncer got free. I've been looking for him. When I came after him, I found you." He looked at Pumpkin Joe. "I've been watching all you fools out here for an hour, including you, you stupid old man. I come out here a lot at night. I have since I was a kid."

"Dumping fill in the slough would've gotten you a fine," Nedlee said. "It's not a matter for guns. You wouldn't have gone to jail."

Keith laughed then, the same mellifluous laugh of the commission meeting where Eldon had first met him, the laugh of the party where Eldon had interviewed him, the hale laugh over the phone. "Not the fill, Joe. Not the fill."

"*You* killed John Henspeter," Eldon said.

"Right," Keith said, and Eldon felt as if he were falling down an elevator shaft.

"But you couldn't have killed your stepmother and Ellis Weems," Enola Gay said. "You were too young."

"Dad wasn't," Keith replied with great simplicity. "Dad killed them this very month, in the very way I killed John. He made me watch, so I knew how to do it. He told me I was an accomplice."

"You were a boy," Nedlee said.

"Dad had a way of always sounding right. He had a pretty hard fist, too." Keith's voice was firm and level. Eldon listened for some hint of madness but was terrified to hear only a penetrating intensity.

"I didn't betray him even after he died. He was the only family I had, after all." Keith jerked Bouncer's rope. "I kept at my taxidermy, too."

"The anniversary of the murders—that was the anniversary you were talking about at the party," Eldon said. "You always unveil another stuffed animal on the anniversary of—"

"Yeah. That was a good profile you did, Eldon. All your stories were good. When I read how Bouncer found my stepmother's foot, right in the anniversary month, right after he was *raised from the dead,* and saw his picture in the paper—well, I knew I had to have that little dog in my special collection."

Eldon winced. "Right next to the bald eagle."

"Well, I'd have kept him in the closet," Keith said. "And taken him out to look at him and pet him."

"You made friends with Jasper to get the dog," Eldon said.

"Yep. And I finally got to snatch him."

"But why'd you kill John?"

"John found out about what Dad had done. I told him about it one time when we were drunk." Keith shook his head disgustedly. "I didn't think he was sober enough to remember—but he did."

"So that's what turned Henspeter's thinking around."

"He turned on me," Keith said bitterly. "Started acting as if losing his eye was my fault. He was blackmailing me to save the damned trees. I liked him—he was an outsider. But I couldn't let him stop Dad's project. John fought me, but I was too strong. Way too strong—what's that?''

Bouncer pricked up his ears and whined. Eldon's ears were still ringing from the Mauser's concussion, but after a moment he picked out a familiar, thumping rhythm.

" 'Rock of Ages,' " Eldon said. "Paavo's concertina. That's not cops—the Church of the Rising Dog is out there. They found the trunk. And they want Bouncer back."

As if in affirmation, fire from an automatic weapon chopped across the top of the trench. Somebody was getting better. And closer. The concertina played mockingly on.

"No way!" Keith cried, lunging up to blast back with the Mauser.

Hot cartridge casings showered onto Eldon's hat. A huge, billowing bat's wing sailed into the trench with a frightening hiss like a giant snake. Dark, choking smoke enveloped them. Eldon realized it was one of Henspeter's smoke grenades, billowing acrid clouds. Bouncer made his break. The little dog sprang up over the lip of the trench. The rope slipped from Keith's fingers and Bouncer was gone, headed for the concertina music.

Keith whirled and fired at the smoke canister. His prisoners scrambled in all directions, screaming. Eldon started up the side of the trench but someone shot at him from out on the landfill. He reversed course and dodged back around the corner of the trench, dragging Enola Gay with him. They ran pell-mell back up the cut.

A bullet whizzed past Eldon's head. Keith was chasing them. They should have gone over the top and braved the congregation's half-assed gunfire. Now there was no time to scale the road's sides.

They broke out onto open ground. Eldon saw that the edge of the landfill and safety lay ahead. Over the edge and into the trees. Eldon saw the dark hump of his van beyond—

A burst of gunfire cut them off. They veered away across the landfill and dived behind a hummock. The weapon's muzzle flash waved as if the operator were spraying a fire hose into the air. It was the AK-47 again. Whoever had shot at them from the construction site had moved up and was firing over the lip of the landfill.

"Lay low," Eldon said as they crawled behind a low mound. "The sheriff has got to come soon—"

There were three fast shots from the trench. Keith was popping away with the Mauser. Eldon and Enola Gay flattened themselves as Keith and the AK-47 gunner traded shots. Pop-blap, went the AK-47. The Mauser snapped in reply. Pop-blap. Pop-blap. Snap, snap. They're both terrible marksmen, Eldon thought.

They were safe for the moment but cut off. They could not reach the van ahead of them, and to retreat across the landfill would be to invite getting shot accidentally by the gunmen out in the darkness.

"I grabbed the LAW," Enola Gay said breathlessly.

"What?"

Enola Gay held up the tube that Keith had dropped.

Eldon watched in astonishment as she pulled a pin from the rocket launcher's back cover, then flipped the cover off with her thumb. The LAW's front cover and sling fell away, too. Enola Gay seized the tube with both hands and yanked in opposite directions; the launcher extended with a click. She briefly reversed pressure, to ensure that it was fully extended and locked. Then she threw up the trigger-arming handle and the plastic front- and rear-sights and set the LAW on her shoulder. She gripped the launcher overhand, fingers resting on the flat trigger on top of the tube.

"Watch your eyes," Enola Gay said. "I'll fire when I see Howell's next gun-flash."

The AK-47 gunner let off the rest of his clip in a roar of fireworks. Keith's Mauser flashed in return. Enola Gay raised herself on her elbows and fired the LAW.

There was a blinding flash and a WHOOSH! that lifted Eldon's hat. A dazzling white star zoomed away across the landfill. Eldon saw Howell in the rocket's glare as it flew over his head. An instant later, there was a tremendous explosion as a gasoline fireball illuminated the landscape.

"You hit my van," Eldon said.

In the light of the blazing van, Eldon saw Keith try to fire the Mauser, then throw down the empty pistol and spring over the berm. No one fired at him. Enola Gay jumped up in pursuit.

Eldon followed. No one shot at them. As he reached the edge

of the landfill, he saw the man with the AK-47—Ambrose McFee—desperately fumbling with a new magazine. McFee goggled as he recognized Eldon.

Enola Gay flew over the side of the landfill. Eldon followed. They floundered in the soft dirt. Enola Gay tripped and rolled down the slope. A shape in a top hat lunged at Keith Howell from the darkness—One-Square, attacking with his cane. Keith dodged over the bulldozed earth on the edge of the slough and splashed into the shallows.

He's getting away, Eldon thought, and then Howell screamed.

Eldon screamed, too, when he saw. Howell thrashed in the water, trying desperately to shake a huge, black, cablelike thing from his hand. It glittered evilly in the flames of the burning van. It was so long that it hung down into the water as Howell screamed and pranced; he lost his balance and fell, then sprang up shrieking. Another one of the things had clamped itself to his ankle.

"It's John's wolf eels!" Enola Gay cried. "Saul Alinsky and Emma Goldman! I told you they were territorial!"

Eldon heard sirens. A sheriff's car swept in, red and blue lights flashing, fixing Howell in its searchlight as he staggered out of the slough.

"Get your hands up down there!" a voice called above them. Eldon turned to see Art Nola atop the landfill, pistol ready. Pumpkin Joe was with him.

Eldon realized that Nola could not see him clearly and raised his hands. Enola Gay raised her hands, too.

"That van was the best car I ever had," Eldon said as another searchlight fixed on them. He spoke mainly to drown out Keith's yells. "It may have been funny-looking inside, but it ran perfectly."

"I'm a lousy shot," Enola Gay said. "I'm sorry, Eldon."

"You've got some explaining to do."

"Don't worry, I can explain everything."

23

Keith's wounds were bloody but not serious. Medics bandaged them under the watchful eyes of sheriff's deputies while Enola Gay tearfully embraced Pumpkin Joe Nedlee. The wolf eels had escaped into the slough.

"I went straight down the rut and took a jog I know about," Nedlee said. "I brought the deputies back. I told you I know Schumacher's like the back of my hand."

"Where are the Endos?" Eldon asked.

"Up on the landfill with Jasper and his pals," Nola said. "Ronnie's got a hole in that cockeyed helmet from friendly fire, but they're okay. Scattering probably saved all your lives."

"Good thing you showed up when you did," Eldon said.

"We were on our way to pick up Howell," Nola said. "He wasn't home so I figured he'd be here, thanks to you."

"Thanks to me?"

"For coming to me about Pumpkin Joe's shoes. Keith also has size-fourteen feet. I matched his footprints with the print found at the Henspeter murder scene."

"How?" Eldon asked, thinking how good it would be to have the answer in print at lunchtime tomorrow.

"Remember how it rained the day we found the bones? Keith left lots of footprints in the mud out here in the landfill. He was always hanging around. Wasn't hard to put two and two together."

"It's a hell of a story," someone said. Eldon looked down at Ambrose McFee. "I never had so much fun in my life," McFee said. "I haven't fired an AK-47 since I covered that survivalists' convention in Idaho. And I didn't have to give away the basketball comps, either."

"I hope you're taking notes," Eldon said, "because I'm kind of tired."

"Notes! Who needs notes with an angle like this?"

"The crime?"

"The dowsing rod!" McFee said. "That's how Jasper found the trunk."

Fiske will never get tired of telling about this one, Eldon thought. He turned to Art Nola, who was examining one of the Endos' broken plates. "New," Art said disdainfully, and tossed the plate aside.

"Art, listen—I don't want Ronnie's parole revoked. He was trying to help me."

"What is it Ronnie did?"

"He—" Eldon realized that no one save he and Enola Gay knew that the Endos had ever taken custody of the trunkful of guns. The weapons had been handled by so many people tonight that the presence of Ronnie's fingerprints proved nothing.

"Nothing, Art. He and Joline helped catch a killer."

"Yes, they did," Keith Howell declared.

"Has he been Mirandized?" Nola asked a deputy. When the deputy nodded, Nola told Keith, "You don't have to say anything, and anything you do say may be used against you—you understand that?"

"Sure. But I want to talk. I already told all of them about it, so I should tell you. Eldon will have it in tomorrow's paper anyway."

"All right," Nola said. "Somebody get his statement."

"I'll tell everything," Keith said, aglow with the anticipated pleasure of making a fine presentation. "Including the part about Chaucer."

"What about Chaucer?" Eldon asked.

"Dad killed them under a tree, Eldon. How could I do less when it came to John?"

"You spiked that tree the other day, too, didn't you?" Eldon said.

"In John's honor," Howell said sarcastically. "I never much liked that foreman anyway."

"But that only drew attention here."

"I didn't like my father, either. He broke my stepmother's ankle. But you probably guessed that I didn't like him. You're a perceptive guy." Keith smiled, and Eldon understood why he had really killed Henspeter and would now confess: to get even with Harmon Howell. Keith had turned upon his father at last.

A strobe light flared. Eldon looked up, blinking spots, expecting to see a deputy shooting evidence photos. But it was Marsha Cox, grinning like a mink. "You look a sight, Eldon."

"Just get here?" Eldon asked, trying to sound casual.

"We—that's Louis and I—were having coffee after a movie and the patrol cars came down the street, full out," Marsha said. "So I jumped in the car and followed. I'm afraid I left poor Louis in the coffee shop."

"Louis is your boyfriend, Lieutenant Beamish of the Coast Guard?"

"Yes. Louis. Louis Francis."

"I didn't know his first name."

"You owe Louis some thanks." Marsha took Eldon's sleeve and guided him to one side, where she slipped him a folded sheet of paper. "The registration hits on those weapons. Louis checked the serial numbers through the Coast Guard."

"Marsha, I will write Louis a thank-you note on flowered paper."

"It would be very good if you did."

Eldon unfolded the paper and read it by the headlights of a patrol car. The automatic weapons were registered in the name of Enola Gay Hansen. The LAW and the Mauser pistol apparently weren't registered at all. Eldon recalled Loretta Starbuck's warning about a dangerous lady.

Enola Gay sat watching Nedlee give his statement to a deputy. Eldon went over and said quietly, "If you don't mention that Ronnie and Joline had the guns, no one will be the wiser."

She nodded. "Okay."

"That was a hell of a shot with the LAW."

"It was a lousy shot, I told you."

"Maybe it was a lousy shot for somebody like you, who's had practice." Before she could deny it, Eldon held up the paper. "These are the registration hits on John's weapons. Except it turns out they're your weapons."

"Ah. How did you find out?"

"I told you not to try to beat me at my own trade. Now, where did you learn to fire a LAW?"

"In ROTC. In college. That's where that LAW came from. And the smoke grenades."

"Illegally?"

"Well, they don't give them away."

"And the other stuff?"

"I collected it. Over the years, after I dropped out of school and came back to Oregon. I like guns. Got some of them in trade for mechanic work. They're all duly registered, you know. Except for the LAW, of course, and the Mauser. The Mauser is the 1932 version, fires twenty shots—rare and nasty. I got it from a Canadian trucker; he had a lion and a unicorn tattooed on each arm, with *A Mari Usque ad Mare,* the Canadian motto. 'From Sea to Sea.' He had marvelous arms." Enola Gay's eyes flashed behind her glasses, and Eldon realized that he was enjoying speaking with her, yet again, this final time.

"Why didn't you tell me they were yours?"

"Because of what I had them for. And because I wanted you to track down John's killer. I knew you were the man to do it—if it was a big enough story."

"Thanks. But I'd have done it anyway."

"I know that now. But I had to keep you hopping. That's why I fired the bullet through your front window."

"You did that—?"

"With the Mauser. Before John's funeral. There was plenty of time to go and get it, come back and fire the shot and then go back to my house and put it away in the trunk. But after I'd done it, I got to thinking that the bullet might be traced, and I couldn't have the guns around." She smiled. "I knew you might catch me, you see. You're quite a capable man."

"Thanks. You're some woman, too. But what *were* the guns for?"

"For nothing, really—not anymore. But for a while there, after I quit school, I was a radical feminist."

"Radical feminists don't carry guns."

"These did. It was a group in Arizona. I was pretty young. I think I mainly liked them because they liked guns."

"But you quit."

"I got to thinking how much I liked men. I realized I could have men and guns both. That was about the time I met John—the women I went to Mexico with were two other women in the group. It wasn't a very hard choice to move back to Oregon, once I'd taken up with a man. I'm still a feminist."

"I just wish you'd told me straight out. I wouldn't have minded."

"But you do mind."

"I mind being lied to, especially when it comes to my work."

Enola Gay looked at him sadly. "I guess this is it. You got a hell of a scoop, didn't you? And I got my revenge. And maybe got my daddy back."

"I did get a hell of scoop," Eldon admitted. "And we saved the old-growth trees. I just wish you hadn't lied."

Enola Gay stood and brushed herself off. "Well, I'll tell you why I lied, Eldon." She touched her index finger to the tip of his nose. "Because you never can tell with men."

Eldon thought he saw her eyes glisten behind the aviator glasses. But before he could be sure, "Rock of Ages," played to a polka beat, floated down from the landfill and McFee yelled, "Yay, go Rising Dog!"

Paavo the Finn stood in the searchlights pumping his concertina, while Cap'n Jasper triumphantly danced with Bouncer. One-Square, Beanpole, and Wheelie applauded. Bouncer pranced on stubby hind legs, following his pirouetting master, and for a moment the accidental refraction of a headlight backlighted the risen dog in a holy glow. The glow caught the Finn, too, and made him look even bigger than usual.

Eldon saw that Enola Gay was watching Paavo with an eager smile. "Lotta *sisu* there," Eldon said.

"You're right," Enola Gay said. She had that same excited look that Eldon had seen when she had danced with Paavo at the Sons of Eiden Hall. "He dances really well." She started forward.

Eldon thought of Test Bravo's mushroom cloud and of Enola Gay's name and then of Rosenak saying that the rule of thumb was that there was no rule of thumb. Good luck to you, Paavo, he thought, suddenly conscious that every muscle in his body ached. I'll bang out my story and sleep for a week.

He went to the smoldering wreckage of his van and poked it with a toe. I'll have to get another car, he thought.

Something glinted in the twisted metal. Eldon picked it up—the eight ball that had topped the van's gearshift, warm from the explosion but unmarred. He put it in his pocket; it would make an appropriate souvenir. He didn't want the Mauser bullet he'd dug out of his kitchen wall after all.

Then rain spattered Eldon's face, and his spirits lifted. Whenever it rained, he slept long and deeply.